PERFECTION

There were eighteen narrow laces at the back of
Hannah's bosom bodice to undo, but Gray
managed them with skill. The first man in
Hannah's life had taught her how good a man's
hands and lips could feel. He had made her squirm
with frustrated pleasure. But he was a memory as
she had gazed down to see Gray's big, sure hands
and what they held so reverently.

His hands trailed along her ribs, reached her waist,
traced and cupped her hips and buttocks, and
paused. She was entirely bared to him now, and
dared not look where he did.

He suddenly raised himself on his elbows, and
gazed down at her. "There is something different
about your body," he said, "It's perfect."

Again she felt the old fear, the old shame, until he
went on, "You're perfect. Absolutely perfect . . ."

THE SILVERY MOON

The
Silvery Moon

Edith Layton

AN ONYX BOOK

ONYX
Published by the Penguin Group
Penguin Books USA Inc., 375 Hudson Street,
New York, New York 10014, U.S.A.
Penguin Books Ltd. 27 Wrights Lane,
London W8 5TZ, England
Penguin Books Australia Ltd, Ringwood,
Victoria, Australia
Penguin Books Canada Ltd, 10 Alcorn Avenue,
Toronto, Ontario, Canada M4V 3B2
Penguin Books (N.Z.) Ltd, 182-190 Wairau Road,
Auckland 10, New Zealand

Penguin Books Ltd, Registered Offices:
Harmondsworth, Middlesex, England

First published by Onyx, an imprint of New American Library,
a division of Penguin Books USA Inc.

First Printing, January, 1992
10 9 8 7 6 5 4 3 2 1

Copyright © Edith Felber, 1992
All rights reserved

 REGISTERED TRADEMARK—MARCA REGISTRADA

Printed in the United States of America

Women's entire being, mental and moral, as well as physical, is fashioned and directed by her reproductive powers . . . It is easy to understand, therefore, that if these powers be never completely developed, there will and must be an arrest of development of her mental and moral nature.

—*The Practical Home Physician Illustrated*, 1888

SPECIAL NOTICE TO PATIENTS

Having devoted my time and study since I commenced the practice of medicine to the treatment of all the special diseases of both male and female, affecting the generative and nervous systems, particularly all those diseases and discomforts of the female sex . . . I can promise all those sufferers speedy relief. But there are many who may wish to consult me by letter, as they live at a distance, making a personal consultation very inconvenient. . . . All communications should be accompanied by my usual fee, in all cases, *five dollars;* which may be sent by cash, check, or postal office order . . . I find that mail offers facilities for a confidence between the patient and the physician by which they may inform him of many delicate matters that they never would divulge at an interview.

—*Woman, Her Diseases and Treatment*, E. Smith, M.D., 1880

ON THE RELATIONS BETWEEN MAN AND WIFE

In the first moments of wedded life, the constant and unreasoning abuse of the privileges of a husband can not but result in evil consequences for both parties. . . . Let there be, therefore, caution and moderation used in this all-important relation on the part of the husband, as he alone is apt to be the transgressor—for we cannot suppose a case, except in the rarest instance, when the wife is at fault.

—*Everyman His Own Doctor*, J. Hamilton Ayers, M.D., 1880

Chapter One

COLORADO
September 1889

The audience was filled with men who were used to talking at a roar and singing with a howl. But they were very still now, and as respectful as if they were in church, although they looked a great deal happier than if that had been the case. Still, they only shifted in their seats; the only sound they made was when they moved their legs and accidentally set their spurs to jingling, that—and a few occasional coughing spasms, common this time of year, and commoner still among men who chewed and smoked tobacco as much as they did. But even those unavoidable outbursts were hastily subdued. They didn't want to miss a word.

Thompson's Palace was filled to capacity. Eight hundred some odd souls: miners, ranchers, hands, townsfolk, cowboys, drifters, as well as some of their ladies—and many more of that sex that had never thought of themselves as such in all their lives—leaned forward to hear everything going forth on stage in front of them. Because the troupe that was appearing to-night was straight—as the handbills proclaimed—from New York, London, and Chicago, and the soprano on stage was getting ready to sing. Even the dullest among them knew that, because not only had she stopped talking to the villain of the piece, but she'd turned to the audience clutching a rose to her ample breast, and the orchestra had begun to play something slow and sorrowful. Most everyone recognized the song the moment she began to recite its lengthy preamble. There was a collective sigh from the audience, and a wave of tilted-brimmed Stetsons dipped in contented head shaking. The song had nothing to do with the plot, of course, popular tunes never did. But "A Rose From My Mother's Grave" was a great favorite.

Audiences were always drab, compared to what was set before them. But this audience, composed of roughly clad men who had never cleaned up much higher than tidy, and whose female companions were either dressed as plainly as themselves, or done up in strident primary colors that were swallowed and sunk to black in the darkened theater, looked as though they were another species altogether from the brilliantly glittering actors before them. The gaslight footlights and spotlights glowed, and even when they flickered, they glanced off the set, striking up the golds and reds in the painted drop behind it, enhancing the set almost as much as they did the painted face of the soprano.

They sat in silence and listened, but as the song went on, the silence began to be broken by muffled sniffling, and then by occasional muted sobs. A man was never ashamed to be moved by sentiment, after all, and this was a song about dead mothers, broken promises, and yesterdays never to be reclaimed, and it struck a common chord in all of them. One tall, lean, hard-eyed wrangler near to the stage had begun to listen with a cynical smile that was nearly a sneer on his handsome face. But by the time the soprano really got her back into it, and was hitting the highest registers as she quaveringly described the way the roses were being flung upon the grave itself, it could be seen, even in the dim light, that his face was drowned with flowing tears.

An older man sitting next to the wrangler put out a hard-palmed, calloused hand to give the wide, shaking shoulders an awkward pat.

"Take 'er easy, friend," he murmured through his

own tear-drenched mustache, "hit's only a song she's singin', after all."

"Oh, I know," the cowboy finally managed to say, under cover of the wild applause that had broken out at the end of the song. "But *damned* if it don't get me every time," he sighed, wiping his bright blue eyes with the back of his buckskin sleeve as he cleared his throat. "Still," he said more cheerfully, "that ain't nothing. You ought to see me during the last act of *Hamlet*. Never fails. I swear I bawl like a baby—funny, it's not so much Ophelia's death that moves me, or Gertrude's, and not Claudius's, of course, but when Laertes falls to the floor beside Hamlet—well, all I can say is that by the time Fortinbras comes in, I'm lost . . . gone . . . ah . . ." He paused, blinking at the old ranch hand's wide-eyed stare.

"Shore," the old man said, edging away to the farthest reaches of his own seat. "Uh-huh," he said, before he made a great show of pointedly turning himself and all his attention away to the stage again.

The tall wrangler cleared his throat, and fell still. Then he pulled his hat lower over his eyes, shifted in his seat, and stared at the stage as well, but with such intensity an observer might think he thought he was about to see the story of his own life presented there.

Well, so he'd forgot again, Gray Dylan thought with a mixture of annoyance and amusement at the situation and himself as he peered out from under his hat brim and pretended to pay attention to the soprano's next offering. He noted, from the corner of his eye, how the old fellow next to him put up a shoulder and drew himself up in his seat like a maiden who'd been propositioned. But the song had genuinely moved him, and the old man's sympathy had taken him off guard and unlocked his lip—damn, he thought ruefully, how could he have forgotten that out here, a man might weep at a sad song as easily as at a sad story, and more power to him, but a show of a little bit of learning went a long way to alienating his fellowman? It should have been bone bred in him, he thought in disgust. His pleasure in the night fled, and he decided to leave, too, just as soon as the soprano took her bows. But after she did, a comedian in an absurd bonnet came waltzing out on the stage, prancing to the rousing strains of "Where Did You Get That Hat?" Gray sank back into his seat and forgot himself, as did the rest of the audience. Because soon everyone was joining in the chorus—if they weren't laughing too hard to do so. And that, he thought, when the comedian was done and he gave him his deserved applause, and the old fellow next to him forgot himself enough to exchange pleased grins with him as he did, too, was the magic of the theater, and the reason he was here.

He remembered that other reason when the chorus girls, all in spangles and smiles, tights and scanty excuses for skirts, came out to dance and sing the finale.

But when the curtains closed on the last encore, the lights in the theater came up, and the audience, dazed by reality, blinked and remembered they had to look for a way out, he glanced down at himself. Then he remembered that he'd only had time to wash the dust off his face from the trail before he'd come here tonight. Even if he'd cleaned himself up as best as he could, he still wore leather and cotton, buckskin and denim, not wool and silk. There was no way he could pay a visit backstage the way he was dressed. And no point to it. Timing was everything in the theater, even for a member of its appreciative audience. Just as the best seats were taken by the time the curtains parted to show the performance, admittances to the best after-theater shows were quickly arranged soon after those curtains closed. He knew that by the time he could get back to his hotel, change, and come back again, the best girls would be taken. He sighed. When the last bows were being taken, he'd thought he'd seen a wink in his direction sent from a particular pair of painted, sparkling eyes. But even so, he guessed he'd sleep alone tonight.

It wasn't until he rose and stretched his long body that he realized, with surprise, that it ached with weariness. And so he supposed, as he waited to move on out of the narrow aisle, that he didn't mind missing his favorite after-theater treat tonight, after all. It had been a long day, and he'd been on the move since sunup. He'd have been asleep long since if he hadn't spied the posters for tonight's variety show as he'd ridden into town at sundown. The idea of seeing a show, as ever, had enticed him. The performances, as always, had given him the illusion of energy. But he really was beyond tired now. And so the wry smile he wore as he waited to leave was only partially due to the taste of sour grapes.

He nodded to a few familiar faces in the small lobby of the music hall, and stepped out of the crowd and into a cool evening. Once on the street, he paused to send a rueful glance back to the stage door that he saw being opened to admit a few well-dressed gents from out of the cluster of men that waited there. He shrugged and began to stroll back to his hotel. Only to stop abruptly when he heard his name called.

"Hey, mister," the boy who'd chased after him said. "You Mr. Dylan? Well," he said as Gray nodded slowly, his hand at his hip, because being suddenly called out in the street, even in a big town like this, even by a boy, was not always a welcome interruption in this part of the country, "then Miss Joy says how come you dint come back to say hello like she 'spected you to? She seen you at the door, and then seen you leavin', and she's said as how I should run and catch up and tell you she's awaitin' . . . By ginger!" he cried, catching the coin he was tossed. "This is mor'n I got for puttin' up all them posters! Thanks, mister!"

Pandering oughtn't to pay more than hard work, Gray thought bemusedly, a bit shamed at the lesson he'd just taught the boy. He was still thinking it when the guard at the stage door let him in at the mention of his name, while a few dozen other fellows were left clamoring for entry. The coin he slipped the man was worth more than the one he'd flipped to the boy, and though the smile it was greeted with was not as wide, the coin disappeared just as fast.

He touched his hand to his hat, as he paused at the opened door to the crowded roomful of shockingly half-dressed girls, his quick glance netting him a deliciously bewildering display of pink flesh, sequins, and dark tights, along with the scents of competing perfumes and the glimpse of so many different smiles, shapes, and colors of hair and lips and . . .

"She's next door, Cowboy," the woman nearest to the door answered after she quickly looked him up, priced him, and turned him down, all with a regretful smile, and all in a moment, as a practiced member of the chorus had to learn to do.

"Well, but the last time we met, you shared a dressing room just like that one," he explained when he turned and saw the small, voluptuous titian-haired woman standing in the doorway of her dressing room next door, watching him with a slight frown on her lovely painted face.

"Umm," she said thoughtfully, trying to remember if that was so, and deciding it might well be, for though she'd never forgotten him, he'd a way of making her forget her circumstances every time they met. She relented, put up her cheek for him to kiss, and deciding to challenge him just for the fun of it, murmured sweetly, "Yes? Was that in Denver? Or Leadville?"

He touched her proffered, powdered cheek with his lips, and grinned down at her before he took her into his arms and took her lips at the same moment as answer, because he didn't remember, or care to. Or need to. Because it was a long moment before she heard some of the girls from the adjoining room giggling and remembered where they were, even as she forgot all her anger at him. She stepped back from his embrace, and pulled him into her room, closing the door behind them. He took off his hat and held it in front of him, as though he were bashful and contrite, not just because the room was so small there was no where else he could put it.

"Your own room! You're going places, Joy," he said admiringly, letting his glance rove over the tiny room as though it were a palatial suite he was viewing. And then he stood and gazed down at her with such appreciation it was almost as sweet as applause to her.

She looked away from where he stood, his fair hair glowing in the lamplight, his lean face showing clear and clearly sensual appraisal. "But . . . your clothes, Gray," she said slowly, to pay him back for almost making her forget that she knew he could act as well as she could. "What has happened, my dear?" she asked. "Are you coming down in the world?"

It almost didn't matter if he was when he looked at her that way. He grinned, causing two lines to appear in the tanned cheek to the left of his quirked smile, and one to the right of it.

"Aw, honey, it's so sweet of you to care. But it's only that I rode into town today with some cattle. There's a man I want to see about a bull—improving the breed, dull stuff to you, I know—and by the time I'd got them settled, and myself as well, there was no time to change and still see the performance. But I didn't want to miss you," he said, staring down at her lips.

"But . . . I'm not mentioned on the bill, Gray," she said softly, clutching her dressing gown closed at the neck, turning aside as though she were hurt and not just trying to show him her left profile, her best side.

"And I wasn't with 'Henderson's Touring Revue' when we last met, either," she added with a little broken catch to her voice to cover the slight gasp she gave as she felt his large, warm hand come to rest lightly on her shoulder.

"Didn't you think I'd ask?" he murmured, letting his lips brush the charming profile she showed him.

She didn't and he hadn't, and they both knew that, but they were both enjoying the game they were playing. He turned her around and kissed her for a very long time, long enough to undo her robe, and almost undo her entirely. But, he noticed, when he opened his eyes to look for a place to be more comfortable with their sport, the room wasn't big enough for them to lie down in, even if there'd been a bed in it. The wall was likely too thin to take the pounding it would get if they leaned up against it, and he doubted very much if she'd let him take her onto his lap even if the spindly chair in the room had been strong enough to support the two of them. In any event, he was sure she'd insist on the usual procedure: dinner and flirtation, offers, rejections, and more fervent offers, and then, and only then, when honor and illusion had both been satisfied, could he be. Because only then could there be a trip to a room and a bed. It had been, after all, weeks since they'd last met. Or months, he couldn't quite remember. He sighed and drew back from her, glad that he'd at least been able to remember her from her name after the boy had told it to him.

"Where can we be alone, darling?" he asked.

It took her a moment to recover herself enough to answer. He always did that to her, that was almost the nicest thing about him.

"Dinner?" she asked.

"Yes," he agreed. "Where are you staying?" he asked eagerly, because he doubted Henderson's Touring Revue could afford his hotel, and didn't want her there anyway because that would mean his room, and he wanted to get some sleep tonight, after.

She smiled coyly and turned, drawing her dressing gown up over her shoulder again, and peered at him over it. "Oh, but think of my reputation," she breathed, using the exact words, tone, and stance of the ingenue in *Her Atonement*, before she asked slyly and in a more natural voice, "Where would you suggest?"

"Then never my place!" he exclaimed, with an almost believable show of horror. "Not if it's your reputation at stake!"

She scowled at how ill her art had served her, and thought of how to get around the trap she'd set for herself. A night in his bed might lead to another, since she knew that a clever woman installed in a man's bed might maneuver herself into becoming a permanent fixture there—or a semipermanent one—at least until the end of this run. And who knew what might happen after that?

"How about that handsome dining parlor up the street?" he volunteered enthusiastically.

Her eyes narrowed.

"How about Folgers?" she snapped, because that was the most expensive hotel in town, and she thought he was probably staying there, too.

"But I'm in all my dirt!" he protested.

She smiled in spite of her chagrin.

"How you do talk," she said, shaking her head. When he looked at her curiously, she explained, "I know it's only that your daddy was English, but sometimes when you say something like that I swear I think we're doing *Romeo and Juliet*."

He'd forgotten that he'd ever told her that, it had probably been at a moment when he wasn't responsible for what he was saying. It bothered him, he wasn't used to being intimate to women he was only intimate with, so he said quickly and in a deeper western accent, "I only meant that it's a fancy place, honey, they'd never let me in dressed like I am. Let's try that place up the street, I'm starved, I can't wait . . . for dinner," he said passionately, giving her a heated, all-encompassing look.

"My hotel's got better food, and it's not fancy," she said curtly, giving it up because it was true. She was withal realistic, before she chided him by protesting, "It would never do to be seen just up the street with you so late at night," because she was, even so, always an actress. "Now, scoot, I must dress," she said on a teasing smile, giving him a gentle push to the door, because she knew that the getting into clothes was never so pretty a procedure as the getting out of them, especially since she'd have to lace herself up tightly if she wanted her new blue gown to look good. And she wanted to look very good to him.

He waited outside her door, seemingly oblivious to his surroundings. Which was more than could be said of those around him. One of the members of the chorus peeped out their dressing-room door to see if the gent she'd agreed, by note, to an assignation with, had arrived yet, and seeing Gray standing there, drew in her breath. Then she wilted. He couldn't be her gent, of course, because he was no gentleman. But she couldn't help staring.

He wore the everyday working garb of an ordinary ranch hand, the kind of man that filled all the theaters around here, the kind her more experienced friends told her to stay away from, since they didn't have more than the clothes they wore. But the way he wore those clothes! His broad shoulders filled out his cowhide jacket, his lean hips and long legs made the common denim trousers he wore seem as elegant and graceful as if he were in evening dress; she caught a glimpse of an ivory handle at the wide belt that circled his narrow waist, so it might be that he wore a gun as well as boots and spurs. But it was difficult to fault any kind of clothes when they adorned such a form.

It was more than what he had on, his face was too tanned and scarred to be that of a gentleman. Although, she admitted on a stifled sigh, the white scar on his chin only called attention to its perfect shape, just as a longer, darker one on his cheek spoiled its symmetry but emphasized his high cheekbones. His nose was long and narrow, his lips, full and shapely, if he'd had a beard and burnside whiskers instead of only a mustache as flaxen as his thick overlong hair, she supposed his scars would have been concealed, but then the clear, clean shape of his face wouldn't be as visible either. And then, there were those sky blue eyes.

There was too much character in that face for him to be a villain, even if there was too much experience in it for the young hero. He wasn't quite an Adonis, although he looked quite a man: too hard-bitten for *Hamlet*, she mused, staring at him from the concealment of the door, fascinated, too young and attractive for *Rip Van Winkle*, but maybe an *Enoch Arden*, she decided, and certainly a swell Mr. Rochester for *Jane Eyre*, and a peach of a boyfriend for *The Bride Forlorn*.

But then she stopped casting him in her private play. Because Miss Joy Fenwick, their newest ingenue,

stepped out of her dressing room and took the cowboy's arm.

The chorus girl gasped, causing her bosom friend,
Miss Daisy Denton, who was preparing to accompany
her tonight with her own admirer—at least so far as
dinner—to look at her curiously.

"Miss Joy's taking a vacation, do you think?" she
asked her friend, to cover over the way she'd been
caught goggling at the fellow. "It isn't like her to give
up profit for a pair of blue eyes."

Miss Denton squinted into the faint light of the corridor to watch the departing couple, and saw the slight
hitch in the man's gait as he dipped his fair head to
hear something the woman said.

"Some vacation!" she said, as much in chagrin as
admiration. "I'll bet it'll just feel like a week in the
country, too! Trust her to know how to combine work
and play. Only two years in the chorus, and her singing's no better than her acting, if you can call it that—
and she's got her own dressing room. Now this. She
was born lucky. And smart! Don't be a dopey. That's
Gray Dylan."

"Who?" her friend asked.

"He owns everything hereabouts," Miss Denton
said enviously.

"A dopey, am I?" her friend asked on a sniff.
"Well, how should you know, Miss double-dopey,
when we've only been here for a day. This is not New
York, you know."

"He owns everything there, too," Miss Denton
sighed.

"Oh," her friend said sadly, though still not quite
convinced, since in her experience, and it was considerable, a gentleman with money looked like one—
which was to say, not very much like a gentleman,
and not at all like a leading man of any sort, and so
not in the least like Gray Dylan.

She hadn't wanted him to leave, which was flattering. But the sight of the number of bills he'd left on
her dresser had soon consoled her, which was decid-

edly less so. Still, Gray thought much later that night as he lowered himself to his own blessedly big, empty bed at Folger's Hotel at last, it was money well spent. Miss Joy Fenwick had been as pretty as a man could want, even more obliging than pretty, and as appreciative of his talents—or talented enough to seem to be—than any man had a right to expect. When the time came.

But that time had been a long time coming, he thought on a sigh. Because it only came after a long dinner, longer strings of compliments, and other intricate wordplay meant to convince him she didn't usually do the kind of thing she usually did, and to convince her that he didn't doubt it for a minute. That was tedious, but it was also a form of theater, and necessary for both of them. Without it, she'd be purely a woman who sold herself for money, and not what she was: an actress, who could almost beguile him and herself into believing that was all she was. That, after all, was what he valued most about her, and all her kind.

Pheasant, steak, wine, conversation, and compliments—it was a long way around to get to what he could have for less money, and a short walk up a gilded staircase in any one of a number of elegant houses not a block from his hotel. But then there'd be no way to escape knowing he'd only rented a body for however many hours it took him to ease his own. There wasn't much choice in such matters. A good woman didn't lay herself down without getting a man's legal promise that he'd keep her doing it until death did they part. If a bad woman didn't charge for her services, she'd either have an angry husband or some other problem a careful man wanted no part of. And any kind of woman at all was a rarity in this part of the country, Gray thought, and he was a bachelor and this was, after all, a short business trip that a man might lighten with pleasure . . .

He looked at his watch and frowned at how his unusual disquiet was keeping him awake, even after his hard day and his evening's exercise. And then took a cue from his actress friend by pretending it had all been exactly what he'd wanted. And by welcoming one illusion, he found it simpler to slide into less deliberate dreams, and so got down to the business of the night at last, and slept.

They leaned on the rail fence and watched the cattle, and pretended that was all they were considering. The thick-bodied older man beside Gray was dressed no differently than he or any of the workingmen on his ranch, even though between the two of them they'd enough money to trade and buy diamonds and rubies instead of the heavy-necked cows they were studying.

"I see what you mean," the older man said eventually. "Not enough in the hindquarters compared to your lot. But mine got them deep chests, and real power in them back legs."

"Sure," Gray said. "Their chests are as pretty as any chorus girl's, John, but now, those legs . . . steaks don't need muscles." He shook his head, and as the other man turned bemused eyes to his, Gray added, "Now, you get a spur from the railroad nearer to here, John, and you can do without those powerful legs and let even more go to the chest and flank, where it counts."

"And you might be able to arrange that?" the other man said.

"Might," Gray agreed, nodding, turning back to look at the cattle again.

"*If* I send over a bull or two—so you can keep experimentin' with your herd the way you do," the other man said casually.

"Hell, no!" Gray said, turning around as if amazed, his sky blue eyes lit with seemingly innocent wonder. "That'd be fine with me, John, but what would Josh say? My big brother's a New Yorker now, the only bulls he's got any interest in are on Wall Street! Hell, no," he repeated with much regret. "Be more than fine with me, but my brother doesn't concern himself with any cattle that can't pull his fancy carriages down

Fifth Avenue now—and you know how big brothers are.'' He sighed.

"Might be interested in mines, though, do you think?'' the man he'd called John said after a long silence.

"Might just,'' Gray agreed absently.

"Say—The Gypsy Queen up in Ashcroft?''

Gray said nothing for a moment, then shook his head.

"No, doubt he'd go for it,'' he answered. "Word is that Ashcroft's just about played out.''

"Ah,'' the older man said, "not many people know that, keeps himself up on such things, does he?''

"You bet,'' Gray said with animation. "No flies on Josh. But now, maybe . . . that new one up at Aspen, The Silver Girl, why that one might take his fancy.''

" 'The Girl?' With all the silver it looks like she's going to be spittin' out? For just a word in a railroader's ear about a spur?'' the other man asked with incredulous laughter in his voice, before he spat on the ground.

"Well, seeing as he's on the board of that particular railroad . . .'' Gray answered, before he added, "Plus say, some thousand—maybe, thirteen hundred shares in it. No more, of course, because Josh don't own the damned thing, just some of it. Doubt he'd offer more. You know him. But, of course,'' he said with more vigor, "I'd throw in some of these gorgeous girls of mine that we're looking at for you to add to your herd. Say . . . aw, what the hell, all of them. I'm not such a hard businessman as my big brother.''

"Hard man, all right, your brother,'' the other man said after a while, and then stretched out a calloused hand. "Done, then.''

"Well, fine,'' Gray said, shaking his hand.

"Of course,'' he added slowly, still holding the older man's hand, "if you wanted five hundred more shares, you could offer a half interest in that other mine up at Aspen—The Big Time. It hasn't shown much, still Josh is a gambler, sometimes.''

"Didn't know anybody knew about The Big Time.''

"Well, I was out at Aspen and had a look around. I like to gamble, too. Can't afford to like my brother, of course, but I'd bet he'd offer you another five hundred shares for a straight partnership in it," Gray said.

"It ain't safe since that cave-in . . . you must been the damn fool they told me was having a crawl through there last week!" the older man said with a frown.

"Well, she needs some new timber, all right, and new blood to explore some more, but I'd guess my brother would think she might just do."

The older man nodded and shook Gray's hand once more, before they unclasped hands.

"Your brother's a shrewd one, lucky for me you're the one I had to do business with, Gray, ain't it?" he said after they fell to studying the cattle again. "He's sure clever—never would think you're the one he sent to college back East."

"Yeah," Gray said sadly, "he kept me a schoolboy for years. Never will let me grow up."

"Shame," the older man agreed, keeping his face still, although his eyes sparkled. "Still, you're a man grown, Gray. Ah, speakin' on that, care to stay to dinner?"

"Thank you kindly, John," Gray said with every evidence of sincerity, "but I got to get back home. Royal's watching the place. He's a good man, but Josh'd skin me if I went larking off too long."

"My Melanie will be disappointed, you've always been a favorite of hers, you know."

"I'll be sorry to miss seeing her," Gray said with evident dismay, "but like I say, I got to get back."

"She up and got herself engaged to Duane Carter last week, sure I can't talk you into stayin', after all?" the other man asked with only the slightest hint of a smile.

"Little Melanie? Why, she can't be more than . . . Lord! She's got to be nearing nineteen now. Congratulations, John," Gray said, taking his hand again, though he frowned as he did. "Damn!" he said. "Just think, all this time I thought of her as a little girl. Guess I let her slip through my fingers, didn't I?"

"Guess so," the other man agreed. "Don't know who was sorrier about that, her ma, or her. But she couldn't wait forever. Surely is a good thing your big brother is such a fiend with numbers, Gray, since I remember you was at her eighteenth birthday party just last spring. Didn't happen to take any drama classes back at school, did you, son?" he asked, not bothering to conceal his smile now.

"Me?" Gray asked, grinning back at him. "No, my interest in the theater is strictly that of an appreciative audience, John."

"*Awful* appreciative, from what we hear."

"The only thing sadder than a heifer without her calf," Gray said solemnly, "is an actress without an audience."

"Damn, but I'm glad Melanie got herself hooked up with that Duane, after all," the other man said, shaking his head as he nonetheless smiled.

And so was Gray glad as he rode away. Melanie was a nice girl, which made her about the only kind he didn't need.

But a few days later, as he neared his home, he wasn't so sure just what it was that he needed. It had been a long and tiring journey back. No roads could make fast work of the trip across the mountains, and somehow, no matter how he yearned for home, it was hard to hurry when he was riding through them. The smell of the pines—the air itself made him as drunk as anything he'd ever had from a glass. Still, he'd made decent time, because he'd been so preoccupied with his thoughts that the beauty of the land around him didn't distract him as much as it usually did.

Melanie getting married! He couldn't stop thinking about it. Not that he minded. He was genuinely glad for her, she was a sweet child, and for all she'd grown up handsome enough, she'd not been either clever or handsome enough for him to take for more than an hour at a time. And while that was enough of a span of time for his commerce with most women, it would never be enough for marriage, and that was all that was good enough for a good girl like her. She'd certainly wanted that, it had been in her every word and gesture at her birthday party—Lord!—she'd been sweet on him ever since he could remember—but the problem now was that he was forced to remember a time before she'd even been at all. He'd been ten years old the day he'd heard she was born. Now she was going to be married and would soon have children of her own. It was so sobering a thought, it robbed even the intoxicant of the high reaches he traveled through of its power to lift his spirits. But there was another he looked forward to.

He'd been riding the edge of his own wire for hours, and when he finally looked up to the endless blue sky to see that he was riding under the high wooden arch that bore the name and symbol of his home again, he waited for the familiar surge of exhilaration he always felt at coming home. It came. But more faintly than usual, and he'd a disturbing notion that it might be because it felt too familiar.

Maybe, he thought, it was diluted because it was becoming too commonplace an experience. He'd just come up from Denver and Aspen and Leadville, but he'd traveled up past Fort Laramie, then across the Casper just this past summer, too, and before that to Chicago and New York only last spring—all for business and pleasure—and down to New Orleans for pure pleasure just before that. But lately it seemed the pleasure had been tainted by the fact that he'd been seeking it so hard, and the business itself was no longer the pure pleasure it had been.

What he needed, Gray decided as he rode down the long road to his home, was none of the things he'd sought, neither drink nor sex nor triumph at business—but good hard physical labor. Because work, like all those other diversions, drove everything from a man's mind but his performance of it. Only it left a man feeling good about himself afterward.

He paused at his house just long enough to drop off his carpetbags, leave his horse at the stables, and get on another. Then he rode out toward the northern reaches of his land, where he knew the men would be.

This time of year they'd be moving the herd in closer to home, preparatory to selling off excess stock and weaning the last calves, in order to thin the herd down hard for winter. Those ranchers who had survived it had learned some bitter lessons during the terrible winter two years ago. But he'd not gone far before he saw a familiar paint with a tall, thin rider coming his way.

"You're back," the man said when they came abreast, and they clasped hands hard as the man's thin, solemn face broke into a wide white smile.

"And ready to go. What can I help you boys with?" Gray asked, with a matching smile.

"Nothing. The weather's been real soft and easy, and we got most everything nicely in hand, boss," the thin man said.

He was a tall and rangy man, with the sort of outsize bones that would never have enough flesh on them. His hair was a dusty brown beneath his Stetson, and his clean-shaven face had a leathery tan, he'd a wide, narrow-lipped mouth, and a thin narrow nose to match his other spare features; only his surprisingly expressive hazel eyes gave his face animation.

"Well, but the 'boss' wants some work to do, Royal," Gray said on a laugh.

"Just lazied around up in Aspen, did you?" Royal asked. "No climbing down mine shafts or crawling up mountains, as usual? Guess you got all those scrapes on your cheek playing, huh?"

"I went to the theater near there," Gray said agreeably. "Actresses are so fierce . . . oh come on, Royal, what are a few scrapes? You know climbing and tunneling isn't work for me. 'Fie upon this quiet life—I want work'! Boss me no bosses either, there never was a ranch that couldn't use an extra hand, especially in the autumn."

"You said it pretty enough, but I guess you got a first," Royal answered, as he guided his horse back toward the main house, "because I was just coming in for the day."

"And if you're coming in, I can bet my immortal

soul there's no more work," Gray sighed, and turned his own horse to accompany him. "So be it. You can catch me up on what's been going on here."

"Let's see," Royal said. "Old Henry's got a sore tooth and has been taking down about a quart a day for it, so I guess if you really want work bad enough, you can bully him into getting the damned thing drawn before the other boys knock it out—along with some others—because all he's been doing is whining. Boyd got something interesting at Celia's house in town, so everybody's staying away, and Celia's almost as sore about it as he is, which is to say, considerable. Steady had another litter, and they're all spoke for already. . . . And there's a couple of letters from your brother waiting for you on the hall table."

"And they all say, 'Come to New York,' " Gray sighed.

"Wouldn't know," Royal said.

"Yes, you would, without looking," Gray said with some annoyance, "because they always say the same thing. 'Opportunity's here, society's here, civilization's here—you've got an education, and a good man to take care of the ranch, so what are you doing back there?' Lord, he's the best brother a man could have, but for all I make sport of it, he never does forget he's a big brother."

"Maybe it's just that you never do," Royal said.

"Maybe it's the same thing, then," Gray said.

"There's that," Royal agreed.

They rode on in silence until Royal spoke again. "Well, maybe you can tell him that you may have to run the place yourself soon," he said softly.

Gray slewed around in his saddle to stare at his foreman.

"I'm thinking of buying that land I've been thinking on. One of these days I'm going to have to go off on my own," Royal said.

"What for?" Gray asked, amazed.

"Well, I'm not getting any younger . . ."

"You're two years younger than me!" Gray exclaimed, "You're only twenty-seven."

"But that's considerable. Time for a man to be thinking about settling down and making his own home. Hell, don't look at me that way, Gray, I know I owe you and Josh . . ."

"Owe what?" Gray interrupted. "You've been working for us over ten years, since you first drifted in here, and working as hard as either of us, too. Whatever you've gotten for it, you deserve. I never saw anyone work so hard, even when you were just a skinny kid you shamed me with it."

"You?" Royal laughed. "I think if you could figure out a way to work in your sleep you would, Gray."

"But I always knew you *had* to work. That's a big difference, you know," Gray said quietly.

"Always seemed to me you thought you had to, too," Royal said with equal seriousness. "They tell me you was trying to break horses when most boys were trying to get up on ponies. I've seen you hanging out with the hands when you could've been giving orders from the front porch. I learned from you as much as I worked for you—both of you. Not only did you take me in when I had nothing . . . but I've got a good bit of money now, and not just from my work. You and Josh showed me how to invest . . . Lord, what ordinary ranch hand knows about investments?"

"You were never an ordinary ranch hand," Gray said. Then he said impatiently, "All right, who's the girl? And where in hell did you meet her? If you say Celia's or Big Sally's, I'll have to pound some sense into your head. A man gets lonely out here—but not plain crazy. You can't settle down with a whore."

They'd reached the house now, but Royal only reined up and stared at Gray.

"What girl?" he asked, genuinely startled.

"The one you're going to settle down with and leave us to build that home for," Gray said.

"Well, I ain't met her yet," Royal said. "I'm only saying that I got to thinking it's time I did."

Gray sighed again and stared at him, before he slid down from the saddle and threw his reins to Royal. He laced two hands at the small of his back and stretched. "No, it's time you did something else," he said, wincing as he looked up at Royal. "When was the last time you took a break? Thinking about women is one thing, but when a man starts to thinking about settling down with one that he hasn't even met, it's sure that he needs to do more than think about them. Next time I leave this place, you're coming with me."

"I don't think theaters and whorehouses hold my answer, Gray," Royal said with a smile.

"They sure as hell might help you ask a better question," Gray said as he limped away to the house.

Royal's smile slipped as he watched the fair-haired man make his painful way up the short stair to his house. When Gray limped as badly as that, it meant he was in considerable pain; he must have done some hard traveling.

Gray took the three steps to his porch, silently cursing each one as he did. His leg ached most, but it was only adding its bit to the symphony of discomfort he felt. But for all he wanted a seat that didn't move beneath him, he wanted one in a hot bath first. He paused in his hallway before he attempted the long stair to his bedroom. Not because of the pain in his leg. He picked up the letters from the hall table, and stood holding them in his hand as though weighing them, although there was nothing he wanted more at the moment than to read his brother's words. Because there was no one he loved more on the earth.

His brother was a decade older than he himself. A self-made man, one who'd gone to work at men's jobs when he'd been a boy; a man who'd given up his youth so that his younger brother could have a chance to enjoy his, a man who'd sacrificed what he'd wanted most in life: an education, so that his brother could have one. Now Josh Dylan was one of the richest men in the country, and so then, too, was his brother. And now Josh lived in New York City, where he directed the family fortune he'd made, and he wanted his brother to come live with him—to help him, as he said in every letter he wrote. As if Josh needed any help, Gray thought with a wry smile.

There was no man on earth Gray loved more. Yet though Josh had never been less than reasonable with him, there was no man on earth Gray feared more—or at least, no man's deeds. Because he never knew how he could measure up to him, although he'd spent his life trying. Trying, he thought, as he looked up the long stair he'd have to climb in a moment, even though it seemed he'd have to break every bone in his body to do it, and still not succeed.

No, brother, he thought, sadly staring at the letters, in New York, I'd just be what I've been all my life: Josh Dylan's lucky little brother. Here, I'm your brother, but by God, at least they know how hard I try to be more. He let out his breath and faced the staircase. The horse that had crushed his leg so badly it couldn't be set right had been too wild for him then; just as the stair in his house was too high for him now. But he'd gotten on one to prove a point, and he'd refused to take down the other to make another.

He gathered up his mail and his carpetbag, and clenched his teeth. And had got halfway up the stairs when he heard his housekeeper cry out in alarm.

"Why didn't you let me know you were coming?" Mrs. Ryan keened, watching him with distress, knowing too well to offer assistance. "I'll have old Ryan fetch your bath," she mumbled as she hurried away, offering the only help she could.

It was only when he was undressing that he found the paper he'd stuffed into his pocket before he'd left town. It was that paper he read as he finally sank into his hip bath. And that paper that made his grave face brighten at last, when he picked it up again after he'd read Josh's letters.

Because it was a handbill listing new performances to be presented at the theater where he'd just seen that pretty little redheaded actress he'd spent a night with—Josie?—no, Joyce—or something like that, he thought, as the memory of her face receded with her name. The handbill spoke of pleasures even more ephemeral than the meeting of bodies, and yet in a way, more satisfying, because it reminded him of a better way of escaping from himself.

That's where he'd take Royal, and soon, he promised himself. As he sank into the water and felt it leach the pain from his limbs, he thought with a smile, that with all he had, and that was a lot, he needed more. But that unlike Royal, he knew what it was. And that for both of them, the play would, indeed, be the thing.

Chapter Two

NEW YORK
September, 1889

The audience was on the stage. There were some four
dozen of them, some sitting on folding chairs, some
standing, but all appearing to be very much at ease.
Because they all were performers of one sort or another, and they were, however anxious to hear what
the man before them was saying, on a stage, after all.
There was no one in the darkened audience to see
them, only some few who'd come along to the theater
with them waiting and watching from backstage. But
since they were performers, that was enough to keep
them on their toes. That, and the presence of each
other, of course. And certainly, and most of all, the
presence of the dark, thin young man who was addressing them.

"You've all been called back today," he repeated in
his rich, velvety voice, "but sad to say, we've not
reached a final decision as yet. However, fear not!"
he said, raising one long, thin hand to quiet the mutterings that had begun. "We do not waste your valuable time. We shall come to that decision later this
very day. Our final say is not so important as yours,
because in this case, you see, my dear friends, it is
your decision we must have first."

He seemed to approve the murmurings and looks of

surprise and confusion the assembled company exchanged with one another, because he let them go on for a while until he stopped them by saying, "Yes. That is so. There are some things about this booking you must know before we take a step further together. Please!" he said imperiously, with nothing of pleading in his voice as some suspicious mumblings began. "Allow me to explain."

He stood before them, saying nothing, until they were shamed into silence.

He was a slender young man of middle height, dressed all in black, lean to the point of emaciation, or else it was just that his white face and pompadour of thick jet hair emphasized the starved planes of his aesthetic face. It was entirely an actor's countenance. Because the mobile mouth and flexible brows all acted in concert with the bold, dark eyes and constantly moving body to bolster every word he spoke in his fluctuant, mellifluous voice. A few inches taller and he'd be a matinee idol, some present thought. But then, as he drew himself up and cast them a scornful glance because he'd not gotten the complete silence he'd demanded, they saw their eyes had deceived them—he might already be that few inches taller, and he'd be a better villain because there was so much cruelty in those hard ebony eyes. But when he smiled upon them for their cooperation at last, they realized that they were wrong again, because such great compassion and sympathy was radiating from his gentle smile and limpid, soulful eyes. By the time he spoke again, some had already perceived that he might be anything he wished to be, because although he said he was a producer and director, he might also be perhaps the greatest actor of them all.

"You will note that each one of you has a replica present—or at least, a passable one," he said on a chuckle.

At that, a little cherub of a girl with fat yellow sausage curls shot a look of purest spite at another child at the end of her row of chairs, this one with a headful of midnight ringlets. A deep-bosomed blond woman narrowed her eyes at a similarly voluptuous dark-haired one nearby to her, and a handsome young gentleman regarded an even handsomer one with more than the usual loathing that competing actors ordinarily display.

"Yes," the dark young man agreed. "You are rivals. Semifinalists. We've not made a final decision because it may not be necessary. Some of you may fail the final audition, but alas! some of you may not have the will to succeed even before that. Because this is no ordinary play we're casting for. No, this is a tour, and a tour is not like a run anywhere in this great city," Kyle Harper said in such sudden, booming tones, he startled his audience into disregarding each other and giving him complete attention again.

"Not only does it mean a guaranteed three months' work, room, and board," he said as the first disappointed mutterings of "tour" was heard, and then suddenly stilled at the sound of that heart-stoppingly wondrous offer, "but it's a unique experience. Some of you know this, but others have never gone on the road. I heard someone sneer, 'tour,' " he said, as everyone of his audience cringed, or tried to look innocent or unconcerned, or looked away from his murderously scathing glance altogether. "But mark you, the 'tour,' " he sneered wonderfully, "is not the humble undertaking it once was."

"Then why didn't you advertise it as such in the casting call?" a bold gentleman from the back row called out, echoing the unspoken question so many of them had. And then was sorry he had, for bold as he'd been, Kyle Harper's eye was bolder, and far back as he was, it was not far enough away to escape that withering glance.

"Because, my dear sir," Kyle said with aplomb, "I am not a fool, and know the reputation of the very word 'tour.' And I wanted no second-raters applying for my company. If you are such, please feel free to leave. Ah, but," he said as the theater remained still as a churchyard, "were you such, you wouldn't be here now, would you?"

He chuckled and they all felt enormously relieved.

"No," he went on, "no, the touring company is no longer a pathetic cluster of cannots who slink from the cities to perform before chickens and hogs. No, because America is growing. I grant you it is difficult to believe, but only a small part of it is here in New York City," he said on an engaging, conspiratorial smile. "And so I—we—will be bringing theater to America— the newest, richest . . ."—he paused as if he found the word as delicious as they all did—"yes, *richest,* Americans—those in the golden West. The mine owners and ranchers, the cattlemen and railroad czars. The Silver Circuit has had the stage to itself out there too long, my friends. Those who join us will also be performing upon the stages of those beautiful new opera houses that have been built in the West—those magnificent new citadels of culture—in such boomtowns as Denver, Leadville, and Aspen, and then will return with me in triumph to begin the new decade in New York! Because those who join us will be members of the new 'Golden Circuit'!" he cried.

He waited until the echoes of his voice had died away. And then spoke into that profound silence.

"Those who come with us will make their names and their fortunes," he said with such quiet conviction that even those who doubted it did not doubt him. *"If . . ."* he said, and paused to smile in a most unpleasant way, *"if* they're professionals. Which means in more than their skills. Which means they accept that traveling is not always easy, but that they must perform every day anyway. The show must go on, especially on the road. When we hand out our bills, the audience comes at great expense to themselves, and they don't like to be disappointed. If they are, I am. And if I am, I promise you, you shall be. For we shall be our own self-contained kingdom, bringing our own sets, stagehands, cast, and crew to create our own wondrous world wherever we go. And since we shall be far from home, I'll be in the position of being the king of that magic land: I will be your father, your confessor, and your helpmeet. A kind, loving, compassionate one. *If*

you choose to come with me. *If* I choose you to come
with me.''

He could have raised them as an army then, and they
would have marched off to war against anyone he
pointed at, the young woman watching from the wings
thought with sincere admiration. She came from an
acting family, and had seen Booth doing Brutus from
her cradle, but seldom had seen such a performance.
She darted a quick glance to her pupil, Lottie Lesley.
Yes, Lottie was watching Kyle Harper as if she were
playing Lady Ursula, and he, the lead, in *The Mes-
merist*. Well good, Hannah thought, then Lottie would
do her best and she might get the job, and then she'd
finally be able to pay what she owed. Which meant,
Hannah thought with rising delight, that she herself
might at last be able to have a dinner that her landlady
hadn't half cooked.

She was doing sums in her head, thinking of the
debts she could pay off if her star pupil finally did pay
her accounts in full, when a dissident voice pierced
the stillness, and shattered the mood.

"Well, *we* should never have come if we'd known it
was a *tour*," the great-bosomed lady in black bom-
bazine cried. "New York *is* the stage, elsewhere a
mere waste of time, and we did not come here to waste
our time. Come, Isa!" And rising from her chair like
leviathan from the waves, she gripped her umbrella in
one hand and her cherubic little blond girl in the other,
and marched from the stage, her heels pounding like
drumbeats as she departed. The blond child looked
back as she was propelled forward, and so saw Kyle
Harper's smile. It might well scar her for life, Hannah
thought with unease. If it didn't, then his comment
certainly would.

"Possibly, madam," he called to her retreating
back, "because you haven't the time to waste. Puberty
awaits you in the wings. Infant prodigies ought to be
within calling distance of childhood," he added in a
not very confidential aside to the others. "Dear Isa
may be playing *Little Lord Fauntleroy* today, but I'd

wager she'll be ready to stand-in for Lillian Russell by next week.''

When the laughter subsided, he said coolly, "Any others? If you leave now, I promise you may leave unscathed, as well as unemployed, I am a fair man. Fare thee well," he said with an air of great unconcern as, after a moment's hesitation, several others slinked away.

"Now then," he said, as he looked at those remaining, "to work, perchance to be hired, eh?"

"One question, please sir," a young fellow called out. "I see that grand comedian, Lester Claxon, here. And my old friend, Fay, just there—is a soprano. I see some dancers, as well. And a prestidigitator, I have seen his act. Surely you cannot need us all, I can think of no play that would."

Hannah was as much struck by this as the rest of them, and she stopped thinking about the much needed winter coat she'd buy if Lottie got the part, to listen to Kyle Harper's answer.

"Ah, my observant friend," he said on a vulpine smile, "I hope you can act as well as you see! But I surely do need you all. New times call for innovations, do they not? We're going to tour the West to bring them theater: which means all the theater arts. We shall not be precisely a variety show, nor a dramatic ensemble, nor even a burlesque. We'll present playlets and songs, magic and dance, even humor. Who can resist a night of drama, music, laughter, and tears? We'll have it all. We'll give the world a new concept, that new word 'vaudeville' an even newer meaning, and ourselves, fame and fortune! But not if we don't make a beginning somewhere, right? Come, let us begin. Perhaps the actors first, since they are so observant?" he said charmingly.

Hannah occupied herself watching Kyle Harper make swift work of auditions. The inquiring young actor did get the job, his open face made him a perfect stock hero; an older, dignified-looking gentleman who might be anyone's dream father was hired, along with a skeletal-looking fellow with a lush mustache, who'd

make a convincing villain even if he couldn't act, and
a few assorted all-purpose men were signed on as well.
Before the female dramatic roles were even heard, the
one remaining child, the dark-haired girl, got the nod
for infant roles, if only by default. And then those
aspiring to ingenue were called forth, and Hannah
stiffened.

An ethereally fair young girl did the usual monologue from *Romeo and Juliet*, but though she was
lovely enough to make eyes water, her voice was a
thread, the sort, Hannah thought with relief, that no
lessons—nothing short of surgery, in fact—could remedy. There was a look of regret in Kyle Harper's eyes
as he let her go and called the next actress to her mark.
This was fairer competition, Hannah thought, because
the young woman, although only merely attractive,
seemed to feel the words she was saying, and made a
stylish, if not a beautiful, *Ophelia*. And then, after
dismissing her with a speculative look, Kyle called
Lottie up. Hannah actually held her breath. But Lottie
said it all perfectly. As if, Hannah thought a bit sadly,
it really mattered in her case.

Lottie had worn a vivid peony pink frock, so she'd
command the eye, but a man would have to be blind
not to note the way she'd cinched in her already tiny
waist so that her truly impressive breasts could better
be seen. And when she'd whipped off her great belled
skirt to show the stage pantaloons she wore for the
role she was to do, the gasps the men gave were not
so much for the cleverness at having come prepared in
costume as they were for the curving hips and limbs
that went on display. If not the most impassioned *Portia* ever, she was probably the most voluptuous one.
Kyle Harper grinned.

After a few more girls were scarcely attended to as
they tried for the job, Lottie got it. Hannah sighed,
now it was entirely possible that she might not only
be able to have that lovely restaurant dinner and the
new coat, but if she was careful with the rest of the
money owed her, she might actually be able to stay on
in her rooms until Christmas. She hurried to Lottie's

side as the older women took their turns at auditioning.

"Congratulations!" she breathed as Lottie struggled
to refasten her skirt.

Lottie nodded her thanks as Hannah said a little hurriedly, glancing down to check her lapel watch, "I'll
be running along now, I've another pupil coming at
three . . . ah, I imagine you'll be leaving on tour soon,
how many more lessons do you think you'll be able to
fit in before you do?"

"Whad d'ya think I yam? Loony?" Lottie laughed.
"I got the jarb, did'n I?"

"I mean, that is to say, you'll get new parts, and
you'll want to get them right, won't you?" Hannah
asked, not liking the supercilious smile on Lottie's
carmined lips at all.

"But I," Lottie said with great care, enunciating as
carefully as Hannah had taught her to do, "cahn do
ahlmost anything I attempt, cahn I not? For I am an
actress, am I not? Cheez, Hanner," she said with a
more natural curl to her lip, "can't let a meal ticket
go, canya? Gettin' greedy, ain'tcha?"

Hannah grew pale. "No, Lottie," she said, "I don't
believe I am, nor do I think you do either, not if you
think about it. But it's not necessary. If you feel that
way, now that you have a position, you can pay me
what you owe me and I'll be on my way."

Lottie stared at her.

"I know it's a large sum, but you usually get an
advance when you go on tour, and if it isn't large
enough, we can work out some sort of payment sys-
tem, you can mail me what you can from week to week
. . . well, every two weeks then," Hannah said, as
Lottie laughed.

"Here," Lottie said, reaching into her handbag and
drawing out some bills. "That should do it."

It was Hannah's turn to stare. "Lottie," she said
when she could, as Lottie turned around to watch the
dancers begin their auditions, "this is . . . this is only
payment for three lessons. I've been giving you them
for weeks . . . here," she scrabbled in her own hand-

bag and pulled out a notebook and riffled through it
frantically. "August 7th and 9th, two on August 12th,
August 14th, and then that long session that I agreed
could count as only three on August 16th, and . . .
and . . . Lottie," she said, so agitated she stammered.
"L-look here, here it is: the total is eighteen lessons.
You've only paid for three!"

Lottie turned and grinned. "So what?" she said
with the impudent smile Hannah had taught her for
audition for the ingenue in *Springtime Girl*.

"So . . . so . . . but it's *eighteen!*" Hannah said,
suddenly seeing a little nasty tilt to the smile that she
hadn't taught, and finally understanding why Lottie
hadn't got that part.

"Yeahr? Well, prove it!" Lottie said triumphantly.
"Whad'd'ya gonna do? Sue me? Run afta me? Yeahr?
Get owda here," she scoffed.

Hannah trembled with rage. She'd given Lottie lessons on the understanding that they'd all be paid for
when they came to fruition. They'd decided that on the
day Lottie had come to her little studio to beg for
acting lessons. It wouldn't be easy for a shop girl who
aspired to the theater, yet Lottie's fervently voiced
dream had touched her heart—even if that same rough,
coarse voice had grated on her ear. Still, Hannah knew
the theater, and knew Lottie's spectacular looks and
natural theatricality would get her in the door, and if
only something could be done about that voice . . .

But she was supposed to be an acting teacher, wasn't
she? It had been a challenge as well as a charity, disguised as a gamble. Now it seemed she'd known more
about the theater than human nature. She still couldn't
quite believe it.

"You're jesting, aren't you?" Hannah asked with
sinking hopes as she saw Lottie's sneer. "But you *owe*
it to me, Lottie, you do!"

"Wouldya quit it, hah?" Lottie screeched. "Shut
yer fly trap! An' leam me be!"

"How very entertaining," a not very amused voice
cut in. "And here I thought we were auditioning the
sopranos *after* the tenors. Or could it be you wish to

sing as well as be our ingenue, Miss . . . ah, Lesley? But surely that was a burlesque song you were just singing, was it not?'' Kyle Harper asked, as silence fell over the stage and the diminished audience of those hired on and those few still waiting to audition looked on.

''Wouldya beleeve it? She gimme a few poynters an' she wants ta bleed me white fer it ferever,'' Lottie cried out in her normal hoarse, flat tones. ''The crust of some persons, huh?'' she said somewhat more quietly as she saw Kyle Harper's expression. ''It is certainly something, ain't it . . . ah . . .'' she said before she fell still.

He passed a hand through his hair as he swung around to see that all the rejected ingenues had left the theater. Then he snatched up a thin book and stalked over to Lottie. Hannah, who'd been standing in the shadows, shrunk even farther back, but his burning eyes were on no one but Lottie. He flipped the book open, thrust it at her, and pointed to a place with one long finger.

''Read!'' he commanded.

''Er,'' Lottie said, as she swallowed, cast one sidewise look at Hannah, another up to Kyle, and then bit her lip as she looked at the book again.

''. . . Er, here?'' she asked, and as he gave a brief nod, she cleared her throat and read, in a much softer voice than she'd used moments before. '' 'Tis known before: our prep-preperashun stanze in expectashuns of them,' '' she read. '' 'O dear Fodder, it is thy bizzness thad I go about, therefore great Franze . . .' She stumbled on, until he cried, ''Enough!''

''Enough,'' he sighed. ''Ah, William, forgive us,'' he said to the ceiling, before he stared down at Lottie again. ''Alas, Cordelia. Cordelia—the very heart of 'Lear'—'Lear' the heart of any touring company . . . you play her like the rump of it,'' he said flatly. ''And yet, and yet you virtually *sang* us Portia. How comes this?'' he demanded.

Lottie paused a moment, and then, after daring to

meet his eyes, said sullenly, jerking a thumb behind her, "Hadda teecha. Her. Miz Roberts."

"You trained *her* to do that sublime Portia?" he asked Hannah wonderingly, and then his eyes opened wider as she stepped out from the shadows.

"Well, she really has the most amazing facility," Hannah said at once, determined to be fair. "Rather like a parrot, actually . . ."

"*Very* like a parrot, or some other jungle creature," he said, taking Hannah by the arm and steering her aside so that he could talk to her privately, and see her in a clearer light. His own face cleared as he did.

The young woman before him was dressed in gray, and more neatly than fashionably, at that. But no garment was needed to point up her loveliness, not to his practiced eye. She was slender enough to scarcely need the stays that held in her trim waist, and yet even the pilgrim color and cut of her high-necked gown couldn't conceal the lush contours beneath. Still, in her case, the eye was only momentarily distracted by her form. She'd clear white skin and masses of smoky dark hair that neither her strict hairstyle or hat could wholly subdue, since here and there silky wisps, like wanton shadows that mocked her efforts, escaped to tease at the margins of her face. In fact, he thought bemusedly, half her attraction lay in the fact that she seemed made for bed matters, even as the other half sternly sought to repudiate it. She'd winged dark brows and a small, serious nose, and great dark eyes that seemed surprised by her lush pink mouth; it really was the most remarkably sensuous mouth, he thought, nodding his approval at the small sharp white teeth that showed as she spoke again.

"The altercation was because I'd given Miss Lesley several lessons that she decided she need not pay for," Hannah said worriedly in her clear, expressive voice. "But indeed, I have the records here," she added, holding up her little leather notebook in one gloved hand.

He disregarded it. "You give acting lessons?" he asked.

"Indeed," she said eagerly, nodding, because she thought she might yet retrieve something from this disappointing day. One never knew who might send business one's way, and this gentlemen would certainly know a great many actors, many more would-be ones. She extracted a card from her handbag and offered it to him.

" 'HANNAH ROBERTS' " he read. " 'STUDIO FOR ELOCUTION, DRAMATIC READINGS, AND VOICE TRAINING. Special attention given to Speech Impediments, Debilities. Reasonable rates, patient instruction, experienced tuition for Ladies, Gentlemen, and Children.' And household pets?" he asked gently. "Come, my dear, this is all very well, but it is all nonsense. Why are you not on the stage, where you belong?"

"I have no wish to act," she said hurriedly. "I quite enjoy my role as preceptor in the theater arts."

"Perhaps that is because you have no experience of it—or a bad one. My dear," he said in a softer voice, for when he wished, his whispers could be heard across the room, and now she was sure his voice went no farther than her own ear. "You have a place in my company as of now, you know. As if I would keep on that . . . that parrot of yours, when I can have an actress such as yourself!"

"Oh no," she said in a matching whisper, her eyes wide. "I do have such experience—much experience of the theater, Mr. Harper, and want no more, I assure you. I come from a family of actors, but I am a teacher and a good one, I believe, and happy to be so. Or at least," she said with a small smile that almost beguiled an answering one from him, before he caught himself at it. 'I'd be happy if my practice of it would just pick up a little bit, and my clients," she added, casting a significant glance to Lottie, "would pay me what they owe me."

"What experience in the theater?" he asked, amused, 'I've been in the New York Theater since the day before forever and never heard of a Roberts family. Of course, I do know several 'Roberts,' " he mused. "Let's see, there's Winthrop Roberts, but he's

old as the hills and never wed, and . . . ah yes, Ada
Roberts, she's your age and a professional orphan.''

"My married name is Roberts. I'm a widow. My
former name,'' she hesitated before she lifted her chin,
looked him in the eye, and said, "was . . . Darling.''

She winced as he blurted explosively enough for all
eyes to turn to them, "Darling? Darling? Of course!
Those eyes, that hair. You're *his* daughter. Good Lord,
my child, why not say so at once then?''

She didn't smile at the sound of a man so near her
own age calling her a child. Instead, she flushed, and
turning her head, said low enough so that her very
tone was a reprimand for his calling attention to their
conversation, "Because 'Roberts' is my legal name
now, and because I wish to prove that I can succeed
on my own, whatever my name. Can you understand
that?''

"No,'' he said honestly, because success was the
only thing he did understand, and any road to it not
taken amazed him.

"But it's so,'' she said mutinously. Then she composed herself and put out her gloved hand to him,
adding, "And so I thank you for your offer, but I must
go now.''

"Go penniless, and go alone, and go unpaid for all
your pains?'' he asked, recovering himself as quickly.
"Because even if she agreed to pay you, she could
not. Well, but I won't hire her. Would you?'' he asked
as she stared at him.

" 'O Fodder!' indeed,'' he said with a quirked smile
at her distress. "Can you see it? Or rather, hear it?
There's nothing wrong with seeing her,'' he said.
"Blondes with such, ah, obvious graces can get away
with a great deal on the stage. And she has a certain
flair,'' he conceded, "but not with that voice, and that
diction. Even New Yorkers won't buy a Desdemona
who sounds like she comes from a barge in the East
River and not Venice. And certainly, a western audience won't. They won't understand a word . . . unless,
of course, you're willing to continue coaching her. For

pay," he said quickly. "Handsome pay," he added as he saw the hunger for the offer clear in her eyes.

"But she . . ." she began, as he cut her off to say, "is doubtless vile, and I don't blame you for not wishing to associate with her again. But if you know the theater, you know that actresses are not valued for their own personalities but rather those that they can put on, and this time you will be working for me, not her."

It was reasonable and it was fair, and aside from that, she didn't know how she could go on as she was if she didn't accept his offer. It was actually a gift from a suddenly attentive heaven, she thought on a sigh.

"Very well," Hannah said courteously. "I'll do it. Only give me the parts you wish her to get right, and tell me how much time I have, and I'll do my best."

"Ah," he said, taking her hand in his firm clasp. "But you've all the time in the world, my dear, or at least three months of it, which is as you know, almost the same to an actor. Because you'll be coming with us, of course. Well, we are a repertory company," he said to her blank stare, "and if I decide it's time for a change of scene, I can't have an ingenue who murders *Macbeth* as she performs in it, simply because her instructor is miles away from the scene of the crime, can I?"

And though it was the last thing she wished to do, she knew it was the very thing she must, because there was no hope for it, she thought dazedly as he shook her hand, he was absolutely right. But that hardly made it better.

Still, Hannah thought when she got back to her rooms, took off her hat, and stood surveying the work she had to do, it could be a great deal worse. At least she'd be able to pay the rent on her rooms and so have them when she returned, and if she didn't go, it might well be that she'd lose them even before the new year. And then she'd have to go creeping back to her father and mother, begging houseroom . . . with Father being so extravagantly noble about forgiving her for striking out on her own, and Mother being trium-

phantly so . . . No, she thought immediately, stooping
to collect her playbooks, beginning the sad business
of packing at once instead of after dinner as she'd
thought to do—traveling with a dozen Lottie Lesleys
would be preferable to that. Anything would. Almost
anything, she thought, sinking into a dispirited little
heap in the center of the room, all her playbooks in
her lap. Because she reminded herself how she'd gotten herself into this very predicament.

Some girls married young in order to run away from
home. She'd married early so as to try to have one.
An only child of two magnificently self-involved parents, on the move with every new booking they secured, she'd always longed for what she'd seen her
parents able to enact on stage, but never experienced
in reality: a stable life in a real home. One that would
be far from the theater, a place like the ones she read
about in *Little Women* and other of Miss Alcott's
books, or like those she'd seen portrayed behind the
footlights since she'd been old enough to dream of a
better life. It didn't have to be an elegant place, such
as the kind she'd seen created for *School For Scandal*
or *The Mighty Dollar,* for example. No, it might even
have a humble parlor like the one she remembered the
Beacon Theater set up for *East Lynne*—something filled
with samplers and rag rugs and glowing firelight, a
home that was so warm and welcoming, the audience
could understand, after one look, why a girl would
truly weep to be exiled from it. And a kitchen, a real
one, only very like the one she'd seen at the Savoy for
The Old Homestead: a place fit for unimaginably do-
mestic wonders to be done in; a room in which mirac-
ulous things, like the actual baking of pies, could be
performed. And a front yard filled with real, not card-
board flowers. But most of all, whether elegant or
homely, it would be a home like none she'd ever
known: one that wasn't rented or temporary. With
someone in it like no one she'd ever known: someone
who'd love her for herself, and not for her reaction to
themselves.

John Roberts had come backstage one afternoon

when she'd been seventeen. He'd come to deliver a parcel from his mercantile store, only that. He hadn't even tried to scrape up an acquaintance with any actress there, he'd only ogled them as if they'd been creatures from another world, which of course, they'd been to him. But so she'd found him to be to her. Because they'd started talking. And then walking out together. He was no more than average-looking, and she could not, even now, remember even the cleverest things he'd said. But he'd listened and looked at her as she'd never been attended to before, and he'd said he never cared for any other girl as he did for her. She'd no reason to disbelieve him, because for all he was and was not, he was certainly no actor.

They hadn't known each other very long, nothing like the year she'd heard girls from the outside world required for a proper courtship, when she decided to marry him, as he had asked. And at once. As he had not. Because when Father had finally noticed their courtship, he'd laughed at the very idea of her making a life with a man from outside the theater, and one with such meager prospects, at that. It had done what John's courtship had not had a chance to do. It decided her. And so by the time *Julius Caesar* was done with its run, and it was time to move on, she'd moved out and into holy wedlock with John.

Father had come to the hasty wedding and wept at being made to feel so old, as Mother had grieved at losing an able pair of hands backstage. To give them their due, they'd said it was because they'd expected so much more from her. John only wanted a wife. At least she knew she could be that.

But she was wrong. Because not two months after their wedding day, John had finally raged up from out of their bed, telling her the truth, at last, about her deficiency as he'd packed. And then, still avoiding her eye, had left her and the city forever. She could hate, but scarcely blame him for it. It couldn't have been easy for him, he was not that much older than she was, although vastly more experienced of the world—and women. How should she blame him for refusing to live half a life with her? And all because of something so profoundly intimate and embarrassing that she still could not so much as think of it without blushing. A thing neither of them could have suspected or helped or even discussed before they were wed, much less at any length after—a thing she'd been born with—or was—she'd never got the terminology straight. It hardly mattered. It was certainly enough to know she was imperfectly made, and so for all her charms, useless as a wife or a prospective mother, as well as unable to grant him what he most wanted from her.

She understood that part of it absolutely. There'd been enough difficulty to establish that fact even before he'd spoken. Isolated as her life had been, she'd no other female to confide in—certainly not her mother—and had been unsure of whether she had to go to a doctor, and then afraid to, and then it was unnecessary. He'd been to see one, he said. She was not, she was given to understand, a complete woman, and certainly, even after all that embarrassment and pain, all too obviously not his wife. It was because of a mistake of nature, imperceptible to her eye even if she'd the courage and the means to look, or the knowledge to know what she'd see if she did. An error of nature's that she'd not known about, but one of great magnitude for him—and her. Still, she understood his decision even as she wept for it. After all, hadn't she run from a life, however attractive on the surface, that offered her nothing she really wanted?

It was ironic that it turned out she was so like everything she'd tried to escape from. Because it seemed to her that she was like that magnificent cake she'd coveted when she'd been a child, the one she'd seen her mother carry on stage one night . . . only to discover after the show that it was literally only for the show, being nothing but a perfect fraud with wooden layers and painted icing.

She'd no course but to conceal the fault as she did the hurt of having it, which wasn't difficult since it required only that she never again permit anyone mental or physical intimacies with her. And since she'd never had the one and couldn't achieve the other, she was safe enough after she went back to the backstage of her parents' lives.

John Roberts had done better, though his life had been briefer. Because he'd taken up with some woman in Philadelphia, and produced a son with her before his hot temper had gotten him into a saloon brawl that took his life and widowed her. He'd left Hannah nothing but a hard lesson, and alone, even though she'd returned to her parents when he'd first left. What else was she to do? Now the very idea of marriage was absurd. Even if she were the sort of woman who had no morals, which she was not, the thought of a lesser and more profitable affiliation with a man—such as many girls in the theater had with their admirers—was equally ridiculous.

Once, a few years later, when a particularly charming young Tristan had seemed uncommonly taken with her, she'd stolen out to buy a medical book, which had told her nothing she didn't know, and more she couldn't understand. He'd been diverted by a more accommodating ingenue by the time she'd finished reading it, but by then she'd begun to accumulate more medical books expressly written for the common man and woman. There were dozens available; people didn't trust doctors, even if there'd been enough of them around to trust. There were fewer doctors that one could even think of speaking to about that secret, shameful subject usually covered in chapters titled: "The Generative Organs" or "Women's Difficulties" or "Words of Advice on Marital Matters." Soon Hannah estimated she knew more about the evil consequences of self-pollution, the various diseases of womankind, and the way to birth healthy babes, than any female of her age in New York City. But nothing more about her problem. And as all the diagrams of intimate anatomy were done in cross section, it was even impossible to recognize anything she possessed. She gave it up.

Some time later, when a truly kind as well as determined older gentleman from *She Stoops To Conquer* sought her company, she found a new book by a doctor whose offices happened to be not two blocks from the theater they were at. There were dozens of testimonials to him from satisfied patients in the book; he wrote in a kind, agreeable manner. Best of all, at the conclusion of his book, after the usual chapters on diseases, the evils of unfortunate habits, and the rigors of childbirth, he'd written a personal note. For a fee of five dollars, he stated that he would diagnose and prescribe for any woman's ailment that she described to him by letter, because he realized so many lived too far from his New York City offices for any other kind of consultation to be possible. And because, as he wrote with exquisite discretion:

"I have found that the mail offers facilities for a confidence between the patient and physician by which they may inform him of delicate matters that they would never divulge at an interview: matters that they have long worried over, and yet dared not consult their family physician about."

Since Hannah's family physician changed with each theater they played, and she was sure whichever one she consulted wouldn't hesitate to share her confidences with her Father—and that, she could not bear to think about—Dr. Smith's offer was a godsend. She passed the better part of three nights revising her letter until it was a model of delicacy of feeling and euphemism. Dr. Smith's eventual reply was no less a masterpiece.

He reviewed the several things that could be her problem in language that only her reading of several dozen medical books enabled her to understand. He then wrote with genuine sorrow, that in her case he believed her particular problem would need a personal examination in order to diagnose. Then he wrote:

"But, of course, as you are now a widow, the problem need never concern you again. Should you remarry, your husband might wish a finer diagnosis, and in that case, I would urge you to overcome your understandable and laudable scruples and fine sense of modesty, and come to my offices immediately for a thorough examination, Sincerely.''

Men continued to find her attractive; it had to do, she believed, with things she'd little to do with—her eyes, the way they seemed fascinated by her mouth . . . She learned to disregard them. If she felt so much as the stirrings of temptation, she knew enough not to. She acquired a reputation for virtue. She knew it for wisdom.

She acquired more. She plotted and planned another escape. It wasn't that her parents were cruel or unfeeling, only that she'd learned by hard experience from an early age onward that they were quintessential actors, and so thought only of themselves and simulated every other feeling. It suited them, but she was weary of that. Nor was it that she didn't love them, but only that she knew they scarcely noted or needed her mite of adoration. She wished for more, even if it was only to eventually deserve her own love for herself.

Times were changing, these days a woman might try to support herself, if she must. Of course, it was scandalous, but she was, after all, from a theatrical family. She might have inherited some of her parents' selfishness, if not their brilliance, she thought, because if she were only to be a helpmeet of theirs, she saw little reason to continue to be, at all. She reasoned they must have passed on some of their courage to her, too, since an actor must have that or be nothing. Because after six years she'd stored up enough money and confidence to strike out on her own.

Which was, she conceded sadly, looking about her small studio now, certainly what she'd have done literally this time if it weren't for Kyle Harper's offer. It turned out that few people in New York City needed or wanted elocution lessons, at least not from her. There were too many well-known actors and actresses reduced to giving lessons in this city of theaters. And since there would never be any given by the woman who might be able to make a success at it—the one named Hannah Darling, a lady with a famous name that fairly shouted her experience and talent—she'd never have a real chance at it. But just imagining the look on Father's face if she'd taken his name and not his advice had been enough to keep her up nights. That—and the thought of her growing debts.

Because after six months at her new profession, she'd only three clients: little Harry Platt, the butcher's boy, whose stuttering irked his father so much it had almost caused him to lose a finger; Mrs. Harrison, who cherished dreams of reciting poetry at her church group so stirringly as to make Reverend Ames weep, before he proposed to her for her fine sensitivity; and, of course, the feckless Miss Lesley. Three clients, one of whom disliked her intensely. Not very much to show for having lived almost all of twenty-four years, Hannah thought wistfully as she sighed, arose, and began to make neat piles of that which she'd take, and that which she'd leave behind.

But she'd passed most of those years in the theater, and had a knowledge of it which was equaled by few women. And so she straightened her back as she straightened up her room, and remembered, at least, to keep that thought. Because she didn't doubt that where she was going, she'd need everything she could take with her.

Chapter Three

Singing on a train was no different from singing in the bath, it took faith in one's talents, even as it gave an entirely wrong idea of them. The Lord gave talent, rehearsal preserved it. One might be able to not eat for a day and live, not drink for a day and survive, but only two things were invariably fatal: not breathing for an hour, and not rehearsing for a day. An actor who didn't know his lines was like a peacock who'd lost all his feathers—a queer bird that wasn't good to look at, not good to hear, and not even better off dead, since he was too tough to eat and too big to bury fast. Kyle was full of adages like that, and those he didn't know, he made up when the need arose, which was every five minutes, or so it seemed to his newfound troupe.

He made them work all the way from New York to their destination in the West as much as he'd made them work back in New York. Since they hadn't had much time to rehearse before they'd left, they didn't object. Nor did they mind the myriad scripts and musical scores they were handed to look over, they were professionals, after all. But when they fell to looking out the train windows and seeing the rapidly changing scenery: the sudden dearth of houses, the increasingly empty vistas, the landscapes that weren't enlivened by

human hand or eye—that was when they resented his
urging them to work. Because that was when they
wanted the time to fret and brood.

"I never saw so much nuttin' in my life," Lottie
sighed as she gazed out the window at the deepening
dusk.

" 'Noth*ing,*' " Hannah corrected her absently, as
she matched her sigh.

"Oh no! My books say there are many jackrabbits,
elk, and antelope on the high plains, as well as deer,
and bison, Indians, and countless new settlers," Little
Polly Jenkins, their "infant prodigy," said brightly.
She spoke with irrepressible good spirits she seemed
to believe were expected of her, but which, as their
resident comedian, Lester Claxton, often said when
she wasn't within earshot, more nearly insured her
never surviving to adulthood.

"*Wonderful* houses that will make for us," Nelson
DeWitt said, bending to peer out the window. "Just
how does one appeal to an elk—or rather, *elkess?*" he
added quizzically, turning to grin sidewise at the ladies
who were clustered by the window, causing even little
Polly to blush. For though he was very handsome, in
the slightly exaggerated way of all leading men, for a
wonder, he seemed almost as nice as he was nice-
looking, for all he was a leading man.

" 'Music hath charms to soothe the savage beast,' "
their all-around villain, Frank Dupree, misquoted
wryly. "A few rounds of 'Home on the Range' would
probably do it."

"Yes, or 'Never Take the Horseshoe from the Door'
and 'With All Her Faults I Love Her Still,' if that
doesn't turn the trick," Nelson put in merrily.

"That's 'breast,' " Maybelle Ansonia, their digni-
fied older woman, corrected them. And when they
turned to look at her, she added, shaking her silver
head in her best mother-of-the-clan manner, " 'charms
to soothe the savage 'breast,' was what you meant to
say."

"In your case, certainly," Nelson said, grinning and
making a great show of ducking should she take of-

fense, as he added, "but Frank's an engaged man, so he's better off staying with 'beast,' I think."

"Please! Think of the child," Polly's mother said reflexively, scarcely looking up from her knitting. Then Frank said gallantly, "Very true, but a man's a man for all that," and he bowed to Maybelle, stroking his mustache and arching an eyebrow in the grand manner.

"That's as it may be," Maybelle said in a lofty way, while she nonetheless smiled as she smoothed the massive bodice of her gown. She added gloomily, "But I don't sing, nor do I wish to charm livestock."

"It is most awfully empty out there . . ." Hannah agreed softly, for she'd been staring out the window as they'd been rehearsing, watching the evening creep over the barren land, sowing it with shadows. Her sad little comment quieted them. She felt, as well as heard the sudden silence that had fallen over them, and blinked, for the light in the railway car contrasted with the cool shades of purple and gray that she'd been staring at. Seeing the somber faces gazing out at what had hypnotized her, she added quickly, "But I daresay that's because of the hour—why it's actually blue out there now. Twilight is such a sad time. I've never seen it properly before. In New York there's no time to see the sunset and the moonrise."

She saw the huge new moon continuing to rise, banishing the blue twilight, but flooding the landscape with an even eerier silvery light, and went on, "We hardly ever look up really, except to see if it will rain, we just see the sky brightening behind the buildings before the dark comes over everything. If we see that at all . . . Why, right now, the gaslights would be being lit, people would be hurrying home from work— or out to dinner, the traffic would be beginning to pick up . . ." She swallowed hard against the unexpected lump of homesickness that threatened to close her throat and added, too brightly, "How lovely nature is, after all."

They remained still, each lost in thought, until they

heard the omnipresent background sound of clattering wheels increase as the door to the car slid open.

"Ah!" Kyle cried as he entered the car and startled them back to reality. "Not rehearsing! So you've all got your parts in *Her Fatal Charm* down pat. And so speedily! I can scarcely wait to hear you." He settled himself on the edge of a chair and looked up at them with great expectation.

"We haven't," Maybelle admitted, "we were merely . . . taking a break."

"Breaking your hearts, more like. What is this? Come, come," Kyle said, rising and pacing down the center of the long aisle before he swung back to confront them again. "My songbirds in the next car are in as high spirits as they are in voice right now. Ah, but I see . . ." he said wisely, cocking his head to the side, "that's just it. We've the singers and the comedians, the magicians and the dancers in there. All the lively arts. You, my poor fellow tragedians, are likely exhausted in spirit after enacting the trials of those you portray. Such, such is the price of drama, my friends," he said sympathetically.

Since none of them, not even Polly, felt the smallest twinge of sympathy for the stock characters they played in *Her Fatal Charm*—a playlet to do with the tribulations of an erring daughter, a drunken husband, and a greedy landlord, that they all agreed wasn't a patch on *East Lynne*, although it was stolen from it as deftly as copyright laws would allow—they fell still again.

Kyle still wore his outsize look of sympathy when Hannah spoke up.

"We . . . we were taking a break and observing the twilight, merely," she said.

"We were wondering whether we'd have anything in our audience but tumbleweeds," Frank said.

"We were thinking of New York," John Wills, their lead middle-aged male, said.

"*Polly* was learning her lines," Mrs. Jenkins volunteered, earning her a sour look from everyone, even Kyle.

"Ah," Kyle said on a long, audible sigh, "I am

lucky that none of you were my forefathers or mothers.''

He let them regard him doubtfully before he went on.

''I'd never have tasted oysters if you had been. Imagine!'' he said in a such a thrilling tone that they all were willing to imagine whatever he proposed, even the possibility that he was being sincere. ''If any of you had been the first man or woman, upon seeing your first oyster—a rock, some of you might say, or a barnacle, another would guess—and then whatever you thought it was, you'd have tossed it away. Because it was an ugly thing, ridged, hard, and shelled, covered with a beard of weed, brine, and sand. If you'd seen a gull cracking one open and feasting on it, you'd certainly not have bothered to try one once you'd seen the naked, pulpy thing within. But what you'd have missed! What I'd have missed! Something rich, meaty, and tangy. And nourishing. And some say, ah—in deference to dear Polly—invigorating.''

They smiled as he went on, ''Now look at what you're doing! The same thing. You look out the window and see nothing but brush and grass, and are immediately prepared to fly back to the city, where everything is apparent, where the spirit of adventure means crossing a street against traffic. Oh dear!'' He sank to a seat and seemed to lapse into a despondency so profound that even those who knew his usual gambits began to worry for him. Then he bounded up again and pointed a long finger at them.

''Tell me!'' he demanded. ''If you lived out there, in among the rocks and the mountains and the grass, what would you want most in life?''

''Ah, . . . company,'' Hannah said, seeing the finger aimed at her.

''Entertainment,'' Maybelle added immediately in turn.

Kyle pointed at each of them, and they each responded in their turn and according to their own temperament, or what they thought he was after them to say: ''Excitement,'' ''Civilization,'' ''Friends,''

"Crowds," "People," One even putting in a weak: "Umm—interesting things," when all other city pleasures had been mentioned.

"Exactly," Kyle beamed upon them. "Just so: theater," he said triumphantly.

"All of those things mean theater, and they need theater," he said. "Out there—somewhere beyond your eyes, are people who need you, and who are willing to pay—and well—to see you. Oh, my friends," he said rhapsodically, "I have seen the theaters they've built to entice you. As fine as any in any city I've seen—no, some are finer. Tabor's Opera House in Denver—a gem worthy of London town. Red plush and gold curtains, a stage that an elephant could waltz upon, the audience swagged in gilt and hung with velvet, electric lights and a backstage—" He kissed his fingers to the sky, as though bereft of words to describe its wonders. But not for long. "And the opera house in Leadville! Not to mention the new jewel in the crown of the new West—the Wheeler Opera House in Aspen . . . friends, they are thronged every night of the week, no matter who's playing there, because they're starved for us.

"Who is starved? All the people of the West you cannot see from this train. Those too wealthy to want to live on the tracks—where I believe you expect them to," he said on a laugh as they smiled with him, "since, as you haven't seen them, you don't believe in them. And others who must live in the new cities: those who run mines and refineries, and the fortunes made from them. And all the other men and women the new prosperity has brought together. Now, do you wish to look out the window and pine for the city you know, or accept that I've seen the ones you will know, the ones that breathlessly await you?"

But now the landscape outside the train was obscured by the blackness of night, and only their own dimly reflected images could be seen, ghostlike, on the windows. The only visible reality was within the brightly lit, onrushing train.

"I think we can go over that renunciation scene again, Lottie. I'm willing if you are," Nelson said.

"Oh yeahr . . . Oh yes, certainly," Lottie said, rising and taking up her script again.

Kyle smiled and watched them for a while before he ambled down the aisle and off into the next car again.

Only then did Maybelle leave off pleading for her husband not to throw their erring daughter out into the storm to say excitedly, "I didn't know we were going to play the Wheeler! It's the latest thing!"

"Or the Denver Tabor," Lottie said with her eyes wide.

"But we won't play any if we don't get it right," Frank said. Then he doused his radiant smile and growled, "Not another day, my beauty! The mortgage is due tomorrow—unless my payment is collected . . . tonight."

Kyle stood outside the door to their compartment and smiled, before he slid the door to the adjoining car aside. He heard the silence long before he saw all the woebegone faces before him.

"What's this?" he cried at once, striding into the car. "My songbirds molting and my dancers wilting? Come, where is your magic, Mr. Howard? And your jests, Mr. Claxton? Or like Yorick, have you expired? Look at your long faces! Ah, I see what it is. I've just come from the tragedians, and they're merry as the day is long, but then, my fellow variety stars, I know how hard it is to be gay all the time. Such, such is the fate of the clown—you must smile, though your heart be cracked. But why ever on earth should it be?"

"We were thinking about New York," one little dancer said softly.

"Good heavens!" Kyle cried. "How glad I am that none of you were my forefathers—or mothers!"

This time he waited until they all wore matching puzzled looks before he began to explain.

Dinner that night was a merry affair, with all the players together having such a good time of it that the other passengers were heard to observe that dining with

them was as good as a play. They worked all day in
groups according to their talents, but they played each
night as a theater company, ensemble, in every sense
of the word. Only three days out of New York City,
and there were already two liaisons absolutely confirmed: a winsome young brunet dancer had moved
into John Wills' compartment with him, and a very
young tenor seemed about to do so with Maybelle.
Mrs. Jenkins might cluck her tongue at the scandalous
goings on, but only because she and Polly would be
the ones evicted if he did, since there was no other
solution: he shared quarters with three other male
singers, so Maybelle could scarcely move in with him.
Although, as Mrs. Jenkins said spitefully, she probably would if they'd let her. Mrs. Jenkins might look
after her daughter's morals, but there were things even
Polly knew. After all, she'd been in the theater since
she could toddle.

Both Frank and Nelson seemed to be vying for a
chance to supplant Hannah as Lottie's roommate, that
was, when they didn't seem to be trying to evict Lottie
so that they could secure a place in Hannah's compartment. Amusing as they were, flattering as it was
as well, and gratifying, too—if only for the look on
Lottie's face when she saw the game they played—
when dinner was done, Hannah was only too glad to
rise and leave them a clear path to her pupil. Knowing
Lottie as she did, especially after sharing cramped
quarters with her, she pitied whoever won. She
doubted the bliss of carnality was worth the pain of
living so close to Lottie, and was actually pleased to
think she might soon be ousted from her quarters. She
didn't think she'd mind sharing a compartment with
anyone else, and had it in her mind not to protest at
whomever Kyle suggested—until he did, after he'd invited her to sit and take an after-dinner cordial with
him.

He eyed her appreciatively. She always dressed in
good taste, with a bit of theatricality to save that taste
from boredom. Tonight she wore a deep blue gown,
ornamented by nothing but the shape it displayed. Its

stark simplicity was highest drama: high at the neck, tight to the waist, and bustled lightly in the back. It was a rich, warm velvet that belied the stern fashion, and by showing up the purity of the creamy skin it encased, set a man to wondering about relative textures. His gaze went to her hair, and without thinking of what it was he must say, he said first what he wanted to, which was as strange and disturbing a thing for him as it was for her.

"Why do you wear it in such a puritan fashion?" he asked, gazing at her tightly bound hair.

"Why . . . because it looks more professional so," she answered, taken aback by his question as well as his frown.

But he was frowning at himself and his lapse and not at her, so he answered more roughly than was his usual way.

"It looks like a professional matron's at the Tombs," he said gruffly. "Your profession is the theater." He saw her hands flutter up to her hair as her eyes widened, and relented. "You might not wish to be taken for an actress," he said on an engaging smile, "but there's no need to look so fierce. You've lovely hair, and I should think you'd be able to appear to be whatever you wish to be taken for without such a masquerade."

"You may be right," she admitted. "It's only that as I am on my own, I don't want to appear to be fast."

"But you're not alone now," he said gently. "You're a member of a troupe. That's what I wanted to speak to you about. I've watched you. You're very good with *la* Lesley. Astonishing, that. It's like waxing a dirty floor, actually, how you make her shine! One could almost forget what lies beneath the luster."

She felt she should protest, but his phrasing was so apt, all she could do was to laugh and make little sounds of denial, while all the while she felt a great surge of relief because someone saw what was actually going on. Lottie resented her as much as she needed her—which was to say, a great deal. It wasn't only her spite and anger that plagued Hannah, it was the way

Lottie flaunted her desirability and bragged about her conquests, the more so when she realized that her haughty, mighty tutor and roommate had no beaux. A woman without a man or the promise of one was nothing at all, in Lottie's opinion. And since it was such a widely held one, there was never anything for Hannah to do but fall silent when Lottie brought the matter up, which was often. Or leave the room, if she could, when she was challenged by the nastier things in Lottie's arsenal.

Just last night, Lottie had undressed for bed, and then for the first time, suddenly showed dismay at her usually proud and brazen display of her nakedness. She'd gasped, making a great show of trying to cover her ample breasts with her little hands, so inadequate to the task. Then she'd stared, wide-eyed, at Hannah, explaining that she was trying to spare her sensibilities . . . or desires. All Hannah could do was gasp, before she managed to retort about preferring true Guernseys if her tastes ran to *that*. But Lottie didn't know what a Guernsey was. In fact, as Hannah went on to rage, she'd have trouble with the word "cow." But she was asleep by the time Hannah thought of a really good reply, so there was no satisfying revenge exacted for that bit of cruelty. Or any others, Hannah thought sadly. The stupid, she decided, were as safe as the smug when it came to insults. But since Hannah had vast experience with both sorts of people, she was soon asleep as well.

Kyle's words were balm. And he knew it.

"Still," he said thoughtfully, "you do well, and the sooner she gets into her parts, the sooner you'll be free of her. Then, you've only to wait about and see what we might require her to learn next. I expect to do very well with this tour, but all my outlay has gone into it. I'm not a rich man," he said sadly, brushing at his jacket's velvet sleeve as though he were trying to keep such an expensive thing in good order. Then he gazed up at her from large, pain-filled dark eyes and said sorrowfully, "And while I do not begrudge what I pay you, and am aware of how I lured you here

with us, and never, I promise you, intend to displace
you . . . ah, my dear Hannah, since you shall have so
much free time, I wonder if I could prevail upon you
to take up some other few little duties, as well? For
the truth is that just now I can't afford one more member of our little family—even if I could find anyone
else so suitable to the task as you."

"Oh, but that would be fine," she cried, and then
whispered, so the others couldn't hear their conversation. "Please don't apologize. I understand. In fact,
I'd find idleness embarrassing. I know the theater,
and know how many tasks there are to do. Indeed, I
did so many of them for my parents. Do you need
another dresser? Or someone to help with makeup? Or
props? Or costumes? Or making script notations? I'm
very good at all those things, I promise you," she
said, for all of it was true, though she didn't usually
brag about it and hadn't intended to volunteer to do
half of it. But he looked so abject. And he'd done the
one thing she could never resist: he'd needed her.

He smiled and put his hand over hers. It was, she
noted, forgetting the glass he'd just held, cold. He must
have been very nervous, she thought, smiling back at
him. She had, he thought again, wonderful lips, smiling only made them more tempting. He almost leaned
forward to taste them to seal their bargain, until he
remembered where he was, and what he hadn't estab-
lished as yet.

He always had a helper when he ran a show. And
always a female one. Not only because they were the
only ones happy to work for nothing more than his
approval. He might even have paid them, if he had to,
because unlike many men, he liked females very
much, and for more than their most obvious talents.
Which was never to say that he denied himself them.
No, his assistant was always also his lover, it made
things simpler. It saved time to give instructions from
bed, and was pleasant to have someone to share his
troubles with night and day. And a show always meant
trouble. But his last assistant had expected to stay on
with him past the run of his last show, then on into

the next, and just as he'd reminded her when he left her: permanency was never anything he required, desired, or had promised.

Now the position was open again. He always waited a week or so into the new show to make his pick. Hannah was his first choice. She was bright and desirable. And experienced in everything he needed. He considered himself very fortunate.

"Yes, yes," he said, matching her excitement, "I need someone to help with all of those things, and even more. Someone to take notes for me, and make note of things that I might miss. Much more than an assistant, I need a helpmeet, a friend, someone to work intimately with me. Someone lovely, clever, and true. You're of the theater, you know precisely what I mean. And you're a widow, so you know only too well what loneliness is," he added, lowering his voice to velvet. "I can't give more than my entire appreciation and devotion in return—for the run of the tour," he said urgently. "But life itself doesn't offer more guarantee—at least I promise I'll be grateful until our ways part again. Say you will, Hannah, do!"

"Oh, of course," she said fervently, caught up in his drama.

"Oh good!" he said happily, taking her hand. "We'll move your things into my compartment tonight. Well," he said, seeing her arrested expression, "from the look of things, Nelson will be taking your place in Lottie's compartment presently—at least her bed—and three *is* a crowd. We'll be a much more comfortable twosome, I promise you."

"What?" she asked, withdrawing her hand from his.

"Ah, we'll do very well together," he began, nonplussed by the look on her face, and as astonished by that as he was by his own uneasiness.

"I-will-not-*stay*-with-you," she said, spacing each word distinctly, her fine dark eyes glowing, her lips thinning to merely delicious, he thought, watching, fascinated by her fury. "And if this train were not moving now, I would step off it."

"Oh. You're not attracted to me," he said, so genuinely puzzled that he didn't have to think of how to show his complete lack of comprehension at her distress.

She relented. "That isn't it," she said fairly. "You're a very attractive man. It's only that I haven't thought of you that way before this. I never do. Or would. I don't do that sort of thing." She saw his confusion and sighed. He deserved honesty, because, she saw, he hadn't meant to insult her. If they'd been people from the vast outer world, she knew he'd have to be a cad or a bounder to make such a disgraceful offer to her, much less presume she'd go along with it. If she were of that world, she knew that even to speak of his offer, if only to object to it, would be to be exactly what he'd thought her to be, and so to be beyond the pale of polite society. But the theater was not polite society. And so if he were of that world and she an actress, his offer would be merely practical, and insulting only to someone such as herself.

But this situation was nothing like any of those. He was of her world as she was of his, and so she knew he meant nothing insulting by his offer, and thought it might be possible to make him understand yet.

"My marriage," she said, as she always said to those men she respected when they offered her any kind of liaison, "was dreadful. *Dreadful.* I never want to start that again. I could not. I therefore avoid such . . . doings with men. However kind or handsome they may be. Do you see?"

"Oh," he said, and sat back to study her.

She was either telling the truth, which would be a great pity, he thought, or telling a lie, which would be an even greater one, because she was so convincing it would mean she'd have to be the greatest actress he'd ever known, and she refused to act onstage. Or so she'd said. But then, she'd said some very odd things, and it was very early in their acquaintance, wasn't it? Change was the only constant he knew. If he couldn't have her in one way, and that was by no means certain as yet, then he could try for another. Because no pleasure was as great as finding a new talent he could make into a star, which could make him into a millionaire. Because nothing was so pleasurable as money.

"Understood," he finally said. "But will you take up your other duties? If I find you a room with a less demanding roommate?"

She gave him a long, level look. He gazed back with his most transparently opaque look of sincerity.

"And I won't importune," he promised.

She thought quickly. She had meant everything she'd said. Not working behind the scenes was harder for her than working. He obviously still needed her for more than his bed. And where else could she go if she alienated him now, after all?

"Very well," she said.

"Good, you'll stay with Peggy Callahan. She's with wardrobe," he said, neglecting to mention that Peggy *was* wardrobe, "and has her own compartment. Had, that is to say. But she won't mind sharing. She's young and shy, and very sweet. You'll have no trouble rooming with her, although," he said with great sympathy, "your bed is likely to be oh so cold at night."

"I will endure," Hannah said.

"I was afraid of that," he answered. And they both laughed so merrily, and looked at each other with such affection, that everyone in the company was amazed when they blithely went off to separate compartments that night.

The two gentlemen stood at the rear of the theater and looked around them. The fair-haired one nodded with satisfaction, as if he'd just bought the place, and not just excellent box seats in it. The raw-boned, darker-haired fellow next to him was so occupied with shifting his shoulders and turning his neck that he scarcely seemed to take in the splendor of the theater or the audience that was filling it.

"Royal," the light-haired gentleman said in an amused undertone, "you sure no one back at the bunkhouse put ants in your traveling bags? I've never seen so much squirming outside of an overturned rock.''

"They didn't have to. Things is itchy enough, thanks, Gray. These are the new duds you told me to get. You sure I'm not supposed to go on the stage instead of into the audience in them?'' his companion answered in an aggrieved undervoice. "It's all right for you," he said, eyeing Gray, and seeing, despite the scars on his tanned face and his slight limp, that he somehow even moved right in his clothes. He was every inch a tall, spruce, exquisitely correct-looking gentleman, his light hair and silver waistcoat pointing up the sober perfection of his evening wear.

"You look like you was born in Mrs. Astor's backyard," Royal commented. "Or lived there, and you would've if your brother had his way. But this is a damned uncomfortable getup for me. No wonder you came home after school back East. When I think those poor folks have got to wear suchlike everyday . . . You sure this is a good idea? I'm not so mad on seeing *The Corsairs* anyhow. Never heard of it.''

"It's got costumes and girls in tights, what more do you want, Shakespeare?'' Gray answered absently, looking around the ornate theater with something very like love.

It was an enormous place, as big as any of the playhouses he'd been to in the East. It had a raked orchestra made up of ornate plush seats, two gilded boxes at either end of the great stage, and a series of vivid murals of the muses on every high and gilt-edged wall; great golden pillars with paint-embroidered margins upheld the horseshoe balcony, and the closed curtains were rich and voluminous swags of cream and gold, the kind that promised to open up on a wonderland that would fit such a theater.

"Well, yeah, Shakespeare wouldn't be too poor a notion,'' Royal said, putting his finger inside his collar again in the hopes that it would save at least what remained of the tender skin on his neck from being scraped off.

"Too bad,'' Gray said without a trace of sympathy.

"Nothing like that's playing tonight. Come on, we'll get you seated in the box and you'll feel better."

"Feel better?" Royal asked incredulously once he'd taken his seat and discovered that he could be looked on by the audience as well as those onstage. "Damn, Gray, this is . . . this is . . ."

"Excellent," Gray said, his eyes sparkling in the reflected footlights. "Or at least it will be when the lights go down. You can see everything onstage clear from here. No chance of thinking some girl's a beauty and then finding out, once you've arranged to buy her dinner—and everything else she's offering—that the face you loved is back in her dressing room."

"Now lookie here," Royal said, forgetting, in his chagrin, his self-consciousness at being in new clothes and on plain view in front of hundreds of strangers, "I think I've about had it, Gray. I allowed I could use a break from work. I came to Denver and to that fancy hotel, and put these dude clothes on because I like a good play, and if you said a man's got to dress like a fool to get in, well, I could. And I did, didn't I?"

Gray smiled at his companion. There was nothing wrong with Royal's new clothes; his tight black frock coat and trousers were in the latest style, his shirt was white, and his waistcoat nicely embroidered with gold leaves. His hair was combed back and ruthlessly subdued with macassar oil. He looked very well, in fact. But even so, he looked out of place, and Gray had to admit his long-boned body looked even better in his usual flannel shirt and denims.

"But if you're trying to make me think I can just take my pick of the actresses I'm going to see tonight," Royal went on, "well, I think you been out riding without a hat too long, friend."

"That's what I said the first time I was taken to the theater by someone who knew the ropes. And that someone was my brother," Gray said with a reminiscent smile. "But that's just the plain truth. Of course, times have changed. Not every girl is willing anymore. Some are married and some have other gentlemen, and one in a million has other ways to have some extra fun and make some extra cash. And one in two million, as my brother found out,'' he said with a quirked smile, ''hasn't got the inclination. But that's the way of it, Royal. You'll see. So far as the clothes go—well, they go a long way, because there's not an actress here who'd stop to so much as have a chat with a cow-puncher, and that's another fact.''

''You're talking about more than a chat,'' Royal said on a sigh, discovering that if he leaned back and sat on the edge of his spine, he could stretch his long legs out far enough for something close to comfort. ''If that's it, I don't see why we just don't go to a parlor house, and skip this whole show. The theater's for watching, and a . . . well, Lucky said there's some beauties in Mattie Silk's parlor house here in town,'' Royal said in a low gruff voice, his color rising. ''Pretty ones and with good manners, too. And Jennie Rogers has got a house of mirrors, he said. Not that I'm keen on seeing myself, but, damn, Gray, the girls there are supposed to be like real ladies, too. So why fool around pretending to court a girl, taking her to dinner and all, when all you want's down the street for less trouble and more honest, at that.''

Gray's clear blue eyes grew dark. ''Because,'' he said, ''the play's the thing. Fantasy makes it better. Listen, Royal, if you want to go to Mattie Silk's or Jennie Rogers', fine. But I won't go with you. Because no matter how 'ladylike' the girls are there, they're only whores. You'd be doing just the same thing you'd be doing with one of the girls from a hog ranch.''

Royal winced. The hog ranches were houses set up outside of remote army camps, where the oldest, ugliest, washed-up prostitutes plied their trade, because the men they serviced hadn't any other choice.

But Gray frowned for a different reason, it was a fair question and deserved a more thoughtful answer than the one he'd given. He considered it. The first actress he'd known had also been the first woman he'd known, for all his fantasies, he'd been uncomfortably chaste until he'd come to New York when he was eighteen. Although he'd been considered a handsome

youth, women were scarce at home, good ones were
unobtainable, except in marriage, and bad ones too
obviously available to any man willing to wait in line
at their cribs and parlor houses. He'd been a great romantic, as well as a fantasist, then. Ada had been an
actress, and a jolly girl, as easygoing in bed as she'd
seemed on the stage, and being his age, they'd seemed
to have a lot in common aside from their sport. She'd
been a good teacher, never commenting on his inex-
perience, and he'd liked her as much for that as for the
experience she'd given him. There'd been other actresses after her, but none he remembered—not only
with such fondness—but at all.

But he'd finally come to know the other kind of
woman a man could buy, as well. When he'd come
back home to Wyoming Territory on school vacation,
he'd been restless. Now that he knew what he was
missing, it was harder than when he'd only dreamed
of it through illustrations in his *Police Gazette*. One
night his need had sent him to a parlor house in town.
He'd been astonished to find the experience better than
pleasant, much more than he'd expected. And all because he'd found a shy, dark-haired little beauty named
Lita. She'd been so quiet and gentle, he'd have been
content to merely hold her hand, but he'd paid for a
great deal more. And she had supplied it. For the rest
of the summer, he'd come to town once a week, always
to see her, only her. He refused to think of how she
passed the week without him, he passed his, thinking
of her: of the pleasures she offered so shyly, of her
sweet smiles, of her sudden, helpless look of rapture
when she was in his arms. She confessed her father
had sold her into her trade. Gray had lavish fantasies
of taking her away from it, at first. At last, he'd decided that he had to. Even if it meant defying his
brother and not finishing school, he couldn't leave her
to her cruel fate.

He confided in old Rusty, a ranch hand he'd known
for years. Rusty didn't even try to discourage him, so
afterward, he decided it was Rusty who'd arranged it.
It hardly mattered, he'd needed his eyes opened, how-

ever painful the surgery. Because when he came to visit Lita the following week, the madam told him to go on up, she was waiting for him. And when he opened the door, he saw her at work with two strange drifters. Both of them at the same time. And the worst part of it, and there were so many bad parts he couldn't sort them out for months after, was that she'd been wearing that same helpless look of rapture he'd loved, for them.

"The difference is . . ." Gray said softly now, speaking again at last, "I guess the biggest difference is that an actress can say no if she wants to. And you know it."

"Oh," Royal said, considering it, learning almost as much from Gray's grave face as he did from his words. "Then okay. You're right. I'm just a simple man, Gray. Not like you. But it's a big difference all right."

"Well," Gray said a little sadly, "not really big enough. But it'll have to do."

Chapter Four

The first thing Hannah heard was the silence. The constant thrum and rattle, the vibration that had become so much a part of her head that it seemed natural for her very teeth to buzz with it day and night, was gone. She'd woken to a blast of blissful silence, and a strange lack of motion. They'd come to a stop. They rested at a stop. They'd arrived.

She poked her head from out of the covers and pulled back the window shade a crack. Then she hung her head down and spoke through the tangle of her unbound hair.

"Peggy! Look! We're here!"

A groan was her answer, and then a quilted heap arose from the bed beneath hers, and a small hand pulled the shade back from the bottom.

"Faith! Yer right, Hannah dear. We're here. Quick!" Peggy cried as the quilt leaped to its feet. "Get yerself dressed fast! No telling when they'll be tossing us from the train so they can go on, don't want any porters coming in here while we're in our alltogeythers, . . . altogethers," she corrected herself hurriedly. "Do we now?"

Hannah stared down at the animated quilt that was rushing about the cramped space of their tiny compartment. Even standing upright, it didn't attain very much of a height. The ginger crop of curls that topped it barely came up to the top bunk, Peggy had not much stature. But she made up for that in energy, for the quilt was shifting and dancing as Peggy attempted to dress from beneath it, as she always did. For though she said it was because of the chilly mornings, Hannah had observed how she undressed half in the cupboards in the evenings, and realized that Peggy found even semiprivate nudity embarrassing. When Hannah had laughed and asked her if she averted her own eyes when she undressed all by herself, Peggy hadn't so much as smiled. She'd only stopped, considering the matter.

"I dinno, miz," she'd answered wonderingly. "I've never been by meself that long, y'see."

As it happened, Lottie hadn't chosen anyone to share her bed with, after all. She was too wise, Hannah thought, to tie herself up with an actor when she was about to meet all the gloriously wealthy gentlemen Kyle had gone on about. But Hannah was delighted with her own move, she couldn't have found a more dissimilar roommate from Lottie. Peggy wasn't an actress, nor had she any experience in the theater, or on her own. She was a seamstress, at eighteen the oldest child of a large family, and considered herself lucky beyond belief at having been hired on by Kyle. The traveling terrified her, those she worked with shocked her, and the work would have overwhelmed a lesser spirit. But she'd been grindingly poor, had boundless ambition, and a natural talent with the needle. Seamstresses were common enough, Peggy's gift was that she had a truly creative imagination to apply to her work. Hannah didn't know how Kyle had discovered that, but she wasn't surprised that he had. She'd begun to understand that he'd a gift of his own: the ability to discover others' talents. And weaknesses.

Peggy had a generous spirit as well, and far from resenting having to share the tiny space allotted her, already crowded with bits and pieces of the costumes she was responsible for, she was overjoyed at having

Hannah move in with her. Not only was she unused
to solitude of any sort, but, as Hannah quickly discovered, she went in awe and admiration of her new
roommate. Three things accounted for this, two immediately told: Hannah was Peggy's idea of a true
lady—she approved of her dress, speech, and morals.
And she was not an actress. And, as Hannah had only
just realized, she believed her to be courageous. "Ye
stand up to him, y'see," Peggy explained in the safety
of an anonymous late-night, before-bed chat. There
was really no need to explain who "he" was, much
of their talk had been about their mutual employer.

It was in that same safe, comfortable darkness, that
Peggy had dared to make her timid request. She vowed
she'd sew for Miz Roberts till the end of her days, or
until her fingers fell off, whichever came first, if only
Miz Roberts would condescend to correct her speech
now and then, when she had the time, that was to say.
When Hannah said, in all honesty, that she found the
natural lilt of Peggy's speech charming, Peggy had
been dumbfounded.

"Ah no, Miz Roberts," she'd sighed, " 'tis Irish.
And that's a sore trial these days. I want to get ahead,
y'see. My family's countin' on me."

Hannah discovered Peggy to be a quicker study than
Lottie. And she thought her more naturally pretty. It
was true no man would stare after her hungrily when
she walked down the street, it wasn't that sort of
beauty. But she'd a round little face, an impudent nose,
and great hazel eyes beneath long sandy lashes. She
might scorn her freckles and her round chin, but Hannah thought her charming and said so. And won not
only her awe and admiration, but her undying devotion
by so saying, since no one, evidently, ever had before.
Peggy might think her addled or only kind, but as she
explained, she did appreciate the thought—as well as
Hannah's nightly company and daily friendship. For
though she knew she was doing the right thing by improving herself and making enough money to send
home, she confided that now and again, when she was
alone, she suffered fiercely from the homesickness.

Hannah sympathized, she'd known the aching, throat-stopping longing of homesickness, even if it had always been for the home she'd never known. And as she'd not had a friend since the days of her childhood, and then only fleetingly, before the other girl had to move on with her own theatrical family, she appreciated Peggy, as well.

The sun was just up, the hour was early enough for optimism. Peggy flashed her a grin as she gathered up all Hannah's belongings and helped her by packing them into her bags. It might not be such a terrible tour, after all, Hannah decided, as she hurried into her own clothes and prepared to step out and face Colorado. She wanted to see it firsthand, and first, before the others were up and moving out.

She'd seen mountains from the train windows before. Her heart had raced faster, but the porters had told her that was because of the altitudes they were climbing to and the thinner air there, not only her reaction to such astonishing scenery. The towering mountains had looked so near, so unreal in their reality, so very like the painted backdrops for *Evangeline* or *Davey Crockett*, that she couldn't quite believe her eyes. She had to see it without even the distorting glass of a window.

But now as she stood on the platform, she could scarcely see past the depot, much less to the mountains. It wasn't a cloudy day, for now and again the wind blew the gray aside. When it didn't, it didn't take long to realize that no heaven-born cloud had ever smelled like that. She wrinkled her nose in distaste.

"That's money you smell," Kyle said from behind her, somehow managing to take in a deep breath of the noxious stuff as he went on, on an exhalation, "pure distillation of cash, my dear. This is a mining town. Each fire they stoke up to refine the stuff, stokes up the economy. It's silver or copper or some other precious ore. Only gold smells like clear running water, or so I'd think. This precious stuff smells like high finance."

Hannah didn't even honor his remark with a sniff,

and not just because she couldn't bear to deliberately breathe in. It smelled like man's greed and nature's disaster to her. Her face said everything her lips closed down on.

"Anyway," Kyle said, taking her arms and turning so that he could escort her back to the train for their last paid-for breakfast there, "you won't smell it at night, because that's when the fires go out. And so do the miners—for entertainment."

But it was hard for Kyle's troupe to accept what he kept reassuring them one by one as they left the train, stunned. And though certainly no one wished to take in too much of the atmosphere, there were nevertheless many jaws dropped and mouths gaping wide as they trailed off the platform and down the dismal main avenue into town. The depot was at the head of town, the mines and the smelter's smokestacks at the foot, and in between, there was a vast grim, gray huddle of shanties and shacks. The town itself was a long, wide street of saloons and supply stores. And two more of cribs and saloons, for the hardest-working people in town: the prostitutes.

As the troupe paused in front of the hastily erected wooden hovel they were afraid was the hotel, for once Lottie spoke for a multitude—or at least all of them—when she opened her mouth and yowled.

"Ay! Whassis? This ain't no *town*!"

It was wonderful, Hannah thought with sincere admiration, how much contempt Lottie got into that one-syllable word before she went on. "Thisisa damn sewah! It stinks. It's durdier than New Yowk. And where's the goddamn theayter, hah? Where's the 'Gem of the New West'?" she demanded in perfectly mimicked accents. "Doan try'n tell me they got the Tabor Opera House hid someware, puleaze."

"If," Kyle said with icy majesty, before he had to bellow louder than Lottie to make himself heard, "*if* you all would be so kind as to step in, and discuss the matter with me in private—or at least, in semiprivate, I should be glad to explain. Well?"

The troupe straggled in. The interior of the hotel,

Hannah had to admit, was not so horrid as the exterior. The lobby furniture was leather and fairly new, there were decent rugs on the floor, and the wallpaper was a busyness of perfectly clean and satisfactory cabbage roses. It was true that the some thirty persons, the entire crew of them, save for the stagehands—for those two stayed with the scenery, whatever mysterious place Kyle stowed it—crowded the little lobby, but that way at least everyone heard what Kyle had to say without his having to raise his voice. They were grateful for that, at least, when they heard what it was.

He stood in the middle of the room before them: slender, disdainful, and elegant in his signature black.

"People," he said, and then sighed in exasperation. And angry and disappointed as they were, some of them were already beginning to feel foolish for the fuss Lottie had made and they had tacitly supported.

"This is not Denver," he chided them, shaking his head so that his long dark hair seemed to sigh with him as it fell over his high forehead. "Nor is it Leadville. Nor Aspen, Telluride, or even Central City. It is Copperhead, a newly sprung mining town. Not polished or well-known. But then, I remind you, neither yet, are you."

The fact that for the first time he hadn't referred to them as "we" was not lost upon them, and a few shuffled their feet.

"Have you ever heard of a trial run?" he asked with awful sarcasm. "Or were you supposing we'd step, unsung, onto the greatest stages in the West? I thought, that like most troupes, we'd first want to know what the local humor was, what their preferences were for . . . or at least, so it has always worked in the past. Had you a better idea?"

They remained still, considered that, all of them, until the brash senior man in their juggling team spoke up.

"Yeah, fine. But Denver's a pretty big town. And so are the others. I wouldn't think that what they thought here would go over there, anyway."

"No, you wouldn't think, would you?" Kyle asked

sweetly. "Nor, obviously, have you been West. This is not New York. They haven't heard the same jokes, or seen the same sights."

"You said they were so sophisticated," the brash young man persisted.

"So they are," Kyle said haughtily. "But sophisticated East is not sophisticated West."

That was unarguable, not only because no one quite understood it, but because no one but Kyle could claim to have ever been West before. Still, tryouts were a common practice, even if this town was uncommonly drab and depressing. The young man subsided, but he grumbled something moodily to his partner, while the rest of the troupe pointedly ignored him.

"Now, unpack, my dears," Kyle said. "And then we'll meet again here, and go off to the theater together. Time's wasting," he said, clapping his hands together. "Our first performance is tonight. We shall be here two nights—or until we get it right!"

That got them to scurrying up the stairs to their diverse, but still shared, quarters.

But they slowed again when they came to "THE GILDED GARTER," temporary home to "HARPER'S GOLDEN CIRCUIT TOURING COMPANY" as the badly printed lettering on the sheet that had been draped over the saloon's front proclaimed. Because, they realized, it was just that: a saloon—with a long glass window, behind which could be seen an enormous wooden bar, occupied mostly with persons in dusty clothes and with a great deal of facial hair, all staring back at them.

"Have you ever heard of beer gardens?" Kyle asked in exasperation, though no one spoke. "Where do you think Tony Pastor got started? What do you think most of the theaters on the Bowery were when *they* began? Just remember," he said in a low voice before he pushed the swinging doors open, "these towns are only newborn, some two hundred years behind those in the East."

"Make that two thousand," Lester Claxton said sadly as he came in the doors. He was, by far, Kyle's most famous player. Hannah had heard of the comedian's fame when she'd been a girl, and had wondered why she hadn't heard of him much, more recently. The look in his eye as he looked at the bar told her why.

But all their eyes brightened once they'd straggled down beyond the gaping bar patrons, and under the arch of a low doorway. For they came to a wide, high-ceilinged room, floored with shining hardwood and with a hastily erected stage being hammered into place at the far end of it. The long rows of benches would seat at least a few hundred, the acoustics were not at all bad, and when they put up a screen to hide their rehearsal from prying eyes, they could almost believe they were in a real theater again. Until they performed that night.

It was not so much what happened during the performance. That, all agreed, was bliss. The audience of miners and whores was as appreciative and polite as any of New York's four hundred could have been. They sobbed in all the right places during the playlet of *The Drunkard*, and if one miner got so carried away by emotion when little Polly begged her erring pa to come home that he charged the stage with the object of knocking that selfish sot down, before his friends subdued him—why, that was all to the good. No actor could want a higher compliment for overstepping the line of reality so completely. And the chorus of sniveling during the renditions of *A Handful of Earth From Dear Mother's Grave* and *The Pardon Came Too Late* made the room feel like a funeral parlor. Which was fine, since after that, Lester Claxton had them roaring with just a twitch of his mobile brows. If they tended to laugh hardest at his warmest stories, so that he, as a natural performer, warmed them to the point that not only Mrs. Jenkins, but an outraged tenor threatened to march out if he didn't restrain himself, still the audience stood on the chairs to cheer him when he was done. They sang with the songs, swayed in place with the dancers, and then applauded until their poor calloused hands must have ached. That was never the problem. Or rather, it was.

Lottie liked admiration far more than the next girl, but even she was a little afraid to stay onstage after the welcome they gave her. But then they hooted and whistled at Maybelle, too, which was, for those who didn't know her well, like lusting after Martha Washington. All the female dancers and singers wondered if they'd have to call the sheriff in order to get back to their hotel unmolested. But that was nothing to what they saw in the audience itself between acts—both their own and the show's—as Lester commented.

"The thing is," Frank concluded to as many of the assembled cast that could fit into his room at their secret meeting that night, "that it's damned unpleasant to play to them."

"That's only because they were going to lynch you when you said you were going to foreclose," Nelson said.

"That's a damn sight better 'n what I thought some of them were going to do with you, dear boy," Frank shot back at him. "There are far too few women in this town."

"I'll say," Lottie said, darting an ugly look to where Maybelle sat preening herself like a pouter pigeon. But, Hannah thought, she could be forgiven her spite, because for as many offers of dinner and more that she'd gotten after the performance, Maybelle had gotten as many, and neither dared to take advantage of the situation—not in this town.

"Yes, yes!" a male singer cried out, until they shushed him and he whispered, "But now I wonder how many more rattraps and flea palaces Harper's got us booked into."

"I, for one," one of the minor actors proclaimed, "will not go on to many more!"

There was a whispered fever of agreement, until Hannah spoke.

"Still," she said quietly, "if they love you in Denver as they do here . . ."

They decided, before they crept back to their several rooms, to wait and see.

The take was so good, they stayed on two extra

days at The Gilded Garter, although Kyle insisted it was only because they needed the time to get their abridged *Little Lord Fauntleroy* down right. They got on the train with high hopes, but the next stop they got off at made Copperhead seem like Eden. At least they only played there one night. But the next saloon theater they played after that was at the foot of the mountains, and some of the audience looked as though they'd come straight down from them, without, despite what Mr. Darwin said, having had to stop off at humanity first. "I was afraid of displeasing them—literally," the juggler said in disgust, and he and his partner were off and headed back to New York on the next train they could find.

Kyle braced the more gullible in the troupe by telling them he'd actually been planning to let the jugglers go, anyway. And stopped everyone's grumbling when he informed them that they'd each have an extra five minutes onstage, because of the defection. And solaced himself with the reminder that he'd two less mouths to feed.

But after the troupe was forced to play Downey's Superior Saloon the next week, in a town where the water ran rusty as the blood that was spilled by the patrons fighting to get the best seats for the show, they confronted Kyle backstage that very night.

"But children," he said charmingly, "are you sure you wish to go? Ah well then, I'll not prevent you. But how hasty of you to leave me now, especially since we open in Denver in two nights."

And so they got on the train singing, every one of them, even though there was no audience to hear but themselves.

"What do you want when we're done with this tour, Hannah?" Peggy asked sleepily as their train streamed through the night.

They were snugged into companion seats in a darkened railway car; Kyle said berths weren't available for short trips, and they'd been too weary to argue the point. It was difficult to sleep, cramped and tired as they were. Still, they were so close, they had a sort of privacy; they could whisper and not be heard by the others because of the constant noise of the train.

"What do I want?" Hannah mused. "The money, of course. Enough to pay my back rent and my front rent, so I can keep on going when I get back home. And you?"

"Oh," Peggy said softly, and Hannah could almost see her hazel eyes shining with hope as she spoke. "Not just the money, surely. Not me. No, I want a trade, so I can take care of my own."

"Don't you want a husband to take care of you?" Hannah asked curiously, for she'd seen how Peggy sometimes stole glances at Nelson.

"Surely I do," Peggy said sadly, and Hannah smiled, for though she was correcting Peggy's speech, she could not bear to tutor the music from it. "But I'm not fooling myself, not I. I've not got what to offer a fine gentleman, and I'm thinking I'd not settle for less. Why, look at you . . ." And then she fell silent, fearing she'd said too much, for Hannah never spoke of plans for a future marriage, and not of her past one at all.

"But you're only eighteen, my dear," Hannah said, feeling it best to ignore what Peggy had said, and feeling her extra five years as five centuries as she did.

"Ah, but look at you," Peggy repeated sleepily. "You have everything, you do, but it's sure you don't need anyone but yer-yourself, you don't. Why, you're so lovely, you make Miss Lottie want to spit, I seen— I've seen her looking at you, sometimes. Ach, it's turrible," she said, giggling as she remembered the expression on Miss Lottie's face whenever she saw the gentlemen looking at Hannah—rejoicing in it, if truth be told, because Miss Lottie was not only a difficult person to sew for, it was a variety of hell to have to work for her in any way.

"Terrible," Hannah corrected her absently.

"That it is," Peggy agreed, and then, with the freedom that the night gave her, thinking of Hannah's trim figure and soft smoky black hair, white skin, and great

dark eyes, she added, with an admiration so profound
it was untouched by envy. "You're so much prettier—
everyone says so," she insisted, cutting off Hannah's
protests. "Even Mr. Harper. Didn't I hear him say,
'Yes, our blonde catches the eye, but our dark lady
holds it,' the time Mr. Frank admired you when you
was . . . were, wearing that lovely blue dress of yours?
And the silver gown—the one I made for Miss Lottie
for *The Drunkard*—you'd look finer in it. Aye, and
you'd act better in it, too, so everyone says. Why don't
you try it? Just once?" Peggy wheedled, smiling at an
even lovelier imagined vision of Miss Lottie burning
with envy as Hannah tried her part—and then explod-
ing, as Hannah took it over entirely.

"I've tried acting," Hannah confessed, because she
was unable to see Peggy clearly in the dim light, "and
failed at it, miserably."

"No, I cannot believe that," Peggy said deter-
minedly, "That I cannot. Who said it was a liar, that's
certain."

"Who said it was my father," Hannah answered
before she knew she was going to. And then fell silent,
shocked that she'd said it at all.

"Ah," Peggy said on an indrawn breath, before she
went on, "be that as it may. Being a father don't make
a man an expert on anything but one thing, or so my
mother always said—when my father wasn't around. If
you'll pardon me for so saying," she added shyly.

Hannah grinned, but lost her smile as she answered
gently, "But Peggy, my father knows one more thing
than that thing, and that's certain. He's Blayne Darling. That was my name before I was married, you
see."

"Ah!" Peggy exclaimed, sitting up suddenly to
whisper excitedly after Hannah hastily shushed her.
"Sure, and why didn't I see it? Those eyes and lips.
He's the most handsome thing, I seen his posters everywhere since I can remember . . . but still and all
. . ." She quieted and thought a moment before she
said resolutely, "Aye, well, and he may be the greatest

actor of the century, like all the posters says. That don't mean he's the greatest critic, though.''

But he hadn't said it critically, Hannah thought. Far worse, he'd said it with his famous half-skewed smile. Gently, charmingly, the way he said the worst things. And he'd smiled at Mother as he'd said it, and as ever, she'd smiled back at him.

"My dear, oh my dear,'' he'd said to his daughter, his eyes meeting her mother's over her shoulder, "I don't think so. Oh no. Not with the name 'Darling' on the bill, at least. It will never do. Perhaps—with a bit more . . . practice? Or . . . Well, whatever, we can but try. Should you like our help? Not now, of course. Perhaps after this run?''

It was only a little part, no more than ten lines and fifteen minutes of stage time. But it had been her first and last time on the stage. He'd never mentioned the matter again, nor had her mother. Just thinking about it now made Hannah's face flush hot, her stomach grow cold, and her heart beat faster—giving her all the symptoms of stage fright she'd not had on the stage that one time she'd tried so hard, and failed. It was all right for her mother to take small parts so that she might be able to eternally play her most important role—that of priestess to the religion of Blayne Darling—but she herself had more ambitious visions. Enduring amused sympathy had not been one of them. That was why she'd been so glad to have been everything to John Roberts, she supposed. And why it hurt so badly that she'd not been able to be anything to him, either. As if, she thought with remembered sorrow she was usually able to stave off, it hadn't hurt enough as it had been.

Hannah closed her eyes, remembering exactly how it had been. Although she sat as close to Peggy as her elbow, she felt very alone in the wide dark night. She always did when she remembered that for all the embarrassment and suffering she experienced whenever her husband had tried to make her his wife, even then, in the beginning, it had been wonderful to be held in another person's arms. She could hardly remember his face now, but she'd never forget his arms. Or wanted to. There were things she could never have, but if she thought of them all the time, she'd not be able to go on. And so it was astonishing, even to herself, that she seemed to have such a buoyant spirit that she could go on. Some carefully staged kinds of dreaming helped.

Although she never spoke of men, not even to Peggy, she thought of them frequently. It would surprise them all to know it, she thought, smiling to herself at her secret in the dark, but she found Nelson as handsome as any woman in the audience did, and thought Kyle exciting, Frank charming, and there was a baritone with the loveliest smile . . . And all of them, she reminded herself, as she always did when such thoughts raised needs too complex to deal with, were companions only fit for the dark of her dreams.

"Be that as it may," Peggy was saying sleepily, "you can be anything you want to be, that's certain sure."

The tears had finally stopped stealing down Hannah's cheeks by the time she was able to answer belatedly, "No. I can't be what I most wish to be: an actress, or a wife, or a lover. Only a teacher of one of those things, perhaps, and a dreamer."

But by then Peggy was asleep. It may have been that Hannah was, too. Because that was the sort of thing she only always dreamed she admitted, even to herself. Half-awake now, she wondered at what she'd said, if she had. And then dreamed of what she never had, what she almost had, and what she'd never have; and instead of weeping, resolved herself once more. Because she didn't know what to do but go on. And so she sighed, and turned to her side to rest her head, and let the train bear her off to Denver and the onrushing future, however limited it had to be.

"Have you been laying there, frowning and thinking, all this time? It's way past midnight," Gray said to Royal as he strolled into the room from the adjoining one he'd just returned to minutes earlier. "And I

don't think it's because you had such a terrible night,''
he added as he loosened his cravat. ''You looked happy
enough when I left you with the lady. But no woman
ever made you that gloomy,'' Gray mused as he struggled out of his tight dinner jacket. ''Nope, I know
what's ailing you. Damn it, Royal, but the ranch can
run without you. I don't mean that I'd want it to, fact
is, I don't know what I'd do without you. But if you're
laying there fretting about what's happening back
home, I'm not. Mack and Lucky are competent men,
young Red's coming along fine, and anyway, we put
the place to bed for the winter before we left. Now,
will you relax and have some fun?''

"Well, that's just it,'' Royal said slowly. ''It ain't
much fun for me.'' He lay on his bed, with his hands
laced beneath his head, and so didn't see Gray wince
at his words.

"I expect,'' Gray commented, as he began to un-
button his shirt, ''that's because your young lady didn't
turn out to be what you figured. Too bad. I knew you
had your eye on the little brown-haired one in the
chorus, but I swear, her friends said she was a bible
thumper. The world's sure changing,'' he said, shaking his head and smiling, ''and so are actresses. Must
be taking on airs because of Madame Bernhardt. I
don't expect them to look at a local boy, but now two
out of three don't even look at a fine gent backstage
anymore. They're getting so respectable, soon they'll
have their pictures on bible tracts as well as cigarette
cards. Guess your little lady gave you her thanks for
dinner, and that's all. Well, at least you're richer tonight, if a lot edgier. Sorry, about that.''

"Don't be, I'm poorer, all right,'' Royal said, and
said no more on the subject, because neither he nor
Gray were the sort of men to talk much more about
what they'd done with the two women they'd met tonight. ''It's not her fault,'' he said, easily. ''It's just
that I'm looking for something else now, I guess.
Something that means more, you know?'' He looked
at Gray, and this time saw him wince. But this time it

wasn't just because of his words, it was because he was trying to ease off his shirt. Royal rolled to his feet.

"Hot damn," he said, coming to Gray's side and looking at the long, raw scrape that ran in a jagged line over the ribs that Gray was slowly peeling his shirt away from. "How in hell did you do that? Oh yeah, the mine you were looking at today. You sent me off to check feed prices, and you went crawling down mine shafts again? Where's your head?"

"Still on my shoulders," Gray managed to hiss through his teeth as he separated the wound from his shirt, "believe it or not. The mine was no good, and I won't put a penny in it, though I left some hide there. I had to see it though. Seemed too good an opportunity to miss. Josh needed to know about it." He glanced at Royal's grim face, "No, I didn't tell you where I was going. I don't know a better man with a horse or a steer, Royal, but let's face it, a mine's just a hole in the ground to you. Aw, hell, don't look at me that way, this is your vacation anyway, not mine. My life's a damn vacation," he said more cheerfully, looking down at the scrape, and seeing that it had stopped bleeding.

"Sure," Royal said, sitting on his bed again. "Some vacation. Get a whole lot of scars having fun, don't you? Down mines, up mountains, on horses no sane man would spit at—when are you going to find out what play is, Gray?"

"Maybe work's my play," Gray said lightly. "Lord knows I don't have to work, do I?"

"Maybe not," Royal admitted. "But I never saw a man work harder. Maybe you feel you have to, and maybe I even understand that; you don't want to feel someone else is doing for you, not even if that someone's your big brother. But Josh wants you in New York with him real bad. You'd work there, too, but you'd save yourself some pain."

"Uh-huh," Gray said, his clear blue eyes lit with laughter, "but maybe not. Them paper cuts hurt something fierce," he drawled, "and I hear a man can do some real damage to himself with a pencil—never know which ones have splinters on them. No thanks. I'll stay where I am. But not just now. I need a bath.''

He whistled as he walked into the luxurious bathroom that separated their adjoining rooms, but once he'd got the water running, he stopped. And stared so long, not moving, as the water filled the massive marble tub, that it almost over-ran it before he became aware that his trousers were getting damp where it began to slop over the bathtub brim he was perched on. Then he sighed, shucked off his trousers, and stepped into the tub, immersing himself in the pleasure of the hot water, which was so profound, he scarcely shuddered as it covered over his scraped side.

It was a long, muscular body that lay at ease in the huge tub. The down of golden hair that decorated it was neither dark nor heavy enough to hide all the scars it bore. It would have to be a furry pelt to do that. The woman he'd bought tonight hadn't noticed, of course, because like many women with pretensions to gentility—and those were the ones he was most attracted to—she'd insisted on leaving on a few provocative scraps of clothing, and hadn't commented on his nudity at all. It was unsatisfactory, he thought, as usual, and not just because of the hurried, pointless coupling it had been. He wasn't sure any woman would find his naked body particularly attractive, and never believed those that had said they did. It was, after all, he conceded ruefully, a pretty badly battered object.

But unlike the women who'd seen him whole, he was in no position to judge the random cruelties that had left their mark on the otherwise sculpturally perfect male body. There were ancient statues of warriors that were no less maimed and no more beautiful. Only his left leg might be considered truly unsightly. It bore a crosshatched design of thick and thin scars from an old accident, as well as from the surgery that had tried to correct it. But it was as strong and well shaped as the other leg despite its surface, the defect lay too deep to show except when it was stressed. And maybe, Gray thought, closing his eyes, it was the same with the man it belonged to.

Because he felt damned stupid tonight.

Sure, he thought bitterly, he'd convinced himself it was necessary to track down a couple of women to bed so as to cheer up Royal. He always had some excuse for his needs, after all. But Royal didn't need cheering. He needed a woman of his own, one he could build a life of his own with, just as he'd said. Gray could sympathize with that, he only wondered now why he hadn't even tried to. Because that was, after all, what he'd been trying to make for himself for years now. Only on his own. And although he'd come damn near to killing himself trying, he admitted, he still didn't feel he'd made it.

Maybe, he thought, his eyes widening to their most brilliant blue as he gazed blankly into the steamy room, Royal had the right of it, and that was what he needed: a wife. Maybe it was his single state that kept him feeling perennially a boy, eternally in his brother's shadow and debt. It was, he thought wonderingly, as he absently soaped his aching body, a possibility. Only he was in no better position to find a decent woman than Royal was. Their similarities were that they both had enough looks, intelligence, and money to set them apart from other men. But women were scarce, and they both lived on a remote ranch. The difference was that Royal was less experienced with the world outside the West. Gray traveled the country often, had gone to college in the East, visited New York frequently, been to Europe, and had more money than most men in the country—or any other, for that matter.

If Royal hadn't met enough ranchers' daughters, Gray had. If Gray hadn't frequented as many whores as Royal had, he'd bought as many women who'd different names for their trade. But they both needed women, and thought about them even more often than they'd had them. Which was, Gray thought on a semi-sad grin, considerable.

By the time Gray rose from the water at last, he'd decided that maybe it was time for them both to settle down. He didn't think of love, because having never experienced the kind he'd read about or seen his brother share with his wife, he didn't know if it was something he'd ever know. He'd sure liked a lot of women, he thought on a chuckle. But marriage? Maybe if he found one he liked well enough . . . there might be, in that settling down, the chance for the content that had escaped him all his life. It was worth a try; he'd tried most everything else.

He was a man who made up his mind quickly, the more so when the facts were all in, and they were. So much so that he'd an inkling that the idea was not as new to him as he'd believed it to be. It must have been flirting around the edges of his consciousness for some time now, showing up most in the new disappointment he'd found with all his old easy pleasures. The only question that remained in his mind as he stood drying himself, was where to search for the right woman.

He decided he needed a woman handsome enough to make love to frequently, and either passionate or generous enough to let him: someone smart enough to share his thoughts with, and wise enough to help him find his dream. It would be nice if he could like her as much as desire her, it would be nicer if he could like her as much as a friend. He decided, with a sudden sense of wonder that turned to a glow of pleasure, that he'd like her to give him children, too. In turn, he'd give her fidelity, financial security, and as much love as he was capable of. It should do. He was very good at business, and it seemed a fair deal to him.

But eastern girls, friends of his sister-in-law or sisters of his college friends, shivered at the thought of living in the barbaric West. And he meant to stay in the West. Western girls, at least those he'd met, didn't have the elegance he admired in eastern girls. The other women he met were professionals of one kind or another, and while he'd no objection to an experienced wife, he did object to the idea of marrying an experienced whore. But he'd learned not to be a dreamer, and doubted he could find what he'd always needed just because he'd suddenly decided to go look for it. He'd settle for the best he could get. The problem was where to find that.

Still, all problems had a solution. And he didn't mind working hard to find one. Even if that meant playing hard—especially, he thought on a grin, if that meant playing hard.

"Royal," he announced as he strode into Royal's room, waking his foreman and friend from the first stages of sleep. "Guess what? Vacation's over. We're through playing. We're going to find you a wife. And then see if she's got a friend."

Chapter Five

The lobby was full, but it was such a huge place that even so, it wasn't crowded. The many mirrors on all the high walls doubled and redoubled the busy scene, reflecting the red carpets and golden draperies as well as the well-dressed people awaiting their turn at the reservations desk, or simply waiting for whatever other reasons people did when they seemed to be loitering in grand hotel lobbies. Many in the group that stood in the center of the lobby were too busy stealing glances at themselves in the mirrors to properly take in all the grandeur about them. But they were, after all, performers. Hannah had no such trouble. She frankly stared all around herself, as amazed as she was delighted.

She and all the others in the troupe had been so since they'd arrived in Denver this morning. The city was everything Kyle promised. It was no New York, of course, but they hadn't expected that. It was hard to tell just what they'd expected after the towns Kyle had dragged them through so far. But Denver showed every sign of prosperity and civilization they were accustomed to: the streets were clogged by gentlemen's carriages and family coaches, as well as horse buses and farm wagons; there were new, impressive build-

ings and rows of fantastically ornate millionaire's res-
idences, as well as rows of shacks, shanties, and a
huge crib district. The city was obviously new, and
more obviously unfinished, but it was a true city, one
they could recognize. And now this huge hotel they
were checking into, the Windsor, was every bit as elegant as Kyle had promised.

Hannah glanced from the shining wood and marble
reception desks to the plush chairs and divans set out
for the guests, to the potted palms in their polished
brass containers, and she sighed with gratification.
She'd been about to lose faith in Kyle Harper and this
whole endeavor. But here they were. She'd seen many
great hotels in New York City, this one compared to
any of them.

"Do yer think," Peggy whispered nervously, "that
I should stay here with ye? I mean," she said, her
hazel eyes wider than Hannah had ever seen them,
"I'm no performer, nor even a managing sort of person, like yerself. I'm help-like," she tried to explain,
unaware that she'd crept so close to Hannah that her
new friend could almost fancy she heard her rapid
heartbeat from where it obviously was in her throat.

"Nonsense," Hannah said bracingly. "You'll stay
with me, unless Kyle runs mad and decides to get us
all single rooms," she added. She smiled and lifted
her chin higher, discovering that having someone to
comfort gave her more courage, because the magnifi-
cence of the place and it's patrons had begun to make
her feel insignificant and poorly dressed herself. "After all," she went on, "that's the wonder of democ-
racy, if you can pay the rent, you belong. You'll see.
We're all just a bit travel-stained, and these people
have had time to dress up." And down and all the way
around, she thought with a little less confidence, eyeing the plumes on the hats, the furs on the backs, and
the diamonds on the necks of some of the women as
they passed by.

Kyle had got to the top of the line, and now seemed
to be arguing with the desk clerk, who snapped his
fingers and summoned a haughtier gentleman to also

confer with them. Hannah hoped he'd get their rooms
soon, because for all she knew that money was a great
equalizer, she saw several members of the troupe
looking a bit anxious where they stood in a clot with
her and some others, waiting for Kyle to return to
them. A few others, Hannah noted, were standing
apart, looking so theatrically bored that they immediately caught the eye. Lottie did, and she'd also put
on lip rouge, which no actress did unless she was on
the stage, or it was late at night, or she wanted everyone to know her for what she was—which in Lottie's
case was certainly more than theatrical, Hannah
thought with such sudden annoyance that she shocked
herself.

Because she wasn't the only one to have gotten that
impression. And whereas Hannah didn't mind the stout
gentleman with his thumbs in his vest gazing at Lottie
consideringly, nor the old gray-mustached fellow with
slicked-back hair who was ogling her openly, the sight
of two young gentlemen paused in their tracks to look
at her as they left the gilt elevator was quite another
story.

They were both tall, well-made men in impeccable
clothing, the sort one might expect to find in any good
neighborhood in New York City. Except that few men
anywhere looked quite as handsome as they did, and
no men in New York were so tanned. One remarked
something to the other as they gazed at Lottie. He was
a jot taller, and had craggy features in a long, pleasant
face. But it was the other Hannah continued to stare
at, because she told herself, of his splendid coloring.
He'd hair the color of sunlight, and as he watched Lottie, his handsome face grew a smile as bright and
warming as that, too. But, what a pity! Hannah noted,
for he'd a scar on his cheek and another on his chin
. . . It wasn't until his eyes had traveled from Lottie
to assess the group she stood apart from, that Hannah
could see that those eyes were as bright and clear blue
as the western skies she'd been under this morning.
Because now he was smiling and staring directly at
her. In that second she smiled back, as enchanted with

him as he'd been with Lottie. A half second later she realized what she was doing, and rather than scurry beneath a couch, or hide behind a potted palm, she called on all her training and congratulated herself on how calmly she managed to turn and look away.

"Now that you've scared her half to death, can we go?" Royal asked Gray, as Gray stood and watched the dark-haired beauty turn the color of the crimson carpets and then pale as ice, as she primmed that luscious mouth and jerked her head around to stare fixedly anywhere but at him.

"I was hoping she'd faint, so we could come to the rescue," Gray answered. "Don't know how else we can make her acquaintance."

"Wait and find out her room number, maybe?" Royal suggested.

"What a brilliant idea!" Gray congratulated him.

"Yeah. Especially since that's what we decided we'd do with the blonde," Royal replied, grinning.

"Yes," Gray said on a smile. "So let's just get us something essential, like seegars or a newspaper, at that shop to the back of the lobby, and wait until we see them go up. See what a better idea it was to stay here than at The Denver Club?" he commented as they strolled to the hotel tobaconnist's shop. "It's more exclusive there, all right, but it's too damned exclusive for our purposes."

"Our purpose," Royal reminded him, "was to meet decent girls who might be good wives."

"Another reason this is such a fine hotel," Gray agreed. "Two birds with one stone, literally. Because after we find out what we want to know for later tonight, we nip upstairs to the ballroom and meet the cream of Denver society at the afternoon tea we got ourselves invited to, and find out what we need to know for the farther future there. Because some things take time, and other things just take money.

"Didn't you see those cases that were stacked up near our two beauties?" he asked his puzzled friend. "It's a theatrical troupe," he explained, on a chuckle. "Friend, we are in luck!"

Kyle held his hands outstretched at his sides, as if there were a gun pointed at him, and not just a few dozen pair of accusing eyes.

"It's a matter of luck. What else can I say?" he said. "What else can I do? Haul out guns to try and change things—the way the natives might do? You saw me do battle with the clerk, his superior, that fool's superior, and then, finally, the august manager, himself. To no avail. They say we've no reservations. They say they haven't got my telegram, they say they may never have got it, they swear they haven't got enough rooms free for all of us. Well, what shall I do, children? Book a dozen of you in, and the rest elsewhere? And who shall choose those lucky few? That is—if any of you wish to stay on in a place that's so dishonest," he said, on a haughty sniff. "For it's clear to me that they haven't the room because of some local society party they've got going on here.

"Come," he said, picking up his traveling bag, "there's another fine hotel not far away. You'll be comfortable, I promise you. Only not patronized, or cheated!" he said grandly as he strode out of the lobby without looking back.

After a moment's hesitation, one by one, the members of his troupe lifted their bags and followed in a reluctant, ragged line, like so many dispirited ducklings. There was much muttering about Kyle's honesty, and many threats 'to go and ask that manager a thing or two myself,' but no one did. Perhaps, Hannah thought sadly, because no one really wanted to know if Kyle was telling the truth, since there wasn't much that they could do if he wasn't.

Hannah felt as embarrassed as she did uncomfortable. It was one thing to leave an elegant place because you wished to, another to leave because you'd the sneaking feeling everyone knew you weren't suitable enough to stay. She didn't brood about it, because soon she'd another, more physical problem to vex her. The rarefied air made breathing difficult for everyone, even the youngest dancers. Some of the troupe staggered and some wheezed as they carried their cases and followed Kyle along the streets of Denver toward their new hotel.

She only looked back once as they trailed down the street, but she didn't turn to salt or to tears. She only sighed, although it hurt to so wantonly waste her breath. Because she realized that the luxury, the grandeur, and most especially, the two grand gentlemen she'd seen within, were obviously used to much higher altitudes, in every way, than she was herself.

"Vamoosed. Gone and vanished, cleared clean out," Gray reported merrily, when he returned to where Royal was waiting for him. "Seems they either didn't have reservations or enough money to use them if they did. But I've got their name. They may not have money but they sure got handbills, they managed to somehow misplace a few piles of them at the desk. They're 'Harper's Golden Circuit Touring Company: Superior Variety, Blithe Songs and Gay Dances, and Touching Drama,' among other things—says so right here. And they'll be playing at a saloon theater called The Denver Grand Opera Palace and Dance Hall, on the Row, down near the cribs. The bellboy said he'd wear his guns if'n he was me, but thank God, he's not."

Royal shrugged at that bit of information. If the girls had been easily accessible, he could maybe see pursuing them. But since they were going to a gala party now, one Gray claimed would be stuffed to the seams with eligible girls, he could not. It took a full half hour more for him to understand, and then he mentally begged his friend's forgiveness for doubting him.

Royal stood with Gray in the doorway to the hotel ballroom. He noted it was set up for serving punch and tea and little sandwiches, which would not fill a tooth. The place had more mirrors than Mattie Silk's famous house of ill repute was supposed to have, and there were massive arrangements of flowers everywhere. Musicians in the corner played dreary high-tone music that was easily ignored, and though there

were dozens of tables covered with white cloths, only
the older women sat at them. The men and younger
women stood in groups, chatting. Royal could scarcely
believe his eyes as he looked at the young women as
they stood in groups, fanning themselves and laughing
together.

There were dozens of them: young, beautifully
dressed in the sort of floating, frilly concoctions he'd
only seen the like of on the stage, or calendars and
cigarette cards before. They wore gowns made of yards
of white floating stuff, with trains in back of them that
drifted from swagged bustles to make their graceful
way of walking seem like a flirtation in itself. Everything about them was enticing, but there was nothing
outwardly seductive about them. They weren't like any
women Royal had ever known. They'd high lacy col-
lars, and high-dressed hair festooned with flowers. He
was struck speechless. The mere sight of such elegant
ladies made him realize his mistake in coming. Just
looking at them made him feel awkward and ignorant.
And a glance at Gray didn't help. Because it was hard
to tell what he was thinking, he seemed as at ease here
as he did on the back of a horse.

These women were a select group: a minority of a
minority group. Women had always been a scarcity in
the West, although more were coming every year,
along with the new prosperity. But men still vastly
outnumbered them. Royal wasn't sure if he'd ever seen
so many in one place before, even in the biggest parlor
houses he'd visited. Not only did these women look
too rich for his blood, they were likely too rich for
most men in the land. He paused with Gray in the
doorway and wondered if it was too late to sneak away.
It was.

In a moment Gray was noticed, and hailed by an
older man. Seconds later, they were introduced to his
daughter. From then on, Royal knew he'd been foolish
for being ill at ease before. Because now he knew what
it was like to be really uncomfortable.

They were deluged. Within moments, they were
thronged with young ladies. Royal found himself cut

off from Gray, separated until they were each surrounded by a different circle of ladies; quartered and
fenced in by them as neatly as he'd ever seen a working
dog or a quarter horse isolate a steer. It was done fast
and neat, and before he could figure it out, he was in
the midst of a bunch of lovely ladies, all giggling,
flirting, and talking at once. No, Royal eventually realized, they were all *asking* at once.

"Just how big did you say your spread was, Mr. Atkins?" Miss Emmylou Pepper asked playfully, though
her blue eyes were hard.

"Well," Royal answered slowly, "Ain't bought it
yet."

"Mr. Atkins only said he'd his eye on it, silly,"
Miss Loretta Kenyon corrected her friend. "Isn't that
right, Mr. Atkins? Are you planning to run cattle on
it, or just farm?" she asked, saying the word "farm"
like other people might spit.

"Cattle, I s'pect," he answered, getting more close-
mouthed with every question.

"Ah, but there's good growing land here in Colorado," bright Miss Verna-Lynne Percy put in merrily.
"A very nice parcel, right near Twin Pines—that's my
daddie's place," she said, tapping that bit of information into him with her fan, and smiling widely to
show him her best feature, a set of what looked to be
a few hundred large white teeth.

They asked him where he intended to buy, how many
acres it would be, what he meant to do when he did,
and if he'd ever been married. Then they got to asking
what he was "in." When he'd figured that out and
answered, "Cattle," they smiled wider. After a while,
he answered with just a yes or a no or a shake of his
head, which seemed to do just as well, because that's
what he noticed Gray was doing in his circle of young
ladies, and Gray managed to be smiling as he did it,
too.

. . . Nine thousand and nine, nine thousand and
ten—Gray thought, time's up. He'd leave now if he was
by himself. Hell, no, he thought sadly—smiling at
something being said, since nothing sad was ever said

at parties like this—he'd never have come if it hadn't been for Royal, and he owed it to him to stay on a while longer. Wasn't Royal's fault that he'd forgotten what hell these things could be—the way, he supposed, a man made himself forget how much it hurt to visit the dentist until he got settled into his chair again. He had to think of this the same way, he reminded himself. He did need a wife, after all.

This was the best place to find one. These were eligible girls, the cream of the newly rich—the only kind of rich in Denver society. He'd enough money to marry anyone he chose, but there was nothing wrong in marrying rich, if he could. In fact, he thought with dawning pleasure, Josh would be tickled if he brought some more money into the family. Couldn't hurt, money never could, after all. Wasn't Josh always trying to introduce him to the most eligible girls in New York society every time he came East?

"Just look at it like you would if you were looking for superior stock," Josh had said on a grin, the last time they'd argued when he'd refused to go along to a debutante party on Fifth Avenue. "These girls are screened. You know the line you'll be picking from, and you'll be getting a breeder's guarantee that they're clean, pure, and carefully bred."

"Oh yeah," Gray had agreed, nodding. "Just like you did, hmm?" And then before Josh could misunderstand, because he was always ready to put up his fists if he thought anyone hinted an unkind syllable about his beloved Lucy, who'd been an actress when he'd met her, Gray added truthfully, in the exaggerated drawl he always used when he was pushed too far, "Josh, I ain't saying I'll ever find anyone like Lucy, but I've got to try, don't I? And I doubt I'd find her at a debutante's ball."

"Well, I never guessed I could ever find a gem like her in the theater, either," Josh had answered, completely serious for once, ". . . although I'd draw on any man that even hinted that to me, now. But if I could find a treasure like her there, well, I guess a man can find his love anywhere. Even at a debutante's ball, don't you think?''

He'd gone then. And he hadn't found anything but boredom. But that didn't make Josh wrong. He had to give it a chance. Anyway, he thought, looking to where Royal stood dazed and surrounded, he couldn't leave just yet. Might as well see what was being offered here. He hadn't in a long while. These girls weren't as subtle as the girls in New York society, but they'd only had their money for a couple of years. That, he decided, ought to work in their favor. But as he actually began to listen and look at them again, he realized it might have—if they hadn't decided somewhere along the line to be as much like the girls of New York they could. And, he thought on an interior sigh, they'd almost got it right. If they could only learn to mask what they were doing a little better, they'd have it down the way it left him—cold.

Because they were obviously looking for a man to marry, and one with as much or more money than their hardworking past had made—just the same as their counterparts in New York were. Just the same sort of thing he and Royal were about, for that matter. Nothing wrong with that, except it was the "obviously" they'd have to work on, he thought, as Miss Rhonda Hatcher mentioned her daddy's new house and Miss Emma-Lou Anderson shouldered her aside to mention her daddy's newer one—so sharply that they looked like a pair of frilly battering rams knocking heads in the spring rutting season.

"You didn't come to my come out," Miss Holly Ingram complained archly, adroitly edging Miss Rhonda and Miss Emma-Lou aside.

He looked down at the little gold and white lady before him. John Ingram's late-life daughter, his only baby girl. Daddy ran a lot of cattle on his ranch, but made his money in railroads and silver, so he'd had to come to Denver to run it into some more. A fair enough man, who knew cattle, but could talk money. She was petite, with an extraordinarily full bosom for such a slim girl. He'd known her family since forever, but she seemed to have grown up and out very nicely since he'd last seen her. There wasn't a spot left on her winsome face. And since she was the prettiest girl he'd seen outside of a theater in a long while, he smiled down at her and said, "No, honey, I did not. And I'm purely sorry. I didn't see just how much you had come out, you see."

That would have got him the back of one pretty little shoulder in New York, if not worse. When he noticed the way her gold hair was drawn up from the faint hollow at the nape of her white neck, he almost looked forward to following her when she left, and apologizing sincerely. He was genuinely sorry when it turned out he didn't have to.

'Oh you!'' Miss Holly squeaked, tapping him with her fan. "You're a right caution, Gray! But it isn't too late to come visit with . . . us," she added, more softly, managing to tilt her head down and yet her eyes up, so that she could look at him through a fan of eyelashes.

"Well, and I just might," he said as he thought it, but the sudden triumph that sparked those deep blue eyes when she raised her head made him sorry he had.

But after all, it was sort of a competition, he thought fairly, noting the way those eyes could say things Miss Holly, for all her boldness, couldn't. It was the only way a girl like Holly Ingram could get herself a suitable husband. She couldn't go out and find a suitable man, the way he could find any kind of girls. Though men outnumbered women five to one around here, few had enough money to match hers. They hadn't got the idea of looking for a title instead of money here yet, either. But give them a few more years, Gray thought, and they'd be just as pleased to be marrying a pauper "Sir" this, or an indigent "Count" that, as their New York sisters were. Their money was just too new to squander on pure show yet. He couldn't blame her for competing when she thought she found a fellow she liked. She had to be twenty or so, by now. It wouldn't be long, before her folks got antsy enough to demand she get married before she got much older, however coddled she was, and harder to suit.

Curved and scented, gold and white, and obviously interested in him, she was, he decided with a glow of pleasure that made the whole afternoon bearable to him, a distinct possibility. He chatted her up for a while longer, stepping aside with her, turning his back slightly so as to definitely single her out, showing his preference for her until the other girls had no choice but to begin to drift disappointedly away from them.

They talked about weather and mutual acquaintances, and then about other things that didn't matter, but that could be talked about long enough for him to have made his point: long enough to make her mama smile, and yet not quite long enough to get her daddy to go running for his financial statements or his rifle, and just long enough to be sure she'd keep until he next came to town.

He didn't give himself airs, but knew he was a catch. In the East, because of his name and fortune. The fact that his father had been an English gentleman, actually a younger son of a viscount, added luster. The further fact that his father had been more of a gentleman than a businessman, and though charming and well-intentioned, impoverished, didn't matter to anyone but his sons any longer. The most important fact was that he'd left nothing to his boys but a love of education, a sense of fair play, and an insatiable craving to make the fortune that he hadn't—and they had. Or rather, as Gray never forgot, his oldest son had.

Then there were his looks, which East or West, were always made much of by the girls, if not by their fathers or himself. Whether or not the girls around here found him a treat didn't matter as much as the fact that their daddies knew his history, and generally approved of it. They knew he was sharp in business and soft on women; that he wasn't afraid of work, but liked to kick up his heels now and then, and was smart enough to do it quietly. And mostly, that he was rich enough to turn them down if he wanted to—in business or at the pleasure of marrying their daughters.

When he judged the time was ripe, Gray made a teasingly ambiguous farewell to Holly, and then went and collected Royal. He separated him from his admirers with a deft excuse that no one listened to because they were imploring them to stay, and hauled him off out the door.

"Better get yourself a pair of dancing slippers, Beau," Gray said. "Looks like we've got ourselves a belle of the ball here."

"Never," Royal said through tightly clenched teeth as he strode down the hall. "Ain't *never* going to go to such a thing again."

"But they purely loved you," Gray said, trying not to smile.

"In the first place, they don't know me. In the second, Gray, I don't have that kind of money."

"But you do now, Royal," Gray said seriously. "I know that, if you don't. You've invested right along with us, small but steady, for years. It's a considerable sum now, trust me. You just haven't done anything with it."

"Well, I'm surely not going to do the kind of things *they* expect with it," Royal said, striding onward toward the long turning grand staircase that would take them back to the hotel lobby. "Mansions and gowns and whatall and parties and soirees—damn, Gray, I was invited to soirees today. Me! I want a house and some land and the kind of wife who won't mind if I take off my boots at night. Don't laugh, God knows what these kinds of girls expect of a man!"

"What do you expect of them? They can't read minds, and you were about as chatty as a rock back there, weren't you? You haven't given them a chance yet," Gray said, following his fleeing friend so closely that he couldn't conceal his slight halt step. Royal glanced back, then slowed his pace and looked more thoughtful as Gray added, "Knowing you, I'd think that when you meet the girl you want, you'd give her mansions and whatall, and even soirees, if it made her happy. After all, a little evening dinner party ain't much to give a girl, is it?"

"That all?" Royal asked, grinning. "Sounded worse."

"Well, it's bad enough," Gray said, matching his grin. "I'm glad you didn't accept. That's not where I want to go tonight. Let's see," he said, as they took the stairs, "the girls said that Bob Ford's in town, giving a lecture on 'How I shot Jesse James.' They're all atwitter about that, and are killed to go, but their daddies won't let them."

"Afraid of riffraff in the audience?" Royal asked.

"Hell no, they were all riffraff themselves and not so long ago. No, it's revenge in the audience they're scared of."

"That's dumb," Royal said as they reached the bottom of the stair. "Boys are saying Jesse's alive and well and living good somewhere. Bob's his cousin, you know, and they're thinking he's spreading the word too far and too wide for a sane man to do if he'd really killed old Jesse."

"Oh, I know that," Gray said, "though it's healthier not to. So I guess we can write off old Bob, even though there's no danger of discovering any of the ladies in the audience? Now then, where else can we go where we can't find them?"

Royal looked uncomfortable.

"Hell, Gray," he said, "pay no mind to me. I saw you'd got yourself a pretty little girl to talk to today, and if you want to go where she's going, it's okay with me," he said with forced nobility.

"Holly Ingram?" Gray asked. "She *is* a little white and gold honey, isn't she? But she'll keep. She'll have to. If I see her again too soon, I'll have to start shopping for rice. Daddy's a strict man. You approach the Ingrams like you would an Indian camp, slow and easy and with your hands in the air. No," he said, as he paused in the same spot where they'd stood hours before they'd gone to the tea, "better for both of us if we avoid the elegant ladies tonight.

"Ah," he said musingly, looking in the same direction of the lobby as he had those hours earlier, "that let's the legitimate theater out, doesn't it? No Shakespeare at the Tabor then, or any other elegant opera house—if we want to avoid the ladies. There's always other amusements, of course, the ballet, or a parlor house, or a wild West show, maybe?'' he said, staring pointedly at the empty spot in the lobby that hadn't been empty those hours before.

''Blondes,'' Royal said, finally laughing as he remembered who'd stood there then. ''Is that all you can think of? Miss 'gold and white' and that other yellow-headed charmer, too? That actress? Pretty enough, sure, but you might as well make love to a mirror.''

''Like the parakeet Ma Slocum keeps in her parlor?'' Gray mused, remembering the amorous bird that everyone who visited Ma Slocum's café always laughed about. ''I never thought of that!'' he said, as though really startled. ''You mean I can never have a blonde again without it meaning I'm loving myself? I just wish it was as easy and cheap as that, even it if meant I'd go blind and my hands would fall off, like they said in Sunday school,'' he muttered, making Royal laugh again.

''But now you've gone and scared me,'' Gray said. ''Yeah. Could be something in that. I might be better off looking for someone completely different. Uh-huh. Why, there's sense in that. Say, someone dark and sultry—someone with white skin and soot-black hair, and big brown eyes? And smooth, plump, plush lips too, maybe?''

''Okay.'' Royal sighed, ''Harper's Golden Circuit Touring Company it is then.''

No one in the audience could guess that the members of the troupe they were seeing had been raging and fighting only hours earlier. Greasepaint covered tearstains, and cucumber slices mended puffy eyes, and anyway the lighting in the makeshift theater was so bad, they had a hard time making out the exact features of any of the performers. Even if they could have seen them through the thick haze of tobacco smoke.

And no one could guess that the troupe was three persons short tonight—two singers and a dancer having packed and left, in a rage, only an hour before the performance. But as the singers were men and the dancer rather squatty, just as Kyle Harper had said, the crowd in the saloon theater missed them not at all.

They were too busy laughing at the comedian's antics. He was very funny tonight, even to the members of the audience who were soberer than he was, because he had to work off his anger some way, and after liquor, humor was always his way. It seemed nothing short of a fire in the theater could have stirred the audience after that . . . until Little Polly came on the stage and had them all crying as hard as they'd been laughing, because her ''Little Eva'' died so lingering and blissfully. None of them had sharp enough eyes to see that she'd been crying long before she knew she had to die. She'd started before the curtain rose, in fact, like so many others in the troupe.

Because if White's Hotel was not precisely a dump, as the kindest members of the troupe said, it looked like one after the Windsor. And after they'd stowed their bags, they'd gone out to set up the theater for the night's performance. And watched as their horsecar took them right up to the magnificent Tabor Opera House . . . and right on past it. But the blowup hadn't come until they'd actually got to The Denver Grand Opera Palace and Dance Hall and discovered that was where they were expected to actually perform.

Three hotheads had quit on the spot, not even waiting to hear Kyle's explanation. The others wished they hadn't heard it when they did.

''I misrepresent? Me? I never said you were to play at the Denver Tabor, did I?'' Kyle asked in an awful voice. ''Did I? No, never. I remember what I said exactly. I said, 'in Denver' did I not?''

He'd looked around for a denial, but try as they might, not one of them could remember exactly what he'd said, and he began to lose some of his pallor—for though he'd never lost his superior attitude, it seemed there were some things even he couldn't control—and he'd been shaken by their outcries. As had everyone within hearing range. They'd sounded, as one old fel-

low who'd been making his way down the street near
the backstage alley where they'd had their confronta-
tion said, as he flattened himself against a wall, "Jes'
like them painted heathens when they made their raid
near the Platte, back in '65. Only," he added, when
he stopped shaking, "the Sioux wuz a lot quieter."

"However," Kyle had commanded, holding up his
hand for silence, "I beg you to look at the bill on the
door at the Tabor, when you've a chance. Do. Do you
know who's playing there tonight? Otis Skinner, in
Hamlet. Yes. He. Next week? William Gibson, in *The
Virginian*. My friends, in truth, do you think we belong there? No," he said into the sudden silence. "Not
now! But we shall! How many houses have we played
so far? Three, four? Five? Did you know most tours
encompass forty to fifty venues? We shall not do that,
no," he said on a weary smile. "That I would not do.
But we must pay our dues. Be reasonable. Mustn't
we?"

They'd nodded and filed into the saloon theater in
silence. But it was a diminished troupe, in many ways,
that finally took the stage that night. And tearstained
and beaten, they were then staggered to hear how they
were received. Enough so that they, being true performers, became better and better as the night wore
on. By the time the singers did, "Sweet Violets," the
audience was rocking along in their seats to the tune.
They did sweet old songs like "Silver Threads Among
the Gold" to quiet them after "Frankie and Johnny"
set them to cheering, and tried saucy new ones like
"What's in a Kiss?" to pick them up again. "Clementine" had them on their feet when it was done,
but "Drill, Ye Tarriers Drill," almost literally brought
down the house, the audience was clapping and stomp-
ing its feet so madly.

It was a triumph. And, though the company could
not know it, a very select audience. Over three quarters men, and three quarters drunk, they were mostly
hardworking miners from the outside of town, in for a
night of carousing. After the show, they'd stagger to
The Row, Denver's famous streets of prostitution, and

end their night with a girl—or someone of the female
sex who was loosely—and on The Row it would be
extremely so—within that category. The remaining
members of the audience were drifters and tourists in
from the wilderness. There were a few prosperous
whores, or lucky ones, whose protectors or customers
took them to the show. And a few more who found
business in the back of the theater, in several construc-
tions of the word. The audience also contained two
men who were, even though they were casually
dressed, so much better dressed than the others that it
was only their size, faces, and the suggestion of guns
somewhere beneath their fancy vests and frock coats,
that ensured the rest of the audience leaving them in
the peace and plenty that they'd obviously arrived in.

"Very cultural," Royal commented, as they waited
for the theater to empty. "Never thought I'd have to
wear side arms to the theater in Denver."

"Didn't have to," Gray said. "Could have been
robbed, if you wanted."

"True," Royal said. When they finally reached the
aisle, he added, "You want to go backstage?"

"Certainly," Gray said, though he looked more ab-
stracted than anxious to go there.

"Even though it turned out that your dark . . . yeah,
'plump-lipped' lady ain't a member of the troupe at
all?"

"There's always one that gets away," Gray answered lightly. "Sometimes it's even better that way.
How often does inspiration equal reality? Maybe some
things are better left to the imagination. Just look at
Dante and Laura. Or don't. Anyway," he said, smiling again, shrugging off a curious pang of disappointment, "one out of two ain't bad. And I'll just bet she's
got a friend."

Their appearance and the amount of money that
changed hands, got them backstage. A few more coins
got them to Miss Lottie's door. Then Gray's smile won
her answering one, and his softly voiced request gained
her confidence, and the name of the restaurant he invited her to got her instant acceptance. One way or the

other, she thought with pleasure, she would dine at the Windsor hotel tonight. And maybe, she decided, looking at the fair-haired westerner's remarkable face and athletic form—just maybe, she decided when she heard he was staying on there, too, she'd stay there herself tonight.

Finding a friend for his long-faced friend was no problem. Lottie quickly recommended they invite Miss Bliss, from the depleted ranks of the dancers. She was always ripe for a spree, and fortunately not half as good-looking as Miss Lottie. Then, the rangy friend of her own escort having secured Miss Bliss's company, they were all ready to go at last.

Lottie put on her best plumed hat, let the gentleman wrap her crimson silk cape over her white shoulders, and taking his arm, picked up her parasol, her handbag, her gloves, and her skirt's hem, so she could step out with him into the night. She needed only one more thing to make her outfit complete. And then turning, she found it.

Hannah's shocked face was just what Lottie had been looking for. She picked up her head, smiled, and spoke to her disapproving tutor.

"Ta-ta, we're off to the Windsor hotel for dinner, Hannah, dear," she trilled in her best, recently learned accents. Then she added, "And don't wait up fer us, neither!" and then promenaded out the door without a backward glance.

Which was just as well. Because if she had looked back, she'd have seen her escort's face, as he did.

Chapter Six

No one was in a very good mood in the morning. But no one's mood was quite as filthy as Miss Lottie Lesley's was. They were all travel weary and bed-sore. The hotel Kyle had booked them into had looked decent enough at first glance, but like so many things that were attractive only on the surface, the attraction didn't survive past the first stare. The beds had turned out to be as hard as the floor beneath the thin carpets, and what was beneath the beds didn't bear looking into—if the dust balls that whirled out from there when the windows were opened to let out the smell of mildew was a sample of it. And yet despite her high hopes, Miss Lottie had spent the night in that same hotel just as everyone else in the troupe had done.

The evening she'd passed hadn't been good for her purse or her pride. She'd been early to bed and early to rise as she'd gone to bed—alone. The gentleman she'd stepped out with had been just that—a complete gentleman, which was not what she'd wanted or expected anymore than she guessed he had when he'd asked her out. Something had changed his mind. And because she could never see any fault in herself, she'd the darkest notions about what—or who—it might have been that had.

Everything else about him had been just as she'd
thought it might be. Handsome? She'd seen that right
off. More importantly, he'd been rich, just as she'd
supposed from his clothes and his manner. As had
every waiter and doorman they'd seen at the Windsor
hotel. Because no one scraped and bowed and catered
the way they did to Gray Dylan unless he was really
rich, or they were out of their minds. He'd ordered her
lobster! Imagine that, lobster in Colorado!—when she
couldn't even afford it at home. And then everything
else she'd wanted, eight full courses worth, and urged
her to eat it, and watched her doing so with kind,
fatherly concern. The problem was that he'd treated
her like that all night. Even after his rangy friend Royal
had gone off with Miss Bliss. Because it turned out all
he'd wanted from her was a little conversation. And
information.

About the troupe.

Well, so she'd told him. And so if he ever clapped
eyes on Miz Hannah Roberts again, he wouldn't be
surprised to see her mopping the floor or taking out
the trash, Lottie thought with bitter triumph.

"Oh, *that* dark-haired woman? The old widow? My
teacher?" she'd answered, when she finally had to admit she knew who he was talking about when he'd
finally got around to what was really on his mind.
Lottie might not know very much, but that left all the
more room for what she did know, which was how to
know when other people were doing what she did
best: lying. Or as she now could put it: acting.

He'd been interested in Hannah Roberts, astonishingly enough. But after she'd done telling him about
the man-hating, highfalutin, bad-tempered witch that
was Miz Roberts, Lottie doubted he'd ever ask about
her again, much less try to see her. Of course, it hadn't
helped Lottie personally, either. She knew men didn't
like women bad-mouthing other women, and she'd
gone at some length about Hannah Roberts. But since
he hadn't wanted her before she had, she doubted he
would after, and if she couldn't profit from him, she'd
be double damned if any other woman would. Espe-

cially Hannah Roberts, who seemed to be correcting her every other minute, whether she opened her mouth or not, and who always made her feel like less than she wanted to be. She would learn from Hannah because she had to, and someday she'd be able to pass as a lady. But it wasn't in Lottie's nature to ever look back. And Hannah Roberts was a constant reminder of how far she'd already come, as well as how far she had yet to go.

"I dunno why I can't!" she shouted now, in the midst of this miserable morning, because Hannah's last correction was the last straw, even though it was her first of the day. " 'Cuz enyone knows the English doan tawk like us!"

"They 'doan tawk' like pushcart peddlers either," Kyle said, neatly interrupting the argument as he strode onto the stage and stared down his long nose at Lottie.

"You are the impoverished mama of Little Lord Fauntleroy here," he said, looking down fondly at Polly, who looked at her feet and pretended not to be enjoying herself hugely at Lottie's expense. "How can we explain to the audience why our little lord speaks like a little English angel if his mama speaks like a big New York fishwife?"

"It sez," Lottie raged, putting her feet apart and narrowing her eyes as she raised her voice, "that hiz momma is forced to woik to support 'em both. An' she's American, ain't she?"

"American is not synonymous with 'ignorant.' Or 'illiterate.' Who, do you think, taught the little lord to speak—the angels? No, you have to speak sweetly, softly, and correctly. Come, come, Lottie, Hannah's right. You know damned well that the little lord's young, beautiful mama wouldn't screech: 'No yer doant, yer lordship, you mebbe his grandfodder, but yer not takin' my little baby away.' Would she now? I do approve of her vehemence at that point, though," he added thoughtfully. "It's very effective. Keep it in. Umm, the anger, that is," he added, to erase Lottie's look of incomprehension.

"Fine! I believe I was just carried away by the drahma of the moment," Lottie enunciated carefully, knowing when she'd lost, and deciding to make the most of the meager compliment he'd thrown her amid all the insults.

"Good, good," Kyle said. "Throwing oneself into the part is very good indeed, so long as one never forgets who one is supposed to be at the moment of being thrown. Now!" he exclaimed, addressing the others, "if we can get the diction right and the parts down cold, we may be able to do the 'Little Lord,' as soon as next month—in Leadville. Yes, my chicks, Leadville. What a dull name for a roaring town! The precious ores and coins that flow from that blessed place . . ." he sighed, "with so many lonely home-sick miners there, the 'Little Lord' ought to have them sobbing in the aisles."

"And do we play Tabor's Opera House there?" Frank asked quietly.

"Ah, um," Kyle said, and then raised his head and stared at his suddenly silent and attentive audience—composed of everyone in his troupe within earshot.

"No," he admitted at last.

"That does it!" one of the male singers cried in outrage. "I'm out. And off. Home. New York City here I come. Hildy?" he shouted to his girlfriend in the women's chorus, who was standing, watching Kyle with a fervent expression of hope.

"Not the Tabor in Leadville, no," Kyle said, as though he hadn't heard the outburst. Hildy sighed and turned away to join her outraged boyfriend. But she paused as Kyle spoke again.

"No, we'll be playing The Golden Nugget, which is directly—directly," Kyle said with emphasis, "across the street from the grand old Tabor. So you see it's a good location, on the best street, better than any house we've played yet, in fact. I've got us a decent hotel and expect at least a good week's run there. And then, I promise,—and you may look at my schedule if you doubt me—" he said, looking fixedly at Hildy, and then so accusingly at her choleric boyfriend that he had to glance away from that dark and knowing stare, "good bookings all the way to our triumphal opening in Aspen.

"Yes!" Kyle said thrillingly, his eyes alight with excitement. "Aspen. A fine big town—nine million dollars of silver mined a year there! Twelve thousand exquisitely rich souls living there. And it just so happens that our opening will coincide with the opening of the newest, grandest hotel in the Rockies: the Jerome. Electric lights, stained glass, indoor plumbing, and chefs from France. Everyone will be there for it. Everyone. Not only the new wealthy West, but the old wealthy East: financiers, society—moguls of every stripe: beef barons from Chicago, railroad barons from New York, even real barons from Europe. Everyone's arriving for the grand opening on Thanksgiving Day. It will be written up in all the papers. Well, after all," he said with a secretive smile, "the Jerome will fill an aching need—there has to be somewhere fit for the big names to stay when they go to the Wheeler Opera House—which just happens to have opened only last spring, and which happens to be not a block away from it.

"I'll not lie to you," Kyle said suddenly, harshly, "not all of our venues will be pleasant until then . . . Lucrative, yes. But pleasant . . . ? Still, I promise you this," he said with passion, "if you play well and hard for me, I will even now, right this moment, with however many witnesses you wish looking on, go to the telegraph office and book us all rooms at the Jerome, for that grand opening. I have a connection, you see," he said almost shyly.

Five of them were immediately deputized to accompany him to the telegraph office—the number the company decided was too many to bribe without someone eventually spilling it. And those five returned with the happy news that Kyle had actually sent the telegram. And then they showed the one he'd got in return. They'd confirmed rooms at the new Jerome for it's grand opening. Shared rooms, to be sure. They'd have to be doubled and tripled up to fit in. But they'd be there. All of them, even Hildy and her impulsive boy-friend. All of them except for a character actor named Willy Kidd, who had packed his bags and left, saying that telegram or not, the day he'd trust anything Kyle Harper had to do with again, even if it was written in blood and not ink, was the day they'd have to commit him. And speaking of blood, he muttered as he snapped his traveling case closed before he marched off to the railroad station, he'd sooner bargain with the devil than Kyle Harper, because all the devil would be after was his soul.

But after a moment's unease, everyone accepted the defection, because Kyle reminded them there was now to be one less room that had to be triple occupancy on that great day when they finally got to Aspen, and their deserved reward.

Royal stood half dressed and hip shot, one sunbaked brown arm on the lintel of the door, staring into his closet.

"Packing to leave?" Gray asked, and was sorry for it if he was, since he'd miss him. But he himself couldn't leave as yet. He'd unfinished business in Denver.

"No," Royal said thoughtfully, running a hand across his bare chest, the contrast between his lightly tanned chest and his dark hand a startling one. "Just wondering if I got a clean shirt."

"Have one of mine," Gray offered more cheerfully, as he took up his towel and finished toweling dry his freshly washed hair.

"Might have to," Royal commented, as he gazed into the closet and without turning, said, 'I want to look as good as I can. Which ain't much, I'll grant. But I want to do the best I can. I'm thinking of going back to the opera house tonight—to that Harper's Review again."

"Oh. As it happens, so am I," Gray answered, and then added too casually, "you must have really liked Miss Bliss last night."

"Nope," Royal said. "Couldn't stand her. Seen someone else there though."

"Interesting," Gray said, and waited.

"You surely must have enjoyed Miss Lottie's company, if you're going back again, too," Royal commented instead.

"No. Actually not at all. I got to bed early and alone last night, if you remember," Gray answered tightly, draping his towel around his neck and staring at Royal's broad bare back, as though willing him to say more.

"Like me," Royal said, turning at last to see that Gray's flat voice was matched by the look in his eyes. "And so I guess you're going fishing again tonight—like me. . . . Ah, but . . ." he added, with the first hint of a smile, "I ain't angling for no dark, ah—'plump-lipped' lady, myself."

"Oh well, then," Gray said, grinning widely, "you can have two shirts."

"For a minute there I thought you were going to hand me a fistful of knuckles, not a shirt," Royal commented as he ambled along in Gray's wake, following him to his room, "but I can't figure why. You got the looks that drive the ladies wild. I'm just an old cowhand."

"There are things you've got to learn about ladies. So take a lesson from someone who, if not older or wiser, is at least more experienced with the breed," Gray said with as much mischievousness in his eyes as there was pomposity in his voice. "For a start," he said as he rooted in his wardrobe for a shirt, ". . . with all their airs and graces, there's not much difference between what you'd call a lady and what you know as a woman—not if she's worth getting to know at all. That being the case, there's really not so much difference between them and us. After all, a gentleman's just a man who knows when he has to hide the fact that he's just a man. Same thing with ladies.

"Now, Number One," he said, raising one finger, "there's no accounting for what kind of man drives women wild, just like there's no telling what makes a man hanker after any one woman. Remember Jake Jeffreys? The man never washed, never talked, and never earned a penny in all his days, but when he died, three widows showed up—all of them bawling for him at once.

"Two," he went on as Royal laughed, remembering, "there's something you have to learn about yourself; you can fit into my boots as well as my shirts, and if you didn't spend most of your time with cattle, you'd see the ladies like you just fine. True, you've got a three-colored hide, like most cowboys," he added, turning his head to smile as he stared at the contrasting tones of his friend's arms, torso, and the margin of skin that showed at his navel where his towel was tied, "but it's clear the ladies like what they can see. So you've got as good a chance as I do with any woman we meet, friend.

"And Number Three, and best of all for me: Miss Lottie said that my plump-lipped lady's a man hater, and shrewd, mean as a rattler, and stuck-up, to boot. Which means," Gray said, grinning as he handed a shirt to his perplexed friend, "that I'm in luck. Because if you understand the lingo of that particular breed, it means I can still pick them, even from across a crowded lobby. See," he explained gleefully, "getting a recommendation like that from a woman like Miss Lottie, means that the lady I was asking after must be something really special!"

"No," Hannah said firmly, because she knew her own mind. "Thank you," she added, because she'd been brought up to be polite. "I don't walk out with strange gentlemen," she explained to the blond man, because he seemed to be waiting for her to say something more, and although he really didn't deserve to be given a reason for her refusal, she was feeling generous. It was very flattering that he'd asked; he was, after all, extremely handsome and well dressed. And though she was as ashamed as pleased about it, it was even more gratifying that Lottie had seen him do so—

before she'd walked off with a sniff and a swirl of her skirts.

But what she had to say was as honest as it was sadly true. Because she just didn't go off with strange men that came calling backstage, and wouldn't, even if she didn't know that her handicap would make such encounters as eventually senseless as they'd be immediately immoral.

"I'm only asking for the pleasure of your company at dinner," Gray said quietly. "In public, and in plain sight. I'm from Wyoming Territory, ma'am," he added gently, looking as sincere and shy as a six-foot and some, fair-haired, tanned, tough, scarred, and superbly handsome male could. "Wyoming—where they invented lonely. But now I'm in town for the week, and so are you. So where's the harm in it?"

The harm was obviously shining clear in those half-mocking, half-earnest bright blue eyes, and in the insidious smile that quirked that well-shaped mouth, Hannah thought with a trace of delicious panic such as she hadn't felt for years, and he knew it as well as she did.

She blushed, lowering her lashes over her eyes as she hadn't done since she was very young, and even as a scornful interior voice taunted her by giving her an unfavorable review as an overage and inept ingenue, she answered in just that breathless sort of voice, "We haven't met. Not formally. Nor do we know each other. Nor will a dinner in plain sight make up for that oversight, you know. I'm so sorry, sir, but I'm not an actress, nor are all actresses available for such . . . arrangements, either."

"I know that," he said on a true smile. "M' brother married an actress. Up in New York, where he lives now. And I swear there wasn't a prissier lady between here and there than she was. Led him a fine dance, till she waltzed off to the preacher with him."

"Ahh, *that's* where I know the face from. The dialogue was familiar, as was the presentation of the lonesome cowboy. Very effective, by the by," Kyle commented, from where he stood lounging in the shadows of the backstage hall, watching the pair. "Although I do believe your brother did it better," he added, sauntering toward them. "But he'd a broken nose to add verisimilitude to the character. You've a scar or two, but it doesn't compare. But then you were a college boy when we last met, weren't you? and I doubt you can completely cover over all that eastern polish you've gotten since. Graham Dylan, is it not?" Kyle asked, drawling the "Graham" as "Gram," English style, as had been originally intended, not "Gray-ham," which accounted for his nickname, as Americans said it.

Kyle offered his hand as another man might offer a thrown gauntlet, "I don't forget names once a face gives me a clue. Yours, I'll confess, escaped me at first. But it's been a decade or more. And you've changed in most things but your tastes. When last we met, you were canvassing the backstages for dancers and bit actresses. Now you've escalated to trying to induce my assistants to come play with you after the play. Your taste has improved," he said with a mocking smile.

"Why, thanks," Gray said with an air of amused calm that didn't match the look in his eyes. "And Lucy's doing fine, thanks for asking. The last time you saw her she was a blushing bride. Now she's got four kids, one smarter than the other. Can you believe it? four. They sing and dance and herd dogs and ponies at their Long Island home, because nothing else but sea gulls roam there. They live in New York City the other half of the year. My sister-in-law used to be a star in Mr. Harper's company," he explained to Hannah. Then he looked to Kyle and smiling, said, "I'll tell Lucy you were asking after her when I write next time. She'll be so pleased. Why, I guess she thought you'd forgotten her entirely since you never wrote or called. So you see," he said, turning to Hannah again, as Kyle for once seemed bereft of an easy retort, "now you know my name, my family—Lord, ma'am, you've got a full reference—the only reason to refuse me now would be pure cruelty."

Or common sense, both Hannah and Kyle thought, as Kyle recovered and told Hannah quickly, "Oh, but I thought you and I and Frank would go over that bit of his and Lottie's tonight," before he fell still, instantly ashamed of himself for such a clumsy, awkward ruse.

But Hannah thought it protective and endearing of him. And as she'd been searching for a reason to deny herself the exquisite pain-pleasure of a new acquaintance that could only lead to an old familiar pain, she said brightly, "Oh yes, I'd almost forgot. Sorry, Mr. Dylan, but my previous promise comes first."

"I understand," Gray said, and a glance at his face showed he did, and more, as he added, "tomorrow night, then?"

"We're leaving tomorrow—early, for Aspen," Kyle said triumphantly.

"Why so am I!" Gray said with a wonderful display of pleased amazement.

"Via Central City," Kyle said.

"My route exactly," Gray said with pleasure.

"And Leadville, a most circuitous path, you will agree," Kyle said.

"Most," Gray agreed pleasantly. "Lucky thing I've business there, too."

And before Kyle could ask where, or Hannah could give way to the laughter that was welling up in her, he added, "So I guess I'll see you there, ma'am . . . Mr. Harper."

And on that deliciously ambiguous note, touched his hand to his hat, turned, and strolled away, leaving Kyle to simmer with the knowledge that he'd just mouthed a perfect exit line. Then, Kyle noted with chagrin, he made an even more dramatic exit because of the slight limp that had gone unnoticed before. As she noted it now, Hannah's laughter was quelled, although her expression held no pity at all. No, Kyle thought gloomily, it held something far worse: interest.

Kyle hadn't made a move toward Mrs. Hannah Darling-Roberts since she'd told him it would be unwelcome. It wasn't her words that discouraged him so much as all her unvoiced body language, the way she behaved when they were alone and working together: the way she edged away from a seemingly accidental elbow touched to the side of her breast, the way she backed off from a conversation that grew too close, the way she stepped aside when a whisper became too confidential. A man who read faces and movements as well as other men read books, Kyle hadn't needed words to deter him. But now, this look of longing when she looked after Graham Dylan . . .

Kyle hadn't lost many women to other men. It wasn't because of his looks, he knew, and certainly not his money, no matter how he wished that could be the case. Nor was it even his personality so much as it was how well he knew the women he wanted. A man who wished to succeed in the theater had to know art and artifice and over all, human nature. That, he did. Though a dreamer, he'd a strong streak of rationality, so he never set his sights higher than he knew he could achieve. But he was only a mortal man. He'd miscalculated and misjudged sometimes, and so lost some women he'd tried to keep. One, in particular, to that man's brother. He hadn't loved her, but then he'd never loved any woman in the way that the plays he presented, presented that human emotion. Nor had he regretted it; from what he could see, true love involved self-sacrifice and self-denial. Very good subjects for theater, of course, but hideous in real life he had thought, and real life was a thing he avoided if he could.

That long lost young woman Graham Dylan had reminded Kyle of had been a professional more than a personal loss to him. Because she'd been a stepping stone, one he'd badly needed to cross the abyss between obscurity and success. Hannah was another such; he needed her now, and that need was a kind of love in itself. And as for other kinds of love, why, she was certainly lovely enough for any man . . .

"That sort," Kyle said comfortingly as he watched Graham Dylan fading into the shadows, "are found backstage, everywhere."

"Oh, but I grew up in the theater," Hannah said, and laughed, so that she couldn't say what she thought next—that he was wrong, for since she had, she knew she'd never found that sort before, anywhere.

"He'll find someone else before the moon sets," Kyle said so confidently, she bit her lip and clenched her hands hard so that she wouldn't hit him as she suddenly, and shockingly, longed to do.

But as it turned out, he didn't find someone else. Or even look to. At least, that's what he himself told her the next night. And the next, and the next and the next, and the one after that. After Friday's show in Black Hawk, and Saturday's, and Sunday afternoon at the hotel there, and then after Tuesday night's show in Breckenridge. Each time before he asked her to walk out with him again. And she again, refused him.

The hotel in Central City, if not as fancy as the nearby Teller House, was clean and comfortable, and high on a street near to their theater. If that theater wasn't the stately and elegant opera house, this time at least that was a fact they'd accepted before they'd come to town, and so a lamentable, but not unbearable one. And if the hotel was hard to reach without panting, it was because everyplace in town was. Hannah began to believe that every street went in only one direction—up. Although she knew that was impossible, her legs and lungs didn't. They were high in the Rockies now, and the town had been cut into the side of one of them.

If it was hard to walk, it was harder to sleep, tired as the hotel's occupants might be, because the hotel was in the center of the mountain-girt town, and the miners who lived there didn't go to sleep after the show as Hannah and Peggy were trying to do. The miner's night's out were all-night affairs, and the ladies that accompanied them were no ladies at all. But the miners paid a good bit of the good money they'd just torn from the earth to see the troupe perform, and lack of breath and lack of sleep were small prices to pay for such success. So instead of sleeping at once, Hannah and Peggy had learned to chat above the distant sounds of laughter and singing until the hour was late enough, if not quiet enough, for them to drop off.

Tonight it was especially difficult. Not only were the miners in high spirits, and their female companions obviously well supplied with bottled ones, but a brilliant moon rode high, drenching the night with liquid silver and filling their small room with an uncanny light.

"Do draw the curtains," Hannah said from the depths of her pillow, after she'd turned it over seeking a comfortable spot for the third time. "I can't sleep with such a light, it feels like my bed's onstage."

"Oh, aye, it's powerful. I'll wager Mr. Harper wishes the theaters here had such a light as the nights do," Peggy said on a laugh, rising to her knees to pull the curtain across the window over her bed. Then she gasped and cried, ". . . Why, look at that! Hannah, come look!"

Hannah clambered out of her bed onto Peggy's, and knelt there, blinking as she stared out the window. It took her eyes a moment to adjust, but even though the moon lit the streets below, it was a shallow, silvery light, making everything it touched shadowed and illusionary. All she could discern were the shapes of the revelers, and she didn't recognize one of them.

"What is it?" she asked, turning to look at Peggy. And saw that she was staring upward at the sky.

"Ah Hannah, have you ever seen the like?" Peggy sighed. "So close you could touch it. And 'tis a full one, too. Make a wish over your left shoulder, and it'll come true."

It was a blanched and startling moon that loomed over the town, so big it seemed to fill the sky, and it was as silver, round, and full of mysterious runes as the face of a foreign coin. Hannah shivered slightly at the beautiful but alien sight, and laughed to dispel the strangeness of it.

"You wish for me," she said lightly, seeing Peggy's round face grow solemn as she turned and peered at the moon from over her shoulder.

"Oh niver!" Peggy said, aghast. "You must do it

yourself. Then niver tell a soul what it was you wished for, else it won't come true. But it will, you'll see. Oh do it, Hannah.''

"Very well," Hannah said, for she was of the theater, and could never flout a good superstition. So she turned and gazed at the staring moon, and made the first wish she could think of: to be loved and love in return, like any normal woman, for now and ever after. And after that incandescent moment of hopeless dreaming that Peggy called a wish, she turned back to reality with the same resignation that she always did.

"Done. Now, I think you ought to close those curtains," she said as she clambered back into her own bed, "or you'll be wishing you did when you fall asleep at breakfast."

Peggy giggled and drew the curtains closed. Hannah heard her settle into bed, and heard the miners laughing again as well, and knew it would be awhile until they got to sleep this night, moonlight or not.

"They're in full voice tonight," Hannah said on a yawn. "Speaking of which . . . did you hear Sally try to hit that high note tonight? Oh my, three breaths to get out one C, no wonder mountaineers yodel—they must have to," she said, stretching in the dark, hearing the covers rustle in the most comforting way. "I don't know why Kyle just doesn't stay with recitatives until we get used to the height and air here."

"Mr. Claxton says it's a treat the way one beer acts like three here, because of it. He says a man can save a fortune getting drunk. And that he'd stay forever if he could just figger out a way to pay for that one beer, if he did," Peggy said, giggling.

" 'Figure' out," Hannah corrected her absently, "and he ought not to even have that one, you know."

"Oh, I know, none better than I know," Peggy agreed softly, all laughter fled. "My father's that fond of the bottle, too. Well, at first it was because he couldn't get work, and then it was he couldn't get work because of it. Now he's took . . . taken off, and who knows where . . . which is why I work for Mr. Harper, you see."

Hannah had guessed it, because Peggy had said as much, if never so precisely before. Their previous talks in the long, dark western nights had brought their lives out clear as either wished the other to see. Some things, after all, couldn't be said to any other living one, even if their relationship was increasingly becoming a big and little sister one, with Hannah in the role of the wise elder. Only a few years actually separated them, but Hannah had a life in the theater to guide Peggy by, as well as a considerable, if limited, education in the classics. Even more importantly, she'd been a married woman. That gave her seniority no years could equal. But in spite of their differences, they'd an underlying equality of gender and innocence, and more of one of temperament and morality than either did with any of the other members of the troupe.

Peggy was as grateful for Hannah's friendship as Hannah was glad for hers. The other women in the troupe were performers and tended to disregard Peggy. But they looked at Hannah with awe, or suspicion, or else, and worst of all, treated her with false friendliness because of what they thought her influence might be with Kyle. Knowing actors, the men, of course, even the most charming of them, Hannah did not trust at all. As for Kyle . . . it seemed he might actually be trying to be a friend, too, but knowing the theater as well as she did, even if she didn't know men as well, Hannah couldn't quite trust him either.

But Peggy had no ambitions for anything but security, and and no motive for friendship but the need of a friend. Although Hannah could wish she'd more education so that they could share more, living with Peggy showed her clearly as what she was: kind, gentle, and yet with a streak of practicality that astonished Hannah, and sometimes even tilted their relationship so that it was Peggy who was the wiser. Stage born and bred, Hannah had never encountered the like before. Reality was, after all, antipathetic to the very idea of theater, and to find common sense in it was as rare as finding a humble leading man.

"My father never drinks before a performance, for

fear he'll slur his words or his makeup," Hannah said softly in reply to Peggy's confession. "So he almost never drinks at all. I'm not sure I wouldn't prefer him getting tipsy now and then so I could see what he might be like when he's not onstage. But then, he always is," she sighed.

"No, no," Peggy said emphatically, "you never mean that, Hannah, that you never do. I can tell you that. You wouldn't want to see the drinking—nor when it takes effect—when the crockery gets tossed about as freely as hateful words do—and his eaten dinner, too, in it's own due time," she added sourly.

Hannah had to smile and was glad that Peggy couldn't see it. She was sure the girl was sincere, and that it was true. But still, the thought of her own father raging as anything but King Lear on the heath was amusing. He claimed to have gotten blind drunk a few times to know the way of it, but even his "Drunkard" was a mannerly, charming fellow—a "sublime and sympathetic sot" as one of the papers had written, which was why the matinee ladies, even those of the Temperance set, loved him so.

"No, a man who's a boozer's no good to himself or his loved ones—and a woman who's one? Faugh!" Peggy spat. "They don't bear speaking of, they don't."

"Ah, but," Hannah said in a dark, wheedling voice, "a drop of fine French champagne, my dear, can never do a girl a bit of harm."

After she got over the shock of hearing what had seemed to be a vile seducer's voice in her own bedroom, Peggy giggled, only stopping to breathlessly exclaim, "Ah, Hannah, if you'd only take to the boards, you'd make Miss Lottie look like yesterday's porridge, you would, I swear it, you would."

"I offer the girl a sip of champagne, and she offers me a life of sin upon the stage," Hannah said mournfully. Then added, in Peggy's exact accents, "Och! What's this world comin' to, I ask you?"

It was several minutes before Peggy could speak again, but after her yelps of glee subsided to chuckles, she was silent for a moment, and then said, in a very different grave little voice, "Hannah, my dear friend, 'tis about sin I wish to speak to you."

It took a moment for Hannah to realize no jest was forthcoming, and that gave Peggy time to phrase the question she finally dared to ask.

"I need your advice," Peggy said seriously. " 'Tis about a gentleman."

Hannah swallowed hard. It would be a pity if Peggy had fallen for the blandishments of John, the reedy tenor that had been in the habit of intercepting her in the backstage shadows, worse if it was their womanizing leading man, for though a charming fellow, he was far less serious about the women he used than he was about the makeup he put on and off each night. But whoever it was, Hannah thought sadly, he would end this lovely friendship she'd found. For she knew that when a girl found a fellow, the last thing she needed was the company of another girl, until, that was, the fellow either married her or shabbed her off; and in this world the latter was the rule, and the former, not much better. But Peggy deserved some luck, Hannah thought, and hoped for the best as she waited for her to go on.

"Y' see," Peggy said carefully, "this gentleman's been asking me out of late, and though at first I said no, as well I knew I should, he keeps after asking, and asking, and well, with all the way he's gone about it, polite and kind . . . He don't ask for me to come with him at night—well, surely not after the piece of mind I gave him the first time he asked that!" Peggy declared with satisfaction, before her voice gentled and she went on, "He asked for me to come walking, or riding with him in the broad daylight, on Sundays and such. Just to talk. And I believe him.

"I know that sounds pure folly," Peggy said defensively, though Hannah hadn't said a word, "for I'm well aware that I'm just a poor dab of a seamstress, in an acting company, far from home and hope of fair play from any rogue or devil, or so they think! But I'm no fool, and he's a gentleman to his fingertips, and

only asking after my company. And I only want to say
yes—just for a day that I can remember for always
after. Because I am just a poor seamstress, and I know
it, and know such an invitation will not come my way
again. What do you think, Hannah dear?''

"Why, I think that would depend entirely upon who
he is," Hannah said carefully. Then she prompted,
"Who is he?''

"Well, but you don't know him," Peggy said, "for
he's not in the company. No. He lives here. Not just
here," she said in pretty confusion, "he's from Wyoming Territory, he says. And he's no miner or common cowboy, that I'll swear. But he's no Johnny
Backstage, neither!" she cried. "That I'll take me
vows on, too. He came backstage back in Denver, and
here I thought he was lost and looking for some girl
in the dressing room, because that's where I'd seen
him the night before, with Miss Lottie and all, when
I was with you. But no, he says he was looking for
me. Because he'd seen me and couldn't forget me. Me!
Aye, imagine that!

"Well, I couldn't. And so after he tells me what for,
no, I says, of course. What sort of girl did he take me
for? To step out with a backstage admirer like a tart!"
she scoffed. "But he was back the next night, and the
next. He's even here now. He followed us . . . me.
Imagine that," Peggy breathed wonderingly. "And always so polite and soft-spoke', and well dressed, and
marvelous handsome, too. And for all I keep saying
no, all he keeps saying he wants is my company for a
few hours in the daylight. Imagine!''

It was curious, Hannah thought, how one forgot exactly what pain felt like until it came again. Hunger,
pleasure, and other emotions could be remembered
with fairly good accuracy, but the precise dimension
of pain was always a surprise when it returned. Which
was the only reason why, her mother always said,
women continued to have children after they'd had a
first one. Only not her mother, of course, she was too
wise for that. And not herself, of course, because she
wasn't a real woman, actually. But she'd not felt such

pain in her throat and her breast in a very long while. At least she'd the bitter comfort of knowing she'd been right—she'd never met a man like Gray Dylan before. And she hoped to never again.

"I think" she finally managed to say, because Peggy was awaiting her answer, and she'd a fair, if not an easy one to give, "that you might go, if you wish, in the daylight as you say. But that you'd better be very, very careful of where you go, and be sure you can get back from there alone if you have to."

"Just what I thought myself!" Peggy said on an exhaled sigh. "And so what I said to himself, exactly, too! So he says I might take a friend as a chaperon, for if it made me easier, he'd prefer it. He wants to take a carriage and drive out of town to show me the mountains in autumn, for he says there's no lovelier sight in the land, and what have I seen of his home but cities and theaters and hotels? And he's right! So who shall I take, I'm thinking? Who else? Ah, will you come, Hannah dear? Please. It's just for an hour or two together. Oh, I know it's a onetime thing, for what's a gent like that to do with a girl like me? Especially when he finds I've been telling the truth about myself. But I think it's a thing I'll never forget. And safe as houses if you're there, too, for though he's big and strong as an ox, I should think from the look of him for all his fine clothes, what can he do with the two of us?"

No more than he's already done to one of us: which is to kill hope, Hannah thought. Then she was instantly shamed by it. For she was old and wise enough not to have been fooled by the softest words or the bluest eyes, wasn't she? And then she was bitterly glad that at least he'd done it early on. Because she knew very well that no man ever seduced a woman as well as her own fantasies did. And that was, after all, the only place she could be fully seduced.

So why not go? Why not be Peggy's chaperon? Since she could never be much to a man, at least she could be of use to another woman. Her thoughts raced as her heart did: How could she tell Peggy that her handsome

gentleman had repeatedly asked her out, too, without
it sounding like spite or cruelty?—which she supposed
it would be if she divulged it now, when she was aching so badly. But at least she should try to save poor
Peggy from him. For herself there'd be more than virtue as it's own reward, there'd be the extra prize of
that most exquisitely perverse of pleasures: the wrench
of regret and rejection to be lived through once again.
It would give her the fuel for the silent battle of wits
she'd need to wage in order to show Peggy with her
own eyes what a deceitful, faithless fraud Gray Dylan
was. And most of all, what else could she say now,
after all?

"Well, yes. Why not? I will," Hannah said.

She was instantly rewarded for it by the sound of
Peggy's contented sigh, and then by a pang of pain
that sliced through her temples and her heart.

"You're a true friend. Thank you," Peggy said in a
choked little voice.

"Yes, well, and why not?" Hannah repeated to herself and Peggy, for there really wasn't anything else to
do or say yet. Because there was no sense in tears,
even if there'd been luxury of solitude for them, and
no point in them really, she told herself, even if there'd
been a realistic reason for them.

She was on the brink of sleep when she heard Peggy's voice again.

"Do you want to know what I wished for?" Peggy
asked sleepily.

"I thought you weren't supposed to say, or it won't
come true," Hannah said, thinking of the cold and
beautiful moon, and how insignificant her impossible
wish had been in the face of it.

Polly giggled. "Ah, but I can tell now. For it's come
true already . . . thanks to you, Hannah dear," she
said on another comfortable little sigh.

Peggy was long lost to sleep as Hannah lay awake,
envying her. Not for the wish come true, but for what
she herself had lost so long ago: simple problems with
simple solutions. She discovered wishing to have been

a painful luxury, too. Because wishing itself holds hope, she realized wearily, and all she was left with now was the knowledge of her one omnipresent, simple, and simply impossible wish.

Chapter Seven

Hannah was completely prepared for the outing. She had a firm, cool smile in place, and carried a book, a shawl, and a purse full of odd bits of things to sort through so as to look occupied if the scenery and the book palled. She was also wearing her best day dress, a fetching one made of heavy brown and lilac satin, crossed high at the neck and trimmed with intricate pale lavender silk fringe. She only wore it, she assured herself as she adjusted her charmingly tilted lilac and feather-strewn hat, because it also had only the merest hint of bustle, and so would be the most comfortable to sit in for hours. She'd have bodily comfort, at least, she thought as she took one last glance in the glass, congratulating herself on the expression of polite disinterest she'd perfected the night before.

That expression was so at variance with her exclamations of delight and words of praise when she turned from the mirror to see how Peggy had dressed, that for a moment Peggy was worried that she looked a fright. Her own gown of yellow and cream satin was in charming taste and good style—if Peggy had other doubts about herself, she was at least sure of her fashion sense and her ability to wield a needle to copy any of the masters of fashion. Otherwise why would Kyle

have hired her in the first place? Or so she reassured
herself as she kept her suddenly worried eyes on Hannah's uncharacteristically unsmiling mouth. Because
for all that now Hannah was saying lovely things about
the way she'd swept up her sandy hair and crowned it
with an impudent matching hat, her face was set still
and hard as she said them.

"Thank you, but I'm worrying because . . . och,
you look so . . . grim, Hannah dearest," Peggy faltered.

"A touch of a headache, nothing more," Hannah
replied.

"Why then, we'll make it another day, to be sure,
there's no need to suffer for me . . ." Peggy exclaimed, though her heart was sinking, for she'd been
up half the night entreating all the saints for good
weather.

"Nonsense!" Hannah snapped, deep into her role,
but her head did ache, since she'd been up half the
night praying for an early blizzard. "The fresh air will
clear my head."

And looking so unapproachable that Peggy didn't
dare dispute her, Hannah sailed from the room, promenaded down the hall, and descended the stair led by
her uplifted nose, her head held so high she almost
caught her foot in her skirt and tumbled the rest of the
way down. Even that wouldn't change her expression,
she decided, placing a trembling hand more firmly on
the stair rail, for it was her only protection. So, with
a prayer of thanks for her upbringing in the theater,
she marched into the lobby armed with the best pose
to affect, trying to look like a grande dame from *A
Lord's Lady*, never knowing that since her face was
shaped for smiles and not icy disdain, she looked more
like a mannequin than a haughty dowager.

She was angry with the jolt of unbidden pleasure
she felt the moment she saw that familiar tall, bright-
haired figure in the cluster of people waiting in the
lobby. Then she forced herself to remember how
swiftly he'd taken a yes from another after all her noes;
how it hadn't mattered to him which lady had said yes.

Oh, Peggy would have her eyes opened today, she silently promised with grim spite that helped her pin an insincere smile on her compressed lips, vowing nothing would remove it short of a major disaster. Another major disaster, she corrected herself, her heart skipping as he stepped forward and smiled at her.

He was wearing proper casual clothes, checked trousers, and a tightly fitted Norfolk jacket, though the hat in his hands was a Stetson. But all she'd eyes for was his tanned face, so she averted her gaze and fussed with her gloves so she wouldn't be forced to stare at those well-shaped, lying lips.

"I don't blame you for being vexed, ma'am," Gray said at once, with unmistakable laughter in his voice, "but I'm not a man to let my chance go by. The second I heard you were going to be chaperon today, I started polishing my best boots."

She gasped and her eyes flew wide.

"How dare you!" she hissed in a heated whisper, after glancing back to see that Peggy had been halted in conversation with a tall, raw-boned fellow.

Gray's eyebrow raised.

"I knew you didn't want to walk out with me," he said slowly, puzzlement and what looked very much like hurt growing in his clear blue eyes, "but I didn't know you'd go into such a taking. My mistake, ma'am," he said, putting on his hat. "But," he added, all amusement fled from his voice and face now, "if you'd be so kind, I'd like to know just what I did to get you so angry—for another time, or another lady— if not just for my vanity's sake, I guess."

"Surely," she whispered in an embarrassed rush, gesturing with a tilted head toward Peggy, "even you know that this is scarcely the time to discuss it. And since I doubt we'll ever have another time, I can only suggest you think about it. Oh!" she said, stamping one foot at his look of complete confusion, "How could you? How can you? Even here in the West, surely there must be some glimmering of civilized behavior. To ask two ladies out with you, and accept the first one to agree, and then to appear delighted that you've got the other as well . . . and then, to top it all, to volunteer to disappoint one when the other is reluctant to go along with your nefarious schemings. You . . . you, sir," she said, pulling herself up so that she addressed his cravat directly, "are beyond vile. You make Bluebeard seem constant!"

"Hannah," Peggy said excitedly from somewhere near her shoulder, because Hannah suddenly found her vision narrowed to a thin tunnel of light sufficient only to show her the contents of the overloaded purse she was fumbling in for a handkerchief, "this is Mr. Royal Atkins, the gentleman I was speaking of."

"Ma'am," the tall, raw-boned fellow Hannah's gaze flew to said in a deep smooth voice, "I thank you kindly for coming along today. No way Miss Peggy would've budged without you. Here's my friend, Gray Dylan, he'd be pleased to come along, too, so's you won't feel out of place. I know him forever, ma'am," Royal added anxiously, seeing Hannah's arrested expression. "He's my boss and my friend, and true as the day is long. I promise you. Honest."

" 'Beyond vile,' " Gray mused half to himself. "Must be around the corner from atrocious and at the intersection of hideous, or in an even lower rent district. I'm afraid Miz Roberts wouldn't want to be caught dead in a boneyard with me, Royal. Looks like you three will have to go on by yourselves."

Peggy looked frightened. Royal's long face fell. And Gray Dylan, Hannah noted with a mixture of shame and chagrin, looked not half so unhappy as he sounded or she felt.

But floundering in embarrassment helped her find hidden resources. She discovered that she'd been raised to the occasion.

"A foolish mistake, a mere misapprehension of mine. Pray forgive me, Mr. Dylan," she said, lifting her head, this time trying the Grand Duchess of Ruritania from *The False Count* and getting it exactly right. "And if it is not too late to change my mind, I should be delighted if you would accompany us."

They all smiled; some in relief, some in relieved

confusion, and one in genuine amusement, for she'd
done it so perfectly, she'd even left in the heavy Baltic
accent.

The trap Royal had rented for the occasion was a
shining black surrey, scrupulously clean, with the scent
of new leather still so strong, it even rose above the
smell of the horses pulling it. It was a mild day, and
the top was taken down so that the four passengers
were covered by only a brilliantly clear Colorado blue
sky. The ladies unfurled their parasols, and the surrey
pulled away. Royal held the reins, Peggy sat stiffly
erect on the seat beside him, and Gray and Hannah
sat directly behind the pair. If it hadn't been before,
propriety was served with a vengeance now, for though
never properly introduced by a third party when they'd
first met, none of the parties within the coach could
have so much as scratched their nose without a pas-
serby seeing it now. Certainly no one could have
guessed that the two ladies were from an acting company, and the gentlemen were two wealthy bachelors
out on a spree. But even so, no one in the coach
seemed able to forget it.

Hannah's apology had been made and accepted. But
she was even more warmly forgiven after she'd whispered, red-faced—the grand duchess having departed
for parts unknown as Gray helped her to her high
seat—"I didn't realize . . . you see, Peggy kept telling
me about a western gentleman who came backstage
every night, asking her out . . . so you see . . ."

Still, Gray's reply, made under a quirked mustache,
"Lovely opinion you have of me," didn't make future
conversation any easier, the more so when the only
thing Hannah could think to answer was "But men
who come backstage, after all . . ."

That made her rethink the wisdom of going out with
men who come backstage after all, and Gray, for all
his flippancy, couldn't think of a way to deny that truth,
and regretting his words, decided to wait it out until
the conversation took a turn that truth needn't follow.

Which was a good decision, except that as they be-

gan to pull out of the city and off into the long road
that led toward the higher mountains, he realized that
the conversation hadn't just lapsed, it had, after a few
weak comments about the weather, completely expired. Hannah was studying the roadside with theatrically rapt attention, which he could understand, in
light of their last words together. But Royal was staring at the team he drove as if he'd never seen the like
of such animals before this afternoon, and his little
lady, Miss Peg, was sitting as if she'd been placed on
tacks. But aside from the sliver of uncovered nape at
the bottom of her upswept hair that was turning an
increasingly bright shade of red, she showed no other
signs of life that Gray could recognize.

Gray knew that if he spoke first, he'd have to explain
he wasn't the kind of man that lurked around stage
doors, but since he was, he wished he were sitting in
back of Royal instead of Peggy, so he could kick his
friend into speech.

It was Hannah who finally broke the silence, despite
all her inclinations not to, but only because she had
to: silence was the most painful sound to any actor's
ear, and she'd inherited her parents' fear of it.

"The mountains are magnificent," she said, loathing herself as she did, because it was more than trite,
and wasn't something anyone would deny and served
no purpose but to make noise. "We don't have anything like this back East, do we, Peggy?" she asked
a bit desperately, trying to get Peggy to say something,
anything, other than the "yes" and "thank you" and
"I see," that had been her contribution to the afternoon so far.

Peggy made a muffled sound that might have been
anything from agreement to a cough, and Hannah went
on, almost defiantly, "Well, but I'm a child of the
cities, and so I suppose we could have a mountain high
as Ararat on the New York border, and I wouldn't
know of it."

The biblical reference moved no one but Gray, who
chuckled and said, "But you've got some Catskills I
remember from my Washington Irving."

"I do, too," Hannah said, diverted. "But I'd for-gotten they're ours, and in any case, they're not a patch on these," she admitted, turning her great dark eyes to Gray before the interest in his caused her to look away again.

The sun calls up autumn in her eyes, there's brown and russet there, he thought entranced, but her hair swallows up sunlight; it transmutes it to moonlight the way its edges shine like silver.

"Well, mountains are more than scenic, they're nec-essary. At least to some folks. Royal and I get a little anxious on the flatlands, seems we're used to seeing a mountain in the distance anywhere we look, right Royal?" Gray asked with such false joviality he winced, and wished he could halt the carriage and walk off and leave himself there mouthing facetious noth-ings.

Royal's answer sounded much the same as Peggy's last one, if a little deeper in tone.

Another awkward silence fell. It was a sparkling au-tumn day with the scent of pine growing stronger with the rising temperature of the afternoon. The surrey drove down a long, twisting road, the aspens at the side of it were wearing yellow fringes, and the sky was so blue it hurt; in the distance the only sounds were those of birds and the low murmur of water in hidden brooks, and the reason he could hear every drop of water that raced over the stones in them, Gray realized, was because no one in the surrey seemed to be breathing, much less talking. It was more than awk-ward because it was becoming foolish. Gray thought of a dozen things to say, but when he looked over to Hannah to say them, all he saw was a parasol atop a pretty dress, and when he looked forward, all that greeted his eyes were Royal's stiff neck and the back of Peggy's parasol.

To hell with the lot of them, Gray thought, and sat back, giving up, disliking all his companions, a thing he found much easier to do when he couldn't see Han-nah. He remained still, although he was complaining loudly enough inwardly about women of the theater who thought themselves better than the men who were their livelihood. Women who presented faces to the world that were far superior to anything that went on behind them, and whose dark mystery always faded in sunlight—before he'd a grim thought for their victims: men who were hopeless daydreamers, constantly fooled by them in the night and so always doomed to disillusion in the clear morning light.

They rode on in silence. Hannah glanced at Gray, raising her frilly parasol so she could pretend it was the dazzle of the sun behind his bright head she was protecting her eyes from, and not his glowing eyes. In doing so she suddenly discovered that if she gazed right at the edge of a frill at the bottom of the opened shade, she could see his face and yet not those eyes. She knew she was only safe as an ostrich with her head in the sand, but at least she felt more comfortable avoiding his direct gaze. There were, after all, some actors who couldn't focus on their audience, but were fine so long as they kept their eyes on the middle distance and pretended there was no single one out there to judge them.

Freed from self-consciousness, she found herself free to be annoyed. She was angry with Peggy for sitting like a stone, annoyed with Peggy's taciturn "gentleman" who might be a rancher but had less conversation than a milk cow, and positively furious with Gray for a number of reasons that made no more sense than his silence did. After discovering her mistake, she'd found herself thrilled to be with him, and then saddened anew at the futility of it. She felt sure that vivacious chattering would lead him on to imagine things she'd no way or intention of pursuing. But he might at least try to pursue, she decided, irrationally angry at his solving her problem so neatly. There was no reason for him to sit and wait for her to entertain him, as though she were being paid to do so, simply because she came from an acting troupe. But the silence was unendurable. Hang the lot of them, she decided. I'm not going to sit like a stuffed goose until its time to go back.

She spoke suddenly.

"How nice that you like your mountains so much," she said sweetly. "So wild, so rugged, so fitting . . . now I think of it, there's something about mountains that defies civilization, isn't there? Why, just think! There's not a great city in the world that's built on a mountain. Seems that we "flatlanders' have the edge, culturally," she said, wondering if they'd the wit to know whether to be flattered or insulted, and not caring which they decided on.

"Rome," Gray said immediately. 'Seven hills of'— you know. And Pompeii. And San Francisco. And all the Mayan capitals in Peru, for a start."

"The Mayans are extinct," she said quickly, hoping he'd forget about the other cities she'd forgotten.

"So they are," he answered, remembering what had happened to Pompeii an instant too late, and hoping she would, too.

"I'm not very good at geography," she admitted, before he could think of more.

She saw his lips turn up, and spun the parasol so she'd not be tempted to look into his eyes.

"Neither am I," Gray said, "but I've been lucky enough to visit some places that I'd have forgotten if I'd only seen them on a map—Oh, no," he said, forestalling her. "No, I won't talk about them. There's nothing more boring than a man who goes on about his travels, is there? Because no matter how interesting they are, sooner or later he'll be talking about something historic, and he'll say, 'and from there I went to luncheon and had a most remarkable stew . . . or was it Venice where I had that? Had a great many peppers in it, I recall, and bits of onions . . . or was that Rome? No, Rome was the noodle dish. At any rate . . . no! It was a ragout I had there, now I remember'!"

She laughed. And he grinned at her laughter.

"Or the lady who remembers a world capital by the shawl she bought there," she offered, as he countered, "And the gent who's so interested in the life story of his guide he doesn't remember a thing about the Colosseum.''

They began talking about foolish things people said about places they'd been. He'd made the grand tour, but she'd seen every American city in the East that had a good size theater. He'd been to college and spoke French fairly well, but she'd teethed on Shakespeare and Molière, and knew how to mimic any known accent of mankind. They'd a great many interest in common, and both loved to talk. But they laughed more than they talked, and that was considerable. They only stopped when they realized they were the only ones talking. But that was a long time later, when Royal finally stopped the surrey.

"Seems like a good place to stop," he said. When they heard his voice, they realized it was the first one they'd heard but each other's since they'd set out.

It was a good place to stop, at least, Hannah couldn't imagine a better. They were high on a mountain, but there was a natural slope leading to level ground where they hitched the horses, so they didn't feel like mountain goats when they stepped on the grass when they left the surrey. They were beside a grove of towering aspen whose leaves shivered in the slightest breeze, and so sliced and scattered the light beneath them into dancing, sparkling bits. A walk to the edge of the grass showed a vista of frowning mountains above and gentle valleys below. They were not up high enough to panic, or low enough to keep constantly looking up; it was a perfect place for a picnic. But no one was thinking about picnicking.

"Seemed like a good place to stop," Royal said uncertainly as he looked at Gray where they stood near the surrey, apart from the women.

"Or start," Gray said in a harsh whisper. "I don't expect you to do a song and dance, but where's your tongue? You didn't say be damned to that girl. Made me do all the yapping. I felt like Scheherazade back there."

"Miz Roberts didn't mind," Royal said.

"Damned if I know if she did," Gray said impatiently. "She's got the manners of a debutante and the manner of an actress, so how should I know? But why didn't you open your mouth?"

"I didn't know what to say," Royal said abruptly, turning his back on his friend and reaching into the boot of the surrey to take out a basket. Then he turned and met Gray's steady gaze, and his lashes concealed his own hazel eyes as he said, with as much confusion as despair, "Damn, I didn't know it would be this hard, neither."

"What's so hard?" Gray asked, genuinely puzzled.

"Talking to her," Royal whispered.

"Why? She's pretty and young and appears to be scared half out of her wits by you. She seems like a nice girl. Just talk to her."

"Don't know how," Royal said, rationing his words as he became more upset. "Well, damn it Gray," he said in a burst of loquaciousness. "That's just it. She's a good girl."

Gray frowned in incomprehension. Royal sighed and then beckoned Gray over to the side of the surrey where he pretended to be searching for something so the women wouldn't hear them, and said in a hoarse, pained whisper, "I never talked to a good girl more than 'how do' and 'nice afternoon, ain't it?' Well, where'd I find one? Sure, I've had lots of women, but they was just whores, and all they said was how much and 'honey you was real fine.' She's a good girl."

"Didn't you have a sister?" Gray asked, astonished, because for all the years he'd known Royal, they'd never discussed this aspect of women.

"Nope," Royal said, his tanned face showing ruddier as he did.

"Well, then, your mother," Gray said.

"Died young, m' aunt raised me, and she was a holy terror. Yeah, really," Royal said with the vestige of a smile. "She talked to God and the preacher, and never did more than pray over me. That's why I lit out when I was old enough to go it on my own. I want to talk to her, Gray," he said with difficulty, "but what in hell do I say? I know how to lay a woman down, but nothing else. I never had one for a friend," he shook his head and smiled at the inanity of that thought before his smile slipped. Then he said softly, "I'd sure like to have her as a friend, even if I know there couldn't be nothing else. She's sure special, ain't she?"

Gray glanced over the little woman Royal was staring at. All he saw was a round-faced, freckled girl with an unremarkable figure and a mass of sandy hair. She'd a friendly face, he decided, a not unpleasant one, but only that. But he knew how much it meant to Royal to agree as he nodded and said, "Surely a fine-looking woman."

His eyes were on Hannah before he'd done speaking. She looked as lovely in the forest setting as he imagined she'd look on a stage; her dark good looks were more than attractive, they were dramatic. In fact, everything about her—her way of dressing, of speaking—was just exaggerated enough to make everything she said and did seem larger than life. She might swear she was no actress until her last breath, but there was an aura of excitement about her that transcended even the fascinating one of suppressed sexuality that lured him, and spoke louder than she did; there was no mistaking she was of the theater.

But what else was she? For the first time, Gray wondered if he'd ever know. Even more surprising, for all his success with women, for the first time he wondered if he'd ever known much more of them than Royal did. Because he, too, had had no sister, and though he'd adored his gentle, doting mama, she'd died before he'd come to manhood. And now he saw that though he'd had more liaisons than he could count, and many of them for longer than a night, most of them, he had to admit, had been, however nicely done, about little more really than how much and 'honey you was fine.' He was glib and liked women, never had any trouble talking to them, and had had some of the best times in his life with them. Still, now he stood and considered the matter, and realized he'd never had a woman as a friend, or at least not as he thought of as a man as such. Or even ever thought of having one as such before.

He looked at Royal with new respect. He was a canny trader, and knew truth, in whatever guise, was always a valuable commodity to acquire. But he didn't have time to refine on it now. His friend needed advice. His immediate problem, at least, was easy enough to solve. He could teach Royal how to talk to a woman, the incomprehensible rest would be up to him.

"You know how you talk to me?" Gray asked. "Well, talk to her just like that. No, I mean it," he said to Royal's incredulous stare. "If you're not hell-bent on getting under her skirt, then you don't have to flatter and coax and lie. Just talk. Talk about things like you'd talk about them to any man. Just avoid cuss words, and the subject of sex and cigars. Well, aside from the obvious, their brains work like ours do, don't they? Talk about things you'd like her to talk about with you. What would that be?"

"I want to know more about her," Royal said simply, turning his head to stare at Peggy again.

"Well, there you go," Gray said cheerfully. "Ask her. Just up and ask her. That's all. There ain't nobody," he said, slapping Royal on the shoulder, "man, woman, or not-quite-sure, who don't love talking about themselves."

And so when they went to join the ladies, after they'd spread out the blanket and taken out the wicker basket full of food, and Royal was sitting up alongside Peggy on one side of it—the two of them like tent posts and just as comfortable looking, as Gray whispered to Hannah from where he reclined on the blanket next to her on the other side—it was Gray who then turned his head as it rested on his hand and looked up at her. And the very next thing he said, was: "Now then, enough of them. Tell me all about yourself, Miz Hannah Roberts."

They drove back to Central City in silence as the sun slid further into the west. They'd eaten every scrap of food the hotel had packed into the basket, and even if the men had the lion's share because the ladies were too tightly laced to take on more, they were all, as Royal observed, "full as ticks." And so, full and sleepy in the last of the golden sunlight, lulled by the pace of the horses, and stilled by the intoxicating draughts of thin air they'd breathed all day, they rode back as they'd gone out, in silence. Only this time it was a contented one.

The men saw the ladies to their hotel, and left them as the sun set. Which was, Hannah and Peggy realized as they hastened up to their room, the time when they were most needed. Hannah threw off her air of lassitude along with her shawl, and scrubbed her face with water to wake up and prepare for her working night. Because it was, as she said as she groped for a towel, now the time of day when both bats and actors came out.

"And other dread cray-tures of the night," she said on a grin when she saw Peggy smiling. "So we'd best get busy. As she struggled into a less expensive dress for work, she remembered her duties. "You my dear," she said over her shoulder, "have got to let out some seams in Polly's doublet. She popped a few last night. I think the air agrees with her. If she gains more weight, we'll have a bigger little lord than we need, but I haven't the heart to tell her to eat less. You're only young once, and before she knows it, she'll be stuffed into a corset with the rest of us."

"What a crowded corset that would be, to be sure," Peggy said on a grin.

Hannah's laugh was as much surprise as genuine amusement, for though Peggy had the merriest of temperaments, she seldom made jokes. But now she saw that though Peggy's pleasant face was wreathed in familiar smiles, there was a new dimension to it, too. Her hazel eyes sparkled, her very skin seemed more translucent. Happiness? Hannah wondered, or love, or just fresh mountain air? Whatever it was, it transformed her from just a pretty girl to a very pretty one. Hannah was glad for it, and sorry, too, because if it depended on the smile of a man, it was ephemeral as innocence and just as fragile.

"And that red skirt of Mary Holiday's needs mending," Hannah went on, forcing herself to forget the matter so she could attend to business. "And then, I'm sorry but you must drop in on Lottie—she's been whining that her gown for *Midsummer Night* is too plain and won't show up at all—yes, Kyle wants to get it ready for Aspen, even though I think it's too soon for her, and would always be too much for us to do, but I don't have the running of things."

"Hannah," Peggy said, still smiling so widely she forgot to conceal the tiny gap between her two front teeth that she was usually so ashamed of. "Oh, my dear Hannah, but wasn't it a glorious day!"

"Yes, yes," Hannah said distractedly. "We'll talk about it tonight," she promised as she caught a glimpse of herself in the mirror and tried to make a last-minute adjustment to her hair. But Peggy's sudden change of expression was clearly reflected behind her. It wasn't her expression of hurt confusion so much as the eloquent way her small shoulders slumped that made Hannah spin around. Then she crossed her arms in front of her, leaned back against the vanity table, and sighed.

"Very well," Hannah said with an encouraging smile. "Tonight's a year away then, isn't it? Tell me, what did he say?"

"No, no, you're right, I'm that foolish," Peggy said. She began bustling about the room in a whirlwind of ineffectiveness, looking for things to pick up and put down again, before she stopped, shrugged, and said, "Och, well, but you see, I never walked out with a gentleman before."

Hannah's pretended smile widened into one of real relief, "Ah, so it's the novelty of the situation, and not the fellow himself that's got you into such a twitter."

"Oh no," Peggy said at once, a faint high flush coming to her round cheeks. "It's never just that. He's not like anyone I've ever met before."

"And you've met so many gentlemen," Hannah said.

"Well," Peggy said, straightening her spine and looking at Hannah with an unconscious haughtiness, " 'tis true, I haven't walked out with a gent before, but that don't mean I don't know them. I've four brothers, Miz Hannah, and more uncles than I know what to do with, and there's the neighbors, too—we live on top of each other at home, and what's one person's business is everyone's, and they've all got friends— yes, I know a great many men, I do. But none like Royal Atkins, that I'll swear. He's kind and handsome and has a good heart, too."

"Splendid. And what else do you know about him?" Hannah asked, though she hated to. But although she disliked being devil's advocate, she knew an unhappy affair was the last thing Peggy needed. When she saw Peggy's chin come up, she'd a moment to worry and wonder if she'd challenged her because Peggy's having a happy affair was the last thing she herself needed.

"I know a good bit about him," Peggy said proudly. "He's an orphan and has got no family at all, and he's worked for Mr. Dylan's family for most of his grown life so that he's ready to strike out on his own now. And he's got a bit of land that he's thinking of settling on to raise cattle and horses and especially palomino horses, which he says are the prettiest on the face of the green earth; and he had a spotted dog named Bango when he was a boy—and he loves fried chicken and biscuits, and he plays the harmonica."

Hannah blinked.

"Heavens!" she said, when she could. "I'd no idea. You do know a thing or two about him, don't you? I didn't hear you two talking together at all."

"Well, and that's maybe because you and Mr. Dylan was laughing and joshing so much," Peggy said.

"Yes. Well," Hannah said. "But still, one swallow doesn't make a summer. You've only gone with him once."

"Aye," Peggy agreed sadly. "And who knows if we'll meet again, for he said nothing to me about it

when we parted. But still, I'd this afternoon, didn't I?
And I thank you for it, Hannah, I do.''

"Don't thank me," Hannah began, relieved that she
was "Hannah" again and not "Miz Hannah," but
Peggy interrupted her to add, "for you know I'd not
have walked out with him by myself. No, even the
nicest fellow can get the wrong idea of a girl that way.
And if he did, why, he'd not be that nice to her anymore.'Tis the way of the world," she sighed. And she
said more briskly, "But now then, you and Mr. Dylan
never stopped laughing. It was a treat to watch you.
Are you going to see him again? What sort of fellow
is he?''

"He's a rancher, and he lives in Wyoming, and he
loves the theater and he's been to college and to Europe and he . . . Hannah paused, realizing that she'd
laughed a great deal and had a fine time, but even after
all that time in his company, she didn't know much
more about Gray Dylan than that.

"He's a very slick character," Hannah said finally,
"and I certainly don't expect to see him again, because I don't believe he's used to such tame entertain-
ments as picnics, and not by word or gesture did I
imply I was used to anything else. Quite the contrary," she said, remembering how she'd changed the
subject whenever the conversation had drifted toward
anything to do with men and women and what they did
together. Then remembering how often it had, her own
cheeks flushed as she added, "I'm glad I hadn't your
hopes when I set out, or I'd be very set down now.
But you had better be careful of your fried-chicken-
fancying, harmonica-playing Mr. Atkins if you see him
again, because birds of a feather flock together, you
know.''

"Och, but wouldn't that maybe mean it's Mr. Dylan
who's not so bad then?" Peggy answered, and Hannah
was amazed, but it truly did seem as if Irish eyes did
smile.

"And she's got four brothers, too," Royal said as
he sat across the table from Gray talking about Peggy

while he wolfed his dinner so that he could go on talking and still appease other more mundane hungers. "But she started sewing early and makes more money than any of her brothers now. And sends most of it home to her ma. Her ma sews, too."

"And has a bunion on her big toe on her left foot, too, you'll be telling me next. Lord, Royal, you know everything but her grandma's first name—no, I don't want to hear it if you do," Gray said as Royal tried to speak. "She's turned you into a regular chatterbox," he said wonderingly. "Yet I never saw such a pair of clams when we started out. What did you do? Use sign, like Indians?"

"She just needed some warming up. She never walked out with a fellow before," Royal said, and seeing the amusement in Gray's eyes, added with a look in his own that would have made most men reach for their guns, "and I believe her."

Gray held up both hands as though surrendering, and said, "I wasn't going to say a thing. But if I was," he added, lowering his hands as Royal lowered his lashes in embarrassment, "I'd remind you that you only walked out with her once, and that she works in the theater."

"She sews," Royal said flatly, addressing his steak. "Miz Roberts works there, too, and you were having a high old time with her. Near broke your neck trying to for the last couple of weeks, too, Peggy says."

Gray had a sudden, eerie premonition that he'd be hearing "Peggy says" for a long time to come. Well, why not, he thought, she seemed like a good girl, or at least one that wouldn't harm Royal. And for a certainty, the way Royal was talking and acting, he'd never harm her. No, his intentions were abundantly clear. Gray would have preferred Royal finding a girl from a rich family so he could improve his stake with his marriage, but he could hardly disapprove of him disregarding that, as he himself had all these years.

If he felt any slight unease, it was that his tongue-tied friend had found out his girl's whole history down to when she lost her first milk tooth, or so it seemed, and all he himself had found out about the mysterious Miz Roberts was that she was wonderful company, very smart, had a fine sense of humor, loved the theater and distrusted him with some intensity. It wasn't as though he hadn't tried to discover more, but she was as adept at changing the subject as she was at making him laugh. If there was going to be any joy forthcoming from those quarters, he mused, pausing to reflect on just which quarters would bring the most joy, it would take time to discover them. Maybe more time than he had. Or at least, more than he was willing to spend, for it occurred to him that he'd all the time in the world for anything he wanted.

Royal clearly didn't.

"I'm following along to Leadville," he said before he took a mouthful of bread and gravy.

"You like their version of *Little Lord Fauntleroy* that much, do you?" Gray asked.

"God, no," Royal said. "It's poor. Poorer when you see it a few times. Though Peggy says they'll be doing *A Midsummer Night's Dream* next."

"Bet you can hardly wait," Gray said.

"Don't care if I ever see it," Royal answered. "But I'm seeing her again."

Gray nodded and took a swallow of coffee, waiting to see when it would occur to Royal. It took three seconds.

"Gray," Royal said, suddenly putting down his fork and knife, and looking steadily at his friend. "She's a good girl a long ways from home. So, no matter what, I know she won't come out with me alone. Can't blame her," he said with as much pleasure as wonder. "So . . . would you . . . ? Damn," he said when Gray only smiled at him. "I'll ask you proper. I'd hold it a favor. So . . . you coming?"

"Oh. Well. Yeah. I suppose I have to, then," Gray grumbled, delighted.

Chapter Eight

They stood on the raised wooden sidewalk outside the theater, and though it was narrow, they managed to stay in a clump together, like schoolchildren on an outing. It might have been because the gentlemen didn't want to get their shoes ruined by the mud in the street, and the ladies wished to protect their hems, as well. But the men had boot scrapers back at the hotel, and the ladies had sewn on hem protectors. They were used to it by now, this was the West, after all, and the members of the Harper troupe were getting to be veterans here. But they stayed in a cluster, apart from the other theatergoers, because they weren't used to being in the audience and not on the stage, and perhaps even more because they weren't used to frequenting such theaters, onstage or off.

When they filed into the little lobby and looked up the plain high stair that led to the mezzanine floor, they relaxed. They'd heard the Tabor at Leadville was a little gem, but such a *little* gem couldn't transport them to the realms of envy they'd feared. Their theater, across the street, was no more or less than any of the other saloon theaters they'd played. But they'd got into town a day early, so someone's suggestion of a look-

see at the Tabor tonight had been met with instant
approval by all.

A coach ride around town had shown them that
Leadville was a booming town with its fair share of
streets of fine mansions and quality stores. Civilization had come to it with a rush, along with its silver
mines, for it boasted a half dozen newspapers and over
a hundred saloons. But most of the sprawling town
was filled with those who'd made it the success it was.
A night at the theater was always preferable to any
other sort of sport for most members of the troupe,
but especially so here. Because a night out on the town
anywhere else would mean being surrounded by thou-
sands of miners. That hadn't appealed to anyone but
Lester Claxton, who never cared who he drank with,
and as this tour had gone on, he had been drinking so
much he'd never notice who he drank with, either.

"Coals to Newscastle, come along you red-hot thes-
pians," Lester quipped now as he led the troupe up
the steep stair, and they laughed at his jest, until they
got into the theater, and then they fell still as their
faces suddenly became grave. It was a gem. They grew
silent as worshippers at a shrine as they stood in the
red-carpeted aisles and gazed around themselves.

Who better than they could know the charm of the
raked orchestra that spread out into a fan to the back
of the hall, so that despite the several white and gold
supporting pillars, everyone in the house had a good
seat? What other eyes could evaluate the impact of the
rich gold swagged curtain that hung over the neat stage
flanked by two huge birdcage-styled boxes? Who but
another performer could take a comfortable seat in a
flocked velvet chair with cunningly wrought-iron arms,
sit back, and gaze up at the domed ceiling to see the
painted cherubs cavorting in the blue firmament there,
and then know, from the second the orchestra struck
up, that the acoustics were made for angel choirs, or
at least, could make the merest whispers sound like
one? When the curtain rose, before the drama even
began, there was scarcely a dry eye in Kyle Harper's
troupe—although when they saw the beautifully lit,

painted backdrop, they really should have been grateful that the lights in the theaters they played were too weak to show the wrinkled, inappropriate sets they had to act before, instead of being consumed with envy and shame.

There was no sawdust on the floor. Although the audience was packed with hard-faced workingmen, most of them were sober, or if they weren't, they didn't keep shouting out, celebrating it. No bar girls roved the audience, distracting them. No, the prostitutes there were on a night out, too, so they sat the way they thought ladies would, and were even more postured than that, to drive home the point of their hard-earned leisure and elegance.

The play was well acted and well received. There were so many dazzling changes of scenes and sets that it was hard to tell just how good the actors were—but they were. When it was finally over, and all the encores had been called for and given, the Harper troupe applauded just like the rest of the audience. But as they filed out again, they were the only ones on the verge of suicide.

"I've got a pal in the company," one of the singers said, as they descended the stair. "There's a party backstage and we've been asked in."

It was a measure of the general despondency that no one replied, except for Maybelle, who asked dully, "Do they have any openings?" and when the answer, "Good Heavens, no, do you think I'd be here if there was?" was given, there was utter silence among the company. And so they left as they'd entered, together, and even if they hadn't looked theatrical, the company would have stood out from the rest of the departing audience, since they were moving as if they were a funeral cortege caught in the midst of a Mardi Gras.

It was a good thing their hotel was next door to their own theater, because that way, Lester said when he left them, he wouldn't have far to crawl from the saloon he was going to. Unspoken, but loud enough in all their ears to make some of them go along with Lester, was the fact that the actors at the Leadville

Tabor stayed at the best hotel in town, the Tabor Grand, next door to the theater. But that was across the street, and so, as they now knew, in another world entirely from them.

Even Kyle's impromptu speech about how success in Leadville would bring them greater success in Aspen didn't lighten the mood. His assuring them that their theater, if not the best, was far from the worst, didn't hearten them much. It was true it was superior to any of the city's so called "concert halls," which featured musical entertainment and boxing matches, as girl waiters circulated in the audience, and not so bad as some other variety theaters in town. But that hardly mattered. They'd never even consider playing a concert hall anyway, and didn't care about the other variety theaters now. The truth was that "not so bad" and "better" wasn't the same as "best." And so even his final rallying cries about the promised land of Aspen, their planned performance there, and the opening of the Jerome hotel, only gladdened their hearts for a little while. For as they each filed into their rooms, they knew that Aspen was weeks away, and that for now, heaven was just across the street.

"It was an eye-opener," Peggy said as she finished undoing the many tiny buttons on the back of Hannah's dress, and then turned so that Hannah could do the same for her. "It was that, all right. I never saw the like."

"I have," Hannah sighed. "But I'd forgotten. I suppose one grows unaccustomed to luxury as quickly as one gets used to it. There are theaters in New York just as fine—the Astors, the Morgans, and the Vanderbilts have as much money as Mr. Tabor any day. But New York's only a memory out here, and it's easy to forget and be pleased with less, thinking the poor conditions you see are the best they have—if you don't know any better. Maybe that's why people like to be superior about their home when they travel. It's more comfortable than knowing that if they'd money or position anywhere they were, there'd be nothing to feel superior about."

Hannah took a deep breath as she unhooked the front of her corset. Sighing with relief as well as sorrow, she slid her long nightdress over her head so she could take off the rest of her clothes without scandalizing Peggy, and added sadly, "So it's as well we didn't have the chance to go to a performance at the Tabor in Denver, or I suspect most of us wouldn't have got even this far. I hear it's even grander than this one. Well, but by then Mr. Tabor had met Baby Doe; he only built this theater for his vanity and his first wife."

"Aye, too true," Peggy said, or something like, for she was scrubbing her face at the washbasin as she did.

Hannah waited her turn, her eyes on the window with the shade drawn against the lights of the Tabor hotel and theater, although all her thoughts were on it. The illusion of the challenge of the West and success in that brave new world had sustained her through much. But then, illusion always had. It had been hard to leave New York, harder now to realize she truly was exiled. Loneliness had always been her chiefest enemy, even before her fiasco of a marriage; times like these made her wonder if the war she waged against it was worth it. Illusion was her only ally, but now it was temporarily defeated.

And so when she heard the faint tap at the door, she reacted with as much glee as surprise, rushing to answer even if she was in her nightgown, not caring who it was—even Kyle with another rallying talk, or Lottie with another complaint, would be welcome. But in her mood, the drunken miner or madman, the women of the troupe always worried about intruding on them in the night, would have been welcome.

But it was only little Polly Jenkins, standing on the doorstep in her flannel night robe, alone, and looking afraid. After glancing down the hall to see if Mrs. Jenkins was there—since the only time she ever saw Polly without her mother was when she was onstage— Hannah asked quickly, "What is it Polly? Is your mama ill?"

"Oh no, no, please can I come in?" Polly asked in

a rush of a whisper, looking behind herself, and looking even more fearful as she did.

When they'd hurried Polly through the door and barred it against whoever she was fleeing, they were shocked to discover that it was Polly's mother she'd fled.

"If she knew I was here . . . oh, you mustn't tell her," the girl said in an agonized whisper, looking from Hannah to Peggy, who stood around her in their white nightdresses and with their long hair unbound, looking like two distracted angels hovering about a junior member of their heavenly choir.

"No, of course, certainly not," Hannah assured her, before she asked hesitantly, "Umm, but what is it that we mustn't tell her?"

"It's about my doublet—for Fauntleroy . . ." Polly said, producing it from beneath her night robe and then hanging her head until her black sausage curls covered over her heated face, "I tore it again."

"Why, but that's nothing, nothing at all, my dear," Peggy said at once, inspecting the split seam in the side of the bright blue doublet. " 'Tis the work of a moment, I can run it up right now, if you want to wait."

Hannah smiled at Peggy over Polly's bent head, thinking about the crystalline purity of a child's conscience, when Polly added in a choked, tear-glutted voice, "Won't do any good. It'll only tear again. I bind tight as I can, but they're getting bigger every day."

It took only a moment for the women with her to realize what "they" were, and then they both stared down at the heavily ruffled front of Polly's robe. And since there was nothing to be seen, neither knew what to say.

"They get bigger every day, I swear it," Polly cried in anguished tones. Then she said tearfully, "I'm fifteen, though Mama tells everyone twelve. But I'm small for my age, and Mama's small *there* so she thought I'd be, but I'm not anymore. She'd kill me for sure if she knew I was here, but I knew you'd know sooner or later, because you sew my clothes, Peggy, and you'd mention something to Miss Hannah, and everyone knows Miss Hannah is sharp as can be. So I waited until Mama was asleep and the halls were quiet . . . Can you make the doublet bigger or something, because it's not that I'm a coward or a complainer, like Mama says, but it hurts to bind them so tight. Truly it does. Can you do anything, please?''

Hannah and Peggy looked at each other.

"Surely, if you told Kyle . . . ?'' Hannah began, but Polly looked up wild-eyed and cried, "Oh no! We need this job! It's only for a few more weeks, like Mama says, oh please,'' she pleaded. "I'm scared to even talk about it, the walls in this hotel are so thin, but what else can I do?''

Peggy nodded and went to get her measuring tape and sewing box. "Let's have a look,'' she said when she returned to Polly's side. "Come then, we're all females here, and I can't sew for what I can't see.''

She'd only meant for Polly to open her robe, but with the trusting literalness of youth, Polly removed her robe, and averting her head, quickly undid the drawstring on her nightgown, pulling it down to show two small, firm, uplifted breasts. They were not half so big to the other women's eyes as they were to Polly's own, but upon seeing them, both the older women remembered the pride and confusion they'd felt when they'd first noticed the change in their own bodies. And seeing Polly wince as Hannah gently drew her gown up to cover them again, they both recalled the exquisite sensitivity of those newly formed breasts.

Peggy put down her measuring tape, "I'll let it out, make a double seam, and an extra yoke,'' she said in very businesslike tones as she sat to begin the repairs.

"I don't see why we can't just forget the belt, too, do you?'' Hannah added.

"Aye, long and boxlike, it'll be smart as paint,'' Peggy assured Polly. "Now,'' she said, "you get on back to your room, and I'll have this by morning. Then you get your other costumes to me, and just see how I alter them. No one will be the wiser. But don't bind so tight anymore,'' she gestured to Polly's chest with her needle, ''you hear? Or you'll have pancakes by the time you're twenty.''

Hannah began laughing, and then, for a wonder, so did Polly, and Peggy joined in, so that it was a few minutes before they could let her go back to her room.

''Thank you, oh thank you,'' Polly said fervently, as Hannah opened the door. ''How can I thank you?''

''Hush, no need,'' Hannah said, ''but be quiet, we don't want to wake the neighbors.''

Polly grew still, poised on the doorstep, ''Who's next door?'' she asked fearfully.

''I've no idea,'' Hannah whispered, ''but actresses have a bad enough name. Let's not make it worse with late-night carousing.''

''Oh,'' Polly said with relief. ''I thought it was one of the troupe, or something. I'll go. And thank you.''

''That mother,'' Peggy said firmly when Hannah had closed the door, ''should be shot, she should.''

''I don't know,'' Hannah said, as she climbed into her bed. ''What would they do if Kyle fired them now? How would they get home? Poor Polly's womanly charms are an inconvenience and a danger to her—but then, I suppose every unprotected woman's are.''

Peggy put down her sewing and stared at Hannah. She wanted to refute every painful word she'd just heard, but then picked up her needle again and shook her head, because she couldn't.

The first show went like clockwork, in that it seemed mechanical people were performing in it—or so, at least, Kyle said afterward.

''We got enough applause,'' a singer heatedly rebutted him.

''They even threw coins!'' another put in.

''That crowd,'' Kyle said laconically from where he leaned against a table in the backstage of the saloon theater, where he held the post-performance conference, ''would cheer anything they could focus on. Which wouldn't be much. Anything would please them. We must be better than anything, so we draw audiences, not just entertain those too drunk to stagger away from the bar when the performance begins. *That* is the purpose of this tour. If I'd wanted good enough for a saloon, I wouldn't have bothered handpicking the finest cast I could.''

Several of his performers felt his words fall like warm rain upon their parched pride, but the singer spoke up plaintively again, ''It's not our fault, since Bill and Hildy left last night and took John with them, we sound no-count as a chorus.''

''Odd,'' Kyle commented. ''I didn't know that. I'd think the five of you could cope. How many does it take to make harmony? I've heard barbershop quartets that sounded more than adequate, why, I do believe that Mr. Handel's great *Messiah* only requires four soloists—but then, I'm not a singer, so how should I know? What do you think, Miss Flora?'' he asked his featured female singer.

Miss Flora, very well aware that if anymore of her chorus left, she might as well begin packing, too, said at once, ''I thought we sounded fine. But—perhaps a bit dispirited . . . ?''

''Ah. Just so!'' Kyle said, slipping from the table he'd perched upon to stand and face them. ''The key to any performance, and all: spirit. I'd hoped we'd do so well here, we'd have Aspen awaiting our arrival with bated breath,'' he sighed, neglecting to mention that if they didn't do well enough to be booked for an extra week here, he'd that much less money to pay for their room and board in the town he'd have to play before Aspen.

With the inspiring thought of even his diminished troupe eating their heads off without working for a week, he urged them, ''With spirit, my friends, we can become a legend in Leadville in our own time! Why, with the amount of cheering and laughter and wild applause we could generate, to spill out from behind these swinging doors like radiant light upon the streets of town, we could make those leaving the Tabor across the street jealous of what they'd missed, and vow to visit us the very next night. No, you hadn't thought of that, had you? I thought not," he said as he saw the faces around him brightening, "so I suggest you do now. And that will be all I'll ask of you for tonight."

As they rose and gathered their things in order to leave, he added negligently, ". . . Except for Little Polly, if you please. And you, Miss Hannah."

But four people remained after the others had gone: Peggy, standing a bit aside, fussing with her workbasket as though she'd a reason to, and Mrs. Jenkins, of course, as usual, took the invitation to Polly as one for herself as well.

"Only a thought," Kyle said lightly. "No need to look so defensive, ma'am," he added to Mrs. Jenkins, to get her chin down a notch, "but I find *Fauntleroy* a bit daunting for Miss Lottie's repertoire, ah—please let's keep that betwixt ourselves, ma'am, eh?" he added, with the warmest smile they'd ever seen light his dark face, to the point that Mrs. Jenkins colored in pleasure, and she looked, for an instant, like the girl her Polly was.

"And *The Drunkard*," he mused, "though it elicits much applause, is perhaps not the happiest choice for the venues in which we presently play—or so, at least, the proprietors tell me. A man feels a bit awkward, I understand, ordering another drink, when he's just seen a playlet in which a drunken father is responsible for the death of a little angel like our Polly, here. It is, I'll grant, a problem," he said on a sigh, as Hannah's eyes widened, because she'd never seen any man in the audience do more than wipe his eyes before he'd ordered another. She'd heard bartenders say the play was better than pretzels for business. Temperance leaders might adore *The Drunkard,* but so did every drunkard, since they always thought the moral applied to every other man but the drinking man watching it, as everybody in the theater knew.

"Yes, then what are we to do? I'd thought," Kyle said pensively, "we might substitute *Her Fatal Lover* or perhaps, *The Bridge at Midnight*. They're dramatic, and always leave audiences sniveling. And have no tiresome English accents for Miss Lottie to get right, and no more than the usual references to drunken folly. The only problem I can foresee, is that the girl in them both is a bit older than our dear Polly—a sort of a junior ingenue, as it were. I hesitate to ask this,'' he said with every evidence of embarrassment, which was remarkable really, Hannah thought, for a man who'd probably never felt that emotion, ''but do you think, my dear Mrs. Jenkins, that our Polly could, ah—pad for the part?

''Pray—wait before you upbraid me,'' he cried, holding up one slender hand, before Mrs. Jenkins could so much as blink, ''for though the girl ought to look nubile, I promise she'd never be subjected to cat-calls or whistles as Miss Lottie is, because she'd play a pure young thing merely trembling on the brink of womanhood—not wallowing in it—rather like a sprite, like the girl in the 'Fairy' soap advertisements. Do you see? Do you think she could—stretch for the part?''

Before Mrs. Jenkins could answer, he added confidentially, ''Because one day, I shall need a new ingenue. I hope that will be many years hence, of course. But spring does turn to summer in its course, and when it does, how nice to have a new star that we've trained ourselves ready to step in.''

Hannah's face was as radiant as Polly's, while Mrs. Jenkins, a woman who knew acting, too, seemed to think, and then nodded.

''My Polly,'' she said imperially, ''can do anything. She is an actress. Are you not, my child?''

''Oh yes, Mama,'' Polly breathed joyfully.

''And though it's not quite the thing to say, I might add that the women in our family bloom early, and beautifully,'' Mrs. Jenkins said in a lowered voice, as she pinched Polly to get her to stand straight and stop hunching her shoulders, as she'd told her to do just an hour before.

When they'd done making arrangements for getting to work on the new roles, Mrs. Jenkins and Polly left, the pair of them almost skipping to the door.

Hannah stared at Kyle when they'd gone. ''You

wouldn't happen to have the room next to ours, would you?'' she asked on a tremulous smile, as though she'd realized that just now, and not last night.

"I don't need to listen at keyholes,'' Kyle said with every evidence of hurt pride, since he'd actually listened with his ear to the wall. "I've eyes, you know. And if I'd already spied what Polly so gallantly tried to conceal, it wouldn't be long before the gents in our audience did, since they've been without female companionships far longer than I have.'' Then he paused, realizing that might not be true, which led him to the real reason he'd wanted Hannah present when he spoke to Mrs. Jenkins. Before he could get to it, Hannah spoke.

"Whatever the reason, thank you,'' she said earnestly, her dark eyes warm with affection. "It was a kind and good thing to do for Polly.''

And if things work out, even better for me, Kyle thought, as he disclaimed modestly, "Nonsense. I consider myself in the role of father to all of you. Which is why I wished to speak with you—and you, too, Peggy,'' he added, raising his voice as he gazed to where she fidgeted in her corner. "So come here, and stop fishing about in that basket before you get a pin in those busy fingers.

"Children,'' he said in low, loving, caressing tones, which alarmed Hannah as much as it solaced her, for she knew he was at his most dangerous when he was at his sweetest, "I've heard, through my many sources—'' he paused, as Hannah realized that must have been their adjoining wall, "that you've been walking out with those local fellows, and plan to see them yet again. Folly, folly,'' he said in his deep voice, like the tolling of a bell, "sheer folly.

"Graham Dylan,'' he intoned sadly, as if he were a man reading a name in an obituary, "and Royal Atkins, his foreman. The first a practiced Don Juan, for all his western airs. The man's a chameleon: on Broadway, he's the epitome of a swell and a sport, believe me, I've seen him there. Out here—he plays the lonesome cowboy. And as for the other, what sort of innocent, honest, and hardworking ranch worker, which I'm sure he claims to be . . . takes his orders from a fellow like Dylan?

"My dear children," Kyle began, and for all that Hannah knew he was of an age with the two men he was deriding, there was so much worldly sorrow in his deep voice, she'd an uncanny impulse to climb into his lap and throw her arms around his neck so he could console her for any loss she'd ever had, "it's always folly to mix with civilians. What can they offer you but excitement? And what is excitement but ruin to girls who are on their own, far from home?"

Since both Hannah and Peggy had entertained that thought often enough in the privacy of their own minds, they grew gravely silent.

Kyle touched long slender fingers to Hannah's cheek. "My dear," he sighed, "beware. You know more of the world than Peggy here, perhaps you feel that as a widowed woman you cannot be led astray," he said, and paused. But there was that in the deep black eyes that stared into hers, as well as in his dark and midnight voice that hinted—only that—that it might just be that a widowed woman welcomed such straying, and she lowered her eyes at the shame of that insinuation. He nodded, secretly pleased but apparently saddened, as he went on, "You are yet so young, you may have forgotten that there are some kinds of ruin that can come even to those who are experienced. But what sort of guidance is that for our poor Peggy?"

But he'd overplayed his hand. He'd forgotten she was subtle enough to have felt enough shame at mere inference; now she felt only rage at his impudence. He knew it for a misstep the moment after he said it, for he felt the smooth skin beneath his fingertips grow hot. She jerked her head away and gave him stare for stare.

"Mr. Dylan and Mr. Atkins have taken us for a buggy ride in the clear light of day, and nothing we've done could not be shown on a stage in front of an audience of nuns and orphans. It is not excitement but diversion, and pleasant conversation and . . . and . . .

respect," she said after a struggle to find the exact word, and failing that, a powerful one, "that we sought. And will seek. As often as we wish. Unless, of course, by doing so we jeopardize our livelihoods," she added, looking so heated and wild in her rage, he felt a thrill of pure lust for her for the first time, and longed to take those incredibly swollen lips under his own to silence them and appease this sudden, unusual, unforeseen hunger of his.

But an actor worth his pay never forgets he is on-stage, and knows when the scene is played out, and never takes an encore when the audience is hissing. And too, he remembered a lovely quote to solace him as he immediately stepped away from her and the situation.

Methinks the lady doth protest too much, he thought, and said, contritely, "I beg your pardon, I never sought to give offense. Everything I've said was for your benefit," he said. "Your place with me was never in jeopardy, I only worried for your heart," he went on, and saw indecision replacing her fury as he added, "I shall be still, I only ask your forgiveness, and that you understand my position."

"Well, yes, fine, I see, let's do forget it," Hannah said, and turned to Peggy, who muttered much the same.

But by their silence and their faces as they left him, Kyle knew his words, like those of his favorite playwright, would linger long after the sound of them had died away. And for that, at least, he was content. Rome couldn't be built in a day. But at least, he thought with pleasure, he'd ensured that Dylan and his friend couldn't steal them away in that short a time, either. The only displeasure he felt as he sat and considered the matter, was that he was no longer so sure it was only his diminishing troupe that he so badly needed to keep.

There were several things on Hannah's mind as she stepped into the carriage the gentleman had hired for their outing today. But she didn't mind that in the least.

Because disturbing as they were, they were almost more disturbing than the blue eyes that stared down into hers, and so kept her from being beguiled by them. And were enough to distract her from the amused voice that spoke when she hastily glanced away from those same eyes.

She hadn't needed Kyle's warning to remind her that she knew nothing about Gray Dylan, that he knew nothing about her, and that such attentions as he paid were suspect in a man who was, as he claimed, merely along for the ride to play propriety for his friend Royal. But at the thought of those exact attentions, she was pulled up short. Because as Peggy and Royal began chatting in the front seat of the carriage, she realized that things looked very different here and now, in Gray's company, than they did in her own mind in the dark hours of the night. It was true that he'd asked her out many times, but he'd never asked for more. And since their first picnic, he'd been content to wait for his friend to ask Peggy out again. So whatever it had been to begin with, now it might all be exactly as he said: he was simply engaging in a light flirtation to pass the time while his friend courted hers. She sat still, stunned that after all her worrying, that might be the entire answer. A tempest in a teapot, much ado about nothing, she thought, curiously cast down by this revelation. Until he spoke.

"It occurred to me, Mrs. Roberts," he said, as the carriage rolled down the long streets of Leadville and out past the mines into the untouched countryside, "that though we had ourselves a time and a half on our last outing, I know no more about you than you, I suspect, know about me. And so without wishing to be presumptuous, I have to ask, right now, before we go any further and I make a darn fool of myself, if your loss is so recent that there's no hope for me at this time."

It said volumes, he thought, that she didn't seem to know what he was talking about, at first. Her head came up, and there was such an adorable look of confusion on her face, he was tempted to take her in his arms and kiss it away. If she'd looked dismayed or regretful, or even self-conscious, he'd have had to cut line and take his losses. But that look of sheer incomprehension was as good as an invitation to get on with it, and that slow dawning realization that sprung to her eyes now was much too little, and blessedly, much too late. The way her emotions shone and danced on her face made it an odd sort of face for someone in an acting company, he thought bemused, until he caught himself up sharply and wondered if it wasn't, instead, a wonderful face for an actress. But that, he realized, relaxing as he looked his fill at her as she groped for an answer, was exactly what made all of this so entertaining.

He wanted her, certainly. Royal might go on for minutes—which were hours for him—about the apparent purity of his Peggy. It was not Mrs. Hannah Roberts's apparent purity that interested Gray. But, curiously, neither was it her lack of it. If it weren't for her facade of respectability, he'd not be having this sort of fun. It was this difficulty in getting what he was sure he'd eventually be able to, that made it more interesting. It gave him a chance to learn about her sense of humor and her education, which were far more than he'd needed or expected to find, as well as to discover a genuine liking for her company.

And there was this aura of delicious promise about her. When he got her in his bed, or a rented one, to be more accurate—and he'd little reason to doubt he would, she was a widow, after all, working in a theatrical company, and not as a mere seamstress, as Royal kept harping about his lady—he'd almost be a little sorry for it. Because however promising it looked now, it would end soon after it began, as such encounters usually did. He didn't think he'd enjoy keeping a mistress, that was for married men. Paying a woman on a regular basis for what he always tried to fool himself into thinking was an impulsive act on both their parts, was actually distasteful to think about. But looking at her, right now, he couldn't think of any but tasty things.

So if she'd happened to glance at him before she answered his question, she never would have. But his expression changed when he heard her first words. As always, her conversation temporarily diverted his physical longings.

"My . . . loss," she said softly, looking down at the parasol handle she held in her gloved hands, "was a long while ago, a very long while ago."

"How can that be? Unless you got married real young, like the mountain girls around here do—just as soon as they can dress, or more to the point, undress themselves," he said, to distract her, even though he knew she might be angry with him for saying something so warm, because he hated to see her sorrowing so, especially for another man.

But she was too lost in her reflections to catch that, so he knew she must be entirely lost, as she added, "You see, he died only a few years past, but he left me after we'd been married only a few months. I married when I was seventeen," she said more briskly, belatedly horrified at how easily she'd confided what she seldom did. "I am twenty-four now."

"So old?" he asked, as though astonished. "If I'd known, I'd have brought a rocking chair!" And while she laughed with him, he laughed with relief because she was just the right age for what he'd in mind: too old for protestations of innocence of any sort, and too young to take any of it seriously.

"I don't suppose I've any right to ask why he left," he asked after a moment, because he found he wanted to know.

"I don't suppose you do," she answered, before she answered as she'd learned to so long ago, "but it was because we didn't suit."

Yes, as true and informative as saying the sky was high, Gray thought, and let it drop by saying innocently, "That's what you get for marrying a blind and deaf man, ma'am, for all I'm sure it was a kindly thing to do."

"Where are we going today?" Hannah asked, ignoring his flattery absolutely.

"To a place high up enough to catch the last of the autumn sun, and with brooks for cooling wine in, and flowers for taking home to press in memory books so you'll not forget the day," he answered.

Even before the carriage stopped, Hannah knew she'd never forget it. The mountains knew autumn for what it was, even in this unseasonably mild season. The world was in all the colors of Leadville's lovely theater: blue and gold and white. The aspens fluttered gold leaves overhead, their slender trunks as white as the puffy clouds that occasionally wandered across an astonishingly blue sky. It only lacked cherubs, Hannah thought, and then hastily glanced away from the flaxen-haired man who helped her down from the carriage.

It was a wooded place, with a rushing thrum in the air that made Hannah turn her head to seek it's source, until Gray told her it was the sound of a hidden stream rushing down the mountain. They spread the picnic blanket near to a more sedately flowing stream that widened near where they sat, so that it only made polite burbling fountain sounds as background music for their meal. They ate their lunch in relative quiet; Peggy and Royal seemed content to stay still, and Hannah found herself unaccountably shy of a newly quiet Gray. It was a curiously peaceful silence.

But they soon discovered that the earth knew the date on the calendar even if the sky had forgotten, because the ground was chill, even beneath their blanket. It wasn't long before Royal rose and extended his hand to Peggy.

"Are you ready?" he asked her.

She smiled at him as she stood up.

"Are we leaving?" Hannah asked as she struggled to her feet, with Gray's help.

"No need if you don't want to. Thought we'd go for a stroll," Royal said. "You coming, or staying?" he asked Gray.

"Oh, coming, of course," Hannah said at once, brushing crumbs from her gown and readying to go, alarmed at Peggy's slight frown, and so more determined than ever to walk with them.

"Then, best put these things away," Royal said on a sigh, bending to pack up the remains of their lunch.

"Oh. Have you changed your mind? Are we going then?" Hannah asked, disappointed and embarrassed, understanding, for the first time, how awkward a chore it was to be a chaperon.

"Then, yes. Now, no," Royal said, as he lifted the basket, and Gray grinned at him. "Have to put these things back in the buggy before the critters find them."

"The woods are full of creatures just waiting to share our lunch," Gray explained, slipping a bit of bread into his pocket. "Come on, I'll show you."

"But they . . ." Hannah protested, struggling to free her hand from his light clasp, looking over her shoulder as she saw Peggy and Royal strolling off down a path in the opposite direction, "are going that way."

He stood still. "Yes, they are," he said seriously. "And I think you should let them. Listen. Royal's serious about that girl. You don't have to believe me," he said in exasperation as she craned her neck to see the tall cowboy and her friend Peggy, hand in hand, disappearing around a curve in the path. "Just use your head. Do you think he's the sort of man to throw her down on the ground and have his way with her?"

She spun around to stare at him for his plain speaking.

"Well, he's not," Gray said. "He just wants to get to know her, and maybe steal a kiss or two. She doesn't have a home here, and he's a long way from his, so they can't sit out on a back porch. She won't see him at night, anyway. And we're not in New York, so he can't take her to a ballgame or a zoo, or for a boat ride. Lord! I don't know how they do it in the East, but around here we expect a couple to have a little privacy before they make up their minds for certain. He's dead serious, that I promise you.

"And he's got money," he said, as he began to walk alongside the streambed with her, "and he's a hard worker and very smart, if not formally educated. He'll devote his life to her, and that's one worthwhile life, believe me, if he decides to ask for her. Any reason why he shouldn't that you know?'' he asked suddenly. "He is my best friend, and smitten hard. A man doesn't think too well in that condition. I'd hate to see him hurt."

"Why . . . of course not!" she cried, stopping to confront him. "He'd be lucky if she had him. Peggy's honest, kind, wise, and good. But, she has no money at all, and an enormous family to support."

"Good," Gray said, taking her arm, "he'll love that, because he's got no family at all."

"But surely it's too soon . . ." Hannah protested. "They scarcely know each other."

"Yes," he said patiently, "which is why we're giving them this time together, isn't it?"

They walked in silence for a while. The rushing stream glinted in the bright afternoon light, the path they took was covered with the first of the fallen aspen leaves, gold and bronze, laying like scattered handfuls of loose coins on the ground before them. Gray suddenly stopped, held a finger to his lips, and knelt down on one knee, holding out a bit of bread he'd brought with him. Hannah watched and waited, and then had to clasp her hands together in order not to clap them in delight when she saw a small brown creature, no higher than a leaf, separate itself from a tumble of leaves to come out and stand on its tiny hind legs before them. It held its paws together as if to pray for guidance about what to do as it eyed the bit of bread. Then, in a flash, it decided. It raced forward, took the crumb, and skittered away even faster than it had come, tail high.

"Chipmunk," Gray said, looking back over his shoulder, and seeing her entranced expression, smiled and said, "Come on. Hunker down. You try it next."

"There's two!" she breathed a moment later.

A moment after that, there was another, and soon it wasn't necessary to whisper about how many there were. Because soon after that, she found that though they startled when they first heard human laughter, they learned to ignore it, if the bread crumb was big enough.

"All done, all gone, go back to gainful employ-
ment, varmints," Gray said at last, dusting the last of
the bread from his palms. Then looking at Hannah's
face, he laughed and said, "Oh no, we're not going
back to get them another crumb. They have to take
care of themselves out here all winter, a treat's a treat,
but it would be no kindness to get them used to waiting
for handouts when the snow is four feet deep."

He stood and gave her both hands to help her up. In
the moment when she rose, her numbed knees caused
her to lose her footing, and so she accidentally measured her length against him. She pulled back from
him as quickly as the chipmunks had at first. He smiled
down at her, and she spoke up hastily, for though flus-
tered, she was too aware of the nature of that newly
lazy smile beneath his flaxen mustache. "Four feet?
Does it snow that much here, then?" she asked
quickly.

"Then, yes," he said slowly, gazing at her mouth.

"No," she said at once, and then, not knowing what
to say in light of what she saw in his eyes, she dared
in her panic to put her gloved hand to his lips. "No,
it would be a mistake," she said.

He took her hand and kissed it lightly, and then
tucked it entirely in his, "Feels damned stupid to kiss
a glove," he commented, before he asked, "Why
would it be a mistake?"

Now that they were talking about it, she relaxed.
Once a man got to talking, she knew, the immediate
danger was past.

"Because I'm from the theater," she jested, "where
only the villain wears a mustache."

And then his lips were on hers, and his arms were
around her, and she remembered what an aching eter-
nity it had been since a man had held her so, before
she forgot because she'd never known a kiss like his.
It was gentle, demanding, loving, and lusty all at once.
He was warm and sweet-smelling as the crushed ferns
and bracken around them, his mustache was silken,
and his mouth made her grow hot and cold as she
leaned in deeper to him in a confused, vain attempt to

have him protect her from what she was feeling. But when his tongue finally sought hers, she remembered other intrusive things, and tried to pull away. He let her go at once.

There was as much puzzlement as frustration in his eyes as he stood and looked at her. Letting her go was one of the hardest things he'd ever done, and now he regretted it as much as he failed to understand the reason for it. She'd been warm and willing, and that damned sweet mouth of hers had tasted even better than he thought it could, so it was shocking that he'd forgotten it in the wonder of the scent and feel of the rest of her.

"Was it the mustache?" he asked after, amazingly enough to him, he'd had to catch his breath. "Or that you didn't like the kiss?"

She sought the simplest of her many reasons, and like all light things, found it had risen to the top of all her other roiled thoughts.

"I don't know you," she said.

"I can take care of that," he said, taking her hand again.

"And . . . and, you don't know me," she said in a rush, withdrawing her hand, for that was the truest thing of all.

"You'll have to see to that," he said. "Isn't that what this walk's about?"

"It was supposed to be about giving Peggy and Royal some privacy, because you said he was serious," she said, looking into his eyes, trying to keep her tongue from her lips, where she swore she could still taste him as much as his eyes told her he could still taste her.

"He is. But there are other things a man can be serious about," he answered, finally looking away.

She'd no immediate answer for that but a shiver. And though he looked as though he'd a remedy for that, he only took her hand again, more tightly this time, before he led her on.

Chapter Nine

"I know something about the theater," Gray commented, as they waited for Royal and Peggy to return. He leaned back against a tree trunk and watched Hannah lift her face to the afternoon sun, "And believe me, you were never meant to play a chaperon, except maybe, in some French farce. Because they couldn't have one looking the way you do, unless they wanted to make a point about the stupidity of trying to protect a healthy young man from a healthy young woman. Don't look at me like that, I'm only stating facts. Don't you folks cast to type?"

"Sometimes we play against type," Hannah said, raising her parasol over her face as though she were trying to prevent freckles, not blushes, "so as to make a stronger point. Be that as it may, I've no intention of playing what you want me to. So might we forget it, please?" she asked, with more of a plea in her voice than she'd intended. "I'd like Peggy to have her moment, as you suggested, but I will not stand here and be insulted."

"Well, it was praised you were being, and I think you know it, but all right," Gray said. He then added with interest, "What would you like to stand here and be?"

"Informed," she said, after thinking about it for a moment and smiling at the thought, added, "Kyle—Mr. Harper, said you were as at home in New York as you are out here. You do seem to know and love the theater—for whatever reasons," she added with a grin, "so why do you stay out here?"

"Just what my big brother keeps asking me," Gray answered, staring upward as if for inspiration, before he absently snatched a leaf from the tree he was under and pointed up to the sky. "Mostly because of that. Can you see anything like that in New York? If I could have western days and eastern nights, I guess I'd be in heaven. Literally. Because that's the only place they'd have that. I love this country, I was born here—but my big brother grew up in the East, our family was originally from New York, that's why he loves it so much, I guess."

"But you were educated in the East," she prompted, as he fell still.

At that, he left off studying the sky and looked at her and smiled again.

"Right again. Educated to a turn. Just enough to make me realize what I was missing culturally—here, and aesthetically, there. No, I know not many cowboys toss around ten-dollar words. But then again, not many stockbrokers start itching for the wilds after a week of desk work, either. My education fair ruined me," he said, shaking his head. "But my brother meant the best by it. What else would you like to know while we wait for Peggy to have her moment?" he asked quizzically.

"Well," he went on before she could think what to ask, as he smoothed the leaf between his long fingers. "As far as the basics go, I'm a rancher; I've got a good bit of land decorated with some highly bred cattle, due west and north of here. I fool around with investments, and horses, too. I'm a bachelor. But unlike Royal, fixing to remain so for a little while longer; my brother's preserving the family name just fine by himself—well, not exactly by himself, you understand, my sister-in-law's helping him considerable with that."

He looked for her reaction, and saw she was smiling.

"Your brother must mean a great deal to you," she said, curiously pleased at how often he'd mentioned him. Perhaps it was because she knew that a man who had no respect for a woman would never discuss his family with her, perhaps because she sensed he was being more honest with her than he'd intended. That would mean she wasn't the only one to feel this odd sense of friendship, along with the undeniable, frightening lure of more.

He nodded. "Funny thing, that," he said softly, cocking his head to the side as he saw how raptly Hannah was listening to him. "He's on my mind a lot these days. I guess I'm feeling guilty, and not just because I'm not working. But because he's stepping up his campaign to have me come East—for good."

"You say that with such finality," she commented.

"I suppose I do," he agreed as he stripped a bit of leaf, his head down as he did, so that the brim of his Stetson shaded his eyes. "But that's the way I think of it—like an ending, not a beginning. And that can make a man feel considerably torn up, as m' friend Royal says. I'd like to please my brother as well as myself. He gave up his youth to work for the family, now he's the only family I've got. But for all I love him for it and more, it's damned hard to live a life in his shadow. He's rich as the devil and made our fortune twice over, but he's as kind as he's clever, and that's something. Sometimes I think . . . Sorry," he said quickly when he saw her expression change at his words, "for the profanity . . . and the monologue. But you must be used to that in the theater—soliloquies, I mean. But not on the subject of me. Lord, who started this?" he asked, looking up as though he'd just realized where he was.

"It's your fault, you know," he said after a second, gazing at her, surprised and amused that what he'd thought would be a light flirtation had turned to something very different.

"Lord, you listen as well as you talk," he explained

with a pronounced and satirical drawl. "Must be your training. People on the stage are fun to watch when someone else is talking to them; folks in real life fidget or tear up bits of paper, or leaves, like I'm doing now," he laughed. "But a good actress just listens the stuffing out a conversation, doesn't she?"

"I suppose she does," Hannah said, "but I'm not an actress. I teach acting. I really was listening—and envying you."

"There you go!" he said, nodding. "That's just it. Multiply what you said by as many people as you meet in a lifetime. Do you know what it's like to have everyone telling you about the silver spoon in your mouth, as if you didn't know you had one there? Especially when it's one your brother gave you? It can near choke you."

"Oh, that's not what I meant," Hannah said in consternation. "It's not the money I envied, we weren't rich—but I never went without, I assure you. But I never had a brother or sister, and I would've liked one. Father claimed it was on purpose, because he believed a tree grows straightest where there's no shade. He said trees must twist and turn to reach the sun if they're all crowded in together, and children grow up just as twisted if they have to compete for a place in the sunlight. All he wanted, he always said, was one perfect one. Poor man," she said on a too bright laugh, "all he got was me."

"Didn't want you to go into the theater, eh?" Gray asked sympathetically, thinking of how he'd feel if his daughter took to a life on the stage, and then wondered if he'd lost his mind. It was bizarre to be thinking about the shame of daughters at the same time he was wondering just when he could take advantage of the fact that this lovely, curving lady was in just such a deliciously disreputable profession.

"Oh, no," she answered, laughing outright. "He would've wanted me to go further into it, if anything. My father is Blayne Darling," she said softly.

That shocked him. He dropped the leaf he'd been playing with and straightened.

"Blayne Darling?" he said, remembering the times he'd paid top dollar for a ticket to see the man tear up the stage in a fine passion. He stared at her and shook his head at how blindly he'd been staring at her since he'd met her. There was the inky hair, the fine, sculpted features, the remarkable eyes that had such fire, depth, and feeling. Only the sulky, pouting mouth was hers alone. That, and the lavishly curved body, of course.

"Then, what in h . . . What are you doing here? Alone. In a troupe like Harper's?" he asked incredulously. And then was instantly sorry he had, wondering what dark low sins she must have committed to make even such a sophisticated man of the theater as Blayne Darling decide to cast her off.

She lifted her chin at the tone of his voice, and then somewhat higher at the look in his eyes.

"Silver spoons are capable of choking people of both genders," she said coldly. "I can grow just as tired of hearing, 'You're *his* daughter?' I suppose, as you do of hearing, 'You're *his* brother?' "

But while he was thinking about that, she added in an altogether more subdued tone, "And then, too, I'm not a very good actress, you see, and so I couldn't just keep living with him and envying him for the rest of my life."

That recalled him to her, and there was a new expression in his bright eyes when he gazed at her—a different sort of admiration than the one she was used to seeing there, and possibly an even more dangerous one. Because there was fellow feeling in it.

"Oh, that I do understand," he said. "Darn near broke my neck when I was young, trying to prove I was as good as he was. Let me tell you, it's not necessary. A father can provide as much shade as a big brother, I guess, but the point is that your daddy was wrong. The straightest trees make the best lumber, sure. But timber isn't everything. Artists go for the more interestingly shaped trees, and a bird doesn't care what shape its home is in. Now you've got me doing it!" he complained, grinning at his foolishness. "The point is that a man's not a tree," he said seriously, "and you can't live by what other people think."

"In fact," he went on, "my fine eastern college took four years trying to teach me that a man's only as good as he thinks he is. But I'd already learned that, or should have. And faster, too. See this charming scar?" he said, touching the long, wavering line that creased his cheek and called attention to its leanness. "It took a horse too big for a boy stepping on my hard head to sink that fact into it. He was so high, I had to climb up on top of the corral fence to get on him," he reminisced, "and he stayed still as death, watching me out of eyes that were pure burning coals as I did. He had more teeth, all bared, than I had, because I'd just lost a few to Mother Nature and was waiting for them to grow back. He was wild as the wind. But m' brother had stayed on his back for a full minute, and I'd be darned if I wouldn't."

"But you could have been killed, weren't you at all afraid?" she asked, so carried away by his words and his expression, she could almost see that vanished boy and the wild horse.

"Lord, the state I was in that day, I think I was more afraid I wouldn't be," he said on a chuckle. "But once I was on, he did his best. I stayed on because I was even more scared of letting go. But I was wrong, and it wasn't just this scar and a few others that proved it to me. See, I'd been so careful about sneaking out to do it, nobody ever saw it but the horse, and he wasn't talking," he laughed. "All everyone else saw was me later, bleeding, flat out on the ground. It seemed all I'd been after was the glory, all right, because just knowing that I'd done it didn't ease my pain at all. It should have. And would have, if that had been all I was after. But it wasn't, and that proved it. No, there's no sense in living up to someone else instead of for yourself. Let me spare you the pain of discovery, it's true."

"I know that," she said quietly, "I do. But knowing it isn't the same as feeling it. Can you understand that?'' she asked. Then, after a pause, she asked more shyly, ''Is that how you hurt your leg?''

Startled, he glanced down at his legs, wondering if he'd see some injury there, before he realized that she was talking about his limp. It was so much a part of him now that he usually forgot it, unless the wind was blowing cold and damp.

''That? Yeah,'' he said dismissively. ''And to get the record straight, this pretty one on my chin's from years later, a different challenge on a different day. That was a mine shaft I had no business prying into. Care to see some others?'' he asked on a wicked grin, to change the subject.

But she refused to be diverted. ''Oh,'' she said with a sad, sympathetic smile, ''I see. So you understand very well what I meant about the difference between knowing a thing and feeling it.''

Too true, too close, and much too deep, Gray thought. It had gotten far too dark and deep. It was a beautiful day, they were alone, she was standing only a foot from him, meltingly lovely in a tightly fitted lace and cream concoction of a taffeta gown that looked as though it would be almost as good to touch as skin, and they were talking about the kind of personal things that would make a rock cry. It was all very well to desire the woman, and there were few rules in this ancient game he'd begun with her, but he'd no intention of getting in too deep—mentally, at least, he thought on an interior grin. If he didn't keep it light, he'd be on one knee soon, like Royal. And looking at her, where she stood in the sunlight, he realized it was far more than his knee he wanted to be on right now. She had the most uncanny way of turning him around, but now it was definitely time for him to turn the subject and the mood, if he ever wanted more than philosophy from her. And God and the devil knew he did.

''Yeah. Speaking of feelings . . .'' he said, abandoning his post by the tree and walking the few steps to her. He touched a billowing swell of the heavy dark hair she'd pinned up high on her head, and saw how she sprang back to life beneath his gaze, sparkling with indignation, and if he was not mistaken, desire. And then he lowered his head, and kissed her again. Lightly, at first, even when she started to struggle away from the hands that closed over her shoulders and drew her closer, and then more deeply, even as his hands lightened their grip and drifted lingeringly across her back when he no longer needed them to hold her close.

He didn't want to break the kiss, but knew he must, if only because dimly, in the distance, he heard the sound of approaching footsteps on gravel and brush.

When he stepped away, her eyes opened, and he saw a helpless, hopeless look in them before they flared again.

"Now, hold on," he cautioned her, smiling affectionately, adding, before she could speak, "because another thing that fine eastern college taught me was a rule of chemistry. You can't really steal a kiss, you know—just the makings of one."

It was that indisputable truth that caused Hannah's silence as Peggy and Royal came back, hand in hand, looking as smug as they were dazzled. And the equally undeniable shame and fear of it that kept her quiet all the way back to Leadville.

"Now why do you suppose they asked us to meet them here, instead of at the theater?" Gray asked exactly one week later, as he twirled the silver pickle castor on the table around until it blurred.

"Wasn't Peggy's idea," Royal said. "Peggy says Kyle's giving Hannah a hard time about meeting us."

"You mean meeting 'me'," Gray said with the tracery of a smile as he sat back, crossed his legs, and idly surveyed the other elegantly dressed guests in the dining room of Leadville's finest hotel.

"No, both of us. Only Peggy don't care what he says anymore," Royal said with a note of pride.

"My, my," Gray said with interest, "only the third meeting, and she don't care?"

"Only the third time we're going out somewhere together," Royal corrected him. "I see her every night backstage for a while before she has to go to bed. She can't stay up late when she gets up so early. Not everybody can afford to take vacations like we have. I'm done with it, Gray,'' he said suddenly.

Gray sat up straighter. "Done with what?" he asked, fixing a steady blue gaze on his friend.

They'd remained in Leadville for the past week, but each had followed his own bent during the days: Gray going out to inspect mines, renew old acquaintances, and talk with investors; and Royal riding out to see horses and look at stock. In the evenings, Gray had gone out to dinner with men he knew, or to their homes to meet their daughters, or else he'd gone to the theater. But never to the one where Kyle Harper's troupe was playing. It was hard for him, but he kept reminding himself that deals in business or love were best played with a cool head and hand, and that he was waiting for absence to make a certain heart grow much, much fonder. Lord knows, he thought ruefully, it had worked in his case. He could hardly wait to see her tonight. He was so eager, it was embarrassing, so he told himself it was more than that: his loneliness was increased by the fact that he'd seen his friend Royal only briefly, in passing, at their hotel.

But when he'd talked with Royal at all, they'd talked about everything but Peggy, and knowing his friend, Gray had let the matter rest until he was ready. Now, it seemed he was.

"I guess I'm giving notice," Royal said, as he toyed with his knife and avoided Gray's eyes. "But way in advance," he assured him, as he dragged his gaze from the tablecloth to meet Gray's stare. "Well, I got to get my stuff in order, my place and all."

The continued silence and Gray's unblinking stare made Royal's neck, above it's high, starched collar, grow ruddy, and he added with difficulty, "Well, you know I was thinking of buying the Pritchard place. You even said it was a good deal. Well, I'm gonna do it. But it's got nothing on it 'cept a few head and a few old boys to watch over things. Now I got to get it stocked, but that ain't nothing," he said. His voice grew lower and his face redder as he went on, "I got to get the place mucked out and get some furniture in it and all. And a ring. It ain't no place for a woman the way it stands now.''

Gray's mouth twitched, but he dabbed it with his napkin and said, ''Didn't know you'd need a ring to fix a place up.''

''Damn it,'' Royal exclaimed. Then he lowered his voice and said gruffly, ''You know damn well what I mean, you're just being scaly 'cause I'm leaving. And you know why. I got what I come for.''

''She said yes?'' Gray asked, with an odd feeling of loss with betrayal to color it, because though he'd known Royal's mind, he was surprisingly hurt that his friend hadn't shared his moment of success with him.

''God, no!'' Royal exclaimed. ''I ain't asked. Well,'' he said in answer to Gray's raised eyebrow, ''a man can't ask till he gets everything in line. When a girl says yes, she wants a ring, don't she? And a place to call home. Not just a lot of sweet talk and promises. See,'' Royal said eagerly, dragging his chair closer, ''I got it all planned out. They're going to Aspen for the hoorah for the opening of the Jerome. Peggy says they're all up 'cause they're finally going to play at a good house there: the Wheeler.''

He paused, and Gray had a moment to reflect on the novelty of hearing show business cant slipping so easily from the lips of Royal Atkins, before Royal went on, ''Then they head on home to New York. So I figured that would be the time to make my move. I mean, slip it in with the hoopla and champagne and all, so as to make it stay with her more, you see.''

''I'd think anytime a girl got a proposal, it would stay with her,'' Gray said.

''Yeah. Well. But a girl like Peggy deserves more,'' Royal said. After taking a gulp of water so large Gray could hear him swallow, he added low, ''More romantic and all, girls' set store by such, you see. I want her to say yes real bad. Don't believe I could take it if she didn't, though I'd understand I guess. So I'm sort of stacking the deck. I'm going to have to leave town now to do it right. Then I'll meet up with her in Aspen

when I got it done. Going to get a big ring. And fine
furniture, and the best cattle,'' he added with a trace
of worry.

''It's the cattle that will do it,'' Gray agreed. Then
he laughed and said with absolute sincerity, ''If she
turns you down, she's a damn fool. And you don't
want to be married to one of those anyway, so it would
be all for the best. But she won't. Damned if I won't
miss you, friend.''

As Royal assured him that the new place wouldn't
be far, only a day's ride—at the most an overnight
where there'd always be room for him—Gray began to
wonder how he'd replace him. Oh, either Lucky or
Mack Moran could do the job, and be fine foremen. But
Royal was his best friend, too, and those, he knew,
were irreplaceable. Once Royal had a wife and family,
they'd be his priority. As Gray pondered it, Royal
watched him, and added the worry that he'd hurt Gray's
feelings to his biggest one: That Peggy might refuse
him.

And so when Hannah and Peggy entered the dining
room of Leadville's finest restaurant, they saw two
beautifully dressed, perfectly silent, glum gentlemen
awaiting them.

''Are we that late?'' Hannah said gaily, as the men
stood. ''Oh!'' she said a breath later, stopping and
staring at Gray, ''You look different, but very well.''

'' 'Well?' Is that all? It's elegant he looks,'' Peggy
exclaimed, as Gray ran a finger over the naked upper
lip where his mustache had been.

''Thank you, that's more than I'd hoped for,'' Gray
said humbly. ''I didn't do it for praise, but because I
was told that only a villain wears a mustache.''

That simple statement caused a remarkable color
change in his audience: Peggy was still blushing for
her forwardness, while Royal's face grew brick red as
he realized that he'd been so distracted with his own
thoughts that he'd never noticed the change, and Hannah's cheeks grew pink as she recalled the circumstances following her jest about his mustache. Her face
grew even warmer as the amused look in his eyes

showed he remembered that moment very well. Though thick and silky, the mustache had been so light as to be almost unnoticeable in certain lights, but without it, he looked more classically handsome, younger, and so somehow, more vulnerable. Hannah's smile slipped as her gaze did, when she realized what a dangerously nonsensical notion that was.

"Now, if I'd have known what a tumult it would cause," Gray whispered as he held out Hannah's chair for her, "I'd have shaved it off an hour after I met you."

She didn't answer that, but immediately launched into a story about the performance that had just ended.

"Yeah," Royal put in, anxious to make ammends and show he usually knew what was going on with his friend, "they get better every night, Gray. Now that they don't do *The Drunkard* no more, they got that Miss Flora singing one of your favorites: 'Father's a Drunkard, and Mother is Dead'. It's a treat. You should hear it."

"If I'd know that, I'd have come," Gray said sincerely. When Hannah stared at him, he explained, "No, it's true. I love a little honest sentiment."

"But that's dishonest sentiment," Hannah said, amazed.

"Maybe for you, but not for some of us," he chided her. "I suspect you sophisticated theater folks think that kind of thing is only for us rubes. But I'd always thought an actor or a singer that didn't really feel what he was doing, even if only for the moment he was doing it, would do it badly. So if it's being done right, then somebody onstage must feel the way we do in the audience, right?"

When he saw her bite her full, dusky lower lip as she considered that, he found he had to move his gaze to her lowered lashes in order to keep his mind on his words as he went on, "What's wrong with sentiment? Sometimes it's pure pleasure to wallow in pain, and that's what it's all about. Now, I'm not claiming it's Shakespeare, though even he liked a good weeper every now and then, but it sure gets me every time, and that's the sad truth.''

He smiled, and started singing very softly in a sweet, easy tenor:

> "We were so happy till Father drank rum,
> Then all our sorrow and trouble begun:
> Mother grew paler and wept every day,
> Baby and I were too hungry to play . . ."

Peggy and Hannah couldn't resist joining in:

> "Slowly they faded, and one Summer's night
> Found their dear faces all silent and white;
> Then with big tears slowly dropping, I said: . . ."

Royal added his bass notes for the last line:

> "Father's a Drunkard and Mother is dead!"

They all sang the chorus together, harmonizing beautifully:

> "Mother, oh! why did you leave me alone,
> With no one to love me, no friends and no home?
> Dark is the night when the storm rages wild,
> God pity Bessie, the Drunkard's lone child!''

Gray wasn't the only one to wipe a tear from his eye when they'd finished. There was total silence in the dining room. They sat still, listening to it. Then they looked around. They hadn't realized how their singing had carried. But although they were embarrassed, the look on the faces of the waiters hovering near their table made them bite their lips to keep from laughing, and a glance at the assorted expressions of the other diners and then to each other made their eyes glisten with suppressed hilarity. When a tipsy couple at another table began to applaud, and the other well-dressed patrons in the room hesitated, and then joined in, they gave way to open, hearty laughter at last.

"Now I see the lure of the theater from the other side," Gray said, when they'd recovered themselves.

"So, shall we see you onstage tomorrow night?" Hannah asked.

They all laughed, until she asked, "Or at least in the audience?"

But at that, both gentlemen fell as still as they'd been waiting for their escorts to join them.

Gray spoke up after that awkward moment.

"Ah, no. Afraid not. Royal has some business to finish up, and I . . ." he paused, thinking quickly. If Royal was gone, he'd have to ask Hannah out alone, and he'd the strangest feeling that she'd refuse, if only because she'd want to keep Peggy company. He could wait.

He'd business of his own anyway, he decided. He'd picked up the merest hint of some disturbing rumors about silver that needed chasing down, but paying attention to hints of rumors was what made the difference between rich men and very rich men. And in so doing, his trail would eventually lead to Aspen, dovetailing with theirs. He'd been planning to stay at the Roaring Fork Club there, where he was an absentee member. But a wise man's plans were always subject to change. Waiting to see her until she arrived in Aspen would mean a wait of weeks, and looking at her now, he wondered if he could wait another hour until he'd a chance to hold her again. Just speaking with her gave him enormous pleasure.

Still, one week's absence had won him a wide smile and a compliment. He'd see what more would bring, he thought, never stopping to consider why that decision brought him equal parts of relief and irritation with himself. But then, he was used to being honest with himself.

"I understand you'll be at The Jerome in time for their grand opening," Gray said. "And so I'd like to be the first to invite you ladies out to a real western Thanksgiving dinner with us there. It happens we'll be at the Jerome, too—I've got a friend who could get us rooms even if it meant rolling old J. B.

Wheeler himself out of bed—happens he is old J. B., actually—m' brother had a hand in getting them that railroad spur they needed a few years back,'' he said as Royal gazed at him with sheerest relief and gratitude. ''So then,'' he said, after Hannah looked at Peggy and both nodded instant, pleased acceptances, ''a toast!''

He stood, raised his glass, and said, ''To Aspen. And Success!''

—To all of us, and each according to his own desires—he added to himself, as they drank and then beamed at one another.

They were held over in Leadville. It was a roaring, prosperous town, with new money and the same old needs that men always had for entertainment. For all it's fine hotels and restaurants, the most of it, like most booming mining towns, was composed of hundreds of drab, hastily erected shacks that were the miner's quarters, with their usual plentitude of dirty clothes, dishes, and dogs, and the absence of women and the sounds of their laughter. So the whorehouses and theaters prospered. The troupe was held over for weeks, and Hannah was glad of it.

It mean money for Kyle and the troupe, it meant ample time to rehearse their *Midsummer Nights* for Aspen, and since Gray Dylan seemed to have vanished into the West with the suddenness that he'd come out of it, it also meant Hannah was free to go about her business all day without interruption. The fact that her nights were shaken by memories of him—and if she was lucky enough to fall asleep at last, splintered by dreams of him—was another story. An old one, and one she hoped she'd forget with time, as she'd forgotten all her other old hurts. But the problem wasn't that he brought all the old pain back along with the physical pleasure she'd found in his arms. It was that she'd felt that pleasure; that was what kept her awake almost as much as the memory of his words did.

There'd been a great deal of pain as well as shame in her marriage, but at the beginning there had been pleasure, too. Not the kind of searing, aching, ter-

rifying pleasure she'd discovered at Gray Dylan's
hands and lips, but something very like, something
that had promised that. She'd managed to forget that
by remembering the worst of her times in her marriage
bed. She'd hugged the memories of John's
blaming her, his curses, his bruising hands, and then,
the slap that had finally ended it all. Because, she saw
now, however bad it was, it had obscured the other
part, the best part: the early days when he'd kissed her
gently and most of all, had held her close and handled
her tenderly. It was only toward the end,
when he'd tried his hardest to "have" her in the way
he told her he'd had so many others he'd loved less
or not at all before, and not succeeded, of course, that
he'd grown brutal.

He'd only slapped her the once, that last time, when
he'd tried and failed again to make her his wife. But
she'd used his words to beat herself with ever since:
"You're not a real woman," he said. "How am I ever
going to have children?" he'd asked her. When she
hadn't answered, but only laid there, shaking, after
pulling her nightgown down again to cover herself decently, he'd staggered off the bed and cried, "The doctor said you were imperfect when I told him about us,
but I didn't want to believe him, oh damnation, what
am I going to do?" And so even if he hadn't slapped
her in that drunken flurry, she'd have left him, if he
hadn't left her then. He'd just made it simpler—if the
death and burial of all her hopes for a normal life
could be called simple.

Gray Dylan had brought it all back again. Now he
was gone, and she saw he was right. Sometimes there
was pleasure in wallowing in pain, especially if it
made you forget unattainable pleasures. But this was
more than enjoying a good cry, it went beyond tears
and never seemed to end. Days and nights passed,
and yet it still kept her up and cast her down. The
worst of it was that there was no use to it. Because
even if she got him to like her more than he obviously desired her when he saw her again, it wouldn't
change a thing.

She ought never to have gone along with him for
more than the look of it for Peggy's sake, she knew
that. She should be delighted at this chance to resolve things with dignity, and not the embarrassing
confession she'd have to make if she'd led him on
any further. That was perhaps the worst of it, because she knew she had led him on, despite all her
best intentions. She had no control when he touched
her. Twice now, his lips had silenced her good sense.
There couldn't be a third time, so she should be
pleased at this reprieve. She knew that, too. But just
as she'd told him: knowing a thing wasn't the same
as feeling it.

Still, things could end well. The way it looked,
with Royal constantly writing notes to Peggy from
wherever he went—notes that fired her face and her
eyes—Thanksgiving in Aspen would see the troupe's
triumphant farewell, and Peggy's, too. Hannah would
see Gray once more then, and then no more. The
memories would fade. She'd been granted a reprieve.
She ought to be grateful, she chided herself.

As it was, she was tired and chilled and felt age and
the residue of too many long lonely nights in every
one of her young bones. She gazed out the train window at the mountains fading into early dusk, and drew
her cloak closer about herself. November was not so
kind as October had been.

"Not ' . . . thoid part of a minute,' " she said now,
wearily, " 'third'—roll the *r* as in 'bird.' 'Er,' 'Er,'
'third.' "

" 'Third,' " Lottie trilled, before her eyes narrowed and she frowned at Hannah. "Who cares? You
think any of them's gonna know the diff'rence? Gawd.
Them pigs in Leadville hardly spoke English. You
think anyone's going to know Shakespeare?"

"I care," Hannah said, "and Kyle cares, and Aspen is important. The opening of The Jerome will
draw everyone. The newspapers will be there. *Harper's Weekly* will be there. There will be rich men,
very famous, very important men in the audience
there. We are doing a truncated, diced, sliced, and

expurgated version of *A Midsummer Night's Dream*—a shortened version," she paused to explain, seeing Lottie's blank expression, "because of time limitations, and the fact that we've lost more than a third of the company already. Good heavens, do you think Peggy and I would sit onstage, encased in gauze, pretending to be part of your fairy court if we could help it? The least you can do is learn to speak the part you have. It's the biggest one now. Lillian Russell couldn't want better. But Kyle's right. Titania can't just be killingly lovely, she has got to sound good, too."

"Then, for the *third* part of a minute, hence:" Lottie quoted, her wide blue eyes holding the dreamy expression they had held since she'd heard Hannah say, *rich, very important men,* "Some to kill cankers in the musk-rose buds, some war with rere-mice for their leathern winguz . . ."

"No," Hannah said patiently, and as Lottie snapped, "What? What? I got the stupid 'rere-mice' right this time." Hannah said, "Wing-sss. Wing-sss. Not wing-guz."

"I dunno why we didn't stick with *Under The Gaslight,*" Lottie muttered.

"Because Kyle found out that the most elite ladies club in Aspen did it last winter. We cannot compete with amateurs," Hannah explained—because they might win, she thought sadly—before she went on with enthusiasm she didn't feel, trying to emulate Kyle's highest style. "Just think, Lottie, you'll be the most beautiful Titania ever seen—your golden hair flowing behind you, your gown covered with sparkling jewels—you, the epitome of grace and feminine beauty, with everyone onstage in love with you—Nelson and Frank and even Lester in his donkey mask. Not to mention the audience. Wouldn't it be grand to have your photograph taken that way for *The Theatre Magazine?* or *The Dramatic Mirror?* Or even," she said with sudden inspiration, remembering Lottie's favorite, *"The Police Gazette?* Anything can happen if you're good enough. Because the world's eyes will be upon you.

"Because Aspen," Hannah said with prayer and hope and a sudden, terrible premonition of despair, "will be our triumph. Kyle promised . . ." she said, before she stopped, and shuddered, hearing her own words.

Chapter Ten

They stood in the lobby of the new Jerome Hotel, waiting their turn to sign the guest register, and they wondered. That gent with the side whiskers and full paunch beneath his tweed coat—could he be Morgan, himself? That great-bosomed grande dame with the wreath of red foxes biting each other's tails that was so carelessly thrown about her thick, diamond-draped neck, could she be a Vanderbilt? Her diamond parure certainly looked it—even if few of the company could recognize a Vanderbilt, they could add up a costume quickly enough. But here in this lobby, on this day, all the ladies and gent's jewels, furs, and clothing spoke up clearly in the voice of new American wealth—a wealth legendary enough to rival ancient Byzantium's—to say: Astor, Carnegie, Gould. Rockefeller. And if their clothing didn't say it, their air of command and consequence did.

Aspen was no grander than Leadville, and its grandest new hotel was only three years younger than Leadville's, though its setting in a cupped hollow of the mountains was more scenic. The hotel itself was a modest building of red sandstone; every member of Kyle Harper's troupe had certainly seen finer lobbies; although there were electric lights and a quantity of marble and gilt, flocked wallpaper and fernery, New York had many more dazzling places. But as performers, they knew that the set was only backdrop to the drama. Despite the fact that they were high in the mountains in the heart of the West, miles from civilization and New York, in a place where an antelope head on one wall was considered as fine as a Rembrandt on another, this was where the powerful and elite of the nation were or wanted to be, this week. And Kyle Harper had actually brought them to this shining hour. They were, to a man and a woman, astonished into silence at the enormity of that.

"Take the time to wash and refresh yourselves, and rest a bit," Kyle told them as he doled out their room keys, as, stunned as they were weary with their travels and breathing the rarified air, they nodded and walked to the mahogany and gilt elevator.

Lottie didn't even take a breath to protest having to share her room with Hannah and Peggy, and they, in turn, were too awed to exchange disgruntled looks with each other about it. Once in the room, Lottie found her voice long enough to immediately claim the largest bed, by the window, leaving Hannah and Peggy to gallantly argue over which of them minded taking the truckle bed the least. Peggy exclaimed about their private bath, and Hannah turned on the tap just to feel the hot water issuing forth. She couldn't wait to wash the cinders from the train trip and the dust from the carriage ride off. But even as she was struggling out of her gown, wondering how hard she'd have to fight for the right to bathe first, she noted that all Lottie did was glance in the mirror, pat her hat, announce that she was off to see the town, and sail from the room.

Bless Peggy, sweet Peggy, dear Peggy, Hannah thought reverently as she lowered herself into the steaming tub a few minutes later. I'll hurry, she silently promised as her aching limbs relaxed, because Peggy would appreciate her bath in her turn, too. But her eyes were half-closed with pleasure as she leaned back in the warmth of the sudsy water, and she'd no idea of how much time had passed when they flew open again, at the sound of Lottie's shrieking.

She rose from the tub with such haste she sent water sloshing everywhere, and wrapping a towel around herself, plunged out the door, only to see Peggy looking as stricken as Lottie did. And she didn't believe she'd *ever* seen anyone as stricken as Lottie was now. It wasn't so much that her hat was askew, as it was that her eyes were blazing and her face was blotchy with fury.

"She went to the Wheeler," Peggy began, but Lottie cut in, with more fire and vivacity than she'd ever shown on stage—and that was a considerable amount of high energy emoting, Hannah thought. "The bastid done it again! Damn and double goddamn him!

"I went over to the Wheeler so as to see our go-damned names on the bill," Lottie cried. "And guess what? We ain't playing there! Not tomorrow, like he said. Not the next day, not never! I even ast!"

"Never?" Hannah asked dumbly, with the insane desire to add, "not even—hardly ever?" as they did in *Pinafore*, to lighten the moment.

"Never, never, never!" Lottie screeched.

Hannah nodded. From the second she'd heard it, she hadn't really doubted it, and now every awful implication of it began to dawn on her. She scurried into her clothes, and as soon as she'd gotten into a state where she could be seen in the halls of the hotel, she threw open the door and raced down them, seeking Kyle's room. She hadn't pounded on his door for more than a minute when it drew open. Kyle gazed down at her, looking so arrogant, bored, and annoyed that she knew he knew she knew, she thought, in as much confusion as sorrow.

"I never said 'the Wheeler,' " he said calmly, as she stared at him mutely.

"I said," he went on, after he'd drawn her in and closed the door behind them, " 'Aspen.' I said, 'The Jerome.' I said, 'The world will be there for the opening of The Jerome, and we will stay there and play in Aspen then.' But I hasten to assure you that I never specifically said, 'We will play the Wheeler.' Think on, did I?''

"I don't remember. You know I can't remember exactly what you said," Hannah answered, her eyes on his. "But you also know what we all thought. Oh, Kyle, you've really done it this time. This time the fur will fly. How can I defend you, when I'm so disappointed myself?" she asked in hollow tones. "I know it's my job to help you, but how could you?"

He turned his back on her and paced to the window. His room overlooked the town. He gazed down at the low, red sandstone buildings, the carriage and horse traffic, the city nestled in the mountains that ringed around it like a painted backdrop.

"They may well have believed it," he said, without looking at Hannah. "True. And it may be—it just may be that was not an entirely unreasonable supposition on their part, nor altogether an accidental . . . ah, turning of words, on mine. But tell me, how else was I to get them here? We'll make good money," he said, turning around to face her, but the light behind him was so bright, she couldn't make out his expression. "They'll not suffer from it. In fact, it may be a better booking than some of them ever had—or will ever have again.

"Good Lord, you know the business," he said in an aggravated voice, as he watched her face. "Tell me, how could they have honestly believed they'd play the Wheeler? It's a first-rate house in a boomtown, stuffed to the gills with the richest and most powerful in the land this week. And who are we, after all? We both know," he said, with a shrug of his shoulders, "don't we?"

When she remained still, only staring at him, all her anger and disappointment clear in her eyes, he spoke again.

"They fell victim to their own magic," he said ruefully, "not mine. They believed because they wanted to. That's what this business is all about, isn't it? If a sane man can sit in a darkened theater and come to believe, even for a moment, that another man in a

tawdry costume in a painted castle has just killed a
king, and worry for his immortal soul because of it—
if a painted woman of no morals at all can stand upon
that same stage and get other women to cry for her
endangered virginity—if a man with no more than a
set of mustaches and a good script can set a houseful
of otherwise reasonable people to hissing and booing
him within minutes of making his acquaintance—it has
to be because they all want to believe in make-believe.
The only difference is that our troupe needed to believe in it.

"Be sensible. If they'd thought about it at all," he
said in low, flat tones, quite unlike his normal ones,
"they'd have known the truth of it. And so, having
known all along in some small part of their minds,
they'll come around. You'll see. They'll squall, they'll
swagger, and they'll shriek. One or two may walk, to
be sure. But the rest will come around. And why not?
We'll eventually have the same audience, the Wheeler
can't have them coming back every night. The high-
and-mighty will eventually cover this town in search
of amusement, and we, at least, can provide that—one
way or the other."

"What theater *are* we playing?" Hannah asked,
when she could.

"Ah, as to that . . ." Kyle answered, hesitant for
the first time. Hannah closed her eyes tightly, as though
she didn't want to see what she'd hear.

"Another saloon-theater?" she asked, when she
heard no immediate answer.

"No, no, I said it would be a good house, and so it
will be. . . . The Rink," he said quickly.

"The Rink?" she asked slowly, opening her eyes to
gaze at him in confusion.

"A very good house," he assured her. "Seats more
than the Wheeler, too."

"But . . ." Hannah said, waiting.

"No 'buts' at all," he said with great joviality, before the look in her eyes sobered him, and he added
gruffly, "but when it's not in use as a theater, it's a
roller rink. A small thing. A nothing, you'll see." He

waved a long, thin hand dismissively. "When the seats are put in and the stage is up, it'll be a joy to perform in. They'll love it."

"They will never, never, never accept it," she said, unconsciously echoing Lottie as she shook her head slowly.

"Of course they will. They're performers. They're professionals, they're of the theater . . ." he said with grandeur, before a small, sad smile touched his lips, and he added, ". . . and they're a long way from home."

John Griffin and Jersey Conrad walked down to the train station and then onto the train that would take them back to New York. But John was only an extra alto, and the chorus could get along as four, as Kyle had said, as well as with five. Jersey Conrad had seen his day, and while it had been nice to have another character actor, it was, as Kyle reminded the rest of his diminished troupe: not necessary, merely nice. The rest stayed. They shrieked, they howled, they said dreadful things and threatened worse, then they grumbled and got back to work. Just as Kyle said. But they didn't like it. And Hannah feared worse.

Lottie, for example, Hannah thought as she watched her being dressed for opening night, was not behaving as she ought. Or rather, Hannah thought, biting her lip, she was behaving as she ought, but not as she usually did, or should, considering how angry she'd been. Instead, she'd been unusually calm, almost regal, and although subdued, altogether reasonable. That wasn't like Lottie, nor was the sudden look of unholy glee Hannah caught every so often in her bright blue eyes. Now those eyes gazed at Hannah in the dressing-room mirror, and the slow, small smile that grew beneath them chilled Hannah.

"You look beautiful," Hannah said, to dispel the eerie air of mystery Lottie had grown; for even in her white gauze draperies, sparkling with sequins and gilt, and with all the artificial flowers caught up in her mesh of sparkling, plaited hair, still Lottie looked more a

Borgia than a Titania. Not that Hannah believed Lottie would actually poison Kyle, or even set the theater on fire, like the first wife in the third act of *Jane Eyre*, but she looked capable of it at this moment.

"Ah, is there anything I can help you with before you go on?" Hannah asked her hesitantly, all too eager to be away from that odd, secretive smile.

"No, no," Lottie said with amusement, and Hannah exchanged one frowning look with Peggy, who was putting the finishing touches on the costume, before she nodded and left them in the little dressing room so she could be away to wait, and pray.

There was little else to do this late on opening night. Kyle stalked the backstage, pacing and muttering, attending to last-minute details, and fretting. Hannah waited, as she'd always done when her parents were on, in the wings with hands folded, watching and wondering, knowing it was too late to do anything but worry. But tonight she went to the side curtain and peeked out, to see who was in the house.

It was a huge house. There were the usual masses of poorly dressed men, sitting boot to boot, with their hats in their hands. There was an occasional female among them. But this time the front seats, the best seats, were taken up by masses of the best dressed men and women she'd seen since she'd left New York. She scanned the crowd quickly, row by row, and her eye stopped immediately when she came to the third row, front and center. Royal was there, freshly barbered and in a new suit, with his Stetson on his lap and his long legs crossed. But the seat beside him was empty. Hannah let her bit of curtain fall and stepped back. She didn't need to see more.

Lester came out first, as ever, to warm the audience up. This early in the night, he was still sober, but his antics set the audience to laughing and set the stage for more. Then their lone magician did his turn and made it brief, because the audience was restive. The handbills had promised an: "ALL NEW MAGICAL PRODUCTION OF A MIDSUMMER NIGHT'S DREAM," and a rabbit in a hat or a stream of colored handkerchiefs come streaming out of a skinny chap's pockets didn't compare to the "SPECTACLE, DRAMA, AND FANTASTI-CAL SPECIAL EFFECTS" the bills had also promised, in full color, on every lamppost, all over the town.

Little Polly did her new solo song, and even if her voice wasn't wonderful, her rendition of "Father's a Drunkard and Mother is Dead" was money in the bank, just as Kyle predicted, with any audience. Not only were the miners and ranch hands clearing their throats, but a few of even the fanciest ladies and gentlemen present were softly sobbing when she was done. She took a pretty bow, and then raced backstage to get into her costume as Puck—since Harrison Pompey had quit back in Leadville, an inspired notion of Kyle's had given her the part.

The quartet and Miss Flora came out next and sang old favorites, as well as a few new songs Kyle had picked up in New York, and from listening in the audience at other theaters in Denver. When the curtains drew shut, they stepped out in front of it to do a few more, so the stagehands could struggle out undercover to push the paper and composition trees and boulders that were to be "Midsummer's" sylvan setting into place. Hannah fingered the folds of her costume and sighed as Peggy hurried out to meet her. With a pair of gauzy wings fastened on her back, and her hair covering her face, she, Peggy, and Mrs. Jenkins would be extra fairies tonight. And if the remaining dancers who were not pressed into service in other minor roles, fluttered as vigorously as they'd been told to do as they pranced around Titania, no one might notice that there were very few of them in Titania's court.

But Peggy had no gauzy wings with her. She'd only an expression of sheerest horror on her face.

"She's not going on!" Peggy cried. "She's playing dead!"

Lottie was not playing dead, or if she was, she wasn't playing it very well. But she was playing at something. For she lay back on the couch in the stage manager's room, all in her spangles and gauze, and moaned, one hand to her alabaster forehead.

"It's the atmosphere," Hannah heard her say, as she came hurrying into the room behind Peggy, to see Kyle glowering down at his Titania, while Nelson and Frank, her Oberon and Theseus, crowded around her. "The height. I have altitude sickness," Lottie announced. "My head is reeling, I can't hardly breathe, I can't go on, I am ill."

"But you never were before . . ." Nelson said worriedly. Then Frank said, ". . . Try a glass of iced water, put some on your forehead." Lester took a flask from his doublet pocket, and offering it to her, said, "One nip and you could dance on top of Old Smokey, I promise."

"I cahn't," Lottie said with dramatic emphasis, "I cahn't go on tonight."

"I suppose that I might go on in her stead. I do know the part," Maybelle announced from where she stood to the side, looking like a great velvet-upholstered couch that was standing on end, for all of Peggy's artistry with her costume. But then, the Queen of the Amazons did not have to be svelte. The startled looks she got from all the assembled actors answered her, and she said defensively, "Well, it was, at least, a constructive thought."

"No," Kyle said softly, so softly everyone turned to look at him, "Lottie will go on."

Lottie shot up to a sitting position. "No, I ain't gonna," she said triumphantly, tossing her spangled, flower-strewn hair back from her glittering eyes. "I' m sick as a dog, and nobody's gonna force me to neither."

'No," Kyle said in that same toneless low voice that silenced the other's exclamations. "Nobody can, can they? But if you do not, no one will ever, ever ask you to go onstage, anywhere, again. It's a rule of the business that personal feelings never interfere with our business. Nor does sickness. Nothing short of death does, actually . . . and sometimes I'm not too sure about that either, judging from some performances I' ve seen."

The others chuckled, but his next words, spoken in grim, slow accents, stilled them.

"No, Lottie," Kyle said, staring at her, "we are not seamstresses. Or grocers. Or coal miners or ranchers or shoe clerks or millionaire investors. We are unique among all professions, in that of all the workers in this wide world, wherever we are: what we promise—we deliver. Or we never work in the theater again. If you do not go on this stage tonight, I promise, you will never go on the stage again. It is not just me," he said into the silent room. "I need do nothing. When word gets out, and it will, your career will be over."

The others nodded. He'd said no more, if a great deal more eloquently, than they knew to be the truth. Lottie looked from face to face, her eyes wide and uncertain. Then she rose from the couch and began dragging off her costume with such rough hands that Peggy sprang forward to assist her, to save the costume.

"It doan make no difference," she said, tossing her head. "I got a gennelman in the audience waiting for me. A rich gennelman, a very rich one I met back in Denver, and he follid me here," she spat at Kyle. "He's staying at the Jerome, too, but then he's got a house and a carriage and a diamond necklace with a pair of matching earrings like you never seen waiting for me back in Denver. And so whad do I care? E-nunciate," she spat at Hannah. "E-mote," she shouted at Kyle. "Not me, no more. I played the ratholes 'cause I thought I was gonna go big here in Aspen. An' whaddya know? I'm back inna rathole. But not fah long. You can take your theah-ter and shove it, 'Mister Theahter,' " she cried. "I'm through!"

"Indeed," Kyle said, "you are. Peggy take that costume, every last flower, and come with me. Hannah," he ordered, "with me. Lester, get that costume off fast, and come along. You others, wait your cue," and he strode out the door to the wings.

"Lester," he said as Lester threw down his donkey head and managed to peel off his doublet, mid-run, as he kept pace with Kyle's long legs, "How long can you keep 'Where Did You Get That Hat?' going?"

"That one?" Lester laughed, thinking of the most popular song of the last year. "With two hats from my dressing room: a week. If you need it, two. Get me a couple more hats, I can keep it gong until 1890 is come and gone again. But it's not the best intro to Shakespeare; I'll have them howling, and you want them thoughtful."

"I want them in their seats," Kyle said. "I'll get word to the orchestra, you get your hats. You just keep it going until we say go. Now, you," he said to Hannah, as Lester nodded and raced away, "get out of those clothes, and into those," he pointed to the jumble of gauze Peggy was holding. As Hannah gazed at him with sick shock, he went on, "You know the lines, you know the play, you're very beautiful, and so tonight—you shall be Titania. You must be Titania," he said, when he saw her face.

"I'm not an actress," Hannah said, growing very pale and backing away from the heap of clothing Peggy held, as though she were fleeing a snake charmer offering her an adder. "I teach acting. I'm really very bad, I couldn't, I know I'd ruin it, you'd be so ashamed of me . . ."

"Hannah," he said flatly, fixing her with his dark, deep stare, "I'm drowning."

She wept as Peggy fastened her into her clothes, and had no tears left as the flowers, some with long blond hairs still caught in their petals, were plaited into her own long dark hair. But she held her head high as Peggy shook the sparkles over her hair and face when she was done. With luck, the spots would show the tears as glitter, she thought as she rose and followed Peggy back to the stage, and with a miracle, she'd live through the next hours of this night.

Lester was well into his song when Hannah arrived in the wings again, and he had the audience well in hand. He wore a hat far too small for his dark head, and pranced across the stage as he sang. At his command, the audience good-naturedly shouted out the chorus, ''Where did you get that hat?'' with him.

Hannah stood and thought of the coming playlet. She knew she'd remember the lines and her placement, if only because she'd spent so many hours drilling them into Lottie. But now the thought of going out on the stage in front of that riotous mass of people made her mouth go dry, her hands cold, her stomach queasy, and her legs feel too weak to hold her up. She held her freezing hands together hard, and would have prayed if she could think of anything but her terror.

She made an even fairer Titania than the spectacularly blond Lottie had done, Kyle thought as his eyes roved over her, because she looked ethereally dark and mysterious. But she was also trembling like a tuning fork, so much so that the spangles on her costume flickered and shook, and all the bits of iridescence on her skin and hair fluttered like true fairy dust. Her heart beat so hard he could see it in the veins in the fragile, pulsing line of her neck. He gazed at her, and then at Lester, and at a glance from Lester, nodded, and then tossed a huge mock Stetson to him. The audience roared as Lester discarded the little hat with disdain, and jammed the new one on his head until it half covered his eyes. ''Oh, where did you get that hat!'' they shouted with glee.

''Listen,'' Kyle said, taking Hannah by the shoulders and holding her at arm's length, ''you'll do well. You'll do fine. It's only a little scene, soon done. It's the sort of thing you could do in your sleep.''

''I wish I could,'' she said on a shaky laugh, shivering and sparkling in his clasp.

''My dear,'' he said gently, ''what difference will it make, except to us, here and now? You're not on the bill, and when I announce you after, you'll be Miz Roberts, or Miss White or Black or Brown or whatever you will. You could not have more anonymity if you wore your costume up around your ears, believe me. There's nothing to fear.''

''I know, I know, I know,'' she said wretchedly, knowing she was babbling, but not caring anymore.

"But it's just as I told Gray: knowing is not feeling. And I don't feel right. Ah, for all I wanted to see him, I hope he hasn't come tonight, after all. He'd be so ashamed of me, after all he and I said, he'd think me such a c-coward," she grieved with a broken gasp. "And I am, and I know it, but for all I know, I don't know how to stop this," she confessed, as she kept shivering and gazed hopelessly at him.

The rest of the cast of the *Midsummer Night's Dream* stood in the wings, watching, still as statues of the fantastic beings they were supposed to be; a huddle of fairies and peasants and kings and queens, awaiting the signal to go on stage to become momentarily real. And their queen, queen of all the fairies, shuddered and shook in Kyle's arms. His long face grew still, and he stared down at her with dark and hooded eyes. Then he frowned and looked up and away to the rear of the backstage, and grimacing at someone, nodded abruptly, mouthed a silent "get him," and inclined his head.

"Where did you get that hat!" the audience cheered again.

"She's going to play Titania tonight," Kyle eventually said to someone over Hannah's head, as he released his grasp on her arms at last, "but I believe she's having a crisis of confidence. She mentioned something—am I to understand you've discussed this with her before?"

"I've never seen you looking so beautiful," a too long unheard and thrilling familiar voice said, and Hannah's head snapped up to see the most fantastical vision of all standing backstage with her. Gray Dylan smiled down at her, "You're going to be acting tonight? This is a treat. Lucky that I got up-front center seats . . . even though you never answered any of the messages I left for you today, all day. And there were a few."

Hannah began to protest because she'd never gotten word of one, but then her eyes opened wide and flew to Kyle, as Gray stared at him, too, and added with a wry smile, "I guess it's only natural to have guards at the stage door in a rough town, but my name seemed to close their fists, as well as the door, tonight. And neither love nor money would open them. I thought of something that might, but on second thought, didn't think a dustup at the door would help my cause much. Guess my message finally got through to one of you, though.''

"All things in their due time," Kyle said tersely. "I'd be pleased to squabble with you later. Just now, perhaps you might say something to help put a little heart into our new Titania? She mentioned something about your concept of cowardice?''

"Oh no," Hannah said too brightly, putting her chin up, since suddenly the thought of going out on-stage was more terrifying than staying where she was. "What nonsense. I was just momentarily shaken, believe me. It was the prospect of facing my own . . . wild horse, I suppose," she said with a brilliant smile at Gray. "But I can do it. Why not? It's only a little playlet, and no one has to know who I am, do they? I shall be . . . Miss White, if you please, Kyle. Yes, Miss White will do well. Yes, it will.''

"Are you sure?" Gray asked quietly, his eyes searching hers. "After all, your father might not be pleased with you acting under a new name.''

"How should he know?" she asked airily, hearing another line of Lester's lyric, and wondering how many more there were; hoping he'd finish, and hoping he'd never be done.

"He's in the audience," Gray said.

She was lovely: fragile, yet lush, very much the sprite and the vision of delight Titania was supposed to be, Gray thought. He'd paused when he'd first seen her, as astonished as beguiled at seeing her sparkling and shimmering in the theater's half-light. He'd tried to see her before the performance, and when she hadn't answered his notes, had begun to worry about why she hadn't. But then when he'd seen Blayne Darling in the audience, he'd decided she'd been too taken up with her father to remember him. And though that hadn't disturbed him as much as the thought of her forgetting him for no reason, it had, strangely enough, still stung much more than he'd thought it would. His spirits soared when he realized it was only that Kyle had banned him.

But even before he'd known that, he'd come at once when the page boy had summoned him from his seat, where he'd gone when he'd given up the effort to see her backstage. His breath had caught when Peggy told him Hannah needed him as she'd met him halfway: he hadn't known he could run so fast without breathing. Nor had he realized how long it had been since he'd last breathed until he let out an amazingly long sigh of relief when he'd found her whole and healthy and incredibly lovely. But just now, at his words, she'd gone white as her gauze gown. He'd wanted to see her for days, but hadn't realized exactly why. Now, as he discovered how badly her distress hurt him, he knew. This was a whole new game, he thought with bewilderment, one he'd never played. Because he began to understand it was no game.

"My father, here? Where?" she said, and without waiting for an answer, she pulled back a section of curtain to see him where she might have seen him before, front and center—if she hadn't been looking so hard for another man's face instead. Blayne Darling had likely never been so overlooked before. Certainly, he was not now. He sat in a cluster of well-groomed men and women, leading their laughter, smiling and shouting encouragement to Lester, while all the while holding court, as he always did. She let the curtain fall.

I cannot. I must. I shall, I will not—she hardly knew what she was thinking as she stared at Gray, unseeing.

Lester shot a glance to Kyle, and then, finishing the song, and with no new hat in his hand, he spun around on one foot and hopped off the stage. The spotlight staggered, trying to discover him, and when it did, he'd

plucked a great feathered slouch hat from the head of a boisterously laughing female who was no lady, and clapped it on his own head. He went dancing back to

the stage to the uproarious laughter of the audience,
and leaping up onto it, sang the lyrics once more:

> "Now, how I came to get this hat,
> 'tis very strange and funny,
> Grandfather died and left to me
> his property and money.
> And when the will it was read out,
> they told me straight and flat:
> If I would have his money,
> I must always wear his hat . . . Oh . . ."

". . . Where did you get that hat?" thundered the
audience, delirious with mirth.

"Hannah. Hannah," Gray said, trying to get her
attention, for though he held her icy hand, she seemed
oblivious to him. "Hannah, it's not bravery to damn
near kill yourself trying to prove yourself. There are
other kinds of scars a person can get from that kind of
folly than the ones I've got. Worse ones. On the soul.
Hannah," he pleaded as sense returned to her eyes.
"Remember what we talked about? What other people
believe doesn't count. It's what you think—and if you
really feel you have to make a point, you ought to be
able to choose your own time and place, when you're
ready. You don't have to go out there tonight to prove
anything to anyone. Does she?" he asked Kyle with a
look in his ice-blue eyes that made them glitter like
frost in the shadowed light.

"No, no, of course not," Kyle said distractedly, as
the audience surged with laughter as some other lady
pitched her hat on the stage, and they again shouted:
"Oh, where did you get that hat?"

Hannah took a deep breath. And suddenly smiled a
natural smile. "No, I don't. I know that. And I feel it
as well as know it now," she assured Gray, "but I'll
do it anyhow. I will," she said to Kyle. "I'm fine now.
I will."

She was as determined as she was frightened, but
she was resolved. Let her father mock her, or rue her,
it was all the same to her now. She knew what she had

to do. And so she was shocked when Kyle looked down at her as though he saw right through her and said, "No. You won't.

"You may want to," he added thoughtfully, "and you might do a credible job of it, too. But it would not be a good job. It would be done as a sacrifice, or a dare. No one should use the stage for making a point of their courage. It is not made for that," he added loftily. "Unless, of course, it's someone acting without a limb," he said consideringly, struck by the novelty of the idea, "or some other interesting sort of thing like that. That would bring them in . . .

"But the stage is no 'wild horse,' " he said, drawing himself up. "No, my dear Hannah, this night is not a propitious one for your debut; that must be another time, I think. Fear defies reason and takes one unaware. An actor must be, above all things, aware. Soldiers need bravery. But actors need desire. This is not just some melodrama, however foreshortened, this is *Shakespeare*. Shakespeare. There is a tradition," he murmured, half to himself, "there is a precedent."

Kyle snapped his fingers, "Acting must be an act of love," he said, "or it is just posturing. If you will, my dear, come with me now and take off those clothes."

Kyle exchanged a long look with Gray before he turned on his heel and strode away. At that, Gray relaxed. Hannah began to unhook her costume with numbed fingers. "Are you coming?" Kyle demanded, looking back. After a reassuring smile from Gray, she followed Kyle back to the dressing room as Gray murmured just loud enough for her to hear as she did, "Lord! If I'd known how easy it would be with the right words . . ."

By the time the signal was finally given for Lester to be done, the stage was littered with hats. It had rained hats—it had poured hats, and the audience was weak from laughter. Kyle absently reminded himself to keep that number in from now on as applause filled the theater, swelling when Lester took his many bows, and then ebbing, at last, along with the laughter. After the hats had been picked up and the last of the merriment had subsided to occasional wheezy chuckles, the orchestra struck up again. This time they played the overture to Mendelssohn's *A Midsummer Night's Dream*, and if anyone in the audience was too dense to get that, the stage light went violet, and the first of the fairies came wafting out onstage.

The audience sat in desultory fashion, their coughing and shifting in their seats a sure sign that Lester had been right: "Where Did You Get That Hat" wasn't a good prelude to Shakespeare. The preface Kyle had written to the drastically abridged playlet was read fairly enough, but the 'thees' and 'thous' elicited soft moans and occasional sighs from the restless audience. Not even Lester, tiptoeing out in costume as Bottom, drew their pleased attention for more than a moment. Soon the worst sound—aside from the dreaded cry of "Fire!"—that can be heard in a theater after the curtain rises, came clear: light murmurous conversation. It began to hum throughout the house—until Titania drifted out with a cloud of her gauze-draped, light-footed court.

Then the crowd fell still. Until she spoke, and then they drew in their breath as one.

She was tall and graceful, full-figured and yet lithesome. Pale and dark and glittering with stardust, her every motion was a symphony of languor and eroticism. Her voice, when she spoke, was deep and dark and heavy with the memory of unspeakable pleasures. Her long black hair was meshed with fireflies, or so it seemed. And when she closed her eyes, her jeweled lids struck witch fire in the spotlight. The brilliant flowers on her crown were no less showy and fragile than she; she glowed dark as a midnight sun, and she dazzled the audience.

Gray stood with Hannah in the wings, and they watched, as astonished and enchanted as anyone else in the theater. By the playlet, and by themselves. For they stood side by side, fascinated by what unfolded before them and within themselves. She could scarcely see him in the dim light, only an occasional flash of teeth or the glow of his flaxen hair, and he could only scent the light floral scent that was Hannah, and see the glow of her skin radiant in the twilight of reflected stage light. But neither ever forgot the other was there, they didn't have to look to each other more than once, or twice, to reassure themselves of it. And so, aware of the warm, companionable link they shared, they stood close as one, yet one by one, and at peace for the moment, together in the darkened light, absorbed in the fiction before them. Until Titania roused herself at last, and blinking her stunning eyes, said,

> "Come, my Lord, and in your flight,
> Tell me how it came this night,
> That I sleeping here was found,
> With these mortals on the ground . . ."

And so, awakening, woke them all to reality again.

There was a confused stillness at first, when the actors all fell silent, before it became clear that the playlet had ended. And then the audience rose up, literally. They applauded, and when that didn't seem tribute enough, cheered and whistled, stomped and shouted.

Titania took a dozen bows, and could have taken a dozen more, but fled the stage before some of the more impulsive and besotted members of the audience could surge up on it to give her more than the coins and bills and torn-up bits of paper they'd thrown in a vain attempt to show all their pleasure with her. She passed Hannah and Gray in a rush, her draperies drifting past their noses as she did.

When they got to the dressing room in her wake, they found her slumped in a chair, her long legs bent apart, her elbows on the dressing table, her head on her hands, staring at herself in the mirror.

"Bar the damned door," she said, and Peggy leaped to do it as they heard the sound of excited voices coming closer.

Titania's eyes looked beyond her image and met Gray's blue gaze in the mirror. It seemed her shoulders stiffened then, and her own dark, deep eyes grew cold.

But all that could be seen in Gray's clear gaze was honest admiration.

"There sure is a precedent," Gray said, nodding, "but I'll be damned if I ever saw an equal."

Titania's shoulders relaxed. She nodded, and then dragged off her flower-strewn wig, and ran long, sensitive fingers through the much shorter damp, dark hair that was beneath.

"Thank you, thank you," Kyle said, as he continued to run his fingers over his itching, overheated scalp, "but I doubt Richard Burbage or Will Kemp ever had to worry about getting home unmolested after a performance. Some of the miners around here haven't seen a woman in so long I think they might not mind even if they discovered who I am."

"Hold on. They haven't been here that long," Gray drawled. "We've got some hard-looking females out here, true, and the wind does a job on their complexions, too. But I never saw one with a blue beard showing under her powder and paint! . . . Or at least, not such a dark one," he ammended, with just the right touch of doubt.

"Ah, but none of them have my figure . . ." Kyle said, but the laughter died on his painted lips when he saw the astonished look in Hannah's eyes as she continued to stare at him. He sat up straighter.

"I choose to be a woman tonight because there was no way I could be a reputable man of the theater if I didn't," Kyle said, suddenly very conscious of both the cotton-wadding woman's shape he still wore, and how successful his masquerade had been. Meeting her dark gaze with his own, he added defiantly, "The show had to go on. That is precisely *all*."

"No, it isn't!" Hannah protested. "It was wonderful. I've never seen better. Oh, Kyle, if you could do a Shakespearean production with men playing all the parts, as they used to do, why, you'd make your fortune. I never realized it could be so wonderful."

Again, Kyle's eyes met Gray's in the mirror, and they both grinned, one reluctantly and the other widely, as they realized she'd never understood what he'd been denying.

"I doubt it, child," Kyle said, "times change. It would be like an all-girl *Pinafore*, interesting, but like Mr. Dylan's bearded lady, a curiosity, rather than art."

He smiled to himself as if at a memory, and at that memory, quickly glanced up at Hannah's reflection again. Only to see Gray Dylan doing the same thing with a look of longing on his face. Before he in turn, as though feeling the force of Kyle's stare, gazed back to surprise the same expression on Kyle's dark face as he looked back to Hannah.

Kyle turned around and looked Gray full in the face. As the men stared at each other, each recognized the unspoken claim the other made on the woman that stood between them, and each acknowledged it by their silence.

But she, all unknowing, for if she had, she'd have suffered, since she knew better than both the futility of both their intentions, only laughed with sheer pleasure and said, "Ah, but this is certainly a night to remember!"

Chapter Eleven

Royal bent his head to whisper a word to Peggy, and Blayne Darling, all the way at the head of the long, crowded table, paused in his story-telling and smiled down at him. It was a small thing, a thing of a moment, and a sweet smile, too. But Royal was silenced as effectively as if he'd been publicly censored. So he had been. It had been done charmingly, but it had been done. And it told Gray more about his host than any of his wonderful stories ever could.

Kyle hid his own slight smile in a swallow of wine, but then Kyle was of the theater and had met the like of Blayne Darling before. Hannah showed no expression at all; if Gray had not been sitting next to her, he'd never have known how hard her fingers clenched her napkin. But so they had all through the meal, and she'd eaten little enough of it. Course after course had been brought out to them: game and vegetable soups preceded the service of assorted shellfish and pâtés, which gave way to sorbet and salad, before a round of fish, variety meat, and game croquettes, cutlets and patties arrived to prepare the palate for the main courses. The newest hotel in the West wanted to show its visitors that it knew excess as well as the East did. By the time the turkey was brought out, there'd be no

one with any place to put it, Gray thought—except for
Hannah. Because she'd only moved her food around
her plate as she'd watched her father with all her heart
in her great dark eyes—so like to his, and yet so different: hers showed hurt, and his, only pain. And that,
only when his stories called for it.

Blayne Darling insisted on playing host tonight.
Gray and Royal had planned on taking Hannah and
Peggy to Thanksgiving dinner, Kyle had arranged for
a dinner with his troupe, but Blayne Darling said that
he wanted his daughter and her friends to be his guests.
Since Kyle appreciated having someone else pick up
the bill as much as he did dining with the famous, and
as Hannah was the famous man's daughter, now they
all sat at a long table that was the envy of all the other
guests in the hotel dining room. And Gray heartily
wished for it to be over almost as much as Hannah
did.

They weren't the only ones. Because, Gray noted,
if dinner weren't over soon, Blayne Darling might find
that he could pause until Saturday and smile until his
lips froze, and Royal and Peggy wouldn't notice. Despite their host's charming show of annoyance, they
were slowly becoming oblivious to everything but each
other. But then, they'd reason; Royal had told Gray
that tonight was to be the night.

"The troupe's going home after this engagement. I
mean to see she ain't going with them," Royal had
sworn as he'd dressed tonight. He'd stayed in a steaming bathtub until Gray rousted him out, declaring he'd
taken off his top layer of skin and couldn't afford to
lose more. Then, under Gray's bemused eyes, Royal
had put on a new shirt, new pants, and new boots. At
the last, he'd annointed himself with cologne that kept
his head turning as they left the room, because—as
he'd finally sheepishly admitted—he couldn't get over
the feeling that he'd some French woman following
him, close. He'd put a sizable ring in his pocket, and
all his hopes in his heart. If the girl refused him, Gray
decided now, remembering Royal's nervousness as
well as the man himself, he'd personally have her kid-

napped or committed. But from the way she was gazing at Royal, he'd doubted he'd have to bother.

Hannah had eyes for no one but her father, and that, Gray found, was more than lowering or annoying to him, it was hurtful. Because it seemed he couldn't help but feel her pain. Blayne Darling had embraced his daughter warmly, exclaimed over her beauty, introduced her around to all his many influential friends, and made much of her, acting just as a father should. That was just it. It was impossible for Gray to know just how much he was acting, but judging from Hannah's eyes, it was a performance to rival Kyle's Titania.

"I hear you've been asked to stay on another week," Blayne said. "That Titania of yours is astonishing. I can understand your keeping her close, but on Thanksgiving Day? My dear fellow, is that fair, is that kind?"

Kyle smiled, "My dear sir, no. It is not. But it is expedient. You know your good friend Mr. March would offer her the moon, while your own impressario, Mr. Baker, would add the stars, if she'd sign with them. But luckily for me, she and I have an understanding. She doesn't mind dinner in her room, so long as I come by later with her just desserts."

Blayne Darling threw back his mane of dark hair and gave a full-bodied peal of laughter, very much in the style of his D'Artagnan, Hannah thought. Then he shook a finger at Kyle, "Naughty, naughty fellow. But clever. She is indeed, a find. Shall we see her in New York?"

True sorrow flashed in Kyle's eyes before a more familiar ruefulness replaced it, and he sighed and said, "Who can say? She is of Romany descent. I have her fast now, true. But her moods change with the wind. She's a creature of elemental fancies and desires. I can no more hold her than I can hold the wind in my palm. Alas, that is her glory and her fault, and so I must only appreciate her whilst I may, and live in hope. She will play the rest of this week. But after that?" Kyle shrugged. "Who can say?"

At that, his troupe applied themselves to their dinners with studied concentration. He was giving an even better performance tonight than he did as Titania, because they'd all heard him say firmly this morning and this afternoon, as he had the night before or whenever any of them asked about whether he'd do it after this engagement: "Never, not ever, never again." He'd discovered, to his astonished sorrow, that though he'd do almost anything to survive in the theater if he absolutely had to, there were, after all, some limits to what he'd do to succeed in it.

And so the Harper Company's "Titania" was fated to die, as she was born, in the West. Kyle had sworn them all to secrecy, insuring it when he'd informed them it was their return fare and bonus he was earning for them. If word of Titania's true identity became known, by any means, they'd all walk home, he assured them, and then never walk out on any stage he ever heard about again. If word leaked out, later, as it might—this being, he'd said sadly, a vile and imperfect world—he'd deny it so convincingly, he'd make the tale-teller look like a mug. They didn't doubt any of it.

"A great pity. She'd be a sensation. I tremble just to think of the Scots Lady she might do," Blayne mused, deliberately avoiding mentioning Lady Macbeth by her proper name, in the best tradition of the theater. "But what a hold you have over your people. No one can get a word about her. Not even I," Blayne said, smiling his sweetest smile at Hannah, "and I have connections—or thought I did."

" 'How sharper than a serpent's tooth,' sir?" Kyle quoted, as he glanced to Hannah's downcast eyes as she studied her plate. "Ah, but I think not. Rather, it's a case of loyalty for her word to me, despite the urgings of her heart. Though torn, she remains steadfast. However it appears to you now, you brought up a noble woman, I assure you."

"Yes. She could not love thee so much, sir, loved she not honor more," Gray misquoted gently.

"My word!" Blayne Darling said on a forced laugh. "She's ringed around with defenders. Where are my seconds? But peace—you mistake me, gentlemen, I

never meant to chide her,'' he said gaily, though his
eyes were not amused. It was more than the fact that
Hannah refused to introduce him to the mysterious Titania, or even give him her name so he could pass it
on to his friends. That was difficult enough to explain
to them—though he would, because he could explain
anything to anyone, given time. It was that Hannah,
without saying a word, had got everyone's attention
now. He knew how to change that.

"Your Titania is queen of the night, if not this
night," Blayne said, "so be it. More importantly, shall
you be in town long enough to see me in performance
at the Wheeler? My wife will be joining me in a week,
as will our company, and the week after that, we'll do
our humble best to entertain the good citizens of Aspen. Shall you be there? But give the word, and I'll
leave tickets for all of you."

"Alas," Kyle said as the turkeys were carried out,
"but no. We'll have gone by then, I fear."

Just as she'd already told him, Hannah thought,
avoiding her father's eyes. But then, she'd said it when
they were with all his friends and hers, and she knew
he seldom listened for more than his cue to speak again
when he was in a crowd. She'd been as thrilled as
frightened when she'd seen him in the audience last
night, but now she wondered if he'd come to see Kyle's
troupe because he'd remembered it was the one she
was with, or if it had been an accidental meeting. After all, he hadn't sought her out in New York since
she'd left him. But he might do so in the future, she
decided, since he seemed impressed by Kyle, and even
more so by her friendship with Gray.

Blayne Darling was always aware of up-and-coming
directors; it was his business to be. One never knew
how the wheel would turn, he always said. Just as he
was always aware of who had money, since he believed
that fine feathers made for fine friends in the audience.
And, as he also always said, an actor's best friends,
aside from his prompter and his makeup man, were
his acquaintances with investors.

"Your young man is well-known to me," he'd said,

shrugging a shoulder toward Gray when he'd made his only personal aside to her before they'd parted last night.

"He's not my young man," she'd answered.

"The more fool you are if he's not," he'd laughed. "He looks as if he wishes to be, and the Dylan family is as rich as Rockefeller—or their friends, the Vanderbilts. And with no foolish prejudices against people in the theater—why, his brother married into it, or rather, took his wife from out of it. Harper's very well, but Dylan could buy and sell him before breakfast," he'd added.

"You know I'll never marry again," she'd started to say, until the look in his eyes, half-pitying, half-embarrassed for her, reminded her that he hadn't been necessarily only speaking of marriage. He was of the theater, after all. He'd never understood her prudishness in such matters, since she'd been born and bred to the life backstage. He never guessed it was just because of that life, that she'd such a yearning for everything that wasn't backstage—everything that was deemed good and proper in that world she longed to be part of, that imperfectly seen real world that lay beyond the footlights.

Now, sensitive questions forsaken, if not forgotten, Blayne Darling set himself to entertain them, and so they finished their Thanksgiving dinner with laughter. He told story after story, acting them out wonderfully, and when they'd done and were trying to stand and waddle from the table, it was difficult to tell who was more pleased—the host or his audience, which by now included all the diners in the room.

It was as they were standing, saying good night to the lesser guests at the table, that the moment came when Hannah realized her father wouldn't be making many more farewells to her for a while.

"How do, Dylan," a ruddy-faced, middle-aged gentleman said as he came up to Gray. "Saw you from 'cross the room, but didn't want to interrupt. We've got to do some talking about the Erie, son, and maybe the Oregon-Pacific lines as well. And how-de-do,

Blayne. Haven't seen you since I was last in New York. But I didn't see you with such a little sweetheart on your arm then. I couldn't take my eyes off her all night, thought she was Gray's handful though . . . just his style. But too young for you, old man, and far too pretty.''

"Pretty? Why, where are your eyes, John?" the ruddy gentleman's friend asked, eyeing Hannah avidly. "A peach is what she is."

"Gentlemen," Blayne Darling said, "I present my daughter, Hannah, to you. I won't give you their names, my dear," he said to her, "they're too crafty, by far."

"Your daughter? Good heavens," the first gentleman exclaimed. "Hard to believe, you always spoke of a child. Ho. Some child. Hand him down more than his walking cane, spectacles are in order, old man."

"Just so, time flies," Blayne said lightly, for he was never at a loss for words, even when he was, as he gazed at Hannah with something smoldering in his expressive eyes, something less than pride and more than embarrassment. Whatever it was was gone in a moment, covered over with an expression of great affection.

And then, of course, immediately after, it turned out that there was that appointment he had that he'd almost entirely forgotten. He apologized to one and all, held Hannah's hand, and gave her a kiss on the forehead, very much in the style of Lear with Cordelia, but feeling, to Hannah, more like the bishop sending Joan to the stake with his blessing. Then he left them.

Kyle was quick, but he'd an entire, if diminished, theatrical company to say good night to, and so it was the work of a moment for Gray to steer Hannah out the door, around a corner, and into a darkened niche in the almost deserted lobby, behind a potted palm and near the stair.

But whatever he was planning was changed by what he saw in her face, and then trembling on her eyelashes.

"No, don't," he said, wrapping his arms around her and holding her close. "Ah, please don't. It isn't worth it. It mightn't even be the way it seems."

She let him gather her up close, and she laid her cheek against his chest, all sense of propriety forgotten in the comforting cradle of his arms. Because she knew it was just the way it seemed, and nothing would ever change that or her father, and so it was beyond good to be held so closely by someone who cared. She stayed silent, content just to stand so, breathing in the good clean soap and spice scent of him, feeling the safety of his embrace, comforted even beyond what her hurt had been. She stayed so for a long while, until the sudden sound of his voice reminded her to wonder just what it was that her comforter cared about.

"Lord," Gray breathed into her ear, "what a mass of bones you are! It's like holding a mackerel. No one girl could have so many . . . why," he exclaimed as he ran his hand slowly down her side, "it's all whale-bones! How many whales have died in order to hold you together, I wonder, and why? when you seem so nicely put together without them, or so I'd think, from what I've seen . . . Oh," he said as she pulled away, "am I not supposed to see what I feel? or feel what I see?" he asked innocently, delighted to see the flush of anger he'd provoked replace the sick look of shock she'd worn when he'd first taken her into his arms. She glared at him. And then relaxed, and smiled a wan smile.

"Thank you," she said softly. "It was good of you. I needed a shoulder to lean on just then."

"You can have more, just now," he said, and took her back into his arms.

She didn't move so much as a fraction away, but a second before his lips met hers, she spoke again.

"No," she said, "I can't. Please, no."

It took a heartbeat more, but he did raise his head. Only so far as to look her directly in the eye.

"You could have more than that, too," he said quietly, as she tried to look away from his keen blue stare, and failed. "Now and later. Because I don't just mean for an hour, or a day, or even a year. I'm not at all sure what I mean yet, except that I mean you no harm, believe me. I've never said as much before to any girl and . . .''

"No," she said again, closing her eyes this time. "I can't and won't . . . please, believe me, for all that I've led you on, I haven't meant to. I simply couldn't help it, but I must now, because I can be nothing more to you."

"It's not what you think," he said. "I . . ."

Whatever he was going to say was ended by Royal's loud, imperative call, "Gray? Where are you at? Hey. Gray. Gray?"

Gray stepped out of the shadows and stared at where Royal stood in the center of the lobby, with Peggy at his side.

"Cattle have been called home with sweeter voices," Gray answered with some annoyance.

"Yeah," Royal said, his long face alight with excitement as he went on, "but you was nowhere in sight. Got news. Peggy here has done me the honor of consenting to be my wife. Soon as can be. You going to be my best man?"

"I'm not going to let anyone else be," Gray said, coming forward to shake his friend's hand, before he placed a light kiss on Peggy's cheek. "He's a good man, Miss Peggy. But I'm not altogether sure he's good enough for you. You sure about this? He's mighty big, but I can out-wrassel him if you want to get away."

"Well, of course I know I'm not good enough for her," Royal said at once, as Peggy began to blushingly protest how sure she was, until she saw Hannah, and then she left off in order to throw herself into Hannah's outstretched arms, and they hugged hard.

"Lord," Gray said softly to Royal, as the two women embraced. "That was fast enough. What did you do? Drag her aside, say, 'Will you?' and then start hollering for me?"

"Hell, no," Royal said indignantly. "I told her my mind, and made her my offer. And I kissed her for a spell," he admitted in low tones, before he picked up his voice and his eyes and stared at Gray, "because I'd a right to, at last. But we ain't married yet, so I thought it would be better to get her out in the open before much more went on. She trusts me more than I do. And I got to protect her, that's the whole idea of it, y' see."

Gray's expression grew still and thoughtful as he studied his friend's face.

"Yes. I'll be your best man," he finally said, "but I don't think you need one. Because I don't think you could do better than yourself, my friend."

Endings are all important in the theater; finales are considered all the better for being spectacular. But even they aren't necessarily the last word, because of the tradition of encores. And so the Harper troupe's farewells to each other were long and various and began long before their actual departure did.

Long before their train was to leave for New York, Nelson DeWitt showed everyone his new leaflets. He'd paid a great sum to have them made up in Denver, but even at that, he said, it cost less than it would have in New York, and they'd just been delivered to him. He'd a stack of thin, ten-page brochures, with his picture on the front cover, entitled, "Nelson DeWitt, An American Thespian." He was privately thrilled with them, but said he needed to get everyone's opinion before he could be sure they were good enough to give away to directors, producers, and fans. That was the only polite way he could be sure his fellow performers all got a good look at them, and took a sample apiece. A man never knew where his next job was coming from, after all.

Hannah thought they were dreadful, and so exclaimed as she leafed through one, "Oh, how wonderful. You look so . . . ennobled as Hamlet, Nelson, you really do. I'd no idea you ever played him. Nor Charles Barlow in 'School for Scandal'!" she cried, seeing the next photo, "I am impressed!"

She was only impressed at how badly he looked, affecting the same, jut-jawed pose in each picture, although he wore different costumes in each. Each photograph faced a page of selected reviews. He was a far better actor than the stiff, postured pictures hinted at, but he'd paid a fortune for the brochures, and they were done, so what could she say? Burn them?

"Yes, well," he said with pleasure, looking over her shoulder as avidly as if he'd never seen them, "everybody's saying publicity's the newest thing. The girls can get their pictures on cigarette cards and chocolate boxes, but even men are making their faces familiar these days. They're putting out decks of stage playing cards with theatrical faces now, too, just thought I'd get a self-start this way. A man's got to move with the times, and a picture is worth a thousand words—though I've got those, too—in the reviews."

And all those thousand words say the wrong thing, Hannah thought sadly, because although the camera didn't lie, it couldn't act as well as Nelson could. She flipped through the leaflet, seeing how the camera kept cheating Nelson, robbing him of his living grace and charming smile, emphasizing instead the narrow shoulders and weak chin she'd never really noticed before, and she asked, "May I keep one, please?"

Soon after, Maybelle and her gentleman tenor announced that they'd heard of a *Patience* being done in Chicago, and so they'd be leaving the company at the Aspen train station, not at Grand Central Depot in New York. Two dancers decided to go with them and try their luck.

The day after that, Frank Dupree, their resident villain, collected his mail, and after he'd read it, announced that he'd be leaving the troupe when they got to New York, and taking the next train up to Buffalo. Where, he said with not so much of a twitch of his dark mustache, he was himself going to be married— and then, begin work with his father-in-law in the lumber business. For good, and forever, he said, the look in his eyes forbidding any jests, because he'd have a family to support, and her family felt, as well he knew, that he couldn't do it as an actor.

There was a long, shocked silence after he'd spoken. He received hasty pats on the back from the men, and hurried hugs and quick kisses from the ladies, as they tried to hide their sobs and tears. Then they hastened away from him. They acted as though a dear friend had died. But so he had, to them.

Three days after she'd begun it, Peggy's wedding dress was done, and she insisted that she had time, between performances and meetings with Royal, to sew a fine new one for Hannah to wear to her wedding. And heedless of Hannah's protests, began it.

The next night, Gray tried to get Hannah to come out with him for the fourth time since Thanksgiving, and this time she'd an even better excuse than the other times, because she had to help Peggy finish the dress.

The night the troupe gave their farewell performance, they took their bows, then went out and drank and wept and told each other and themselves the usual lies about their future plans. But they didn't stay out too late, because they knew there was a wedding in the morning they had to attend, before they got on the train to make the long trip home.

Royal and Peggy sat at a separate table and talked in low voices—that was, when they stirred themselves from their dazed content to do more than hold hands. Gray sat at a long table with all the remaining troupe, and joked and sympathized and kept everyone such good company that Hannah couldn't claim he was her escort more than he was anyone else's. She stole glances at his hard profile every now and again, as often as she caught him watching her, and was rewarded with his widest smile when he caught her at it. But in all, he was behaving exactly as she'd asked him to. So she'd nothing to complain about but cruel fate, and she'd done that often enough in the past; so it was hard to know why it was so hard to swallow whenever she thought of all she'd be leaving the next day. Weddings present reminded people of weddings past, she decided, and tried to let it go at that, even though she knew very well she was lying.

It was long after everyone had said good night, when she'd slipped into her nightgown and was staring out the hotel window at a crescent moon so close she thought she could reach out and hang her hat on it, that Peggy spoke to her about more than wedding plans and dresses, at last.

"Hannah, dearest," Peggy said from the depths of her adjoining bed, and from her hesitant voice, Hannah feared she'd talk about good-byes. She sighed, because she really thought she couldn't, not now, not tonight, not just yet.

"May I ask you a question?" Peggy asked softly. "I know I ought not, for all I want to, but you're my best friend, even if my friends from New York were here, you'd be, you know."

Hannah was touched and proud. Until Peggy added, "I suppose you could say 'tis the sort of thing I should ask my mother, but it isn't, I promise you. Och, well, she told me all a girl has to know. But she told it fast and turned her head away as she did, and I don't know to this day which of us was more embarrassed by it, and her having been with child more times than I've fingers on my two hands."

Peggy chuckled, but Hannah's heart grew colder, anticipating what was coming.

"I know *that* part of it," Peggy, "and I trust Royal knows what I might not. But I want to know more than the way of it, plain and simple like my mother told me. I want to know how to make him happy with it. And that's never a thing she told me, ah, well, I suppose she couldn't, could she? Even if she knew . . . but you've been married, Hannah dear, and I thought . . .

"You don't have to tell me word for word," Peggy said, the sudden thought making her sit straight up in bed. "I'm not after embarrassing you, or me. But I— I'm a plain dab of a girl, Hannah, that I am and that I know," she said, cutting off anything Hannah might have protested, "and he's everything any girl would want. And so good to me.

"Why, when he first asked me to wed him," Peggy said in dreamy accents, "I didn't say yes right off. I wanted to, for all I haven't known him long, I'll never know him better. There's no doubting he's the one for me. But I knew my obligations. It broke my heart, but I had to tell him my family needed the money I was making. Never think he only offered me money to send to them each week—as if that wasn't more than enough! No, not he. No, he said he'd welcome them coming to live with us, every blessed one of them. He said the house was big enough and could always be made bigger; the boys could help out, and the West needed women—even if my sisters aren't old enough to be women, and my poor mother's neither a widow nor a wife, still that way I'd always have company. I was so happy—but then I recalled the way of things at home, and asked him if there was a problem with the Irish here, too. He laughed and said, 'Yes—there's not enough of them.'

"There never was a better man," Peggy vowed, "or a luckier girl. But I . . . I'm more than grateful to him. When he kisses me, I . . . ah, Hannah, there's got to be more to it than what my mother said. I see those scarlet women and saloon girls, and I know they know. He's promised to be faithful to me, and I believe it, but I don't want him regretting it. I want him to have the best. And you, you are my best friend, and you were a married lady. I'll be a married woman tomorrow—and though I want to be a lady, I want him to be satisfied . . . Please, can you tell me anything I ought to know?"

Hannah lay very still. What should she say? Her own hard-earned truth? That nature knows nothing of love, and so for all the love in the human heart, still sometimes the body cannot follow the heart? But from all the reading she'd done in all her medical books, she knew that was only once in a thousand, thousand times. She'd speak from her dreams then, and not her experience. Peggy, too, deserved the best.

"Peggy," she said gently, "remember that for all he's a man, he's likely as fearful as you are, if only because he loves you as much as you love him, and wants the best for you, too. So be kind and careful with him, and fair. Let him know what you're thinking and feeling, and never be embarrassed with him as you are with me, or your mother. Because what will pass between you two is sacred—and will be as much fun for him as what the saloon girls charge for, too. Better, because it's given and taken with love. You'll see. And," she said in a rush, "maybe even better yet, because it's free."

She laughed at that, she couldn't help it, and so did Peggy. When they'd finished, Peggy chuckled her good night, and Hannah sighed with relief. Because for all her inventiveness, she didn't know what else she could say. There was only so much she could invent. Holding John had been wonderful, kissing him had been, too, and his fondling had made her yearn for whatever more he could offer. But the rest, the embarrassment and humiliation of failure, she thought as she burrowed into her pillow, was best left, as it always had been, to silence.

"If you don't get to bed," Gray observed, looking up from the book he was holding, and watching Royal stalking around the deserted salon, "you'll never get up on time in the morning."

"I'll go to my room, and let you get some sleep," Royal said, but Gray snapped the book closed and spoke before his friend's long legs could take him from the room.

"No. Something's eating at you. I'd let you pace until it came out, but I'm your best man, remember? I'm supposed to get you to the altar bright-eyed and bushy-tailed, but I've a feeling it might take all night for you to spit it out. I've only known you most of your life, remember. What is it?"

"Damn," Royal said, collapsing onto a hassock near Gray's chair, and putting his head into his hands, "I've got the miseries. Yeah. Gray," he said, looking up and staring hard at his friend. "Listen. It's about . . . after the wedding."

Royal fell silent, and when it seemed he'd not speak again very soon, Gray said, "Oh. I guess you went upstairs for tea every time you went to Misery Annies, hmm? Or Mother Blessed's house? And those times you came with me to New Orleans, you were teaching those girls to play cards when you got them alone in their rooms, is that what you're trying to tell me?''

"Damn it, no," Royal blurted angrily, and then lowering his voice and his eyes, said quickly, "But that's it. See, I never known nothing but whores and suchlike. But now . . . I can't even say Her name in the same breath with them, it wouldn't be right. I don't want to scare her or shame her tomorrow. Damn it, Gray. You've had an education. You know women. I know a man does the same thing with a good woman as he done with bad ones, but . . . but it just don't seem right.''

Gray thought about his answer. He'd no more experience with good women than Royal had, even if, in his travels, some he'd known in a biblical sense had been of a higher class and station in life than the sort Royal had known. He'd certainly no more knowledge of virgins; now that he thought about it, the idea of initiating one was as terrifying as Royal seemed to think. The more he considered it, the more he realized Royal was right—a man could do such wrong things that he could really terrify an innocent, or put her off the thing forever after. But Royal was a good man, and Peggy loved him so absolutely that Gray rejoiced for them. They both deserved the best answer he could come up with.

The problem was that Gray found that though he'd an expensive college education, and an equally expensive carnal one, neither seemed to hold the answer he was looking for. Perhaps, he thought, bemused, because he'd never looked for it before. But he'd been thinking about love a lot more these days. Now he searched his heart instead of his past. Since reality held no answers, his dreams might. He thought about how he wished to love and be loved, and found an answer. He could only hope it was the right one.

"Like I said when you first met her: women aren't that much different from us, except for the obvious, and I think you saw that's so," he said slowly. "But good women are brought up different, that's true—or at least, maybe bad women manage to forget how they were brought up. What I'd do . . . ? Well, it sounds crazy, but philosophers say a man should look into his own heart to find all the answers. So, I'd take that a little further, and I'd try and think of how it would feel to be a girl who didn't know much about what goes on between a man and a woman. Yeah. I think that's it.

"Think about it," he said, leaning forward as he warmed to his theme. "Think about how you'd feel if you had a female body and didn't know what it was for. What would you want touched? When? And how? Then go ahead and do it for her. Well, damn it," he said, as insulted as upset by the look growing in Royal's widened eyes. "Why not?"

"Because that's plumb crazy. Why . . . why," Royal sputtered. "if'n I thought that way, I'd scare her to death, is what. She'd up and die, right there and then. That's why. She ain't no whore. That's what I'm saying!"

"Then you better change your tune before you hear the wedding march, my friend," Gray said, very much on his high ropes, because he'd an uneasy fear Royal was right. "You treat your wife like she was a saint, she'll end up like Ma Carter, in Laredo. She was a minister's wife, for God's sake, before she took up the trade. And she always said it was because . . . well, never mind."

Gray drew a deep breath and thought of his classical studies as well as real life; he remembered the way his brother and sister-in-law were with each other, as well as how his favorite characters in fiction acted, reviewing them in his mind—from Romeo and Juliet to Joshua and Lucy Dylan. And then he was positive, whatever popular opinion might hold, that he was right.

"Listen, my friend," he said with conviction, "a woman feels things just like a man does. If love is right, then the rest of it—what we usually pay for with a woman—then that's right, too. The difference is how and why we do it. When you pay, you're out to get your satisfaction. That's it. When you love, you're out to give her as much as you get. That's the way of it, whether the woman is good, bad, or plain indifferent. And a wife's never indifferent, no matter what some fools in the bunkhouse say. Or at least I don't think you'd want one that was. Now, don't tear my head off, because I'm only asking, and I don't expect you to answer out loud, but do you think Peggy's got no lustful feelings for you? Think she's going to lose them when she says, "I do?" You want her to? What do you want, a wife or an angel?

"Listen, a wife's a woman you love too much to just want once, anyhow. And she wants you enough to stay with you for the rest of her natural life, whatever. Right? So if you love her, you're not going to make a mistake. You can't. Because if she loves you, she's not going to care if you do, anymore than you'd care if she did. Because everybody makes mistakes, and love can correct most of them."

When he'd done speaking, Gray was as impressed with himself as Royal seemed to be. They both sat staring into the fire, thinking.

"Yeah. Well. I thank you kindly," Royal finally said calmly, rising. "Think I'll be going to bed now. See you at sunup. And thanks."

Gray remained sitting by himself long after Royal had gone. Because he was thinking of how easy it was to come up with answers when your only problem was giving them to someone else. And then he sat up longer, thinking of how lucky Royal was.

The preacher was so entranced by the guests that he had some difficulty concentrating on the wedding service. The women were dressed to the teeth, and if he didn't mistake it, some wore paint. The men were elegant and poised, or posed, as no men he'd ever met in his life had been. For all that the groom had looked respectable as he could hold together when he'd first made the arrangements, and his best man was Gray Dylan of *the* Dylan family, up Wyoming way, the guests all were, if the preacher didn't miss his guess, from a theatrical company that was playing in one of the theaters in town. That presented an unforeseen problem. Of a moral nature.

Of course, the theater was evil incarnated, and evil was always fascinating, which was why the preacher couldn't help staring. But some theater was enlightening and ennobling, and so he told his wife when they peeked into the parlor to see the wedding company assembling there. There was certainly nothing wrong with Jenny Lind, on stage, that was. And that Mr. Wilde who'd toured through the territory a few years ago had been everything that was gentlemanly, hadn't he? Wasn't Phineas T. Barnum as American as a turkey? Mr. Edison was recording performers singing, wasn't he? so that soon everyone in America might be listening to grand music right in their own parlors, or so even the December edition of the national church journal had said.

The theater, the Rev. Mr. Howard finally told his wife, may have been wicked once upon a time, but they'd do well to remember times were changing. And just look at the tall cowboy and his shy bride. That lovely couple was no more theatrical than their own calico cat was. Thus reassured, after a hasty consultation the Howards stepped out into their parlor: Mrs. Howard to man the pianoforte and the Rev. Mr. Howard to raise his good book, and theater or not, they were ready to begin.

Royal looked elegant in his new black suit, and Peggy was a vision in her white gown, or so all the guests whispered. Royal made his answers in a deep, mellow voice that would have done credit to any Shakespearean king. Peggy's soft replies were so sweet that every actress hearing them marked them down in her memory should she ever have to do an ingenue again. Before anyone had time to get up a really good show of tears, it was done, and Royal was kissing Peggy, his wife.

"I wish you wouldn't cry, Hannah," Peggy said tearfully when Hannah gave her congratulations, and at the same time, her good-byes. Because although they'd all been invited to the wedding breakfast, the reverend's schedule had conflicted with the New York train's, and they'd no time for anything but farewells now.

"It's only because I'm so happy for you," Hannah lied. "Oh, I'll miss you," she added in truth.

"Not for long, Miz Hannah," Royal said, grinning. "I'm taking Peggy East for our honeymoon. Well, it's the best way to pick up her kin," he said as Peggy gazed up at him with surprise and dawning joy, "and some things for the house. We'll be there in a week or so . . . if you agree, darling," he added very softly into Peggy's ear.

"Oh, but that's everything wonderful!' Peggy cried.

As did Hannah. If for different reasons—one of them being the look on Peggy and Royal's faces, another being for the way she felt so alone when they turned to greet other well-wishers.

"I was thinking of traveling East then, as well," Gray said at her side, startling her.

"Oh. Is it a western custom to take friends on a honeymoon?" she asked.

He smiled. "There's a limit to friendship, even out here. But it's a big city. And one I know. So I thought I might smooth things for them before they arrive. Would you care to help me do it?" he asked lightly.

"Oh. Oh, of course," she said, but before she could explain that was absolutely all she could do, there were more things to say to Peggy, and then Kyle consulted his watch, and they knew they had to be gone.

Royal, Peggy, and Gray went with them to the station, which as Kyle said, was a nice original change of pace from the usual, where the guests go to see the honeymooners off. There was a flurry of hurried final farewells and kisses. Although Gray had the time and the excuse for more, his kiss, very properly, only grazed Hannah's proffered cheek. She'd only a second to note his amusement with her too tardily concealed pang of disappointment, before she had to board. Then she'd only another moment to quickly scan the platform as the train pulled out. But the platform wasn't a stage, so Blayne Darling wasn't there, of course. The train moved on and she waved at Peggy, Royal, and Gray until she could no longer see them, and was glad she was going so fast they couldn't see exactly who it was she stared at until he was completely out of sight.

It wasn't really bad for her until that night. When she lay in her berth and, like an accountant, thought of all she'd gained on this trip, and then realized that she'd left it all behind her just where she'd found it, in the West.

It was a wakeful night. Kyle lay back in his berth and thought of figures. He'd made enough profit to begin something new in New York, and he'd a few ideas along those lines. Thinking along other, equally entrancing lines, he remembered his assistant, the new Hannah, the one who now had no distractions to distract her from him. He'd just have to think of some new distractions for her, he thought, smiling to himself as the train bore him home, because he knew he was a man of endless resources, and not a few ideas.

They left a clear cold night behind them in the mountains. But Royal and Peggy had little need of the hotel's feather comforters now. There'd been awkwardness between them for only a moment, when after a long day of talking and planning, they'd finally come into their hotel room, alone, together. Then she'd stepped into his arms, or he into hers. And then they discovered that shyness could be banished with laughter, and that laughter could pave the way for love. Then he discovered that Gray had been right, even as she found Hannah's advice perfectly true. That was before they forgot all else but each other.

Because in time, he forgot Gray's excellent advice and forgot to act as though her body was his own, instead of only a miracle and his chiefest desire, he was so dazzled by the wonder of it. She remembered to forget she was a lady, just as Hannah had suggested, before she forgot the meaning of any words but ''yes'' and ''Oh!'' Then they were lost in the newness of the oldest act of mankind.

When they became one in act as well as name, he

grieved that he'd brought her even a moment of pain with his love, although she'd wounded him more by suffering it. Then they discovered how to console one another. Finally, only a day and a half night into their marriage, they needed no more advice, from anyone. Because having pleased each other and finding how much that pleased themselves, they were both experts at physical love. They'd never been anything else but expert at the spiritual sort.

As they clung to each other's naked bodies and found ever new comforts there, Royal's adviser lay back alone in his hotel bed, staring at the ceiling, wondering if he'd ever sleep easy again. He, who'd never been afraid of any man, beast or fate he'd ever faced, had found something at last that he feared. Because he'd just realized how alone he was in the night.

He began to wonder if it would always be so, and worried for the plans he'd so blithely made before this revelation. There was more to being a man than his educations, East or West, had prepared him for, and he perceived it was a thing that all a man's cleverness, strength, and courage mightn't be enough to win for him. Because he began to see that a man needed more than himself in order to be a complete man. He needed just one particular woman, but he needed her to love him in return. And though he realized he'd finally found the one, he knew the other was what mightn't come easy—or at all. And so that night he also made the acquaintance of some of fear's old comrades: doubt, envy, and worry, and had the whole of the rest of the night to do it in, too.

Peggy's wise counselor, miles away in a train that screamed in the night as it streamed farther away from Gray, finally gave up. And having always known how alone she was, knew how alone she'd be again, and wept into her pillow for all her bitter wisdom.

Chapter Twelve

"We, like the phoenix, have ended only to rise up again," Kyle said, "but our new incarnation will be much brighter."

Hannah stirred uneasily in her chair. It was partially because she was weary with sitting, the train ride had been long, although it had gotten her back to the reality of her circumstances too quickly. It was also because Kyle was promising something.

"I see you doubt me," he sighed, and looked around the crowded restaurant in Grand Central Depot as though he expected a horde of travelers to leave off what they were doing to stare in amazement at what he'd said. But, as usual, he said it with such conviction that Hannah looked with him, half expecting them to, too.

"I asked you to stay a moment, after the others left, because I'd a proposition to put to you that I didn't want them to hear. About the future. Not that some of them won't find a home with me again in the near future—but because some of them will not. Ah well, but as Mr. Darwin says, 'only the fittest will survive, such is life,' " Kyle shrugged and turned his attention to Hannah again. They sat at a small table in the tearoom at the depot, their traveling cases all around them.

"I've put away more than a bit of money, it was, if not the most glorious, then certainly a most successful tour," he said smugly, neglecting to mention that a large part of the profits had been made larger as the salaries he had to pay had shrunken as his troupe had done. But it had been successful nevertheless, and more so because he'd learned a few lessons in the West, lessons he meant to put to the test now that he was back East. He only needed the usual: luck and opportunity. And this time, in order to do it faster, the unusual: a lovely, knowledgeable, honorable, and clever well-connected assistant—Hannah.

"I've some ideas," he said. "What we did was good, but it could be better. Far better. I'd prefer to do drama, only drama, but I've learned that variety is the spice of theater. Not just vaudeville: music, dance, magic, animal acts, and spectacle, but vaudeville with a tidbit of drama thrown in. Four or five acts culminating in a drama—fun for the kiddies and the weak-minded, with a morsel of the heavier stuff for those who have pretensions. It will work. It *did* work. But I know a way to make it work better," he said, his lean, dark face alight with liveliness.

"There are too many lost opportunities," he said as Hannah listened, caught up in his enthusiasm. "The solution needs vision. I have that. You see, much of the profit we made was eaten up, not by our charming troupe, but by rentals. Theater rentals. The Silver Circuit and all the other trouping companies accept that as part of their natural expenses. But it's unnatural, really. For if a man owned those theaters, and could send his troupe touring through a chain of them as they wended their way cross-country, it would be pure profit. A simple idea, but a revolutionary one. But also an idea that needs the right people to implement it."

Hannah sighed. Now she understood. She had suspected Kyle might offer her another position with him when they got home, and had been half-hoping he would. But now the other half she'd not, had shown up—the reason why he'd offered.

"That would take a fortune," she commented.

"Yes," he said musingly.

"No, she said, rising and gripping her pocketbook, "I will not put in a word with Graham Dylan, even if I ever see him again. Which I doubt. Nor will I with Royal, because if he's got money, he needs it for Peggy and her family. And I will not—never, with my father. Because the truth is," she said, swallowing hard, for it was as hard a truth to swallow at last as it was to say, "that he doesn't care much for me, or my opinion. The whole point of living on my own is to be sure I'll not owe him anything anymore. I'm sorry."

"So am I," Kyle said, taking her hand so that she couldn't leave, "for you. But not for me. I don't need your father's influence," he said, though he would have liked it, but now he knew it was as impossible to have as it would eventually be unnecessary. As Hannah sank down in her chair again, he said vehemently, clutching her hand hard, "Nor do I want Gray Dylan's, I assure you!" That was true enough, the Dylans had a history of raiding his company, and a look at Gray Dylan's face as they'd left him showed him that history might repeat itself if he wasn't very careful. "And though I believe Royal Atkins has enough money to support Peggy and an entire city block with her, I've no need of his support. I can get the investors. I need you for another kind of help.

"This time," he said, with a look in his dark eyes that showed Hannah he'd have dearly loved to pace around the crowded tearoom and made her grateful he couldn't, because he was irresistible once he got to his feet and started emoting, "I'll need a proper office, in a good district. Letterhead paper and a telephone," he said, his eyes glowing, as Hannah caught her breath, because the only man she knew personally with a telephone was her father, "and a secretary—you can play one until we get one," he said offhandedly, "and then we can put a company together again.

"A very good one, this time. But that's not the main

thing. No. The main thing is the investors I will interest in our company, and my plan. And I will, because I believe I know how to now. The odd thing," he said thoughtfully, "is that theater itself isn't the main thing anymore. Publicity is. Fame itself is. And then, too, there are new ways to make money whilst we try to make money. I understand from some of the other troupers I met that there are now songwriters here in New York who'll pay you to sing their songs. Anywhere. Isn't that astonishing?" he asked with wonder. "That way you can make money two ways: singing for the writers and for the audience. Lovely," he sighed.

"But that's all to be," he said with more energy. "That's the point. I need someone like you behind me in this, doing exactly what you've done so well all these past weeks: holding the troupe together, assisting me. Are you with me, Hannah? I'll pay well, better, when I can," he added quickly.

"Well, I . . ." Hannah began. Then he went on, "It will be here, in New York, if that's what's bothering you. We won't need to follow the tour until I get it together and that may take a while . . . Or," he asked, with a great show of disdain, "are you thinking that as you might be marrying soon, you wish to cut your connection with the theater as soon as you can? Or is it that you feel the wedding's so imminent that you don't need to work for your keep any longer?"

"What wedding?" Hannah gasped.

"To Gray Dylan?" he asked sweetly.

"Kyle," Hannah said, as she snatched her hand from his so he wouldn't feel it shaking, for he'd said the thing she could never allow herself to even fantasize about in order to court sleep. "That will, and can never be. Even if he'd the slightest interest in such a thing with me, which I promise you, he has not. The thing is," she said, and turned her head so that he couldn't see how it hurt her to say it, "that I had a very bad marriage. Very bad. You cannot know the whole of it—and that is literally so. So no matter who asks me in the future, I'm resolved: I will never marry again. I'm not being coy. If you never believe another

thing I say, believe this: it is for the best. Nor will I
ever approximate that state with any man, even though
I have been brought up in the theater, I will not and
cannot," she said severely.

"Ah, well," he said softly, "that takes care of the
next question I was about to ask, so I'll forget it, as
you say."

Of course, he never specified which of the two he
was going to ask of her. She might have said she'd no
intention of either matrimony or being a mistress, but
since the point was now moot, it was better unspoken.
It was a disappointment to him, either way. But he
didn't doubt her. She was a great actor's daughter and
a fair actress herself, but to a man who dealt in daily
fictions, truth was such a rarity that he knew it immediately when he saw it. And regretted it, for whatever reasons it was so. She was lovely, even in her
distress. Her averted face showed him the side view
of long lashes closed over those speaking eyes, a
straight nose, and those incredible lips, as tempting in
profile as they were in any other view. A downward
glance showed him a different, equally entrancing profile. He sighed. But accepted it. She was not toucha-
ble, he could only hope she was still employable in
other ways.

"I understand. I rue it, but will honor it. But why
should that change our relationship? I still need you
and want you. Will you be my assistant, Hannah?" he
asked solemnly as he'd ask her to be his wife. For if
it were all true, that position would also link her to
him for life—or until he was done with her.

"Yes, Kyle, I will," she said.

It would be nice to take a hansom cab, and Hannah
felt she could justify it, too. She'd just secured a new
position and had money in her purse that she'd reaped
from the old one. And after Aspen, she felt she was
accustomed to some sort of luxury. But her rooms were
near the Elevated Railway line, and since she'd already
arranged to have her great domed wardrobe trunk sent
on ahead, her two traveling cases weren't that heavy,

and she'd plans for the new money in her keeping. If she'd had to drag her bags through the streets toward Third Avenue, she might have splurged, and succumbed to the lure of the cabs and horses waiting all in a line for passengers outside in the street. But there was a branch line to the Elevated right at the Depot. A hansom cab cost fifty cents for the first mile, twenty-five for each additional, as well as the matter of a gratuity for the driver; the Elevated was a mere nickel, however far downtown she needed to go. She might have to wait for the Elevated, though. But for all she longed to get home, when she thought about the moment after her arrival, when she'd close the door and find herself home, alone, at last, she found she wasn't in that much of a hurry, after all. She took the Elevated home.

When she'd left the city, she'd seen men in light jackets or with them folded over their arms, their arm garters holding their rolled-up sleeves, and all the ladies had worn pastel-colored dresses or white shirt-waists and gay shawls, with straw-brimmed hats shading their eyes. Now everyone was swathed in wool and fur in the several shades of a New York winter; black or brown, or cobblestone, soot and pigeon gray. But otherwise they were the same: their expressions as blank and inwardly directed as they moved just as quickly through the teeming streets. It was she who'd changed. It wasn't so much that she found herself staring at the brick, stone, and steel buildings, astonished to see some rising high above the level of the Elevated itself. It was that all of it seemed unfamiliar now.

The numbers of people around her suddenly staggered her, and the fact that she seemed invisible to them struck her as odd, just as the way their eyes sidled away from hers when they encountered her bemused stare did. Lord, she thought, as she sat and watched the city move by, far below her—a few months in the West, and I have become a tourist!

Then she remembered who it was who always said "Lord!" and remembered that her long vacation from reality was as lost to her as autumn was. The mountains, the brooks, the golden aspens trembling in the breeze beneath a lucent sky as blue as—she shook herself. They had nothing to do with this great gray city or her life. She was lucky she remembered that in time, she thought, her inner visions fading as the outer world pressed in, as she looked down and blinked. Then she stood up and fumbled for her bags, because she'd almost missed her stop.

Her landlady called a greeting, and she had to pause in the hallway and say all the inconsequential things expected of her. It turned out she had to listen more to tales of the landlady's cat and the weather than she had to talk about her travels, before she could decently plead fatigue and go to her rooms. Then she opened her door, and was greeted by the airless, unused smell of unoccupied rooms as she put her bags down. She felt her heart plummet. Everything was exactly as she'd left it, and she'd taken pains to leave it neat.

There were her books, her pictures and her tables, her chairs and her fringed rug, all as if she'd left them yesterday, and all looking as they would if she left them again tomorrow, or ten years from now, or twenty, she thought. At least by then, she mused as she trailed farther into her parlor, she'd have more books to leave. But not medical ones, she decided, staring at what suddenly struck her returning-traveler eyes as the one inappropriate thing in what was otherwise a modest, pleasant woman's home: a shelfful of books entitled: *Women and Her Diseases, Everyman His Own Doctor, The Cottage Physician, The Practical Home Physician, Medicology* . . . and so many, many more. All the fat volumes with their foldout color plates and testimonials, and all with the same advice that amounted to no advice at all for her. A woman ought to have classics and bound volumes of *Harpers* or *Lady's Wreaths'* on her shelves, and not such rubbish, she thought. For that was all it was, and all it amounted to.

She picked up a calf-covered volume and blew off the dust that had gathered on the gilt at the top of its leaves. Not one of the chapters had helped her. Not one illustration bore any more relation to her than a picture of the back of the moon might have done. She knew. She'd looked. Now the thought of it amused as well as pained her. Then, she had been panicky and shamed, her door locked, ears tuned to any unfamiliar sound, her hands hot and trembling, as though she were doing something secret and vile that was detailed in the chapters entitled: "The Solitary Vice: The Dangers of Self-Pollution," rather than just trying to look and see, and know for herself what it was that was wrong with herself. She'd held a mirror up to life, literally.

John had said there was something wrong with her. He'd said his doctor had said it. He'd said he couldn't come into her because she wasn't made right. But every time she undressed and looked in a long mirror, she saw a perfect anatomical illustration of a female. Her problem lay deeper. What she wished to see required more courage than she knew she had, a hand mirror with extra magnification, and convolutions worthy of an acrobat. Perhaps it was as bad a vice as self-pollution, she was sure it wasn't a thing a decent woman would do. Nor a thing she could have done unless she'd been driven by worse than demons—and she was: by confusion and despair. She was fearful, but determined. It was the year she'd received word she was a widow, around the time that she'd met that charming Tristram, a time when she'd been so tempted to know more, to try more, of everything. Or rather, as she knew now, a time when she was unwilling to know there was to be no more for her, not even an answer.

When she'd finally managed to grip the mirror tightly enough in her sweating hands to hold it fairly steady, and discovered how to hold it so she could shed light on the subject, she'd seen herself as never before. And was horrified. The anatomical plates had left out much of life, and it took her a minute to realize that they never illustrated body hair. When she'd taken a shaky breath and disregarded that, and positioned herself so more could be seen, her trembling hands won her wavering glimpses of a welter of pink fringes, as well as smooth portions, folds, and nubs of what appeared to be extra flesh and dark caverns . . . damp, pink, red and black—what was normal, what was not? It was not only dreadful looking, like seeing an internal organ on the outside, but impossible to know what was supposed to be right or wrong in such a jumble.

She'd dropped the mirror, but didn't worry, because she didn't know how she could have worse luck. The problem might lie even deeper, as he'd said, but surely, no normal female looked like that. She felt a flash of acute shame for how she'd have looked to John if he'd ever glanced at that portion of her. But she hadn't known.

She still didn't, and her desire to understand hadn't died. After a few years passed, she began to wonder if her fears and ignorance mightn't have magnified things as much as the mirror had, and decided to dare to see a physician again. She wrote to him in the hopes that he'd request an office visit. By doing so, she'd hoped to outsmart herself as well, reasoning that despite all shame and fear, there was no way she would have denied a physician's request. Then his letter had come, assuring her that an unmarried woman needn't bother discovering the reason for her problem.

But there were other doctors, and the need to know was growing keener. If she could conquer shame and terror . . . She was twenty-four years old and growing older, she needed an explanation—at least, a reason. And perhaps she'd still a fairy-tale hope it could somehow be remedied. They'd invented telephones and electric lights since she'd been born, hadn't they? It was an age of miracles, after all.

Then she'd had to go West. Now she'd returned and knew that it didn't really matter anymore. She couldn't bring herself to shame herself with a strange physician anymore than she could with a man she loved. She didn't know if she could cope with pity if it were offered by the one, but knew now that she could certainly never bear disgust, however well concealed, from the other.

She put the book back on the shelf and reminded herself to dust them all in the morning. She couldn't throw away a book, much less a shelf of them. When she'd lived with her parents, she'd hidden them to hide her disgrace. Now she'd leave them there as a reminder of why she'd sit in her parlor alone every night until the authors of all those books were dead, and she herself near to it. That mightn't banish sorrow. But it would, at least, explain it. And that was all she could reasonably expect. She picked up her traveling cases and set to unpacking. She was home again.

New York had changed since he'd last visited, but Gray would have been more surprised if it had remained the same. The city was growing up in every way: uptown, as well as up high. Each new building seemed to think it had to add a new story to top its neighbor. Gray counted several buildings six and seven stories high as his hansom cab drove past them. He knew better than most how many new buildings were being built uptown where there'd only been fields and squatters before. His brother had laughed when he'd put good money down on the new apartment he'd chosen to be used for his New York visits, even though the plans had looked impressive. "Scout, you just never give up the wild West, do you?" he'd asked, rumpling his hair affectionately, as though he were still the boy he remembered.

But Gray had only grinned, because it was half true. The building had actually been named for the West, they'd called it the "Dakota" just because it was as far uptown and out of the city limits of respectability as that territory was from the rest of the nation. That had been part of its appeal to him. The other reasons, as he'd explained to his brother, had been the nearness to the wilderness sections of the park, where he might ride full-out, and the fact that it was new and daring, and designed by a fine architect. Since he needed a place to call his own when he stayed in New York City, he'd said—ignoring the things his brother had to say about that as he looked around his own spacious town house, subsiding only when his wife murmured something about "bachelors"—he wanted something that was unique.

But now, sitting by himself, he grinned and admitted the truth. As if that mattered. It was the elbow room. He loved the city, but more when he could have the freedom of the West in it. Just as he loved the West, and even more when he could avail himself of eastern comforts there.

In fact, he thought, sitting back and crossing his legs, there was one particular eastern comfort he meant to get to as soon as he could take care of more pressing business.

The girl cried out in sheer pleasure.

"Uncle Gray! Uncle Gray! Uncle Gray," she cried as he swung her up in the air, and straight-armed, held her so, so he could look up into her eyes.

"Woof! One more year and I swear I'll be too old for this. Why, only just last year I could toss you like this—" he said, throwing her an inch up toward the ceiling before he caught her again. "And this," he said as he did it again. "But now I can't no more," he sighed as he did it once more before he put her down, and she giggled, "I'm getting too old honey, that's sure."

"No. I'm getting too big," she corrected him, because there was a trace of seriousness as well as amusement in his face. And wondering if her beloved uncle was really worried or only just funning as usual, she added, "I'm nine now, remember?"

"Nine?" Gray asked, hunkering to his knees so he could tweak her nose with perfect accuracy, "Sez who?"

"Sez you!" she countered, putting her hands on her hips in a perfect imitation of highly offended dignity, " 'cause you was at my birthday party, and you gave me nine pinches to grow nine inches—*and,*" she said, grinning ear to ear, as she put her arms around his neck again, ". . . my Lindy Lou, who is the swellest pony ever, and just like you said: smart as paint and twice as purty!"

"After you finish destroying her diction for the week," a lovely young matron said in severe tones as she came into the room and glared at her daughter, making her giggle more, "I guess you can start on the others."

It was awhile before Gray could be rescued from the avalanche of small children that overwhelmed him. But soon he was able to greet his sister-in-law with perfect dignity. This, despite the fact that he had to do so from beneath the pile of children who'd wriggled onto his lap in the chair he'd collapsed into. His sister-in-law began a flurry of apologies as she pried the younger ones off. But then a handsome gentleman, tall as Gray and similar looking to him, but with his nose slightly bent from an old injury; gold, rather than flaxen hair, and gray rather than blue eyes, entered the room and ordered the children away in a firm, soft voice. They instantly, if reluctantly, complied.

Gray drew some back into his arms and drawled, "Now hold on, Josh, it ain't so bad. At least this time the dogs is locked up, usually they have to be peeled off me, too."

The children left the room, obedient but glum, solaced by his solemn promise to visit with them in the nursery as soon as he'd finished talking to their parents. But they left cheering after he promised to take them into the park after that.

"I wonder if Delia isn't getting a little too old to play touch football," Lucy Dylan said worriedly.

"Well, so's your oldest, but he promised," Gray protested, as Lucy frowned in incomprehension, since her eldest was a girl. "Don't mean to tell me you ain't going to let Josh come out to play, do you?" he added worriedly.

"Just let her try it! I'll run away from home," Josh Dylan threatened as he hugged his wife around the waist. "Pay her no mind, Gray. It's just that she's jealous. Her doctor would have a fit if she played today, or any day from now till spring."

"Lord!" Gray said, eyeing his sister-in-law's neat waist and high blushes. Honey-haired and sherry-eyed, and so lovely that she'd carried the audiences before her even before she'd uttered a word during her brief career as an actress, it seemed to Gray that though she might have added an inch or two here and there, they were all in graceful proportion. She looked as shapely as she'd been when they'd first met, ten years before.

"Another!" Gray marveled. "Congratulations, Lucy," he said sincerely as he planted a kiss on her cheek. "There can never be too many girls like you on this old earth, even if I've my doubts there's any crying need for more like him."

"Like me?" Josh laughed. "Delia's your spit, if not your image, little brother. Wild as the wind and stubborn as a mule. She looks like an angel and sings like one, just like her mama. And she acts from sunrise to sunset, just like she heard her mama used to do. But though she looks like thistledown, she's tough as tumbleweed. The only reason I don't want her to play touch football is because she always wins. And she's always on your team, too."

"But you've got the boys, Josh. It always tickled me to see them right after they were born—looked like he was busy coining little images of himself, the stuck-up thing," Gray confided to Lucy.

Not that there was anything wrong with that, Gray thought. A shading of ivory had begun to mix in with his brother's wheat-colored hair; once he'd thought the classic nose that had set slightly askew after it had been broken years before regrettable, but now he saw it added interest to what would otherwise have been only bland perfection. His older brother was the handsomest man Gray knew, and it was a thing he was proud of, because, as he'd once told Josh sincerely: it was a case of form following function.

They laughed, and gossiped about the children, and then Gray talked about business, because he knew Lucy took as lively an interest in it as Josh did.

"I think he's right," she eventually told Josh, "too many people are getting rich on silver, and that's a reason to start being nervous about it. The rich don't like to be in a crowd, you know.''

"How would you know? You don't even like to be with them," Josh said affectionately, with a look to her that was as good as a caress. "Girl can hold her head up as high as Alva Vanderbilt and Caroline Astor," he told his brother, "yet she don't care to. Not very neighborly, is it? She turns down all their invitations," he said with a look of pride that was completely at variance with his complaining tone.

"Not so!" Lucy protested. "I went to Alva's ball when I was expecting Jarrell."

"You would have gone if you were having him right then," Josh laughed, "even old Gray moseyed East for that one. The world and his uncle was there to see how much money one woman could spend showing another how much she'd be missing if she didn't accept her as an equal. It only cost as much as buying a small country, but Alva had Caroline Astor kissing her . . . fingertips in order to get into that affair.''

"Lord. That was a sight," Gray reminisced. "I never saw so much money wasted, or so many rich men making fools of themselves all at once before. Cornelius Vee's wife going as 'Electricity'—never mind the bulb she held, her diamonds could've lit up Fifth Avenue. And that fool Buckminister going as Julius Caesar: with side whiskers and a beard? And Kate Turner as a puritan when everyone knows she . . . ah," he stopped abruptly, and as Lucy begged him to go on, only said, "Hush, girl, I'm defending, not corrupting you." Then he added, "Why, all that ought to have made you even happier you don't have a social climbing wife, Josh."

"I couldn't be happier," Josh said sincerely, "whatever she decided to climb. As it is, the more she snubs them, the more they want her."

"Now, why didn't I think of that?" Gray asked, as if intrigued. "You mean if I don't look at a girl, and don't ask her out with me, she'll be beating down my door to get me?''

"As if you needed lessons in getting girls," Lucy scoffed, as they all laughed.

But just maybe I do, Gray thought, when he left them that night with a firm promise to return for dinner on Friday. And so maybe I'll try it for a day or two, or three, he thought, calculating that it had been exactly seven days since he'd seen her, and only the Lord could make something good in that little time.

Gray never believed there could be such a thing as too many naked women. Even now, tilting his head to the side, he decided it was that there was too much of each naked woman in sheer square yardage, rather than too many of them. What might be piquant singly, and delightful at closer range, was definitely oppressive in paint and twelve feet high and wide. Despite the green sylvan setting the ladies were cavorting in as they eternally molested a grinning satyr within their massive ornate gold frame above him, there was definitely too much pink and white surrounding him for his taste.

"They are something, hey what?" Gregory Archer asked with pride, "Bouguereau. Longest bar in America, too," he said, unnecessarily gesturing toward the enormous mirrored bar they sat across from. There were twice-life-size gilt metal nudes holding up vases near the great mirrored doors, but they, and the other nude statues and paintings, were the only females allowed through the doors of the exclusively male Hoffman Hotel. Still, for a club that prided itself on being so masculine, it was as preoccupied with the female form as a ladies' Turkish bath on Saturday night would be, Gray thought, but only said, "Mmm. Mite fancy for my tastes, though. No sawdust on the floor. I don't see the cuspidor. Where's a man s'posed to spit?"

"If I hadn't gone through school with you, I'd really believe you lived in a backwoods cabin," his friend said.

"What makes you think I don't?" Gray asked. "You never come to visit me like I visit with you when I come to town."

His friend's pale face colored slightly. "Ah, well.

But I don't come to your town. Nor will I. Not that I believe everything you say, old fellow. But half is enough for me. I'm content to read Mark Twain, Ned Buntline, and Ted Roosevelt on the subject; the nearest I'll get to the wild West is a Buffalo Bill show, thank you. But don't try to pull the wool over my eyes, Grahm," he said, pronouncing his friend's name as an Englishman would and his fellow Americans never did. "You read Voltaire and Plato along with the *Stockman's Journal,* or whatever cow-filled paper it was you used to whoop about when you got it at school.

"But now, look at this place. Convenience, elegance . . . why don't you give up your flat and come live here at Hoffman's as I do, instead? Ah, I know, it's all of a piece," he said in his best almost English accents, which amused Gray profoundly, since his own father had been an Englishman and would likely have gone into spasms of merriment—but suppressed ones, since he'd been a true gentleman—if he'd heard them, "You prefer inconvenience and hardship."

Gray nodded, smiling, thinking of his spacious, comfortable rooms. "Sure thing. Still, I was thinking more along the lines of fun and entertainment tonight. Want to take in a show on the Bowery, like in the old days?"

"The Bowery? Too tame, by half, my friend," Gregory scoffed.

"I think we're both a little too old for the goings on down in Five Points now," Gray said, "and come to think of it, it never was such fun aside from the danger of it. Rather get my head broke on the range than shot off while slumming," he added lightly, though he remembered the desperate poverty of the ramshackle tenements, filthy streets, and wretched saloons they'd visited in their college days with no such soft emotions.

"No, no, we're grown-up now. I've better plans for you," Gregory said smugly. "I contacted Old Peachy and Fredericks, and they're meeting us tonight. We're going to have some real fun. Just like the old days. Come along."

"Peachy and Fredericks," Gray said with pleasure as he rose from his chair. "Thought they were married."

"So they are," Gregory said. "But what has that to do with fun?"

Gray stood with his back to the wall and watched the ball, just like a wallflower, he thought, although there were certainly no other examples of any wilting flowers here tonight. There were floral sprays of diamonds, opals, and pearls in the ladies' hair and at their breasts, and flowers made of feathers and lace, as well, but nothing so simple as a natural one in sight. It was a highly dressed company. The men buttoned to their chins, in their correct black and white evening clothes, the ladies half in their brightly colored, daring, elegant, and low-cut silk and satin gowns. And all of them masked.

Gray wore a simple black silk mask; the sort, he thought, that a highwayman from another generation might have worn, since it concealed everything but his lips and chin. He considered how odd it was that modern-day highwaymen covered what this mask concealed, since stagecoach robbers tied kerchiefs on their faces just under their eyes, instead of above them. He was musing about that, he realized after a while, because he didn't want to keep watching the huge dance floor. This was, after all, a night he was supposed to be enjoying himself.

His old schoolmate, Peaches, had grown so portly that though he hugged his masked lady as close as he could as they danced, that couldn't be as close as he'd obviously like to be; there were many portions of her that couldn't be clutched close, and exposed as they were, Gray found himself wishing they had been. Her gown was low in back and front, and laced so tightly she threatened to spill out of every place that Peaches' greedy hands weren't covering.

Dapper Gregory danced with a woman with bright red hair, although they'd both had so much to drink they seemed to be swaying in place instead of actually dancing. But the floor was so crowded with so many people doing increasingly daring things that no one seemed to notice. Just as no one else seemed to notice where polite, shy James Fredericks stood off in a corner of the brightly lit room. And he, if Gray wasn't mistaken, was already beginning to do whatever it was he regularly paid his partner, his mistress, to let him do.

Which was precisely as it was supposed to be. The annual French Ball at the Academy of Music on fashionable Fourteenth Street had little to do with music, although it certainly was for certain fashionable gentlemen—those who wished to entertain their mistresses, or acquire new ones. It was held masked so that no gentleman—or lady who'd come to spy or cheat on her husband—could be easily identified. Both Fredericks and Gregory were with their mistresses, and old Peaches was looking for a new one. He was in the right place to do it because this event was, Gray realized, just what his father had told him they used to have in the days of *his* father's youth in London: a "cyprian's ball." Or as Gregory had put it, "a night for the demimonde."

But whomever it was for, Gray thought sadly, it wasn't for him. It might have been that he thought his friends were too old now to embarrass themselves so openly, or because he was too old to be other than embarrassed for them now. Because he wasn't enjoying the watching, and he wasn't particularly looking for anyone to participate with. He began to look for an exit. It grieved him to leave his friends, although he began to realize that he'd lost them long since.

"Oh, fiddle. A grump. Now, now, that mustn't be," a light voice trilled, and Gray turned to see a blond woman in a heavily brocaded low-cut pink gown smiling at him. Her scarlet feather mask left a pair of lovely lips bare except for their paint, and those red lips were smiling at him. He looked at what else was bared to his gaze, and then, shrugging, let her lead him on to the dance floor. There was a long lonely night lying ahead of him, after all.

"We match," she said triumphantly, and at first he thought she was talking about how well they fit together. Because her breasts, thrust up by her tightly laced bodice, felt wonderfully good against him, even through his stiff starched white shirt, vest, and jacket. As did the rest of the womanly body pressed so close against his own, pressing ever closer when she felt the sudden involuntary response she'd won from him.

"Our hair, silly," she trilled, when he didn't answer. "We're two of a kind."

She leaned in to him as they danced, closer than he'd believed a waltz could be danced in public; as close, he thought with mild amusement to temper the startling fact of his body's growing desire, as he'd been with some women he'd held for far more intimate embraces. Although, he decided as she attempted the impossibility of moving closer, it obviously wouldn't take long before he could take her in that closer one if he wished to.

Bemused, he let her maneuver him to a less crowded corner, where she swiftly, as deftly as she'd later be pleased to remove his trousers, untied his mask and slid it off his face. She took in her breath.

"Ooo," she cooed, "Look what I've got!"

And then masked his face with her own.

Her lips were wet, warm, and hungry. His hand began to rise, as if of its own accord, to take all that was being pressed on him, when he felt instead, a surge of self-disgust strong enough to shrivel his lust. He stepped back.

He gazed down into the glittering gloom where her eyes would be if they weren't shadowed by her mask, and was glad he couldn't see them as clearly as he'd seen himself in that moment. Those he'd scorned tonight had at least acted through honest lust. He, he realized, had acted from boredom and proceeded through habit. But it wasn't only that. It was what he'd almost been seduced by in that moment.

She was only just what he'd had in his arms. Breasts, hair, and lips. He'd a strange memory of what they might have done together, as though it had already happened, although he'd never done precisely this before. Still, now it seemed to him he'd done it far too many times before, and her masked face was sadly apt, symbolic of all he'd ever known intimately with a woman. And while that had been enough for him until now, it wasn't what he'd come to New York to have. No, nor was it what Josh, or Royal, or any man he respected had. He didn't want to be fobbed off again, not even for an hour, deceived by his body into betraying his heart. He'd enough of anonymous female bodies, like the ones on the Hoffman Hotel walls, or any of these at the French Ball.

"Something I said?" she inquired pertly.

"Something you didn't," he sighed, touching his fingers to her cheek in regretful farewell.

He bowed and left the ballroom. And strode out into the night, through the boisterous streets filled with the exiting revelers, through quieter sleeping sectors of town, to walk his lust away all the way from fashionable New York to his outpost of a temporary home at the northern edges of the city. He was accosted by the myriad prostitutes who patrolled the nighttime streets, but as he'd already refused a better class of one, he'd no difficulty discouraging others.

But even after all that exercise in a dampening wind that set his bad leg to thrumming, and after a thorough sluicing with cool water in his bath, his lust remained with him as he tried to sleep. Because it had never been for the anonymous blond female. He knew all too well who it was he wanted. And knowing it was more complicated than lust, stayed up hours more wondering what it was that she wanted that he could offer her.

Chapter Thirteen

Before he'd made his first visit to New York City, all those many years ago, Gray had studied an etiquette book until it's cover had nearly been worn off. Some things, such as table manners and manners required for house calls, had seemed natural and easy—his mother would have clouted him for eating like a hog, and his father would have been ashamed if he'd dared to lounge or slouch in someone's parlor. But the rules for what, exactly, to say and do at drums, teas, and private theatricals—social occasions that he'd never heard of, much less seen, had boggled him.

For all his mother's lessons and his father's example, Gray was certain a rough boy from the West would put his foot in it somehow, by word or deed. He suspected that, and not just shyness, was why cowboys were always so short-spoken when there were ladies present. Now he was grown and educated, he'd been to New York many times; London, Paris, and Rome, as well. But he purely wished, he thought as he waited for Hannah to come down the stairs of her boardinghouse to meet him, that he'd that old book in hand again just now. Just in case.

He'd come exactly on time and presented his card to her landlady with the right corner turned down to show he was calling in person, even though he knew she'd been expecting him since he'd sent her a note, and had the messenger wait for an answer, the day before. He'd taken off his hat, and struck a negligent, but not slovenly, pose to show he was waiting, but not loitering. Now he stood in the downstairs hall with his hat in his hands and his heart in his mouth, like a raw boy, all nerves and dread expectation again. And he loved it.

Because no other woman made him feel that way, and he couldn't remember being so gladly expectant since he'd waited to see her on Thanksgiving Day. Now Christmas was breathing down the city's neck, causing the shop windows to break out in red and green fabric to showcase their goods for the holy season. He'd seen all sorts of appropriate gifts for her: a silver pin with the masks of comedy and tragedy looking at the world through diamond eyes; a foolish flocked hat with a fantasy of drooping egret feathers that would flatter raven hair as much as snowflakes would; he'd priced a huge silver-ribbed fan as white and feathery as an egret's wing to match the hat, and an iridescent perfumer made of a hollowed pearly shell to wear on her snowy breast. He saw her in white, but then he saw her in gold; on the way here he'd gazed into the shop windows and envisioned her in red rubies and green emeralds, too.

But he couldn't give her anything but his gloved hand when she finally joined him, and that only for a moment in order to bow over her gloved one. Nor would he offer more than his smile, after that. Because he wanted to do this properly. He'd offer nothing until she was ready to hear him offer her his hand and heart, for life. He chafed at society's restrictions, but obeyed them. He'd never courted a girl before, didn't want to ever again, and doubted he'd have to, so he almost enjoyed the foolishness and frustration of it, knowing it wouldn't be for long.

He looked as astonishingly handsome as ever, and so correct in his city clothes that for the first time Hannah rued the fact that her beaming landlady wasn't a suitable chaperon. But then realizing that her mother and father wouldn't have been either, she sighed, placed her hand on Gray's arm, and let him lead her out into the sunlight.

He helped her up the high seat of his gleaming crimson phaeton, and she exclaimed over the handsome equipage as she unfurled her parasol.

"Well, the horses are purely vanity for me, New York or not, I have to have good ones," he explained as he steered his team of grays out into traffic. "And the carriage? Well, I had to cut a dash with you, didn't I? Still, now I'm mighty sorry I don't have a boy in livery hanging onto the back of it, for show, and to let you be easy about your reputation. Even so, I don't think the highest stickler could complain. It would be hard for me to get up to anything in plain sight of the world like this, not to mention this traffic," he muttered, scowling at a hansom cabdriver as he found himself about to be cut off.

She saw his black looks, "It's a good thing you can't wear your guns in public here," she said too brightly, wondering if he were teasing her about her reputation or not.

"Just what I was thinking," he said, neatly pulling ahead of the cab with a triumphant flourish of his whip, "though it sure would cut down on congestion here in midtown, no doubt about it."

They laughed as they painted each other word pictures of shoot-outs and draw-downs between drivers in Madison Square, the center of New York's social world. It had been an unusually warm winter, and today the warmth of the sun belied the date on the calender; sitting up high as she was, with Gray by her side, Hannah felt on top of the world. She wore her best afternoon gown, a fitted one of a dark cherry color to suit the season and her coloring, with a brighter crimson military-style pelisse, whose cut took the gaudiness from its color; and she'd a sloped, veiled, and fruit-embellished hat atop her upswept hair. She'd thought she looked very well, Gray's all-encompassing glance at her when they'd met had verified it.

At this time, and for this moment, however long it lasted, she refused to think of tomorrow and especially tonight. For now, she was young again, with the person she most wished to be with, and to all outward appearances, as normal as any other woman in New York City . . . and much luckier than most, she thought, gazing at Gray's profile. He wore a long black ulster over casual jacket and trousers, and had a low crowned top hat on his head, rather than his usual Stetson. He wore everything fit for a drive in New York City, but she noted, he'd a pair of boots on, and his flaxen hair was longer than most men's, it covered over the back of his high collar. And yet it looked so well that she had to leave off looking at it and study the street ahead.

"Royal and Peggy were thinking of staying at the Plaza Hotel now that its about finished being rebuilt," Gray said, as he steered around a halted horsecar, "so I thought we'd take a look at it because I'm wondering if they mightn't enjoy the Windsor more—it has an American plan, and at least the paint's dry there. We could have luncheon at the Plaza—to test the cuisine," he said quickly. "But since it's just on the edge of the park, I thought we might go for a drive first. It's Sunday, after all," he said, when she remained silent.

But she'd only been trying not to grin, or laugh, or weep for joy because it was such a wonderful idea, and so her voice was unsteady when she said, "Oh, yes," but the glow in her eyes as she did made him nod, and grin.

They drove up crowded Fifth Avenue in a line of coaches, carriages, and horsecars, inching past the reservoir on Forty-second Street and on up past St. Patrick's grand cathedral, and as they did, they complained about the traffic and discussed the weather until there was no way they could condemn the one or compliment the other further. Then Gray commented on what he thought Royal would have to say about the traffic, and when they'd done laughing, they began to talk about what to show Peggy and Royal when they arrived, and they were still laughing as they drove into the park. But even here there was congestion, if, as Hannah noted, of a higher sort.

The unusually clement Sunday had drawn out the wealthy. The narrow lanes were filled with fine barouches and other family carriages, as well as jaunty, sporty curricles and two-seaters. The congestion was complicated by corps of well-dressed riders on horseback, as well as by some daring young gentlemen perched high atop their newest "safety" bicycles, leaving the bicycle paths to weave in and out of traffic.

"After last year's blizzard, I expect everybody's trying to get as much sunlight as possible, in case it happens again," Hannah said.

"Can't store up sunlight or curiosity, I suspect this crew's just trying to make sure they get seen before it happens again," Gray said. Then he exclaimed, "Say! I've had enough of this crawling, haven't you? Let's tie up near the menagerie. We can walk and talk—I think it's our bounden duty to see if the elephants are good enough to show Peggy and Royal, don't you?" he asked, his eyes glittering with merriment.

"Oh, well, in that case," Hannah said, giggling. "Of course." She smiled as she wondered what other delightful things he'd get her to do, claiming it was all for Peggy and Royal, and then stopped abruptly as she thought of what other things he might jokingly attempt with that ruse. And then forced herself to smile again when she saw his sudden look of concern, because she was resolved: she *would* have this day, if no other.

The elephants were chained outdoors so that they might enjoy the sunny day as much as those that came to see them.

"Why don't you have them out West?" Hannah asked suddenly, gazing at the elephants as she strolled at Gray's side. "They could do ranch work, and I'm sure they could manage mountain trails. I read an article about them that said they did in their natural habitat in Borneo, or . . . someplace like that," she said, her voice faltering as Gray turned to look down to her with a bemused expression. "They'd be perfect for laying railroad track and fences, and . . . well, at least, so I should think," she said defensively.

"You know, I believe some foo . . . fellow, did try them once," he said, "the only problem was getting them enough feed, and having them survive our winters," he said seriously, before he went on with more enthusiasm and a suspicious quirk lurking at the corner of his mouth. "Not to mention the problems at branding time! The wranglers, well, they set up a mighty fuss when the cattle stampeded one night and then their mounts did, too—and squashed half the beef into filet steaks before they could round them up again. So I guessed it saved some time, though it surely wasn't pretty. There were some other problems, too— tying them up in front of a saloon on a Saturday night made for a real crowded Main Street, and just think of the spurs those poor old boys had to wear to get their attention! Why, the cowboys could hardly make it to the bar rail if they forgot to take them off, to say nothing of how the ladies complained about how muddy streets was bad enough, but what was in the streets then . . ." He was warming to his subject when a look at her made him raise his hands high.

"Ah, no, don't look at me like that!" he cried. "Murder's illegal, even in New York City, even I know that!"

She relented and let out the grin she'd been suppressing. And then they hung onto each other's arms and laughed like children.

But no one thought them rowdy, or drunken, because it was a glorious Sunday in the park, and there were hordes of parents and children sauntering along the paths, and so a handsome well-dressed couple, even doubled over as they were with mirth, only brought smiles to everyone's faces, and no censure at all. They viewed the lions, tigers, hippopotamus, and the seals, and then Gray saw Hannah shivering, for even though the sun was bright, the day was growing colder.

"Would you like to go to the Spa or the Dairy to get something warm to drink?" he asked.

"No, no," she insisted, tugging her gloves higher before she put one hand into her pocket and the other back on his arm, wishing she'd worn wool and not kid, for warmth, not fashion.

"You should have worn a muff," he murmured, taking her cold gloved hand in his. "May I serve as one?" he asked gently, chafing her hand before immediately putting it into his capacious coat pocket with his own.

"No one will notice, or care—if you don't," he said softly, encompassing her hand completely and squeezing her fingers gently. Warmed to her forehead by her blushes, she nodded, and they walked on.

She put their newfound silence down to their mutual sorrow when they left the monkey house, saddened by the stench as well as the desperate boredom they saw on the all-too-human-looking little wizened faces that peered out at them from behind the iron bars. Even the brightly colored birds in the birdhouse failed to raise their spirits, because to be indoors, however much warmer it was, seemed to be a cruel fate for both animals and humans this day.

But the open air didn't immediately pick up their spirits either. Gray grew grave as he stared at the great shaggy buffalo in their enclosure.

"Time was, and that was before my time," he said quietly, "they owned the West. They covered it like prairie grass, m' brother said. The older hands remember even more of them. Now, I don't guess you'll see any more of them at home than you do right here in New York City. It may be that they'll be altogether gone soon. I don't know if that's progress. Yet, who knows what covered over all this ground before concrete did?" he asked, expecting and receiving no answer but a sigh.

The bear pit cheered him somewhat, at least enough to make him scoff at it, although it made Hannah draw back a pace.

"Now, it's hardly worth putting these poor little critters behind bars," he said, looking down at a pacing black bear the exact size of several of Hannah's more creative nightmares. "No more than cubs compared to what you can find behind any tree back home.''

"Bragging again, little brother? Why, you'd be half-way up one of them trees if you saw one of these facing you back home. Pay him no mind, ma'am," an amused voice said from behind them. "He talks real big when he's got bars between him and b'ars."

"No, that ain't so!" a child's voice cried.

" 'Course it ain't," Gray said in his thickest drawl, turning, smiling, holding out one hand to the gentleman he greeted, while still not relinquishing Hannah's, hidden snug in his pocket.

The man he spoke to must be his brother, Hannah thought, it could be no other. They were of a height, where Gray was flaxen, this man was gold, Gray's eyes were blue and this man's gray, but the same smile played about the same well-cut mouths, and there was that in their every motion that told the tale as well as their fine-boned faces did. The red and gold-haired lady with Gray's brother was exquisitely lovely, Hannah thought with a pang, as beautiful as any woman she'd ever seen onstage, though her cheeks were wind, not paint-blushed, and her lovely mouth was innocent of everything but laughter. An assortment of children—four—Hannah counted, gazed up at their uncle as though they expected him to rise and hover in the air before them. A pink-cheeked nursery maid completed their party.

"Hannah," Gray said merrily, "this terrible liar is m' brother Josh, the beautiful lady he don't deserve is his wife, Lucy; the clever, handsome children are, in size places: Delia, Jarrell, Emma, and Luke Dylan. I'd like you all to meet Miz Hannah Roberts," he said, tightening his grip on her unseen hand as she tried to extricate it from his, so that she had to bow to them all, instead.

"Well met!" Josh Dylan said heartily. "This pack of demons wanted to ride the carousel, then see the animals, then they argued over which ones to see, then they all got hungry, and we were just on our way to get some hot chocolate into them before I dropped them all into the seal pool. Care to come with us?''

"To the seal pool?" Gray asked, gazing down to where his eldest niece was watching him, looking from him to Hannah worriedly. "Wonderful. Let's dunk this one first," he said eagerly, finally letting go of Hannah's hand so that he could use both hands to lift a delighted, squirming Delia Dylan up into the air as his other niece and nephews clamored for similar man-handling. Then, with them all tucked under his arms, or slung over his shoulder, he marched off in the direction of the seals as the children screeched with pleasure.

"Please don't think they're always such savages," Lucy Dylan said to Hannah, as they watched the children squealing as Gray pretended to try to throw them to the seals.

"But she knows Gray always is," Josh Dylan put in with a laugh.

Before she could think of how to answer, Hannah saw Gray finally divest himself of all the children before he quieted them by holding up one hand. "Joke's over. But if you don't cool off," he said, "I'm just going to up and leave. Now come along and show Miz Roberts how polite you can be when I'm not stirring you up."

They trotted behind him in a row, like ducklings, as he returned to Hannah's side. This time he took her hand in full view of everyone, and holding it hard, said, "Now, let's get us some hot chocolate before Miz Roberts gets pneumonia. She's not a rough critter like the rest of us."

Hardly knowing whether to be flattered or insulted, Hannah said nothing. But since he'd her hand again, she merely went along with him, as did the others. As she did, she wondered what she'd say to the elegant couple when they sat down to refreshments, and her teeth worried at her lower lip as she did. Gray had said that his brother had married an actress, but then, Gray told many amusing tall tales. Certainly this natural, unaffected lady could never have been one. Hannah fretted, thinking about Gray's brother and sister-in-law's reaction not only when they heard her occupation, but that she had one at all.

She knew very well that most well-bred people wouldn't expect a woman her age, especially one Gray had invited out for the day and then introduced to them and their children, to have an occupation at all. So she was vastly relieved when she discovered that Sunday in the park was a day for the Dylan children, since the adults gave all their attention over to them—before she began to wonder if that was only so today because they didn't want to speak with her, and had discovered a polite way to avoid doing so.

They sipped their hot beverages as the children talked about their day and their latest accomplishments.

"They're showing off," Gray ducked his head to say when Delia and Jarrell got into an argument over who'd gotten more brass rings on the carousel, "I've never brought them a lady to impress before."

Before she could answer that, Jarrell won the dispute by virtue of getting his little brother to swear to his claim. Delia instantly clouting him for it ended the entire interlude.

"Home," Josh Dylan said quietly, rising from his chair.

There wasn't a sound of protest as the children arose.

"He's a hanging judge, but an honest one, and they know it," Gray explained, his eyes twinkling.

"As you will be one day, scout," Josh Dylan said over his shoulder as he hoisted a weary toddler up to rest there, "then I'll take my pleasure stirring your children up so you can have a chance to be as popular as the plague when you try to restore order."

"We live just outside the Engineer's gate," Lucy Dylan told Hannah as they strolled out into an early winter's twilight. "Won't you come in to visit with us for a while? The children will be being bathed and getting ready for their dinner, and we can have a lovely chat."

"No, Lucy," Josh said decisively, as Hannah was about to demur, and though she had no intention of imposing, her heart sank at the finality in his voice.

"Gray'd find a way to stir up their baths, if I know him," Josh said with a wry smile. "As long as he's in the house, there'll be chaos. If you want to talk, let's all go to dinner, instead."

"I couldn't, I can't . . ." Hannah began to stammer.

"We don't mean to impose if you've other plans—but it would be such fun," Lucy said eagerly. Then Josh put in, "No place fancy, I promise. If I gave my wife a chance to change clothes again, it'd be a midnight supper, and I'm starving."

Hannah hesitated, and Gray asked quietly, "Have you another appointment? If not, would you come with us? I know it's short notice, but we did plan to have luncheon together, and we stayed out way beyond that. I can't take you home hungry. Say yes, please? After all, how else will we know which restaurant to recommend to Royal and Peggy?"

She nodded, but taking a deep breath and all her courage, said clearly, "But I must get home early. I've work tomorrow, you know."

"Hannah works in the theater," Gray said easily, as they strolled on with his brother and his family, and Hannah missed her step as she did her next heartbeat. He steadied her and then added, "I met her in Denver when she was on tour with the company of the fellow she works for, an entrepreneur, name of Kyle Harper."

"No!" cried Lucy Dylan, stopping short and wheeling about to stare at Hannah. Hannah had heard of people with violent antipathy to the theater, but having been brought up in it, had never come face-to-face with such censure before. She trembled and raised her chin. Lucy's face was flushed and her huge brown eyes were wide.

"Kyle!" she said, "I haven't seen him in ten years. Never say you work for him? But so did I! I was his 'Josephine' in *Pinafore,*" she said, before she added, with a tilted grin, as she motioned to her grinning husband, "and although I was never as good as this fellow says, I must say, I think I wasn't half-bad."

"And even the other half was pretty good—or anyhow, pretty," Gray said, and won himself an indignant frown, and then laughter for it.

They parted company, with promises to meet again at the restaurant in an hour. Gray helped Hannah into the carriage, and then amid much waving, they drove away.

"Josh is right, if you stop at your place now, you know you'll want to change something, and then something will have to be changed to match that, and so on, for quite a spell," he told Hannah as they rode out onto Fifth Avenue again. She had a moment's unease realizing how well he knew women, before he went on, "You look perfectly fine, amazingly fine, in fact, to me. So shall we ride right down to the restaurant, and wait for them there?"

It was so simple to say yes to him, she thought with sorrow. But her day wasn't over yet, so she looked up at him, smiled, and said, "Yes."

Hannah wasn't sure whether to be pleased or disappointed when they drew up in front of "ROEBLING'S FAMOUS BEER GARDENS". Because, she thought, as Gray leaped down from the driver's seat in order to come around and take her hand to help her alight, she was either being accepted as an equal or condescended to, and she couldn't be sure which it was. Yes, Gray had told her all of his sister-in-law's history on the way downtown, and Lucy Dylan had been in the theater. But only a few weeks, and only because she'd been an orphan with a lovely voice and no other way to make her way in the world. And she'd been in a Gilbert and Sullivan production, which was like playing in a symphony compared to what usually took place on the stage. And that, only until Josh had lured her away— or, the unspoken, possible implication in Gray's voice said—had saved her, by taking her as his wife.

Now, it was true that the Dylans couldn't invite another two persons to dinner on such short notice, and

Gray did seem to send the children into raptures that were hard to control, and which could be considered unseemly for strangers to see, Hannah thought. But it may have been that the Dylans simply didn't want her in their home. It was also true that they weren't dressed for Delmonico's or even the Rathskeller, or any other elegant dining house. But it didn't always take hours to change clothes, and it was still very early for dinner. And Beer Gardens on the Bowery were often patronized by the wealthy, as a lark—and Hannah could only hope she wasn't being so, too.

It was a clean, cheerful place. The waiter's aprons were spotlessly white, the sawdust on the scrubbed wooden floors was fresh, and the tables were all covered over by gaily checked red and white cloths. The dance floor was circular, enclosed by a wooden trellis, covered over by artificial vines. The band, all in German costume, were a merry lot of mustached fellows who played popular tunes for the customers to dance to. Those patrons Hannah could see were both young and old, and all nicely, if not elegantly attired. They could have been either millionaires, as the Dylan's were, out for a different sort of night on the town, or simply shop clerks out to enjoy themselves as best they could afford to do.

"The sausages here seem to be popular," Gray said nervously, watching Hannah's face, wondering why she'd suddenly frozen over. He saw her teeth fretting her lower lip, and noted the way her fingers clenched on the menu card. "Maybe we should've gone to 'monico's, after all," he said, thinking aloud. "Wouldn't have taken that long to change. But Josh likes to relax on the weekends, he says he gets enough of society all week at work. To tell the truth, I figured we'd check 'monico's out for Peggy and Royal, since everyone should go there once and the food's superb. But it always makes me uneasy, too. Well, a man can have money, but it takes a special sort of man to keep bragging on it, and that's the sort that loves 'monico's best.''

Even as Hannah assured him she'd no desire to go

to Delmonico's, Gray thought of what he'd just said and suppressed a groan. He couldn't have said worse, he decided. Since Lillian Russell had taken to displaying herself at Delmonicos, it had become as popular with theater folk as it was with the rich. Maybe Hannah had been looking forward to it: then he must have sounded like a man telling a hungry friend he wouldn't be able to have dinner with him because he couldn't take a bite—he'd such an upset stomach because of the rich lunch he'd had. Poorly done, he thought wretchedly, studying her downcast eyes with his own bleak blue stare.

"What? They've poisoned the sauerbraten, or did our waiter just die?" Josh Dylan asked as he came to their table. But as his lady seated herself and sent him a warning look, he added, suddenly oblivious to the nervous tension at the table, "Well now, then, let's see what Oscar has on the carte tonight. I'm starved."

They ordered, and Lucy Dylan told them merry tales of the children's misadventures in the bath. She'd just asked Hannah how Kyle was these days, and how he looked, when a tall, perspiring red-faced fellow with truly impressive waxed mustaches appeared at the side of their table, beaming at them, although his light blue eyes were anxious.

"Madam. Mister," he said in heavily accented English, "Goot eaffenink. My pleasure to haff you here vonce more. But. If you vuld be so goot, if you vuld be so kind as to sink for us as you did last time? Zah fellows in zah band unt I vuld be pleased unt proud."

"Wretch!" Lucy accused her husband as her color rose, "So that was what you were doing on the telephone before we left!"

"Ach! No, vee are not on zah line yet," the fellow protested. "But," he added with painstaking honesty, "if you vish to kall 'Henry's Gartens' down the street, zey vill give us zah message qvick."

Lucy laughed, and arose. "For such honesty," she said, with a little bow, "and such flattery, I will."

When the band stopped playing a two-step, Lucy took her place on the flower-decked dais with them.

She whispered to the leader, and in a moment, the opening strains of "Willow, Titwillow" from "The Mikado" was heard. And then Lucy sang. And then Hannah understood that Lucy had certainly been in the theater, and could still be there if she wished. For her voice was pure and true, and she felt all she sang, so her piquant face was alight with love as she did. She wore an apricot silk gown, and though she wasn't slim as a girl, she seemed to be, and her red-gold ringlets shone as did her eyes. The truth was she was every inch a performer, and so her loveliness was both an illusion and a reality, in the best tradition of the stage. The applause when she was done was tumultuous, and she bowed low as Kyle might do.

But when cries of "more! more!" were heard, she grew a mischievous grin. And without asking the band to strike up a note, she clasped her hands in front of her waist demurely, threw back her head, and simply sang. It was a sweet, sad, old country song, and needed no accompaniment but the sighs of her audience as they listened to her.

> "When I was single," she sang slowly and sweetly,
> "Dressed in silk so fine.
> Now I am married—
> Go ragged all the time,
> Lord! I wisht I was a single girl again!"

Her gown was a simple one, but it was of silk, and obviously stitched by the hand of a master. She wore citrine and topaz at her ears and her breast to match it, and her fingers sparkled with diamonds, even as her wrists were cooled with pearls. But as she sang, no one doubted she was the poor, desperate girl who grieved:

> "Five little children,
> Lying in their beds,
> All of them so hungry
> They can't lift up their heads,
> Oh! I wisht I was a single girl again!"

She sang a few more verses, repeated the introduction, and then fell still. The audience of diners erupted into applause, some of them with tears still wet on their cheeks. This time, when she arose from her bow, she grinned like a child, and pointing at her husband, said merrily, "Now, for a real treat, ladies and gentlemen, my husband will sing you a tune!"

Gray roared with laughter, and dragged Josh to his feet. Then he, with a rueful grin, strolled to the stage. He looked down at his wife and whispered, just loud enough for everyone to hear and laugh at, "Later, my dear," in the best tradition of stage villainy. Then he spoke to the fiddler, nodded, and sang the cowboy plaint: "Streets of Laredo," all the verses, in a true, deep voice, and soon had the audience swaying in accompaniment. But he refused all cries for encores when he was done. Instead, he put his hands on his lean hips and called, "Little brother?"

Gray arose. "Have no fear, friends," he said to the others in the restaurant, "the talent stops here. I can't sing a note, even in the bathtub on a Saturday night. But I purely love to dance! How about some of dem 'Golden Slippers?'" he asked the band.

When they struck the opening notes, he offered his hand to Hannah, and as she arose, he announced to them all, "Will you join us?" before he took her to the dance floor and proceeded to whirl her about in lively, graceful fashion, until her hair came down from its pins and she was breathless with delight and laughter.

"You're going to be limping for a week," his brother warned him, as they passed each other on the dance floor.

But before Hannah could insist on sitting down again, Gray answered, "Nope. There's a dry wind from the West tonight and that favors me, and my—ah, limb."

"Oh hush," Lucy cautioned her husband, as they spun away. "Forget about his leg, and just look into his eyes. Why, he'd dance with her tonight until he had to walk on stumps. Don't you remember why?" she asked, pouting.

"Of course, but we found better ways to do it," Josh said with a smile, pulling her closer, forgetting to be a protective older brother, just as she'd wished him to.

Although Lucy might have loved to chat with Hannah, they'd little chance to gossip or talk about the theater, the children, business, or anything else. For when the food wasn't arriving at the table with clockwork regularity each time they cleared a platter, the music had them spinning about the dance floor. When the night was done, the two couples stood in front of the restaurant as boys raced to bring them their carriages.

"Next time," Lucy Dylan promised Hannah. "Next time, we will talk and talk."

"Next time," Gray said to Hannah as they drove away. "Next time, I think I won't share you with anyone."

But though he said it with fervor, he said nothing else until he'd tied his team and taken her up the long stair to her rooms again. Even then he remained silent, and as she searched for something to say to explain why she couldn't invite him in, even though she knew she was no girl, and was a widow, to boot, with no chaperon, he raised a hand and placed it gently aside her cheek. It was such a wide, long-fingered hand, it covered over half her head, so he balanced it by placing his other hand on the other side. Then, holding her face lightly, he tilted her head up and brought his lips down to hers, and kissed her with exquisite expertise, thoroughness, and ease.

It was a long, searching kiss. He didn't touch her otherwise, although it seemed to her that she'd never been so completely loved. And flattered that he wanted only her lips as much as she felt protected by his hands, she leaned in to him, pressed against him, parted her lips beneath his, and let herself, for once, forget everything but his warm, wine-scented, all-encompassing kiss.

He kissed her deeply, willing himself to remember to forget the rest of her that was pressing so close to him, not so much as a fingertip away; the rest that was as delicious as her lips, until he lost himself completely in the kiss and could plan and plot no more.

It seemed to Hannah that he'd been almost casual when he'd begun, but he was breathing as rapidly as she was when he raised his mouth again.

He didn't move his lips far, only far enough to whisper, "May I see you next Sunday? So we can really scout out some places for Peggy and Royal this time?"

"Yes," she breathed.

"And may I take you with me to Delmonico's Sunday night so I can walk in with the most beautiful woman in New York City on my arm?" he asked, lowering his mouth to press a tiny suggestion of a kiss on the tip of her nose.

"Yes," she said, or nodded, she no longer knew.

"And will you come to dinner with me Wednesday? Because on Wednesday nights," he said, bringing his lips to her forehead, "I purely miss Wyoming most, I don't know why, but I do. Will you, please?" he asked, as his lips skimmed down her cheekbone.

"Yes," she said, closing her eyes and ears to all the inner voices shouting no!

He looked down at her closed eyes and parted lips and hesitated. But he knew three was his lucky number, and so didn't push it and ask what lay foremost on his mind and heart tonight. It was too soon anyway. He wouldn't be rash. He'd decided he needed at least a week to set the stage. Instead, he only gave her two more devouring kisses, and left, while he could, without suffering more of what was becoming real physical pain. It seemed, he thought, as he took the stairs down again, that dancing with her had only set his bad leg to aching. But kissing her caused him a riot of discomfort, and not only, he thought wryly as he reached the cold night air and tried to straighten his shoulders, in his heart.

The office behind the frosted-glass door with the golden letters proclaiming "Harper Enterprises, Inc."

had three rooms, which was impressive in such an expensive district. The front room was Hannah's domain, for it was there she sat and posed behind her desk in order to act the part of Mr. Harper's efficient secretary. The room beyond that had a desk, plump leather chairs, a couch, and a wide window overlooking Twelfth Street. It was there that Mr. Harper, surrounded by framed photographs of famous and poised performers enlivened by their inked—sometimes in a suspiciously similar hand—promises of eternal thanks and devotion to Mr. Harper, interviewed prospective investors. The third room, bare of everything but chairs and a table, was for lesser beings. It was the room where the work of the theater was done, and auditions could be held.

Kyle had come out of his room and had been saying something for sometime, Hannah realized.

"I do beg your pardon," she said with a guilty start, "I was just, ah, wondering when real rehearsals will begin."

"When I've a secure lease on the theater," Kyle said. Then gliding around her desk in an unnervingly sharklike fashion, she thought, he said silkily, "But I had thought you'd be pleased at the news. Now that we've got Anderson in our pocket, these pockets are a bit fatter, and you're to be supplanted by a real secretary next week. Is it that you've taken to your chores so well you dislike giving them up? You ought to have spoken up sooner, before I engaged Mr. Dobbs."

"Lord, Kyle," she said on a sigh, "I'm sorry, I was woolgathering. Monday mornings are so difficult."

"Especially after Sunday nights with Gray Dylan," Kyle commented, and though Hannah's shoulders rose, she didn't ask how he knew. He always knew. She braced herself.

"But just imagine a lifetime of Monday mornings," Kyle said with such sympathy that she winced, because he was very good at sympathy, and his fatherliness always made her feel guilty, as though she were in fact, some errant little girl.

"He's delightful company, sans doubt," Kyle said gently, "and very good to look upon, though I prefer my matinee idols tall and dark," he mused, his dark head held to the side. "But he is a millionaire, my child. And never forget, his brother was one in a million. Lightning seldom strikes twice," he intoned in doleful accents. When she looked up, his eyes were dark with sorrow as he added, "See to your heart, Hannah, my dear. I beg you. For I couldn't bear to see you suffer as so many others of our kind do, when they come up against the harsh realities of the harsh real world."

She knew those realities, and knew he was right, and the only thing that kept her from ducking her head like a schoolgirl was the one new thing she knew. And so she murmured something about being careful and not to worry, as she picked up her handbag and pelisse.

"Have a good lunch, don't hurry back, we haven't another audition until two," Kyle said with mournful consideration, taking one of her gloved hands and holding it tenderly, as though he was seeing her off to a funeral and not her luncheon.

But he frowned when he looked out his window to see her crossing the street. She walked with a quick, lively, determined step. Her heels tapped the cobbles smartly as she kept turning her head, scanning the doors for their numbered addresses. Because surely, 102 Second Avenue was not far. And so then the offices of Dr. Margaret Singer, as listed in her new book, *"Women, Her Diseases And Their Cure,"* was not distant. And so then, too, perhaps neither was some new possibility. Which was all she was after, after all, just the possibility of some new possibility.

Chapter Fourteen

The room smelled not so much clean as it did of the effort that had been made to purge it, as if of some great filth. The smell was literally blinding, because it was the first thing Hannah noted as she opened the door, and it made her close her eyes and want to close the door instantly again, with herself on the other side of it. For it was a reek of disinfectants: of camphor and sulfur, ammonia and turpentine, all overlaid with a hint of asafetida. But she walked in anyway. Because she had to. And at least it was not crowded.

Hannah sat gingerly at the edge of her chair in the waiting room, and tried to look unconcerned. She decided to pretend, to ease the moment for herself, that she was there to ask a question about her sister. That was it. Her poor married sister who was suffering from morning complaint and so was unable to come in herself. Just thinking that caused her hands to relax their death grip on the handle of her pocketbook, and she could feel the lines of tension at her mouth ease, too. Yes. She was there for poor Annabelle's sake. If she could act it, she could in some way believe it, if only until her turn came to see the doctor. In that way the other two women waiting—the plump matron on the couch and the thin, anxious girl on another chair—

would see that this casual looking stranger who had just come in was never there to seek a consultation for herself.

But the moment the inner door opened, and a white-smocked, white-hatted nurse stepped out and stared at her, Hannah's imaginary sister perished, along with all her courage.

"Yes?" the nurse asked, frowning and gazing at a paper she had in her hand, and then back to Hannah again.

"I . . . I wish to arrange for a consultation with Dr. Singer," Hannah blurted, and then nervously eyeing the two other women in the office, dropped her voice and added, "I have read her book, but require further consultation."

She held herself stiffly and hoped the doctor wouldn't be free for another year, and hoped she could be seen immediately, and prayed she looked correct enough to be seen anytime at all. She'd dressed with care, after bathing until her skin squeaked. She'd taken off her military-styled winter pelisse to reveal a severe blue walking dress, in the latest style, with its material swagged high in back to compensate for the loss of the bustle. For effect—since she'd excellent eyesight—she'd added a lorgnette on a chain about her neck, had arranged her hair in a high pouf at the top of her head, and set a pert blue hat sailing atop it. Kyle had flattered her for looking dashing, but she'd hoped to look like nothing more than a fashionable, respectable young matron. But few respectable matrons had such a flair for dressing, or moving, as she did, nor such shining hair, nor such alabaster skin and speaking eyes. The nurse stared at her. Whomever the young woman was, she thought, she was clearly, *someone*.

"Indeed?" she said, for though she was impressed, she was still a nurse and so could never let a patient have the upper hand. "And the name, please?"

"Nora Coates," Hannah said promptly, taking the name of the young consumptive in *Stolen Hearts* without blinking.

"If you would be so kind as to wait a moment,"

the nurse said, and after beckoning the nervous young woman to her and handing her a packet of medicines that seemed to make her more nervous, before bidding her good day, she disappeared within the consultation room again.

"I haven't very long today . . ." Hannah began to say when the nurse appeared again, but she was silenced by her saying, "Quite all right, Miss Coates, the doctor will see you now. Mrs. Gaynes," she added over her shoulder as the plump woman shifted in her seat, "your appointment is not until the half hour, and the doctor will see you then."

Hannah had chosen Dr. Margaret Singer because of her sex as well as her book. Surely, she'd thought last night, as she'd stared at the photograph of the stern, but clear-eyed older female that faced the title page, she'd be able to explain her problem to a woman far better than to a man. Especially since Dr. Singer's preface was all to do with the problems of womankind that men just did not or would not understand. The book was dedicated to her own sister, with the lines: "Whose faith in the physical redemption of women by correct living has been an inspiration to me." Hannah had never felt the least yearning to be a suffragette, if only because the problems of females in the real world had little to do with those of women in her theatrical world. But the preface had inspired her, and suffused with female-fellow feeling for the first time, she'd put down the book, jotted down the address, and decided to arrange for a consultation as soon as she could.

Her first sight of Dr. Singer, looking exactly as she had in that photograph except for wearing a white smock rather than a black dress, reassured Hannah, and gilded the doctor with that aura that usually comes with fame or reknown.

The doctor's office was spare, but a glance at the room beyond, with its examination table and glass cabinets full of awe-inspiring racks of bottles and syringes, caused Hannah to jerk her gaze back to the doctor again.

"Sit down Miss Coates," the doctor said at once,

"and please tell me your history and where your problem lies."

Hannah relaxed. She was always very good with rehearsed material. She sat in the chair facing the doctor.

"My health seems excellent. I am a widow of some years standing, Doctor," she said, as she smoothed her skirt, "but my husband abandoned me several years before that unhappy fact. He claimed he could not get me with child—or even successfully attempt to—because of a fault in me, which he did not specify. But as I am now contemplating matrimony again, you can understand I don't wish to have my new husband suffer the same disappointment."

There. She'd said it as discreetly as she could, but she'd said it. She waited for the doctor's words.

"I see," Dr. Singer said, pursing her lips and staring at Hannah with suddenly sharp, cold black eyes. "Did you consult a physician while you were married?"

"Ah, no, I was young," Hannah said distractedly, biting her lip, "and too embarrassed, you see. But my husband saw his physician, and his physician made the diagnosis. And it must be so, because," she said, lowering her eyes, "before he died, he'd fathered a child on another woman."

"I see," the doctor said, studying Hannah. "Your menses, are they regular?"

"Yes," Hannah answered.

"And normal in flow, or painful? Are there any irregularities?"

"Once in a great while they are irregular," Hannah said, blushing, because despite the need for it, this was not a thing a lady ever discussed with a stranger, "and at times, painful, but then I have a spoonful of Mrs. Pinkham's and am fine the next day."

"I see," the doctor said. "How, may I ask, do you pass your time now, my dear?"

"I am employed by Mr. K-Kenneth Howard, a theatrical impressario," Hannah said, catching herself in time. As the doctor only stared at her, she added hurriedly, "My family is in the theater, it is a world I know quite well."

The doctor began to nod wisely. Then she looked at Hannah and smiled. It was a wonderful, knowing, sympathetic smile that warmed Hannah's heart as it raised her spirits, and caused her to return it.

"I see. The theater. The bad hours. The poor diet. The lack of exercise and the lack of fresh air. Do you lace tightly, my dear?" the doctor asked.

"Why, yes, I suppose I do," Hannah said doubtfully, her smile fading, because she'd the sudden idea that things were going terribly wrong.

"No, no, and no!" the doctor said, rising and pacing the room like a small, agitated fury.

She reached to a rolled up chart on the white wall and pulled it down with a snap. She tapped the illustration of a corset with one hard finger. "Look!" she cried, and then tapped an adjacent drawing of a curled up spine shown through a transparent female body, with a welter of colorful internal organs clinging helter-skelter to it. "The evils of constriction! The womb, the bowel, and the stomach, crushed! Throw the corset on the fire, along with fashion's rule. Men do not consider that the flower they admire is being crushed so that they may admire it. Bloomers," she said sagely, "so that the internal organs can breathe free. Bate's waists, flannel union suits, and no more lacing. Lacing! There's your bar to conception, my child, there it is!"

"Ah, but . . .," Hannah said anxiously, "it's not only that I can't conceive, you see, it's . . ."

"Exercise," the doctor said, nodding her head. "Indian clubs and set-ups, daily, for at least an hour. Eight glasses of water a day. Purify the body, within and without. And deep breathing. D-eeeep breathing," she said, illustrating as she spoke it. "No more red meats and wines, they are poison. Water, digestive crackers, as Dr. Graham preached, keep the bowels regular and the pores open. That is the road to health. I will give you a regimen, and you may commence. Next time, we shall see your progress."

"Ah, but," Hannah said, closing her eyes so she couldn't see the doctor's expression as she said what she had to, "How will that help my prospective husband?"

"You'll be healthy and sound when you wed, and will be able to bear him a fine infant, if you follow my regimen," the doctor answered.

"My late husband said he couldn't . . . consummate our marriage, and I wanted to know if I am . . . am, put together right," Hannah blurted in an agony of embarrassment.

"When are you to be wed?" the doctor asked.

"Ah—soon. We haven't set a date," Hannah said, her face burning, her eyes on everything in the neat office but the doctor's face.

"I see," Doctor Singer said slowly, as she sat at her desk again. She made a few notes and handed a paper to Hannah. "There is the diet you must follow, and an exercise schedule. When you are wed, and if you still fail to conceive, return to me with your marriage certificate, and we will investigate further."

She paused, and then stared at Hannah with sadness in her eyes, "My dear," she said sternly as Hannah's heart began to race with shame, "I am a female doctor, and I suppose that's why you came to me. Female physicians have a certain reputation in some quarters . . . I know it, and deplore it. But I do not practice abortion or irregular medicine," she said as Hannah, white-faced, rose on shaking legs and tried to summon the courage to flee.

"I know women in the theater have special problems, but I cannot cater to them," the doctor said, rising to her feet as well, "for I firmly believe that chastity is womankind's greatest asset. A woman's delicacy of feeling, her lack of strong lusts and passions—these are our crowns of glory, not the lure of our external bodies, whatever some misguided and debased men may claim. But it is not men alone who are so unprincipled and misled. My child, chastity is the only road for those who are unwed—and for those in a state of holy matrimony: 'Maternity is the highest shrine of human life, to which true men bow in reverence'—as I say in my text. These pure and noble emotions are what make men revere us, and make us . . . dare I say it? Yes. They make us, in some ways, superior to men. Walk the right path, my dear,'' she said with as much compassion as censure, ''and you shall come to no harm.''

''Did you have a good lunch?'' Kyle asked curiously when Hannah returned.

''Not really,'' she said, to explain her ashen face and shaking hands. She didn't mention that her lunchtime had cost her five dollars—as much as they said it cost two people to dine at Delmonico's—although she hadn't dined at all, and doubted she'd ever be able to eat again.

But the food at the Savarin was so delicious on Wednesday night that she ate enough to match Gray as he devoured his dinner. She could, because she'd left off lacing. And because, as he said, there was something about food that eased homesickness. For just as he'd said, there was also something about Wednesday nights, something that increased homesickness. And that was something she'd suffered from all her life. Except that it seemed she'd found a cure, because he banished all sorrow from her heart all through dinner, and every time she looked at him.

''So we have a theater now, or shall, by the weekend,'' she explained, as they sipped their coffee. ''It's the Evergreen, on Twenty-fourth, between Sixth and Seventh, near Proctor's and not far from Daly's. We've signed some from the old troupe—Lester Claxton is back with us, after his performance in Aspen, Kyle resolved to keep him as our centerpiece—if we can keep him from celebrating after the performance as he did then,'' she sighed. And then brightened and said, ''And Polly Jenkins—remember little Polly? She's growing quickly enough for us to to able to use her as a junior ingenue. We're still looking for a lead female, Titania, after all, has retired.''

They grinned at each other. But then she lowered

her gaze, and began to draw a complex pattern of circles in the slush that was all that remained of her pudding in the bottom of its dessert dish.

"Ah, Kyle has said, and I have thought . . . I might wish to try to act again," she said, and looked up to him with every bit of her doubt and fear in her eyes, before she glanced down again quickly. Because it didn't matter what he thought, after all, it was her life and she had to get on with it. But she felt hollow now despite all she'd eaten, as she waited for his reaction.

"I think that's a wonderful idea," he said slowly. "I think you could be a fine actress, and I think you have to prove it to yourself, if no one else. I know a man, or a woman, can do a lot of dumb things to prove they're grow-up—who knows that better than me?" he asked, chuckling. "But sometimes, living with doubt can be worse. If you see it as a challenge, it'll always be there, unless you try it. Then, win or lose, at least you know you had the courage to try."

It was exactly the answer she'd wanted of him, so it was odd that she had to pick up her coffee cup and swallow her hurt before she could speak again. It was just as well, she thought, as she swallowed past the lump in her throat, that he'd no plans for her that an acting career would get in the way of—like marriage—after all. Ah, but it was wickedly foolish to be hurt, she reminded herself, because although she might be able to do the one thing she'd mentioned, she could never perform the other that he hadn't, even if he had wanted it of her.

"But," Gray said very quietly, "knowing you're capable of doing something doesn't necessarily mean you have to do it forever. I mean, I proved I could ride that horse, but I didn't stay on it the rest of my life, did I?"

The relief that flooded through her actually weakened her for a second. Then she smiled at him. "No. Yes. Oh, I mean I agree," she said, hoping he understood her garbled answer, but from the way he smiled back at her, he knew.

It was early evening when they finished eating, and

it seemed not only too early, but too cold to leave him standing in her hall when he took her home. She'd been on her own for months, but she'd never had a man in her rooms, and so her murmured invitation, "If you'd like to come in for a few moments . . . Not longer, I'm afraid, because of my landlady. I haven't anything to offer you but conversation, but if you'd like to chat . . . I don't usually, but . . .," was as much an attempt to explain it to herself as it was to him, and equally unsuccessful. Because the moment he stepped over her threshold and closed the door, she panicked.

"Hold on!" he said as he saw her eyes widen as she stepped back. "Now, do you, or don't you want me here?"

"I don't know," she said quickly, seeing how out of place he looked in her home. He wore buff and brown tonight, and his tanned face and wide shoulders cramped her parlor and crowded in on her heart. "That is to say," she said, as she continued to edge away, "I want you here, of course. I like to talk with you and it's early yet. And I'm a widow and not an ingenue. But I know even a widow oughtn't to live alone, and I must. Still, you oughtn't to be here, because I live alone. I don't entertain men, and—oh, Gray, I don't want you to think I do, because I don't."

He did the very thing she'd feared, but it made her feel much better. He stepped closer and took her in his arms. Then he simply held her.

"I know you don't entertain men," he said, with laughter in his voice that she could feel shaking in his chest. "Though if you're thinking of going on the stage, I think you'd better reconsider that—no sense having only women in your audience, is there? No, listen. I know. It's all right, I understand. I'll leave now, though Lord knows I don't want to, but it's the long run I'm thinking of. There's no point in making you uncomfortable now. All right?"

He looked down to see her response, as she looked up to nod her head, so it was only natural that their lips should meet. Which must have been how it happened, she thought, because she couldn't think who'd started it. It was how it happened, he decided, because he hadn't meant to make it worse for her, no matter how good it felt to him. But he was the one who ached when he had the sense to pull away, at last. Because he was the one who'd discovered she wore no corset tonight, and the thought of that made him realize, in some small corner of his mind not occupied with delighted lust, that if he didn't leave now, he mightn't be able to do so, gracefully at least, later on.

She obviously wasn't willing to take him to her bed now, but he thought he might be able to seduce her. He knew how she felt about him, although she'd never said it, he could feel it, literally, and she was no virgin child. But he disliked beginning their life together with a seduction. He wanted wholehearted cooperation now, and later. She was his lady, he no longer doubted it, and he wanted her to know it in every way.

She was beautiful and clever, educated and good— but none of that mattered so much as the fact that he felt right with her, and displaced without her. He could have a wife with money, family, and position—before he'd met her, he amended. Now he could have no other but her. He only regretted that she'd a bad marriage before they met, although if she hadn't, he reasoned, they wouldn't have met at all, and she wouldn't be just who she was. And she was perfect for him as she was.

He even liked what most frustrated him, her stubborn purity. She'd no chaperon, she worked in the theater, and she was a widow, but despite all that evidence to the contrary, he knew, to his growing bodily discomfort and pride in her, that she was prim as she was proper. He doubted she'd had a lover since that terrible marriage that had so put her off men. But he could remedy that—at the proper time, in his marriage bed. Because she also had the fire: it was banked, but it was there. And so he'd resolved to treat her just as he might any respectable virgin girl, and take her to bed only after he'd taken her promise to marry him. And he was equally resolved to be sure of her answer before he asked.

Now he was the one who backed away.

''Sunday night,'' he said slowly, as he stepped back
to the door, his eyes glowing. ''Dress real fine, please,
Miz Roberts, because we're meeting Josh and Lucy at
'monico's and I want every man there to die of pure
envy of me. Well, come to think of it,'' he said, as he
opened the door. ''It don't matter how you dress then,
does it?''

He stepped out into the hallway, grinning as he
thought of what he'd say to her after Josh and Lucy
left them alone, and what he planned to give her that
was burning a sizable diamond-shaped hole in his vest
pocket since he'd bought it yesterday. He hummed to
himself as he took the steps down, wondering if he'd
have to leave her early come Sunday night, or if they'd
find a cure for the miseries of Monday mornings together, as they had for Wednesday nights.

Hannah sank to her favorite chair and groped for the
book she'd left there. There was an address in it she'd
meant to visit before the month was out. Now she
knew it would have to be much sooner than that.

She hadn't understood the book at all, it was all to
do with surgery and had illustrations of appliances that
terrified her simply looking at them. But it was, after
all, a medical text and not for laypersons, and one
written by a physician who was a professor and authority on woman's diseases at a New York hospital.
She'd bought it because all the simpler books had failed
her. But it did, as well. She'd only skimmed it, realizing she'd wasted her money, until a note at the back
caught her attention. Because it seemed that the reknowned Dr. Lewis, when he was not operating, writing, or lecturing, was pleased to give consultations at
his office.

The fact that Dr. Lewis's offices were at the hospital
made things easier for Hannah. Hospitals had telephones, so she could go to a bank and call for an
appointment before taking a horsecar so far uptown on
Friday afternoon. When she marched into the great
echoing reception hall of the hospital, she could ignore the reek of ether and disinfectant by pretending

to be a woman on a mission of mercy, visiting anyone there, because only the desperate were sent to hospitals. With the right expression of kind concern on her face, no one would imagine her a patient come to see a doctor dealing in women's complaints. Then she would walk down a hall to the left until she came to the office with his name on it, as she'd been instructed to do on the telephone, and nip inside before anyone saw her doing so.

She promptly gave the receptionist her name: Mrs. Eva MacDowell, and perched on the edge of her chair for a half hour listening to her heartbeat, until they called her name three times and she remembered who she was supposed to be. She was shown into a cold green room with a chair, an examining table that looked very like the machine in the dungeon that was used to get prisoners to confess in *The Count of Monte Cristo,* and a folding screen to the rear of the room. She stood erect and held her pocketbook in front of her like a lifeline until the door opened. A harsh-faced woman in white came in, and Hannah found herself feeling as thwarted as she was relieved, because she'd been prepared to meet her doctor.

The woman read her a litany of intimate questions to do with her health, relations with the opposite sex, and history of procreation. Hannah would have bolted from the room if she hadn't been asked in such bored tones, the woman checking each question off and entering her answers in the notebook as she did so.

"Now, Mrs. MacDowell," the woman said when she was done, "go behind the screen, and take off everything, if you please. Your dress, your chemise, your petticoat," she said, enumerating undergarments in a bored singsong, "your bust bodice, corset cover, corset, drawers, garters, and stockings. Everything. Put on the gray gown you find in there, and button it at the back. You may leave on your shoes," she added generously, as she left the room.

Hannah's heart was as cold as her fingers as she stood in the center of the room and tried to control her breathing. It seemed all roads had led to this, as she'd always feared they might—to finding herself alone in a cold, strange room in a hospital: the place for the mismade or ill-used, unfortunates of nature and fate in a place of last resort. No one she knew had ever been in a hospital; people with families didn't go to them, those with any choice didn't either. Although she was only in an office in a hospital, she still didn't know if she would stay. She didn't know how she could bear to appear naked before a strange man. She'd never appeared so before her husband until the last days of their brief marriage, and even then, it had been in the dark. She began to tremble, she'd never been so cold.

But then she thought of the warm bright color of a certain crop of hair, and the vivid summer sky blue of a particular pair of eyes, and the vision warmed her somewhat. And she knew that if she ever hoped to dwell upon those things again, she must do what she'd been told to do. For there was no other way that she could hope to discover what her problem was and if it were solvable. Surely, a few moments of shame and embarrassment, no matter how every sensibility shrank from them, were worth suffering for the possibility of a bright future.

She walked behind the screen, took off all her clothing, and put on the gray smock. But when the doctor entered the room and she came out to meet him, she was shaking so badly she thought he must think she suffered from St. Vitus's dance.

The gentleman in the white coat was a balding, unremarkable looking man with spectacles and a full beard. It heartened Hannah somewhat to realize that she wouldn't recognize him if she ever met him again, outside of this place. The strong-featured woman entered the room after him, and stood with her back against the door, watching them.

"Mrs. MacDowell," he said, barely glancing at her as he gestured to the examining table, "if you would, please."

She sat up on the table and squeezed her eyes shut, and kept them so as he asked her to undo her buttons and lie down. But she was trembling too hard to do it.

She couldn't seem to stop shaking even long enough to get into the position he indicated, and she felt hot tears on her cold cheeks as she realized she could not because her body was clenched as tightly as her fists were.

"Just relax, can you relax?" the doctor said as he tried to get her to lower her shoulders to the cold table.

"I c-can-cannot seem to, just yet," she said in a broken voice. "I'm terribly sorry, if you could but wait, I could try, I cannot seem to help it," she explained with embarrassment as she kept shuddering despite all her attempts to calm herself.

"No need," he said, wheeling about and stepping away from her. "The examination would be both painful and unproductive, as things are. No. Return next week, we shall get an operating theater, and use ether in order to perform the examination. It should be interesting, at that. Yes, make a note to inform the students, Mrs. Bailey," he remarked to the harsh-faced woman, "next Tuesday at ten, on regular morning rounds. It ought to be instructive for them. Is it a case of hysteria such as the Viennese journals are now so fond of reporting?" he asked with a slight sneer. "Or a simple imperforate hymen? Or perhaps," he mused, "a truly interesting anomaly?"

"The students?" Hannah asked, coming out of her well of shame and sitting bolt upright. "There will be students present?"

"Medical students, yes. Why not?" the doctor said, adjusting his spectacles as though noticing her for the first time as he gazed at her in surprise. "You will not be bothered by them, I assure you, since you will be asleep, for hours. If you have something correctable, we shall correct it then and there. If not, you will know of it when you wake. But," he added, with the first smile she'd seen from him, "be assured, Mrs. MacDowell, in any event you will be instructive. A very interesting case."

Hannah worked until past sundown on Saturday, which Kyle knew she didn't need to do. But her face was so set with determination, he wisely decided to let the matter be, after a simple inquiry as to her health and state of mind won him a: "Fine, and just fine, thank you. It is not a thing I wish to discuss further, thank you, Kyle; did you want this letter to go to 'Mr. Peacock and Son,' or 'sons'?"

But when he left the room, she went to work again on the other letter she'd been composing since she'd left the doctor's office the day before.

She couldn't submit to surgery with that cold specimen-seeking doctor, anymore than she would allow herself to be viewed, naked and defenseless, before a horde of his students. She knew no women who'd ever submitted to such indignities, or none that would admit they had. Surgery was a last resort for any complaint, since it was so often just that—a last attempt before the end. And for what? What man would want her after they were done—with whatever it was they decided to do? What would she be left with? For that matter, what did she have? Perhaps it was better, after all, not to know and eternally hope, than to know there was no hope.

In any case, if she knew nothing else, she knew she could do no more, and that Gray Dylan deserved more.

There were some things that were simply never meant to be. Her major fault, she decided, had been in seeking what she ought to have known she could not have. Her lesser faults were still correctable. That, she was determined to do.

When she was finally done with the letter late that night, in her own rooms, it was a masterpiece of its kind. She sat, ankle-high in a welter of her discarded, crushed, and torn previous efforts as she transcribed her final version. It spoke from her heart, but it spoke most correctly.

"My dear Gray," she wrote in her finest script, using bits and pieces garnered from frequent references to a copy of *Hill's Manual of Social and Business Forms*, under the Chapter: "Love Letters," subheading: "Unfavorable Replies," so as to coat her own message.

''While I am grateful to you for your very kind invitation to dine with you tonight, I find I am unable, after all, to avail myself of your generous invitation. Nor do I believe I shall be able to do so in the future. I am fully sensible of your most excellent qualities and the compliment paid to me. But there are some things that are not meant to be, however much we should like them to be. Please do find it in your heart to forgive me.

''With the wish that you may soon meet with a companion in every way more able to ensure your happiness, I remain, Your friend and well-wisher. Hannah Roberts.''

The letter would end it, but it would spare his feelings. And that, after all, Hannah thought as she signed it, was really the most important part. For none of it was his fault. He might be insulted, or merely annoyed at her abrupt dismissal. But he was resilient and would recover soon enough. It mightn't even seem such a heavy blow to him, she thought suddenly, fumbling for a new handkerchief.

After all, his newfound gallantry, the way he'd seemed to cease his campaign of seduction, might have even been a new form of seduction. She might have imagined all his other intentions, as he might have wanted her to do. Now she wondered if he'd even be more than peeved at her dismissal of him. Oh, he was interested in her, of course she knew that. But she'd never stopped wondering if the tug of commonality between them seemed as strong to him as the pull of sensuality that she also felt. She might behave properly, but she had grown up in the theater. As for that, as much as all the rest, she was hardly the best he could do for himself, and she knew it. Maybe he did, too.

She blew her nose hard, and sighed. Gray Dylan was handsome and clever, rich and well connected. He wouldn't grieve long, if he grieved at all. Because for all their fellow feeling and even the desire, men, after all, did not take such things as seriously as

women did. And wealthy, handsome, popular gentlemen, she reminded herself sharply, as she felt tears
trickling down her face yet again, perhaps never did
feel the same things that unprotected women did.

Whatever he felt, she decided, snuffling, as she put
out the light, and whatever he'd wanted, she could give
him nothing but sisterly friendship, and that, she would
swear, was the last thing he wanted of her. After all,
she thought fairly, although it was one of the many
things she wanted to offer him, it was the least, if not
the last thing she wanted to give him, too.

No matter, she thought as she finally lay down in
her bed and prepared to sleep, she'd find a messenger
service that worked on the Sabbath and pay their ex-
orbitant price for delivery. A telegram was too chilly
a way to end things, and then too, they spoke of death
and disaster before they were even opened. No, it
would cost her dear, but Gray would get the note, and
he'd get the message. He'd either be angry at her or
disappointed in her, and then he'd soon replace her
with someone more compliant in any case, and there
was an end to it. And she would have gotten to sleep
much sooner if her pillow wasn't so wet.

It was two in the afternoon by the time Hannah
found a suitable messenger service, and it took another hour to persuade herself that the money she'd
save by delivering it herself wasn't half so expensive
as the risk she ran of running into him, literally, if she
did. But at last it was done, and she was assured the
message would be delivered before dinnertime.

It had grown cooler, if not yet cold enough for December, and so she passed the afternoon tending to
her chores at home. She washed some clothes, and
cleaned her rooms, and finally, since she felt her rooms
stifling, she decided to go for a Sunday stroll. She
headed home as evening shadows began to make the
Elevated's shadow creep up the sides of the buildings
to the west of it. Although she was in no hurry to be
home again, she didn't pause to go to dinner, as she
didn't find herself very hungry.

The human mind was very odd, she thought, as she

came to her own doorway again. For she'd half hoped
to see his carriage waiting there as she turned the corner. No, it was the human heart that was so strange,
she decided as she came into her rooms after finding
that he'd left no calling card either, because she discovered herself as shaken and dismayed at the obvious
success of her letter as she'd been at the idea of its
failure.

She sat in her darkening parlor and contemplated it,
and wished she'd stop weeping as much as she wished
she'd stop waiting for the sound of her landlady tapping on her door to announce a visitor. Because she
began to understand that so long as it remained Sunday, she would suffer so. She would fantasize about
his coming despite all she'd written, until the day was
done. At eight in the night, she realized, she'd be expecting him to come in haste, angry and urgent, demanding to know her real reason for breaking their
appointment. At ten, she might still be sitting here,
waiting to hear he'd appeared downstairs, hearty and
happy-go-lucky, to jolly her out of her sullens and coax
her to have dinner with him as she'd originally promised, despite whatever foolish little female crochets
had possessed her. And cursing her own imagination,
she realized that she'd even be awaiting his call at
eleven, or midnight, when he might come disheveled
and drunken, boozily asking for a more lucid explanation for her refusal.

No, she wouldn't be free until the sun rose again,
she decided. And so she settled into her chair for a
long night's wait to kill her expectations, and end all
her fantasies.

That was why she was both surprised and not very
surprised to hear light hurrying footsteps on her stair,
followed by a knock on her door, only a few minutes
later. But it wasn't her landlady who was standing there
when she opened it.

Nor did he look disheveled, amused, drunk, or angry. He was dressed in impeccable evening clothes,
and he'd his cape thrown over his arm. His face bore
an expression of bewilderment.

"What have I done?" Gray asked the moment she opened the door, his eyes searching hers. "Lord, Hannah, what in the world did I do?"

And then she knew it was worse than anything she'd fantasized. Because as she gazed into his eyes and saw the hurt and confusion there, she knew there was some pain and embarrassment she'd no right to run away from. And so she had to tell him no less than the truth.

Chapter Fifteen

"I think," Hannah said softly, staring at the visitor who stood in her doorway, "that you'd better come in. That is to say," she added, recovering from her surprise enough to note his surprise, "would you like to come in, Gray?"

"No, actually I wanted you to come out—with me, tonight. Until I got this note," he said, holding it out for her to see, as though he still thought she might deny writing it. That was only one of the wild fancies that had occurred to him as he'd raced his horses downtown. But he'd mostly thought that it might have been something he said, or someone had said about him. Even then, it didn't make sense.

Now he saw she'd been sitting in the dark, and yet even the light from the hallway was enough to show him she'd been crying. He'd a sudden urge to take her into his arms to comfort her, but suppressed it so violently his hands clenched to fists at his sides, because at the same time he wanted to shake her for believing the worst of him, however it had come about. He wasn't perfect, he mightn't even be good enough for her, and he knew it. But he'd never done anything to cause her pain, nor would he. He stood on her doorsill and waited because he no longer knew what else to do.

"I owe you an explanation," she said, her chin coming up. "I was a coward before—all this time before. It's nothing you've said or done. It's something I shouldn't have done, or at least, it's something I should have said. Please come in," she said quietly, "it's not a thing I can explain in a doorway."

He followed her into the parlor and waited while she lit the lamps, and then sat in a chair she indicated, his cloak still in his hands, his hands still clenched hard, especially when he saw traces of the ravages of her sorrow on her face. She looked almost as bad as he felt, and when he realized that swollen eyes and tear-stained cheeks didn't make her any less desirable to him, he felt even worse. Because now he knew he was in for it, this was the one woman he wanted, all right, and she had more power over him than he'd known he'd given her. Still, he didn't mind that half so much as the pain he felt at seeing her distress, and if he couldn't console her, he didn't know what he would do.

She sat opposite him, folded her hands in her lap, and gazed at him. One of the things about her that delighted him was the air of high drama that clung to her: how she so often seemed to be unconsciously enacting life as though it were a part she was playing. He only realized that now because that aura of excitement and theater was absent tonight. She was still beautiful, nothing could change that. But she was sad and composed, and somehow diminished, as he'd never seen her.

"Gray," she said at last, "I'll try to explain as simply as I can. When we met, I'd no intention of walking out with you, remember? I was, I suppose, more or less maneuvered into it."

"And you're angry about that now?" he asked, amazed.

"No, no," she said at once. "No. If anything, I'm angry at myself for it. You see, I oughtn't to have gone on seeing you, no matter how pleasant I found it. I was married once, you know, and it was dreadful, and I never intended to become involved with a man again. I know,'' she said in a rush, suddenly fearful she'd presumed too much, or at least fearful that she'd let him know she had, ''that you've never asked for more, but lately we've become so much more . . . that is to say it seemed to me, lately, that you—that I—that . . .''

''You're right,'' he said, cutting her off, ''I was—I am going to ask you to marry me.''

All the color left her already pale face.

''Oh Gray,'' she said in tones too truly tragic to be theatrical. ''Oh Gray,'' she said, and put her face into her hands.

He rose and came to her side, and kneeling by her chair, put a hand gently to her hair.

''Here,'' he said, and somehow, although she was waving him off, she found herself weeping into his collar, and then she was in his arms as he picked her up for a moment, before he sat down with her on his lap.

''Yeah. Better,'' he said, holding her close as she turned her head into his shirt, ''because now you don't have to look at me. Sometimes you can say more that way. But at least I can hold you as you do. Why?'' he whispered into her ear, causing her to shiver as well as weep, ''Why should you cry, honey? If you don't want me, you can just tell me. But I suspect you do want me; I'm not that high on myself that I can't see when someone doesn't care for me. We understand each other fairly well, Hannah,'' he said as he smoothed some of her soft storm cloud of hair back from his lips. ''That's why I want to marry you. That, and about three hundred other reasons,'' he added, smiling as he stroked her hair.

She stopped weeping.

''You can't,'' she said, moving her head to the side so that she couldn't see him even if her eyes were open; although she took comfort from him, for he'd his cheek against her hair, and she'd her hand on his heart.

''My husband left me because there's something

wrong with me," she said in a small, flat voice, and could feel his body tighten beneath her. "I don't know what it is," she went on, "I wish I did. I've tried. Just look at all my books," she added, and felt his head move slightly as he gazed at the shelves of medical books she gestured toward.

"It was embarrassing to buy them. How the clerks stare at you!" she said on a shaky laugh. "But I could do it because I always pretended they were for my mother. Not that I could tell her," she said on a sniff. "Ah well, but you met my father, can you imagine me confiding in him? Especially such a thing? I don't know if he'd be amused, amazed, or ashamed, or . . . Anyway," she said in a sadder voice, "I'm not even that close with Mother, she'd never keep a thing from him, even if I'd dared to speak of it to her. The books didn't tell me anything," she went on. "I did write to a doctor who wrote one of them years ago, and he wrote back and said an unmarried female oughtn't to be concerned with such things. I tried not to be."

She hesitated, before she said, "But after I met you, since I've been home, I've been to see two doctors. One thought I was some immoral creature from the theater, after Lord knows what sort of profane advice. That wasn't so bad as yesterday . . . the other doctor, just yesterday told me . . ." she paused, and he could feel her swallow before she said, ". . . he said I was too tense to examine and that I should come back next week, and he'd give me ether and have all his students watch. Oh, Gray, for all I wanted to know, I could not!"

She was trembling as he tried to soothe her by murmuring that of course, she should not. But his mind was working feverishly.

"Just what is it that you need to know?" he finally asked, and then realizing how foolish that sounded—because if she knew she wouldn't need to know—he struggled to find a way to phrase his question so as not to embarrass her, but so that he might understand. It was odd, he thought, as he reveled in the feel of her as she lay curled so close to him, that a man could bed a woman, even a lady, without embarrassment, but that it was so damned hard to talk about the same thing with one. She spoke before he could rephrase his question.

"Our marriage was never consummated, John said," she whispered into his shoulder. "He said it was because there's something wrong with me. He said I'm imperfect, and his doctor said so, too. He must have been right, because after he left me, he fathered a child on another woman. I know," she said on a muffled wail, "because I traveled to Philadelphia for his funeral and saw the boy. It was his image, Gray, there's no doubt of it."

"Why couldn't the marriage be consummated?" Gray persisted, uninterested in the child. "Why did he say he couldn't?"

"He said . . . he said I wasn't made right, that's all he said," she answered.

After a moment of silence, as he wondered what he could ask next, she added, in such a small voice that he held his breath so that he could hear her, close as she was to him, "From the outside I look normal. I know that. But the inside . . . I looked with a mirror once, and I don't know. How should I know?"

"Sure, that's right," he said, soothing her, before he realized, for the first time, that it was. It was a natural fact that a man's private parts weren't all that private. A woman's might well be a mystery to her if she was a lady. It was a thought that had never occurred to him before.

They sat very still, her sobs subsiding, his hand moving slowly over her back and her hair as he thought.

"When did it go wrong?" he asked at last.

"Ah, when he couldn't," she said, and then remembering, she fell still, fighting to find a way to say it as a lady should, or at least so that she wouldn't die of shame as she did.

"Just tell me about the first time," he said, "however you can."

It was a thing she'd never mentioned to any other

woman. It was a thing she'd never said to a doctor. But here, close in the arms of the one man she'd have for her life, if she could, she somehow found the courage, if not all the words, to try to explain. But she kept her head turned from him.

"It was our wedding night, of course," she said, and he nodded, thinking with a grin, despite all his confusion, that she was one of the few women he'd ever wanted to bed who would have said "of course" about that. "We went to a hotel, here in New York: The *Amsterdam*. Not the best hotel," she said in more normal tones, "but a nice one, and one we could afford. John had arranged for a bottle of champagne to be brought to our room, and we raised a toast to the future. And then, after he'd another glass, he said, 'Guess we'd better turn in, if we want to get an early start tomorrow.' He'd saved up and we were going to Niagara Falls," she said, pleased to find a thing she could talk about that didn't shock her, and thinking his sigh was one of relief because she'd begun speaking of it.

"So I went into the bath to dress for bed, and then John did. And then," she said, remembering, "he had another glass of champagne and came to bed. But after a few minutes, he got up again and had another. And then, after a time," she said, her voice growing lower, "he said it wasn't any use. I was probably too tired, and good night.

"In the next two weeks, he tried and tried. It wasn't until a week later that he said he thought there might be something wrong with me. He stayed a few weeks more, but then he left. I would have left him," she said, "because he'd begun to drink too much, and he—he struck me that last time he tried."

Gray tensed before he realized how futile it was to want to kill a dead man. He thought about what she'd said, and everything she hadn't, and then he sighed again.

"That doesn't tell me much. Hannah, honey, I know you're a lady. But can't you try to forget that for a second? Just for a second? It's important, if you want me to understand. I . . . I don't mean you have to tell me everything . . . damn it! Yes I do. Sorry. Sorry for cursing," he murmured. "But what happened whenever he 'tried'? Can you bring yourself to tell me?"

It was harder than trying to lay back on the doctor's icy examining table, although she lay so comfortably in Gray's arms, but at last she managed to whisper, "He'd push and prod, and then he'd get up and walk around the room or have another drink. Sometimes it hurt and sometimes it didn't, but after a while it was so painful, I wanted to weep, even if it didn't hurt. Do you understand?"

He murmured something insubstantial, and then asked, "Listen. I don't know how to say it politely, but ah—you mean to say . . ."

"I mean to say he never came into me," she said.

"And he could?"

Her head came up. "Why shouldn't he?" she asked.

"I mean," he said with as much impatience as concern for his language, even as he damned the fact that ladies and men couldn't speak the same language about the act of love. "I mean, he was ready?"

She gazed at him in puzzlement.

"You didn't look?" he asked.

"It was always dark," she said, the way she'd said "of course" before, "and, and he was always in his nightshirt," she added defensively, color returning swiftly to her cheeks, as she lowered her eyes from his expression of shock.

But he seldom made love to women with his clothes on, unless they insisted, or there wasn't time—and had forgotten, if he'd ever known it, that most respectable people did all the time. And some very unrespectable ones, too, he thought, remembering the cribs and houses that catered to the poorest drifters back home, where they said a man could leave his hat on, along with everything else, so long as he at least took off his spurs before he hit the bed. It was a tale he wished he could share with Hannah, because he could imagine her laughter at hearing it. That was the problem, and the joy of her. She was proper, but not prim; he'd

swear that once he knew her intimately, there'd be little he couldn't get her to say or do. Because although
he knew her notions of propriety, he thought he knew
her very well, too. It was so damned important to her
to be respectable, to be like the world she'd envied for
so long. But once she was sure of herself and her man,
he knew she'd want to please him and herself and think
the world well lost for love—especially as it was a
world she hadn't been brought up to.

But there were things they couldn't discuss simply
because they hadn't done them yet. Now he wondered
if they ever would. His arms tightened around her. He
held her, but couldn't have her; he knew he'd never
been closer to losing her no matter how close they
were now. And he couldn't bear the thought of giving
her up.

"Then he just up and left?" he said, for something
to say as he thought furiously.

"I helped him pack," she said. "I wanted nothing
of his, nothing. Why, I even threw his bottles of Dr.
Pierce's Peruvian Elixer and Dr. Chase's Celebrated
Syrup and all the rest into the suitcase so hard they
almost broke, and just thinking of the mess it would
make if it mixed in with all his bottles of macassar oil
made me laugh for the first time since we'd been married. You don't use macassar oil," she remarked suddenly and shyly, gazing at the overlong hair at his nape,
glad to forget the past in order to remember how his
hair always felt as clean and soft as it looked, not slick
or caked with dried oil as was other gentlemen's.

"Lilac tonic does for me," he said absently. But
then, his cheek against her hair, he mused aloud, "and
you always smell like flowers and rain."

As she turned her head to smile, he looked down to
her, and their lips were so close it seemed only natural
that they touch. It was simply a meeting of mouths,
but it was never that simple with them. But the intense
joy of it, which was as startling and considerable to
both of them as it always was, lasted only a moment.
Because he pulled back, thinking, through the haze of
pleasure, that it was wrong to take advantage of her

now—as she pulled away despite, or because of the ecstasy of it, not so much because of the morality of it, but because it was wrong to offer what she couldn't give.

Yet, if she gave herself to him, she thought in the next moment, staring at his lips still damp from her own, she'd know: once and for all, she'd know, wouldn't she? He, of all people on earth, would tell her the truth of her condition when he discovered it, wouldn't he? How could it be wrong if it was as much a medical investigation as an act of true love? She leaned forward to him again, delighted to find such a wonderful, simple solution to all her problems at once—only to turn away at the last, when she thought of the exquisite shame of having him not only discover her flaw, but having to conceal his disgust when he did.

He was too busily trying to summon enough resolve not to take her mouth again to notice her own struggle. And after he'd won that inner battle, too busily occupied with finding the control necessary to keep her on his lap without startling her by how intensely he'd reacted to her, to notice her aborted offer. They gazed at each other in mutual despair and frustration.

"But we can't end it now," he said, and though it was only a thread of half a thought, she understood.

"No, not now," she agreed absently, although she knew it was the wrong thing to do, not only to say.

"You are so very lovely," he breathed, shaking his head slightly as he touched her soft, dark hair again.

She traced the thin scar on his lean cheek with one finger and then gazed at his mouth again.

They both realized it at the same time. He looked away and coughed even as she sprang up from his lap. Because in a moment they'd have been back where they began, and though they both wanted to be, they knew now where that would end, or rather, would not. And neither of them was ready for that.

"Still," he said, rising and tugging at a sleeve, glad of the cloak he'd over his arm, "Josh and Lucy are waiting on us at Delmonico's. We don't have to rush into any answers right now, do we?''

"I have to change my clothes," she said, gazing down at her sadly crumpled afternoon dress.

"I can wait," he said, as he thought: I have to, don't I?

"I'll be quick about it," she promised, as she thought: Don't leave me.

"I swear there are more Indians here than back home," Royal said as they drove down the avenue, "I seen one on every street corner since we got off the train."

"But they're wooden," Peggy giggled.

"Makes no never mind," Royal insisted. "They look mighty fierce to me. Old Henry, back home, looks no-count next to them, don't he? And he's full-blooded. Oh yeah, and he sends his best, Gray."

"Lord!" Gray said as he urged his team around a paused hansom cab. "He must be a hundred and six now."

"Claims to be hundred and twenty and I don't doubt it," Royal said, and smiled.

But then, Gray thought, Royal never seemed to stop smiling. It changed him. He was still bone thin and rangy, and however fashionably he was dressed today, he still wore his Stetson. But his craggy face was always wreathed in smiles now, and one long arm was always around his new wife's waist, as though he feared someone would steal her from him if he let go for a moment. And he hadn't stopped talking since they'd picked him up at the hotel this morning. That alone was enough to make him seem like a stranger, albeit a happy stranger, Gray thought, feeling obliquely betrayed as well as pleased and amused by his friend's obvious newfound content.

They were on their way to a day of sight-seeing. Gray had looked forward to seeing Royal's reactions to New York City, but as it turned out, it wasn't showing his old friend the sights so much as it was driving this new creature, "Royal and Peggy" to see them.

Because Royal hadn't so much changed—much as he had changed—Gray thought, as he'd become one of two. And now he wasn't as interested in seeing the wonders of New York City: the Statue of Liberty, the Brooklyn Bridge, the Elevated lines, St. Patrick's Cathedral, and Grant's Tomb, as he was on fire to visit the stores: B. Altman, Stern Brothers, Bloomingdale Brothers, A. T. Stewart, Arnold Constable, and Roux and Company.

"We got to get our place fixed up fine," Royal explained the moment he climbed in the carriage, "and Miz Atkins here, too," he added tenderly, as he settled himself beside Peggy.

Now, as they drove down Broadway, Royal leaned over, peered down the street, and gave out a whoop. "There it is! Pull her in there, Gray, that's the place I heard of."

All Gray saw was a marquee with the name, "C. H. Ditson, & Company," but Hannah began to smile as they drove up to it.

"I didn't know you were a musician, Royal," she said as Gray jockeyed the carriage toward the curb.

"I ain't," Royal said, gazing at Peggy. "But that don't mean we can't have music, does it? Miz Peggy here needs to hear a pretty tune every now and again, leaving the troupe was hard enough for her, but I got to thinking that leaving New York City might get her down from time to time. We got lots of lonely back home, you know."

"Not anymore," Peggy said softly. And Hannah looked away as Royal gazed down into his wife's glowing face.

It wasn't that Royal ever did more than hold Peggy's hand, or that Peggy did more than caress her new husband with her wide hazel eyes. But it seemed to Hannah that since they'd got into the carriage this morning, they'd been touching in some way; that the two of them were sharing some intimate thing right out in public— a thing that always drew them in, and cast all others, even old friends and well-wishers, out. So she'd often felt with her parents. So she felt more and more with everyone else in the world, Hannah thought and tried to smile fondly at the newlywed pair. Until she caught Gray's sympathetic eye. And then she glanced away, frightened, realizing that in that moment of complete understanding, they too became two who needed no one else, and that it shouldn't, couldn't, be.

She was only seeing him again because Peggy and Royal had come to town and would be both hurt and confused if she didn't come along as she'd promised. Or so she'd told herself. Because she finally had gone to dinner at Delmonico's with Gray, his brother, and his sister-in-law on Sunday night, and had a marvelous time of it despite her misgivings or perhaps, because of them. When she hadn't been trading wonderfully humorous, traitorous tales about Kyle with Lucy, she'd been laughing with Gray and Josh. It might have been even more pleasant because it had been bittersweet: she'd vowed that was to be her last night out with Gray. There was no sense in tormenting herself or leading him on. She could be neither wife nor mistress to him, and she couldn't bear to be less, or want more. It had to end. That was why she'd kissed him when they'd parted that night. But not why she'd clung to him until sense had returned enough for her to murmur good night and escape from the terrible joy in his arms. Now, only days later, her resolve was slipping again. The only thing to shore her up and help her lift her head as Gray helped her down from her high seat was the knowledge that Peggy and Gray were only visiting for a little while, and she didn't have to be with them all that while. That didn't stop her from trembling when Gray touched her, but then, it was cold today, after all. And if she looked away quickly when she saw the way the sun struck his flaxen hair, why then, it was such a bright winter's day after all, anyone's eyes might water looking directly into the sun that way.

"Can't read music," Royal said as he strode past the racks of sheet music after they entered the store. "And can't play gitar neither, so come away," he said as Gray paused by the racks of guitars. "But here we are,'' he announced with satisfaction as they reached the pianos.

"Why, Peggy," Hannah exclaimed, as Peggy ran a gloved hand over the polished surface of the fine mahogany piano that Royal stopped beside, "I didn't know you played."

"I don't," Peggy murmured. Then Royal took her hand and pressed it and said, on a smile, "But she's gonna, and every night, too."

Hannah was grinning at the thought of Peggy laboring over the piano instead of a cookstove in order to please Royal, when a salesman, noting their interest, approached, bowed, and flipping up the tails of his coat, seated himself on the bench of the piano.

"You've a good eye, sir," he said to Royal as he slid open a hidden door in the wood above the keyboard, revealing a paper roll in a secret compartment there. "And," he added grandly, as he poised his hands above the keys, "I hope, a good ear. Just listen. It's our latest model, an Aeolian, and very fine."

He began to move his feet and the piano thrummed, and then the strains of Beethoven's "Fur Elise" were heard. It was a lovely rendition, the sound of the piano sonorous and grand, as the keys went up and down to the poignant melody. But the most marvelous thing of all was that the salesman held his hands high in the air above the keyboard all the while, and waggled his fingers every so often to show how unoccupied they were, as the roll turned, his feet pumped, and the piano played on.

"A foot piano!" Royal proclaimed proudly when it was done, as the salesman winced and murmured, "A player, sir." "Yeah," Royal went on, "saw them in saloons in Denver, and I heard they was making them for the home, too, so you could play them without putting in no coins. The very thing for my Peggy, ain't it?"

"The very thing," Gray agreed. "But what if her legs get tired?" he added wickedly.

"Then I'll do it," Royal said at once. "Or if I'm

busy, we'll hire someone else to. All right, Peggy?"
he asked worriedly.

"Why, with all the sisters and brothers you're taking
on, Royal Atkins," Peggy said, putting her hands on
her hips, "if you had to hire someone, I'd be that
shamed."

"Now, for a player accordion and a player harmonica and a player harp, right Royal?" Gray asked, grinning.

"Why, sir," the salesman said, rising, "we have
the very thing! The latest thing! Pianos with full or-
chestral attachments: banjo, harp, drum, and bells.
They're costly, as they're usually for public places of
entertainment," he said to Royal as he rubbed his
gloved hands together, ". . . however, if you wish to
see them, I'm sure we could find one that would fit in
your home."

"Only if our home was on a riverboat," Royal said,
as Peggy rolled her eyes, Gray began to laugh aloud,
and Hannah tried not to giggle. "Thanks, but the
piano's enough for us. My big-mouth friend here is a
fair hand at the gitar, and we'll have him over to
supper when we feel the need of a string or two."

"Of course," the salesman said slyly, "there are
the music boxes for the home as well, the latest craze."

As Royal began to shake his head and mutter something about not needing such a little sound, neither,
the salesman waved his hand to a section of the store
where several large ornate, and beautifully engraved
oak and mahogany boxes stood upon high stands. They
wandered after the salesman, bemused, as he lifted the
lid on a great golden oak one, withdrew a perforated
steel disk easily a foot in circumference from the stand
beneath, and placed the disc on a spindle inside the
box. Then he turned a crank and flipped a switch, and
in seconds they were listening to what seemed to be a
full orchestra as music swelled from the box, music
so loud, so full of strumming chords and chimes, the
very air vibrated. They heard a rendition of "My Old
Kentucky Home" so beautiful that Gray's eyes were

misty when the two minutes were over and it was done, and the final notes reverberating in the sudden silence.

Before they left, they heard several more tunes; Royal had ordered a music box sent home, as well as the piano, and Peggy had to drag him away from the Edison cylinder phone that had real, if tinny, human voices squeaking from the huge morning glory-shaped horn attached to it.

" 'Tis only a novelty, a toy," she whispered into the ear she'd tugged down to her shoulder. " 'Last word,' indeed! And not half so fine sounding as the piano and the box. And it costs the earth."

As Royal began to protest, she added, "And there's only a few cylinders for it, after all. 'Tis enough, Royal Atkins. Don't buy a thing more, leastwise not for me. Is Wyoming so lonely that you need bring a brass band home? Aye, and what sort of flattery is that to me, now, with you going on all the time about 'lonely,' I might ask?"

"But it's you I'm thinking of," he protested. But she interrupted, "Then think on it: wherever you are, I'm never lonely."

They didn't kiss, but their locked gaze did more, and Hannah looked away, disconcerted, only to see Gray gazing at her with infinite sadness in his long blue stare.

A half day. That was all she'd promised them, and so they had to drop Hannah off at Kyle's offices after luncheon. When she urged Peggy to come up and see Kyle again, Peggy only smiled and said, "Later. When we come to pick you up for dinner. Why Hannah Roberts! You haven't forgot, have you?" Peggy asked, her amusement turning to hurt as Hannah began to shake her head. As she saw it, Hannah turned the negative shake into a nod, and hoped she didn't look like an idiot with her head bobbing every which way, as she said, "No, that is to say 'no, I haven't forgotten' and 'yes, I'll come.' Until six, then."

She was rewarded as well as punished by Gray's look of amusement tinged with sorrow as she waved them good-bye, and they drove off down the avenue. A half day and a dinner, Hannah thought wearily, remembering the look in his eyes as she walked up the stair to Kyle's offices. It was their color, she decided, that—and not the fact that those incredible azure eyes seemed to see to the bottom of her soul. After all, she reasoned, she was used to dark brown looking back at her from her mirror and her parents' faces all these years, even John had had brown eyes. It was the shocking color, that was all there was to it. And with luck, courage, and a special blessing, she'd get through tonight and tomorrow and the days that followed, and then be free of those incredible eyes forever, except in her memory, forever.

She was almost knocked down the stair by the woman rushing past her. She spun around to see who could be so rude, when the whiff of heavy perfume left in the woman's wake told her who it was as surely as the bright hair beneath the oversize hat did.

"Lottie!" she exclaimed, as she clung to the stair rail.

Lottie turned around, gave her one fulminating stare, cried, "Be damned to you, too!" and then, head high, pushed open her parasol and flounced out the door.

"Yes," Kyle said from where he stood at the office door looking down. "That was our delightful Lottie, back from the West with an offer of her services—her less desirable ones—for she offered to act for us again. Her silver king already had an ironfisted queen, it seems. She was tossed out and is back. But not with us. We can do better," he said as Hannah came into the office, removed her hat, and took her place at the front desk.

"I'd hoped," Kyle said idly, as he perched on the desk and pretended great interest in a pen he'd found there, "to do much better."

There was that in his voice that made Hannah avoid his eyes as she fussed with unnecessary things on the desk.

"I realize that other old acquaintance has not been

forgotten, either,'' he said far too casually. ''That was Mr. Gray Dylan who just dropped you off here, was it not?''

''Yes,'' Hannah said. She then said with much less hesitation, ''That was Peggy and Royal with him, too. They've more shopping and sight-seeing to do, but they'll be by tonight, to say hello to you.''

''Be still my heart,'' Kyle said, ''I can scarce wait. Somehow, I will endeavor to. But I was only asking after Mr. Dylan because it seems that you two are still sharing billing—and cooing. Are you, I wonder?''

''See here, Kyle,'' she said vehemently, ''I don't care for such aspersions, not that it is any of your business, in any event. But no,'' she added when he began to apologize, almost sincerely, ''I'm only seeing him because I wish to see Peggy and Royal. There's nothing more,'' she said with all the finality of someone who has finally accepted the truth of her words.

''I only said it because I cared, but I must ever say things I care about flippantly, you see,'' Kyle said quietly, toying with the pen and avoiding her gaze so well she wondered if he really meant it.

''Hannah,'' he said again, after a moment, so spontaneously that she knew this, at least, was rehearsed, ''I've been thinking. We've interviewed so many girls for our lead female, and so far, so few have been so much as interesting: Miss Hart is given to simpering, Mrs. Davenport is a bit long in the tooth, and Miss Wood, although charming, is a redhead—just as Miss Kingston, our premiere singer is. That would be a deathly redundancy. No, we need a contrast, a raven-haired beauty would be perfect,'' he said, and slipped off the desk to prowl the room.

Hannah shut her eyes, but couldn't stop her ears.

''We can't do Shakespeare, not in New York where the best Shakespeareans are—including your dear father,'' he went on, as if they hadn't discussed this days ago. ''You yourself said that *Curfew Shall Not Ring Tonight* would be splendid abridged, and so it is . . . Everyone else has been cast . . . Hannah, my dear,'' he said, "have you come to a decision? Time grows short. We must be running by Christmas week. We're already in rehearsals. Not that we really need them but for timing now. As it's a revue, everyone knows their act, except for the one-act drama. And you're such a quick study. It's true anything can get an audience that week, but there's no reason not to start our run fat with holiday revelers. As Lester so often says, 'cheap laughs sound as good as deserved ones, do they not?'

"It's not such a great thing, after all," he said in a different, eager voice. "Just a part in a revue, in a short drama. You seemed interested just the other day. What do you say? Can you do it? This time with a full heart? You can, if you wish, you know," he said with sincerity. "I believe it would be a great loss to us, and to you, if you did not. Will you?"

She dared to look at him then, because she'd her answer.

"May I have just a few days more to think on it?" she asked. "As you say, I must be sure this time. I will be, I promise, when I know. Just a few days more, please. It may be you'll find someone better by then, anyway."

"Never," he said. "But of course. Think on."

He left her then. And, as he requested, she thought on. But not about the lead in *Curfew Shall Not Ring Tonight*. Instead, she drew ever diminishing circles with the pen he'd left on the desktop, and thought about a pair of sad blue eyes that seemed to know, precisely, the depth and measure of her sorrow.

Foolishness itself, she finally decided. When there was nothing to be done, the only thing to do was nothing, until it was all over. And it would be soon. Ah well, she thought, dabbing her eyes with her last clean handkerchief, suffering was supposed to maketh the artist, as Kyle always said. Well, she decided, as she tried to smile, it ought to maketh something aside from a great pile of wet wash. Perhaps suffering maketh a great laundress, if nothing else, she thought.

She wished she could share the joke with someone.

Chapter Sixteen

It was the first time Hannah had been alone with Peggy since the wedding, but it was as if Royal were still there when they spoke. Because everything Peggy said had to do with him, his tastes, opinions, and thoughts. Some of the lilt had gone from her intonation, replaced by short, flat commonsensical statements that even sounded like Royal. As Royal had become more outgoing, Peggy had become more succinct, and Hannah wondered at such a union, where each had obviously taken on some of the other's best-loved traits. She herself had never copied John, Hannah remembered, for so much as she'd thought she loved him, there'd been nothing about him she wished to emulate. Now she began to wonder if that hadn't been as much a failure as their lack of physical communion, or if it was simply more normal to remain oneself no matter who one loved.

"Lord! . . ." she began to say as she laughed at something Peggy said, before she heard herself and fell still, wondering if she'd ever said that at all before she'd met Gray.

"Now, come along Miz Roberts," Peggy said officiously. "Royal will be here with Gray in no time, and you've not even pinned on your hat."

"Are you sure you want me with you?" Hannah asked as she turned to the mirror to adjust her hat. Peggy had been left to visit with her while Gray and Royal went to pick up some packing supplies for Peggy's family. Which was just as well, for now she'd a chance to see if Peggy really wanted her to go along to where her family lived, rather than meeting them later on some more neutral ground. Because she knew the address, and it was a place where even a New Yorker such as herself seldom ventured.

"I'm never shamed at my beginnings," Peggy said quietly, "nor of my family. Where they live—och, well, now that I can take them out of there, I'm not ashamed of that either. We visited yesterday. They're in that much of a tizzy packing, they'll not be able to poke their noses out till it's time to get on the train with us. So come along, I want you to meet them as much as they want to meet you. Royal says you're like Santa Claus to them: they want to believe in you, but they don't half, you know."

" 'Royal says, Royal says,' " Hannah mocked lightly. "Oh Peggy, what would you have to say, my girl, if they took 'Royal' out of the language?"

"They'd have to take me out of this life," Peggy said simply. Then her eyes brightened and she said, "Oh Hannah, you don't know—or perhaps you do— but there's nothing like it, this marriage business. Och, it's not just the cuddling, though that's grander than I believed it could be: it's all of it. It's like I found the other part of myself that I'd been missing, but didn't know where to look for. Nothing less than that."

Hannah left off adjusting her hat, and lowered her arms.

"No," she said with a little smile, "I didn't know that. I'm so happy for you, Peggy."

They embraced briefly, but when Peggy stepped back, she looked at Hannah sadly.

"I'm still your friend, Hannah," she said seriously. "I've changed, and no denying, but I'm still your friend. Pray don't try to flummox me. You're happy, but you're sad, too, because you think I don't need you anymore. But I do. Royal says that the more you love, the more you can love. Indeed,'' she said, turning from Hannah's stricken look to stare into the mirror and pat her own hat in order to change the subject, ''that's why he's taking on my whole family now, he says. Except for my poor sister Mary, who's marrying the Rourke boy and staying on here, and him with a mean streak a mile wide. And my brother Jimmy, who's going into the livery business with O'Toole, the more fool he. Still, Cousin Kevin's begged a place, and he's coming, so we'll hardly notice the lack.''

''Lord, Peggy,'' Hannah laughed. ''What with sisters and brothers and cousins and automatic pianos and music boxes, you'll have to come back to New York to be lonely!''

''That's a fact,'' Peggy said with great satisfaction.

''Are you planning to come visit, too?'' Peggy asked when they'd done laughing. ''I mean, with Gray, I wondered . . .''

''Wonder no more. No,'' Hannah said. But seeing Peggy's hurt, said in a softer voice, ''Peggy love, not all of us have happy endings. You ought to know enough about the theater to know that. And it's just as well,'' she added on a lighter note, ''because if there were nothing but comedies, people would get tired of laughing.''

Looking at Hannah, Peggy wondered if she weren't getting tired of crying, but was too wise to say it.

''I b'lieve we've left them alone long enough now,'' Royal said, one long leg jouncing up and down impatiently as he watched Gray drive. ''I expect any girl talk Peggy needed is done. Can't you go any faster?''

''Not without killing half a hundred people,'' Gray answered calmly. ''Think she's going to run off when your back's turned, do you? Wouldn't blame her, myself. Lots of better-looking, smarter fellows here in New York for a girl like that.''

''Damn straight,'' Royal said fervently. ''Lucky for me she don't know it.'' He sighed, ''I know you think I'm a plain sap, Gray. I see it in your eyes. He's hog-tied, gelded, and turned to pure drivel, is what you're thinking. Can't hide it. But to tell the truth, I don't care. I never been happier. It ain't just the loving part. Though that's . . . well," he said, glancing away from Gray's bright gaze to look out over the horse's heads as a muscle worked in his jaw, "that's too fine to talk about. It's all the rest, too. The sharing. Damn it Gray, I didn't know nothing before I married her, and I was nothing, that's a plain fact."

"I'm not pitying you or mocking you," Gray said quietly. "I'm plain envying you, Royal, and that's the truth."

"And about you and Miz Roberts?" Royal asked.

"Now I can take all kinds of mush from a newly married man," Gray said quickly. "But you're just too bony and long-shanked to play Cupid, friend. Leave off. Right?"

"Uh-huh," Royal said sadly, because Peggy said those two were perfect together, and he'd thought so, too, but he knew trouble when he saw it, and was as surprised as he was sorry for it.

They were all uncharacteristically silent as they drove downtown. It wasn't just their respective moods: Gray and Hannah edgy with each other and envious of Royal and Peggy, while Royal and Peggy were blissfully happy at being reunited even after such a short separation, and trying not to show it because they were aware of how the other couple was taking it. It was also that it was difficult to find the right thing to say as they drove through the streets that led to Peggy's family home.

There were worse districts. There were parts of Five Points that still looked very like they had decades before, when Charles Dickens had seen them and written: "Debauchery has made the very houses prematurely old. Where dogs would howl to lie, women, men, and boys slink off the street." But the streets they drove through now were not much better. The close-built houses were so cracked and peeling on the outside, it was best not to imagine their interiors. Even so, it was clear from the wretched condition of those walking the streets that those who were within those crumbling walls were the luckier ones. There was not much horse traffic, and few ragpickers with their dogcarts, because it seemed they'd have slim pickings here, buying or selling. Here, the men and women wore their rags, or what looked like worse. But it was the children who were most visible, everywhere.

There was a charitable home for newsboys nearby, but ten times ten of them wouldn't have had enough room for all the children who scavenged these filthy streets. Their faces were as prematurely old as the houses Dickens had written about before they were born. Now, in the December cold, they stood on hot-air gratings on the sidewalks to keep warm, as they eyed the carriage as it drove by—by nightfall they'd fight for the right to sleep where they stood.

Royal's broad shoulders twitched with the effort he made to keep from jumping down and shepherding as many children as he could into the carriage, to carry them away to a land he knew—where there was enough room for them all. Gray, having seen and felt it all too many times before, simply hurried his team on, making a mental note to give even more money to the several charitable funds he subscribed to. Hannah, being a New Yorker, and so having learned from an early age how to be selectively blind, lowered her eyes and hoped Peggy didn't live on each block they passed in turn. And Peggy took in a deep breath, to discover once again, that this familiar air stank to her now after the air she'd become used to breathing only just lately.

Neither Gray nor Royal worried about being accosted by the hard-eyed men they passed. Not only did both of them look as though they'd be able to handle themselves to good account in a brawl, but both had in the past; they came from a hard land, and were used to riding through danger. It wasn't that the city was safer, but Gray had already told Royal to stow his firearms and disregard the envious looks their carriage received. Because, he'd explained, at this hour, members of the professional gangs that ruled this world were either sleeping or already at the saloons where they held court. Even so, their business never involved attacking chance-met strangers; prostitution, graft, and more elaborate forms of burglary paid better, and was withall, safer.

And so, however desperate the circumstances of those poor wretches that watched them enviously now, they both knew—with a twinge of guilt—that they were safe because they were better fed and clearer minded than any would-be assailants. Being the sort of men they were, this didn't make them feel better. But the neighborhood they soon entered did.

The streets they traveled now were increasingly gayer ones. There was still poverty here, but it had not numbed or deadened anyone's spirits. The people here had nothing much, but it seemed they'd hope of more. The houses were just as cramped, and as many children roved the streets. But there was laughter and bright colors, and noise of trade, argument, and living. Here mothers cared enough to scold their children, at the top of their lungs. In fact, all conversation seemed to be carried out in a screech, as those upstairs shouted advice and comment to those below, who responded just as loudly. The streets reeked, but the scents were of cooking: cabbages and chickens and garlic—the spices of a dozen different sorts of immigrant dinners in progress hung in the air.

They stopped the carriage, and Gray paid a youth to watch his team. The boy took the coin, grinned, and sang out a greeting to Peggy when she alit, and she ruffled his red hair as she hurried up the steps to the gray tenement.

There seemed to be a bewildering lot of Callahans in the little flat they entered. Many of them looked like Peggy, most of them were delighted to meet her guests, and all of them talked at once. In time, Hannah came to understand that they all worshiped Royal, thought Gray the most impressive male they'd ever clapped eyes on apart from Royal, and knew everything that Peggy did about Hannah, from all the letters Peggy had sent home. It was as disconcerting as it was amusing—as Hannah whispered to Gray a little later when they walked through the teeming streets behind Peggy and Royal and a half dozen assorted Callahans. Rather like meeting Peggy in disguise, a few dozen times, she said.

"They'll make things lively back home," Gray remarked, smiling. He was as delighted at the notion of accompanying the newlyweds on a shopping tour at the popular Jewish outdoor market on Hester Street as Peggy had been embarrassed by her family's insisting it was the best way to get bargains on staples they'd need for their coming trip. Because Hannah had to cling to his arm to keep from being borne away by the burgeoning crowds. And so however ill-at-ease they were with each other, they soon became informal allies as they struggled on among the currents of people buying, bargaining, and sight-seeing among the pushcarts and shops in the teeming streets.

"Say, have you ever had one of these?" Gray asked, stopping at a great open-mouthed barrel that stood in front of a store.

"Of course," Hannah said with a superior smile, "I'm a New Yorker."

But as she paused, a white-jacketed man with a fierce black beard thrust his hand into the gray-green liquid that filled the barrel and came up with a long green pickle in his red and chapped hand. He presented it to Hannah with a flourish, as though it were a rose. She accepted it as graciously, after removing her glove. And then took a big bite of it before sighing, and saying with every evidence of rapture, "Superb. Just delicious."

"Ah. You've a nose for pickles. It must be a vat of the '89, I hear the year was perfect. We'll have a jar of them, my good man," Gray said imperiously. As the man proceeded to stuff pickles into a jar, Gray studied Hannah's pickle longingly and added, "At least that way I'll get a taste."

She grinned and held out the pickle, and he managed to take a bite without the juice running down his chin and onto his scarf, his woolen Chesterfield coat, or the cupped hand she held beneath his chin. "Ah," he breathed, as he chewed. "You're right. An impudent little vintage, with just a hint of brine and enough garlic to give it body."

They took their jar of pickles and strolled the raucous market streets behind Peggy and Royal. While the newlyweds bought linens and pots, Hannah and Gray delighted in daring each other to taste every sample of every food that was offered them. And as they were offered bits and pieces of every edible thing being vended, they ate bites of potato and onion patties and pieces of herring; slices of salamis and bolognas and wedges of cheese; hunks of bread bearing coatings of fats or jellies, and mouthfuls of all sorts of pastries filled with indescribable compounds of meats and fish.

"That," Hannah said smugly, as Gray swallowed a bite of something in baked parchment, "was liver. As I live and breath, you've just ingested what you said you detested the most, as I recall."

"Indeed?" Gray said with admirable calm, successfully stifling a grimace, for the onions, garlic, and chicken fat had disguised the horrible fact brilliantly, until she'd spoken.

"That," he informed her in turn, three pushcarts down the street later, as she daintily nibbled a tidbit, "is a mixture of sweetbreads and crumbs, as well as onion and garlic. I thought you shared my detestation of any internal organs but your own at dinner."

"Oh," she said, and forced herself to continue chewing as she said brightly, "but it is very good. Exceptions can be made."

"And," he added sweetly, "it is all rolled up and cooked in a length of the unfortunate cow's intestine. That's the crackly coating," he said helpfully, adding, "it's quite true," as he saw her stop chewing.

"Beast," she said, coughing, because she'd swallowed it in her dismay. And then saw his eyes and began laughing so loudly several onlookers joined in because it was such a lovely sound to hear.

They ate their way down the street, buying samples of what they'd liked the best, and then of what they'd seen each other dislike the most, and all for the sheer fun of it.

"Now," Royal said at last, as they turned to make their way back to the Callahan house, "home again. Miz Callahan is waiting on us for dinner."

Peggy and Royal had expected every sort of argument from their friends, but not absolute silence, and then after a glance at each other, absolute and unrestrained mirth.

There was champagne with hothouse fruits floating in it, and pätés and oysters, canapés and lobster patties, sliced and garnished tongues and hams, sides of beef and galantines of veal, dishes of cut-up fowl, meat rolls, and lobster salad. All of it was presented in golden bowls or on silver trays, and that was only on the side of the supper table where Gray was standing. The other end, somewhere down the room, beyond the vases of fresh flowers, had the blancmanges, jellies, creams and custards, fruits and jams, and the biscuits, cakes, and pastries to accompany them. But Gray didn't take a sip or bite of any of it.

He held his champagne glass in his hand and watched the other supper guests at the Fifth Avenue mansion as they filled their plates. Or rather, his brother thought as he made his way through the crowd to get to him, he didn't watch them, because he seemed to be paying attention to some interior scene that interested him more.

By the time Josh Dylan got to his brother's side, someone else had jolted him from his reverie, but not to ask why he wasn't eating.

"I say," the stout, bewhiskered gentleman was complaining as Josh came up to them, "I'm at sea. Are you telling me silver is a good investment, or a bad one? You seem to be talking out of both sides of your mouth, my boy."

The quickly shuttered look that sprang to Gray's eyes told his brother that the only reason the old gentleman didn't have a fist in his mouth was because of his age, notwithstanding the fact that he was an old family friend, but Gray replied calmly enough.

"I said that silver's very big now, sir. As you know. Because if I'm not mistaken, you've got controlling interest in two good mines and a minor interest in one with Horace Tabor himself. All I'm saying aside from that, and that only because you've been fair with us Dylans for a long spell," Gray went on, his drawl becoming more pronounced, which should have alerted the old fellow, Josh thought, to pay close heed to the next seemingly careless words, "is that it looks to me like too many folks is riding the silver train to glory. That always means trouble. Money's not misery, it don't like company. And there's a whole lot of silver pouring into a whole lot of pockets. Now, there's some talk of devaluing it in the future, and sticking to pure gold. Which would bring silver stocks tumbling, which may be why they're talking about it. But, hell, what do I know? It's only trash talk, and I'm only a boy from the West. You own half the East, or so m' brother says . . . why, hello, Josh. I was just speculating on things with William here, but I guess I should stick to things I know, like cattle."

"The things you know," the old gentleman said, putting a finger to the side of his nose, "are things a clever man should listen to. Point taken, young Gray. That's why Josh steered me to you earlier this evening. I'll be thinking about it. Thank you. Or rather, 'thank you kindly,' as you would say—when you're trying to devil me," he said on a guffaw, and bowing, left the two men. But not alone, because they were in a press of people eyeing the supper table, even though their plates were full to overflowing.

"Come on, let's find someplace as empty as your dinner plate," Josh said. "Since you're not going to eat, we have to talk."

They threaded through the crowded room, stopped many times by young women with a flirtatious thing to say to Gray, and gentlemen with a business thing or two to say to both of them. A generation before, talking of business at a society standing supper would have been forbidden. But New York society was becoming a thing of the aristocracy of money as well as lineage, and manners that would have been condemned by the blue-blooded set who had once reigned here had been overthrown. Still, the Dylans, being both enormously wealthy and descended on their father's side from British aristocracy, were acceptable to both old and new society. They scarcely cared, except that it gave them an opportunity to make more money. Having come from poverty, they both cared deeply about that.

They were alone in the room Josh steered Gray to, but it was hardly empty. Their host's library was done up in the latest kick of fashion, and almost shouted of it's currency. The patterned Arabian rugs argued with the patterned wallpaper, upon which dozens of gilt-framed oil paintings maintained their separate opinions; the mantel over the fireplace was crowded with shepherds and winsome seventeenth-century ladies and gentlemen, all prime, if disparate, examples of German and English pottery. Busts and statues were randomly placed beside assorted chairs, and heavy brocaded curtains covered over the windows, while ornate lamps vied with each other to see which could throw the most distorted light out from under their metal, glass, and beaded shades. The only way to find quiet was to shut one's eyes. But Gray stared at Josh directly and curiously.

"We're leaving soon," Josh said, settling in a leather chair and gesturing for Gray to take the one opposite. "Lucy's not too hungry these days, poor girl, so we're going home. I don't know," he sighed. "I love fatherhood, but not when it makes motherhood so uncomfortable for her. Still, she says it's only the first months, and she wanted this one . . ."

"It's real nice of you to ask me here so I could share that with you," Gray murmured. "Is there something you wanted me to do about it? Maybe kidnapping you after the baby's born, so she can get some rest for a year or two for a change?"

Josh scowled. "We saw you sulking, as usual this week, and she sent me to talk to you. She had a lot of questions. Like: why are you looking like a thundercloud, and where's Hannah? Not me. I was just wondering why you were looking at the primest crop of rich, pretty debutantes in America like they had hoof-and-mouth disease, and where's Hannah? We thought she was coming with you.''

"She didn't. I didn't ask her," Gray said, and stretched out his legs before him and stared into the fire that was moodily dying of neglect in the fireplace.

"Look, scout," Josh said quietly, "I guess you might say it's none of my business, but you are my business. I know you're a man grown, but you're my baby brother, and you'll never be that grown man to me—not even when you come to visit me in your invalid chair, and listen to my advice through your ear trumpet. That's the way of it. I was just worried about you. You seemed to have found your lady. And we were glad, because she's a good one, although, I'll admit, I'd dreams of some rich young thing for you. But Lucy says you have to give over some dreams when a better reality steps into view. I think she's right. Now you're alone again. We just wondered.''

Had married people always said "we" half the time, and "so and so says" the other half? Gray wondered, as he answered wearily, "I did find her. But I think I'm losing her. And be damned to your rich young things.''

He closed his eyes and said in a gentler voice, "There's a problem I'm trying to figure out how to handle—but Lord, Josh," he said, opening his eyes and showing his brother the despair in his clear blue gaze, "all that high-priced college education you bought me, and all the higher-priced knowledge I half killed myself to learn isn't helping me now. She *is* the one. But there's problems.''

He rose from his seat and walked to the fireplace. Finding a spot on the mantel free of expensive porcelain, he put his hand there and stared into the fire, prodding the dead end of a log with the tip of his highly polished shoe as he spoke on.

"She's a widow, you know. But it turns out she was

only married briefly—and unsuccessfully. In every way. Her husband said he couldn't consummate it, and he didn't tell her why, and she don't know, and I'll be damned if I'll try to seduce her to find out, because of what it would do to her if he was right, or to us if he was wrong. And I won't have her going for surgery to know why, and that's all these damned priggish New York doctors are offering her. And if you ever mention this to anyone, you're not my brother anymore; much as I love you, Josh, that's the way of it, I swear it.''

"Well, I'm glad to hear you feel that way," Josh said, unperturbed, "because only a low dog would talk about it. But I'm not surprised. Lucy said there was something—she said there wasn't any way she could believe Hannah was ever a married woman . . . You're right, it's a problem. Damn. But, I'd think . . .''

"No!" Gray said, turning around and holding one hand up high, "Don't Josh. Don't you do it. For once, you better not. I appreciate your advice, always have, but see, this is too important to me for it. It's my life, I have to make my own mistakes. If I make yours," he said, smiling sadly, "then I can only blame you for it, for the rest of my life. That ain't half-fair, is it?''

His brother looked at him and said nothing. But he'd a queer pang in his heart, the way he'd felt the time he'd seen his oldest off to school on the first day. Gray had grown beyond him, and he was glad as he was sorry for it.

"Why, it would be like me asking you if you made love with your clothes on," Gray continued, still attempting to explain, and haphazardly seizing on another problem that had been nagging at him since he'd heard about it. He'd been wondering uneasily whether his own preference for only wearing his skin at such times mightn't be an aberration.

"What?" his brother asked, diverted. "That's like bathing with your union suit on—nothing to the point, and about as effective as it would be fun. Although," he added speculatively, "I hear respectable folk do just that. Why, I remember Doc, back home, telling me there's many an old girl married half her life and with a passel of kids, who still don't know how the old man does it—and what's worse," he said, grinning, "she don't know why, neither."

They laughed together, in that moment looking very like brothers. But then Gray stopped, and his head came up. His eyes were suddenly alight with more than merriment.

"Yeah!" he said excitedly, "Uh-huh! That might just be it! Josh, you old hoss, you just might have done it!"

"Done what?" Josh asked.

"Given me some good, sound advice—or at least, a bead on where to get it," Gray said. "Thank you, thank you, big brother, you've done it again. I think I'm going to be leaving town for a while—just a short while, but then I'll be back, and I think I'll know what to do then."

"Of course I've given you good advice," Josh said, rising to take his brother's proffered hand, "even if I don't know how I did it. But Gray," he added seriously, "now don't go off half-cocked, whatever you do. She's a fine girl, and no mistake. But life is long."

"Longer if you don't have what you need in it," Gray said with equal seriousness, "—forget about what you want."

"Boy, look what you done," Josh sighed, holding his brother by the shoulders, and lapsing back into a drawl as he always did when talking to his brother as in the old days, "You done growed up on me."

"Funny, I wasn't even trying," Gray said, and meant it.

He was wearing evening clothes. Black tailcoat and straight-cut trousers, a white waistcoat over a white shirt with a pleated front, and he held his hat in his hand and his cape over his arm. The only color to him was his bright hair, his gold watch fob, and even in the dim light of the corridor, his shining blue eyes. She was wearing an old, formless gown and her hair was down, hanging halfway to her waist. She'd opened the door to the knock, and it was Gray standing there, looking like a man from a better life. His eyes went to her hair, and she wondered if she should ask him in at all. But she knew she had to hear whatever it was he'd come at this hour to say, and so she gestured, and without a word, he stepped over her doorsill.

His hand reached out to her hair, and though he wore gloves and she knew hair could feel nothing, she felt his fingers as they seemed to marvel over the texture of her hair. Someone had to say something, she thought, it was really absurd, him appearing at this time, unannounced, without a word. He seemed almost too sober, so it wasn't that, and yet now that she looked at him, she knew it was no dire emergency either, because the only urgent thing about him was the way he looked at her mouth.

"Gray," she said, and then he kissed her.

He hadn't meant to, but she'd looked so warm and flushed and sleepy, and he'd never seen the glory of that storm of hair unleashed, and once she was in his arms and under his lips, there was no question but that he should kiss her. She clung to him and gave him back as much as he was giving, except that when his hands came to her breast, she didn't put her hands on his chest as well, but only kept them buried in the hair at the back of his neck and sighed into his mouth.

It was so good for both of them that it was several minutes before they got used to it. And then, as greedy as they were giddy with pleasure, they wanted more— which ended it. Because that wasn't a place either one of them knew how to proceed to just yet. It involved a lot of other thinking, and that was the slow-moving thought that kept him from moving further, and her from letting him. She somehow found the wit to step back just as he began to remember why he'd come and let her go from his arms.

"I came to say good-bye," he said.

Her face went white, and so he added immediately, "For a little while, only a little while, there's things I have to see to, back home. Well, Royal and Peggy are going tomorrow, you know, and so I thought I'd help them, too. But I'll be back in no time. Almost on the return train. Before the new year,'' he said as she turned away from him. He clenched his hands to keep from pulling her back to him, and stared at the long silky fall of her hair as it swirled about her back.

"What would be the point of that?" she asked. "I mean to say, why bother?"

"You know why as well as I do," he answered.

"Which means you know very little," she said.

"I came to say good-bye, for a little while," he said again, not knowing what else to say, because the reason he was going was still so new to him. And not a thing he could tell her now, in any case.

She turned back to him and inclined her head, like an empress acknowledging a peasant. As she was so poorly dressed, it was like a gesture right out of *A Heroine in Rags,* one of his favorite plays—the scene where the heroine is revealed to be a princess—he recognized it, and couldn't help but grin.

"Thank you, Your Highness," he said, and took her back into his arms, and though this time she did protest, his mouth swallowed the words, and his hands stroked the anger down until she was breathing his breaths when he finally was able to find the will to let her go again.

"I'll be back," he said, and put on his hat and left.

She raged at him throughout the night—when she wasn't condemning herself.

She ought to have been exhausted when morning came, but she didn't notice it was morning and so felt no weariness. In fact, she dressed with great energy, snapped her hat on her head, and marched out the door to go to work.

She looked magnificent to Kyle when she stormed into the office. And while he didn't entirely understand why she almost shouted the most beautiful words he'd heard in weeks at him, he didn't mind it.

"Kyle. I've decided, yes. I'll take the part, if you'll still have me," she announced.

He put out his hands and took hers.

"Welcome home," he said.

Chapter Seventeen

"Do relax, I could seduce you as well in the theater as in my flat," Kyle said with some annoyance. "I need not lure you here, put on a beautifully patterned smoking jacket, ice the champagne, ooze over your shoulder as you fret over your lines, and coerce you to my couch in order to do it, you know. That's what they do in melodramas of any worth—but please remember the theater presents things perfectly in order to make them more exciting. However, as I'm sure you also know," he continued as Hannah glowered at him, "the thing can be done backstage, on a pile of canvas, between the intermission and the second act. Actually, Lester always brags that he was conceived before the first act, as though that were more than a lovely play on words," he added conversationally.

Hannah lost her look of fury as she began to giggle. It was impossible to be angry at his outrageous lack of propriety. He was of the theater, after all, and not the world she'd been aspiring to.

"Yes," Kyle went on, "and then he boasts that being conceived before the first act is the nearest thing to a virgin birth that he can conceive of in the theater. A *very* amusing fellow—but it's true. At any rate, I asked you here tonight in order to rehearse, because we've little time and much to do. I considered that our being completely alone in an empty theater in the night would be much more intimidating for you than simply coming to my rooms. But then,'' he said with exaggerated hauteur, ''I am not a respectable person, I suppose, and cannot be expected to know the latest rules of modesty that prevail among the refined and genteel.''

Hannah grinned at him over the script she held, but her smile slipped as he added, ''Of course, should you care to share my couch, I'd be more than delighted: I'd be honored, pleased, and gratified beyond mere words. But even so, I'd prefer that you restrain your understandable lust for me until after you've got the part down pat, if you please,'' he said, raising one thin hand to forestall the furious comment trembling on her tongue, ''because, alas, the play comes before play, in my heart, always.''

She shook her head. There was no way she could stay angry, and his smile showed that he knew it very well.

It was late, because they'd worked at the theater all day, had dinner, and only then had time to come to his rooms in order to rehearse the part she'd promised to undertake in a few days' time. She'd trouble with one scene, and it was necessary that it be perfect. She didn't need her costar to rehearse with—she considered him a conceited ass, anyway—only a knowing, patient tutor, just as Kyle had said. It was all very reasonable. But she'd discovered, only moments before, after she'd given him her coat, taken up her script, and waited for him to return to the room, that she was nervous about it.

He'd pleasant lodgings; three rooms in a decent neighborhood, on the second floor of a well-appointed brownstone house near the theater. His parlor was furnished with a plump leather couch, a few plush chairs, several fat glass-globed lamps, and a piano with a gaily patterned cloth flung over it; and though it was obviously his landlord's taste, he'd his own framed photographs of theater folk on the walls and tabletops.

They'd been warm and comfortable surroundings until he'd come into the room again after hanging her coat on a stand in the hallway. Because then, as he'd loomed up out of the shadows of this new setting, she'd seen him as if for the first time, and had thought that he was really a most attractive man, if you didn't know him.

He was, after all, she thought, eyeing him, if not tall, then at least above average height, and if lean, he'd a trim figure. His long dark hair shone with cleanliness, not scented oil, and his great dark eyes were lustrous and surprisingly long-lashed. But it was more than that. He'd an almost aristocratic, long-nosed, fine-featured thin face; indeed, everything about him was lean, almost starved, and spoke of some intense and insatiable hunger. And that, she began to perceive with her newly heightened sensibilities in such matters, was precisely where his attraction lay, because such hunger was in itself oddly compelling.

So far as she knew, he'd been celibate on the tour. But he'd once asked her if she'd like to change that: she remembered that now. Although he'd lived in a single state then, he'd been, after all, extremely single-minded then as well. The men in the troupe had often joked with each other about that singular state. They'd implied it was unusual and unlike his reputation of having little trouble finding a female for diversion, and liking such diversion very much. In fact, Hannah had noted several of the new girls in the show casting longing glances at their director. Lately she'd thought she'd noted a certain overdone coyness on the part of one of the dancers whenever Kyle was near her, and he showed a correspondingly overly pronounced lack of interest toward her at the same time.

But she wasn't here tonight, nor was there a trace of another human presence anywhere in the flat, and Kyle was also said to be fond of having such company live in with him. This might be due to laziness, as she'd once overheard Frank jesting when he'd spoken of a notoriously vain actress Kyle had once been linked with, or because of his omnipresent appetites—however unwise an arrangement, such a man might prefer to have even an icebox handy for his snacks rather than having to eat out every night—as she'd heard Lester answer Frank before she'd scurried away so they'd not discover her, red-faced from her eavesdropping.

The fact was that Kyle could be considered an attractive man, and was, by many women. He was probably of an age with Gray, Hannah realized. And he was never a gentleman as Gray was, and didn't pretend to be.

But he'd read her face before she'd read her lines, and so even if she was still on her guard, at least she could laugh with him now. Until he spoke again.

"Alas, I fear my timing is off, for once. I'm too late, aren't I?" Kyle asked gently. "You've fallen in love with him, haven't you?"

It was his sad smile, his low and velvety tone of voice, and the lateness of the hour that undid her. Hannah nodded, and before she entirely understood what was happening, lowered her guard; she'd yet to learn that a mind could be seduced while one was busy worrying about the body. But it felt so very good to unburden herself, even though she knew that was the whole point of any seduction.

"I suppose I have," she admitted, looking up over her script, "but it doesn't matter. Because nothing will come of it." She rattled the papers in businesslike fashion.

"It seemed to me," Kyle persisted gently, "that he was similarly afflicted."

"That doesn't matter either," she said abruptly, her hands tightening on the script until it crumpled, "because nothing can come of it either—Oh Kyle," she groaned, gazing into his deep, dark endlessly soft, and sympathetic eyes.

It was all soon told. Every embarrassing, painful bit of it. Repetition took the difficulty as well as the reality from the words, as with any part to be played. She was silent when she'd done, marveling over how, once told, it was so simple to tell again even after all these long silent years, when he spoke again.

"Ah. And so, after he discovered all, he left you?" Kyle asked thoughtfully.

She shrugged, and said as lightly as she was able, "What else could he do?"

"He could have asked to marry him anyhow. As I do now," Kyle commented so blandly, she almost spoke again before she heard his words again, and then fell still, staring at him, too astonished to even be afraid of his declaration or the light in his newly kindled eyes.

"Hannah," he said carefully, coming no closer, though his tone of voice as well as his warm looks reached out to her, "I'm not jesting. What is a marriage, anyway, but a meeting of two minds and two souls? Ah well, of course the joys of the meeting of two bodies cannot be discounted. But if they must be—they can be." He smiled sadly as he added, "Although, believe me, the reverse is never true. That's the point," he said.

He began to pace, and Hannah grew alarmed both at what he was saying and how he was saying it; for he'd a way of making everything, no matter how far-fetched, make sense as he said it, and knowing it scarcely helped.

"I need you," he said, throwing her a bright glance, "I've told you that before. You've been a wonderful helpmate to me. I'd thought you might be more—but as you say, that's to be seen, and well may never be. That doesn't change things, not really. You're a dedicated worker, you know the theater, you're good with people—I may be able to persuade them to do all sorts of things," he said on a half smile, "you however, have a way of making them like you, no matter what I've persuaded them to do. That rubs off on me, and makes my path an easier one.

"Now it transpires that you're a fine actress, too," he said, and nodding, added, "You are, Hannah, don't doubt it—or at least, I feel you will be when you stop fearing it. Believe me, my feeling a thing about the theater is as good as knowing it. Yes, I've a wondrous good opinion of myself. But only about the things I know. I do know the theater," he said, stopping in his tracks and staring at her where she stood, amazed.

Each time he took the time to really look at her, he was astonished again by her beauty, because she never used it as most women did, but left it to him to rediscover. He'd learned to ignore it after he'd learned she'd no intention of taking him for a lover; he wasn't a man to languish after lost causes, that was the stuff of drama, not for a man who used that ephemeral stuff to make his fortune. But now, as she stood slender and straight as a shaft of moonlight in her narrow gray gown in the center of his room, he noted her lovely face and form again—the fragility of one as well as the lushness of the other—that contrast that made her so enormously appealing, and restrained himself from taking her into his arms. She looked stunned enough to allow him that, but he was too wise not to know that would take the sense from his words, and this was a woman he could only win with his words. And he very much needed to win her. He spoke the truth and was as surprised to hear it as she was.

"I need a wife," he said quietly. "What transpires in my bed never touches my heart, and that makes life lonely. My life is the theater and I can think of no more wonderful thing than to share it with someone who has also dedicated herself to it."

But then he saw her absolute incredulity, and like any accomplished dramatist, left off telling the strict truth, concentrating instead on words he thought might move her, "Is that what you'll do if you don't accept me—dedicate your life to the theater? Work day and night and dwindle to nothingness in the hours between performances? I can't see it. You have a loving nature, Hannah. You deserve far more, whatever cruel trick nature may or may not have played you. For there's always the possibility that there's little the matter with you that another man mightn't cure—I don't count on it, but in time—if you'd care to see . . . ? At least, you'd always have company," he said, quickly changing the subject as he saw her avert her head, "and a loving heart to sustain your own, you deserve as much, my dear.''

''And you?'' she said when she could, as he waited for her to answer, ''What do you deserve? Don't you think you deserve a normal wife and children, like any other man?''

''I've never planned on it,'' he said honestly. ''I'd be content with a wife I admired—and yes,'' he added when he knew at last that he had to, when he saw her great dark eyes still filled with doubt and disbelief, ''it's true—no sense dissembling at such a time—one with a famous name, who could act as well, could not hurt at all. At least I'm honest,'' he said, surprising himself again by turning aside so he couldn't read what was in her face now.

''So honest that you'll admit you'd seek—certain wifely surcease elsewhere if you had to?'' she asked softly.

''Yes,'' he answered as quietly, ''but only if you asked me to tell you—you'd never know otherwise, that I promise you. Aside from the necessity of it, if it had to be, you're of the theater, so that oughtn't to surprise you either.''

''No . . .'' she began. He cut in impatiently, ''Come, Hannah, why be alone, do you dislike me so much? I confess, I hadn't thought it.''

''No,'' she said, shaking her head, ''I meant, 'No, I wouldn't be surprised.' But . . . I don't know, Kyle, I just don't,'' she said, looking so vulnerable his control broke at last, and he stepped forward to take her into his arms and hold her close. Finding how wonderfully well she felt there, he scarcely dared breathe or move, lest he do more than hold her.

She noted, inconsequentially, that he bore the not unpleasant scent of lemon verbena, and the peppermints he was so fond of. He was slender to look at, and his frame felt light-boned, but his arms were very strong. They were so close, she felt his heart beat fast and hard against her own, and was amazed to feel him tremble as he said, ''Think on, then. Take your time. I'll ask again, never fear. Never fear me, either, Han-

nah. Let me do that,'' he laughed shakily, ''for I'll
always try my utmost never to hurt you.''

He found the control to step away from her then,
suddenly afraid of the truth she'd forced him to admit.
Because for all he'd thought his spontaneous proposal
a clever business move as well as an act of kindness,
he knew it to be far more now, and was alarmed and
not a little frightened at how, for the first time in his
adult life, he'd deceived himself without meaning to.

''Well, and so. In the meanwhile,'' he said, recovering himself, for he was nothing if not adaptable,
''let us rehearse. You're earthly perfection as it is, let's
make you heavenly.''

''Lord, Kyle,'' she said on a nervous laugh, as willing to let the other matter go as he was. ''You'd have
to kill me to do that.''

''Only myself,'' he assured her, taking up his copy
of the script, everything but work forgotten now, ''because if it takes all night, you will get the renunciation
scene down flawlessly—and I so do need my beauty
sleep.''

'' 'Oh Rogue, have you forgotten the lover you have
forsaken?' '' she cried, reading the first line of the
troublesome scene again. '' 'Have you sipped from the
cup and forgotten the intoxicating brew? Alas, alas, I
have not' '' she wailed, finding that he'd been right
the last time they'd rehearsed: remembering reality did
enhance fiction.

'' 'Oh before God, my love, I cannot,' '' she wept
with realistic tears, causing Kyle to smile beatifically
as she read on while remembering Gray, and weeping
for it. But to some purpose at least, this time.

''She calls it her 'sun porch,' '' the older man
grumbled, as he seated himself in a rocking chair and
gestured his guest to another, opposite it, ''but damned
if one ray gets in here anymore, her plants all hog it.
Did you ever see such a jungle?'' he asked with some
exasperation. ''Equatorial Africa, not Wyoming Territory. Built her a fine new house facing the setting
sun, but she brought Connecticut with her all the way

West. Can't see a damned thing but aspidistra and ferns when you look at the windows, but it's night now so it don't matter, I guess. Not much light out here either now, but at least we're alone. It's too cold to sit on the porch, and this is better'n setting in her parlor—Ida's got so many china dogs looking on there, I feel like I'm in a kennel," he complained with a grimace that was suspiciously like a smile, as he always did when he criticized his wife, and took a long drink from his glass.

"Well, now, Gray, speak up, boy. What can I do for you?" he finally asked.

"Sure you don't want to talk about where we should sit for a spell longer before I get to it?" Gray asked easily, sitting back and rocking.

The older man smiled into his glass, but grumbled, "Damned uppity cuss. You always was."

Gray's white-toothed grin gleaming in the dim light reflected from the adjoining parlor.

"And I always did wonder how come you talked just like all the hands and me," Gray mused. " 'Specially once I got to your old school back East, and found nobody else there did but you. 'Pears you and me got a few things in common, Doc, even though you're a learned physician and I'm just a wrangler."

"God save me from such wranglers," the doctor mumbled.

"And me from such old country doctors," Gray agreed.

But then he stopped rocking, put his own glass down on a table, and leaned forward, his hands clasped together on his knees. "Doc," he said seriously, "I need some advice. Medical advice."

"Is it the leg?" the doctor put in quickly, only sitting back again when Gray answered. "No, no, it's not much, but you did your best and it's still there and kicking, all right. No, it's something else."

The doctor eyed the tall, fit man before him and motioned for him to go on.

Gray sighed. "I didn't consult any experts in New York City," he said, "because I'm damned sure they don't know more than you; not about this. Oh, not only because I know you read more medical journals than you do seed catalogs. I suspect that you hide them inside your *Police Gazettes* so you don't ruin your reputation,'' he said on a laugh, before he went on in a quieter voice. "It's your experience, too. Sure, you put me together a time or two—just look at this old leg, but that's not it either. I guess it's just that I trust you as completely as any ranch hand or farmer in the valley does. Although I know half you put out is pure snake oil, for the devilry of it, the other half is solid good medicine.''

"It's not devilry, Gray,'' the doctor said as seriously. "These people wouldn't trust a high-nosed medical specialist. And half of healing is trust. I came out here because I love the West, just like you do. I don't notice you talking New Haven style when you're making a deal or giving out orders, either. That's just good business. For me, too. You can have a language barrier with a man even if you're both speaking English. No, it don't pay to be high-hat if you want to get to know someone. Knowing who it is you're curing is more important than what you're curing them of, most of the time.''

"Yeah,'' Gray nodded. "That's what those New York doctors don't seem to know, that's why I hot-footed it back here. Lord,'' he said, stretching his back, "I been doing some hard traveling. Just to see you. I'm glad nobody's birthing tonight. Because when I'm done talking, I'm going back again faster than I came, if I can. You see, Doc, I've got this friend who's got a problem . . .''

"Tell him applications of mercury will do it, but it hurts like hell,'' the doctor said abruptly, "and to stay away from that kind of woman in the future. I'm surprised at you Gray, you ought to know better by now. Didn't Josh and me tell you often enough? Wash first, and right after, and take a good look at more than her shape before you do anything in between,'' the doctor chided him before he took another long pull at his glass.

"No, it's not that," Gray said. "Nice things you think of me! It's not that I'm too smart not to be careless, but I'm smart enough not to let you know if I was," he laughed, and took a swallow from his own glass before he said, "Lord! That's good. But it's not what you're drinking is it? I know, you see. You're still drinking sarsaparilla and making faces like it was rotgut, aren't you? More than language can be a barrier when you're trying to get to know folks, right? Don't glower at me, Doc, I stole a sip from your glass when you turned your back from setting my leg that time. That first time, when I was a tad," he added, as the doctor grinned.

"Well, don't let it get around," the older man said, "though I expect most folks know it by now. They're just being polite. I got my public image to maintain. If I drank as much as I seem to, I'd be riding on calls underneath my buggy, don't you know."

They chuckled, and rocked in silence for a few minutes, before the doctor said softly, "Out with it Gray, never know when some fool woman will take it into her head to start pushing out a baby. I got two ready to pop, but I want to hear what brought you home. Must be something important."

"It is," Gray's voice came slow and seriously. "The most important thing in the world to me: Doc, I finally found a woman I want to marry. I love her more than I thought possible. It's not just jealousy of Royal—did you ever see the like to that?" he asked, diverted. Then he said more soberly, "Though I fooled myself into thinking that for a spell, and I regret it, because it delayed things. No, I love her, no question about it. She's the only one for me. But there's a problem . . ."

It didn't take long to tell, because he hadn't many facts, only those she'd told him, and he repeated those as he'd heard them. When he was done, the doctor was silent, rocking back and forth, fingering his chin as he thought, and Gray added in a goaded voice, "Now, if I try to seduce her to find out and I succeed, I lose either way it turns out. If there's something terribly wrong, I'll destroy her sure as if I used a knife, and I don't think a man should use his sex as a weapon. But if there's nothing much wrong, I'll have lost her love and her trust. She'll always think I had to try her out first, before I gave my word to love her forever—and who could blame her? She'd be right. That's no way to begin a marriage, is it? That's not love, that's a business deal. But just what in hell am I supposed to do? What do you think it could be, Doc?''

''Could be anything, could be nothing,'' the doctor said musingly. ''She ever say her folks mentioned anything to her about herself before she got married?''

Gray shook his head.

''And they're actors?'' the doctor asked, and then said slowly, ''Well, then we got to figure she's right about that—there's nothing to be seen on the outside, because though I know some folks who'd keep a daughter born with a pecker growing out of her ear a secret for fifty years, you can bet an actor wouldn't keep his mouth shut about something to do with sex.''

He rocked for while longer, before he started chuckling at a thought, and then waved his hand as though to wave it away, as he said, ''She's something, I can tell you. Imagine, having the brass to pick up a mirror to have a look! Not that it told her anything. And that damned fool husband didn't either . . . she ever say he took any medicine?''

''Not that I know of . . . Wait!'' Gray said, remembering. ''Yeah. She said that when she helped him pack, she threw in his bottles of 'Peruvian' something, and 'Dr. Pierce's Golden something,' or the other way 'round—I wasn't listening that close. Is it important?''

''Could be,'' the doctor rocked a little faster, before he stopped and stared at Gray, '' 'Peruvian Elixer' is a nice-Nelly name for what's supposed to be a sure cure for what they call 'men's weakness' and I call impotence. So's 'Golden Syrup'—but all it tells us is that the man couldn't make it, and we know that already. But was it because of him—or her?''

''She said he fathered a child after he left her . . .'' Gray began, but the doctor interrupted, ''Don't mean nothing. Man can perform like a studhorse with one woman and shrink up like a snail on hot rock at the sight of another. Listen, Gray. Here it is, plain as I can see it without seeing your girl, in order of difficulty—for you and her:

"She could have something really wrong, since birth. Something we can't fix. Or she might have something called 'imperforate hymen,' which is only that it's a damned tough one, and needs a scalpel to open it, because no man's that strong. That only means you have to get her to a comfortable sort of doctor with a sharp knife, and there's an end to it. Or it could be that her damned fool of a husband got himself soused on his wedding night—three drinks at least, I figure from what you said she said, and she was so scared she shut up like a clam, so he couldn't do a thing. And being scared of not being able, kept him disabled from then on—it happens. That only means she needs a few drinks herself so as to loosen up, and a strong sober man next time.

"It isn't an answer," the doctor apologized. "It's three of them. But for damned sure, bet on it, it's one of them that's the problem."

"And for your money?" Gray asked.

"Can't say. Wouldn't be fair."

They sat in silence for a time. Then the doctor spoke again.

"Tell you something," he said thoughtfully. "I haven't thought on it before, but from what I can see, we got more cases of imperforate hymen these days than when I was young—or when the world was young, for that matter. A whole lot more, it's a regular epidemic, if I'm reading my journals right. And that's odd. See, it happens once in a million or two, but I been hearing about it once in a thousand or two lately. I'm wondering if it isn't just because they're bringing up girls ignorant of what they used to know, and misleading boys, too.

"Hell, you've been East," the doctor growled. "You hear how they talk and act. Buttoned, girdled, and laced up to the nose—and the brains—all of them. Read one of Ida's romantic novels the other day—they have a married woman finding a baby that 'must have fallen out of heaven onto her breast in the night.' Imagine! That's how they talk about having babies! Tell that to one of my poor girls shouting her head off long into the night later tonight, and she'll tell you a thing or two. "... Falling out of heaven!" Damnation. They're calling piano legs 'limbs,' and even keeping books written by men on separate shelves from those written by women. I swear it! Saw it recommended in one of Ida's ladies' magazines not two months ago."

They laughed before he went on, "But it got me to thinking. Now, a scared woman's harder to get into than a locked safe. You wouldn't believe all the muscles involved, and if they seize up ... man with rape on his mind's got to cut off her wind, smack her silly, or threaten her bad to get to her, and that's the truth. A husband's not likely to do that on his wedding night—I hope. All the proper young gals these days, they have got to be scared blue. They don't know what they're going to be seeing, doing, or feeling—except bad and guilty. Must be as hard getting them to lay down on a bed as on an operating table, at that. The men are just as bad. Half the medical books claim good women don't feel anything but duty. Hah! They should get a look at some real folks like I do. The only difference between a good girl and bad one is a wedding ring. But that's a considerable thing, and maybe it ought to be," he mused.

"Point is," he said abruptly, because Gray was sitting forward, listening intently, "we didn't need doctors to initiate so many wives once upon a time. When they knew what to expect and their husbands expected it of them, too, even the tough ones gave in, if you know what I mean. One in a million in olden days, and now there's a regular epidemic of them, well, what do you think?" he snorted.

Gray sat quietly. And then he rose.

"I think," he said, "that it's time for me to get going. Thanks, Doc."

The doctor arose, too, and asked, "But I didn't give you a good answer, so what are you going to do, boy?"

Gray smiled at him, and it was such a sweet smile that the doctor literally saw the boy again in the toughened, scarred man before him.

"I'm going back, and I'm going to marry her, if I can," Gray said.

"Now hold on, Gray," the doctor said worriedly, stepping into his path. "Damn if you weren't always such a rash boy. Was you listening? I never said it was something correctable. It could be—but it could be something really bad, too."

"I know," Gray said calmly. "But it doesn't matter. That's the point. I came to you for medical advice, and I got it. I was listening, but I was listening to something else, too. Something inside of me that knew the answer from the first. My problem's got more to do with the heart and soul than the regions we were talking about. Of course I know it's a physical problem, too, and there are no guarantees. It could be bad, real bad. But I think the truth is that the worst it could be, would be having to go through life without her by my side."

The doctor stared hard at him and then asked bluntly, "What about kids?"

"What about them?" Gray asked, as he tucked in his shirt and reached for his sheepskin jacket. "You know any way to guarantee any man he's going to have kids with any wife he takes? You do that, you'll make your fortune, Doc."

"Well, what about the other?" the doctor demanded. "A marriage bed's supposed to be used for other things than sleeping—you're a lusty man, Gray, don't forget it."

"I'm not. At least I hope I'm not, nor any of the experience that lustiness got me. And that's considerable. So no matter what it turns out to be, I expect I've got enough experience to be able to figure out something for us to do together at night, don't you think?" he asked on a grin as he clapped on his hat, and then offered his hand to the old doctor. "I'll think of something," he promised, more seriously as the doctor hesitated. ''So long as I have her, the rest will take care of itself.''

The older man shook his head.

''When you were a boy, you damn near kilt yourself trying to be a man like your big brother. Damned if you didn't make it,'' he said, taking Gray's hand at last. ''You finally figured out there's more to being a man than riding wild horses, taking crazy risks, and bedding women, didn't you?''

''Maybe,'' Gray said as he shook the older man's hand hard. ''But then, if you figure that way, that means there's a whole lot more to being a woman than what goes on in a bed and having babies, too—don't it? Don't worry about me, Doc,'' he said, smiling widely. ''And thanks. At least I know the odds now. The rest is up to me. I found my woman, I just have to go convince her of that.''

''Gray, I think you can do anything you set your mind to,'' the doctor said.

''Yeah, but you don't know her,'' Gray answered, and though he was still smiling, it was certain he wasn't joking.

He was beyond weary when he returned to his apartment in New York City. It was night and it was late, but he'd had to drive through holiday crowds all the way from Grand Central Depot. He'd passed Christmas in a welter of small towns, seen through his train window as he hurtled homeward. But at least, Gray thought with relief as he let himself in the door, it was still the old year, and with time to spare. It seemed to him that he'd been traveling long years, since birth: train, carriage, and horseback, and it wasn't just his leg that ached and throbbed as he sat in his parlor and sorted through the mail that had been waiting for him. He didn't bother to remove more than his hat, and sat wrapped to the ears in his sheepskin jacket as he opened his letters.

But when he came to one of them, he went no further. He sat, in his jacket and travel dust, and read and reread the theatrical bill that his brother had sent to

him. It was an advertisement for a new show to premiere at the Warwick Theater that week, a production
given by one Kyle Harper and Company. There was to
be a comedian he knew, a somewhat famous singer he
didn't, a dance troupe, a magician, a dog act, an ac-
robatic troupe, and a chorus involved. All this was to
be capped by a "Sensational, Heart-Wrenching, Truly
Thrilling Performance of the Justly Famous and Moving Play: *Curfew Shall Not Ring Tonight.*" The scenery was billed as being "Magnificent and New to
New York," the costumes as "Appropriate," and the
acting as no more than "Superb" and no less than
"Excellent."

It would feature a new artiste: an actress with a
"Reknowned" name, for it was to star a "Miss Hannah Darling-Roberts."

Josh had circled the name with a broad pen stroke
and written: "Is this *our* Hannah?"

And although Gray sat up in his clothes until he fell
asleep from sheer exhaustion just wondering about it,
he still couldn't say. But he greatly feared he was too
late, after all his haste, and that she'd found her place.
And so it might well be that now she no longer was
their Hannah, after all.

Chapter Eighteen

Everyone in the theater had a task to perform except for the one man who stood in the empty audience, looking up at the stage. If it were a day later and a later hour, he'd have his own part to play; he'd be one of the opening-night audience, and everyone on the stage would be playing to him. Now, they ignored him as they rehearsed and marked out their places, trying to estimate the best angles for their feet and faces. A few minutes earlier, the chorus and dancers had done a lively Christmas medley. Now they were gone, the musicians were taking their break; the tumblers and animal acts were practicing in the wings, leaving the stage to the actors. They had no costumes on, some still held pages of scripts in their hands, and yet the man in the audience soon forgot that as they got more deeply into their drama.

The lone spectator had seen many plays far better than the truncated melodrama they enacted. And he'd seen them performed by such great actors as Booth, O'Neil, Mansfield, Terry and Irving, Drew and Rehan. But there was something elemental about *Curfew Shall Not Ring Tonight*—a tale of lost love and devotion, that never failed to please him. And then too,

Gray could not take his eyes from Hannah Darling-Roberts, the female star of the piece.

She was entirely different from the girl he'd once held in his arms. The Hannah on the stage was beautiful in a new way; everything about her seemed to be magnified, however far from him she was now. Her dark hair drank up the spotlight, her eyes sparkled in it, her voice was pitched to the ears of those who would love her from yards away. She wore an everyday dress and no stage makeup, but there was something newly seductive about her, even in the way she moved. Gray's first brush with the stirrings of adult sexuality had come from looking at a set of much fingered *cartes-de-visite* a french photographer had taken of the actress Ada Isaacs Menken that some drifter had left behind in the bunkhouse. He'd been transfixed by the sight of the reclining beauty's flimsy skirt hiked high to reveal white thighs and long, plump female legs in high-laced boots. He'd never seen anything so erotic before, and seldom since, not even in the best bordellos in New Orleans. Yet now, Hannah, in her ordinary walking gown, high above him on the stage, radiated such sensuality as to leave him as breathless as that ten-year-old boy had been as he'd studied the sensational cards he'd found. No, he thought with growing fear and sorrow, not precisely 'our Hannah' now, at all.

And yet, even so, he was happy for her. Because she was very good. And seemed to know it.

Her voice was clear and confident, her movements smooth and natural, for all their exaggeration. There was nothing of the girl who'd laid in his arms in the wings of a western music hall that cold night, declaring she was brave enough to go onstage even as she trembled from the fear of it. He'd loved that girl, and now wondered if he was selfish enough to love her more than this self-assured, newly emerged professional actress before him. But then she glanced down, and seeing him, flashed a swift grin of recognition and welcome—even though her character was weeping—and he knew that nothing had changed for him, no matter what had become of her in the days since he'd last seen her.

Gray sat back to watch the play. He was amused when he finally realized the lovely little sister of the piece was the erstwhile "Little Polly," and was embarrassed to admit, even to himself, that the only reason he hadn't recognized her immediately was the interesting way she now displayed in her simple gingham gown. But his amusement faded as he thought about it and realized how time was literally flying. It wasn't only Polly's startling new femininity, it was the fact that a new year and a new decade, was only days away. And as the play unfolded, he began to see that his chances might be fading as rapidly. She was good, he thought with equal parts of pride and dismay—she was very good indeed. And all he could offer her was himself. For he began to see that she could win her own fortune.

"I have not forgotten. Shall I forget the spring? Could I forget my beating heart? Oh, Father, let me go. I cannot stay, I must leave now. More depends on this than you can know . . . ," Hannah pleaded.

"Yes . . . ," Hannah's portly "Father" said absently, taking out his pocket watch and studying it. "God Almighty!" he exclaimed. "Look at the time! If you don't let us go to eat now, we'll never make it to opening night," he shouted to the darkened audience. "Here, Kyle, how long do you intend to keep us at it? We had to skimp breakfast, passed up luncheon, and dinner's on the hob now. I can't hear my lines for the way my stomach's growling!"

"Little danger of you wasting away, Renfrue," Kyle said distractedly from the orchestra pit, as he looked up from some papers a cigar-smoking man was urging on him. "What time is it anyway? Ah, yes, well," he said, glancing at a watch the man held up. "The question is if you have it down, my children—and down perfectly? Remember, if you skimp on practice, it will go far worse than skimping on a dozen breakfasts. Hannah, my dear," he called, "I leave it to you. Are you all indeed, done for the day, and ready for the big night as well?''

"We all know our parts and marks," Hannah said, "as for our performances, that's for you to judge. But I don't think we'd know them any better if we practiced all night into the morning.''

"Then you are free, good night. get some rest, and we'll see you dewy-fresh first thing in the morning," Kyle said, and no one protested, knowing his "morning" would be long after noon, as any good actor's was.

The actors began drifting off the stage, calling advice and comment to each other, and Gray stood and came up to the apron. He gazed up at Hannah as she stared down at him.

"Dinner? Please," he said urgently, "I only just got back to town late last night. I have to speak with you. Yes?''

She hesitated.

"We might have some last-minute things to go over, we'll not have the chance for any major changes as of tomorrow," Kyle cautioned her from where he'd appeared at Gray's side.

Indians, Gray thought sourly, had been known to move less quickly, and much less quietly.

Hannah bit her lip.

"Ah, but I thought we'd everything settled, and you wanted to spend some time with Mr. Jackson—so as to see if we have to slip his song in tomorrow night or not," she explained, looking at Kyle.

Kyle glanced over his shoulder with a momentarily worried expression, and stared at the man he'd just left waiting for him. Jackson's new song mightn't be good, but it wasn't bad, or most importantly, difficult to learn. And Jackson was willing to pay a good sum to have it included in the revue; after a few drinks, dinner, and a nice chat, he might be willing to pay even more. Especially if he heard that Harry Carstairs already had a new song in the show. This new breed of songwriters was a delight to work with—they paid to have their songs sung, on the generally correct theory that the more they were performed, the more they'd be performed in the future. Forget about talking machines and box cameras—it was familiarity, not necessarily quality, that made the public's heart grow fonder—that was the most important discovery of the decade, as Kyle was always happy to tell songwriters interested in his shows.

"Ah, yes. Well then, but be sure to get a good-night's rest. Remember, you've a big day and a bigger night tomorrow," Kyle warned her, deciding, from the look of her hesitation with Gray Dylan, that he could spend his own evening with Jackson, since Hannah clearly was his bird in the hand.

"I won't be a minute," Hannah told Gray, and went backstage to get her coat and hat.

Their dinner was the strangest one they'd ever had together. The food at the chophouse was excellent, but not so fine that she had to comment on it so much as she did. That was after Gray explained that his trip home had been hurried, harried, but successful, and before, having exhausted the subject of her approval of the restaurant, she told him brightly about how well the play was going, and how sure she was that she was doing the right thing this time.

"And if your father appears in the audience . . . ?" he asked, and hated himself when he heard what he'd said, even though he was willing to say anything to erase that charming, polite, impersonal expression from her face. She was a very good actress, she'd kept him entertained through four courses, but she'd not looked him directly in the eye once since they'd sat down.

"Oh. But I haven't told him. Still," she said, cutting a tiny wedge from the corner of a cutlet on her plate, "if he comes, so be it. I *am* a 'Darling' by birth and right, and if I'm not good, at least I'll be a curiosity, and Father, being an actor, will like publicity of any sort, just as Kyle says."

"Does he?" Gray asked.

She nodded, and immediately launched into a long story to do with Polly's debut as a young woman.

"As to that . . . ," she said when she was done, and she realized she hadn't gotten the laughter she'd thought the story merited. "She was just asking about Peggy again. I haven't gotten a letter since she went back with you—how is she, and how is the family settling in?"

"I wouldn't know," Gray said, still gazing at her steadily. "I left them at the station. I stayed just one day and one night at home before I got on the train again. Why won't you look at me, Hannah?"

She looked up from her plate and met his eyes at last. They were as blue and clear as she feared she'd remembered, but filled with sadness now.

"Why did you go back then?" she blurted, staring at him.

"I went to see the wisest man I know—in medicine. An old doctor who put me back together many times. I needed him to do it again. He did."

She half rose from her seat, because her first impulse was to flee. Embarrassment made her cheeks grow pink, shame brought tears to her eyes, but her training made her sit again, and her talent made her voice calm.

"I see. Do you think he'd like a photograph?" she asked quietly. "For his records, that is, if not for his curiosity's sake? Although I doubt you'd find a photographer willing to take such pictures, even if I'd pose for them. I'm sorry, he'll have to wait until I'm dead and have willed my body to science. I think I've done now, Gray, I'd like to leave."

"It wasn't just your problem," he said as quietly. "It was mine, too."

She cocked her head to the side, " 'Was'? Yes, perhaps it was. But it is no more. I've given that up, Gray. No matter what your wise doctor told you, it is no longer your problem. Now it's just mine. Or rather, it isn't. No more doctors, no more books—I'm like a child that's been let out of school, aren't I?" she said on a charming laugh. "I've chosen the theater. I'll make my life there. I want nothing else, ever again. It doesn't matter if I do well or not tomorrow night," she said quickly, cutting him off as he began to speak, "there are other careers in the theater than acting for me. But I've decided my future will be in my work, I've done with foolish fancies and futile games."

"You've decided?" he asked softly. "And what about me? I love you, Hannah," he said. "I'll never be done with that. Was I . . . am I simply a futile, foolish fancy to you?"

Her smile faded as he went on, ". . . By the way, my learned doctor had no answers for me. But talking to him, and only him—and he's kept secrets deeper than a well could—made me see there was only one answer, one I'd always known."

She licked her lips and gazed at him, unable to speak another word—if only because a squadron of busboys came to clear the table so that another contingent of them could put a sixth course before them.

"Yes, I think we've finished," Gray said, reaching for his billfold, "at least, here."

He eyed the platters of fowl and vegetables with such distaste, the restaurant's host sprang forward to their table.

"We have to talk," Gray said, ignoring the commotion he'd caused, and the look in his eyes was such that the host relaxed. It was not the food, after all, that was making the gentleman leave so suddenly; it was only that he was after different delicacies tonight. It was only that he was clearly in love. And who could blame him?

They got only so far as the curb in front of the chophouse.

"Don't call a hackney," Hannah said quickly, as she saw him raise his hand, "I live so close by—we can talk as we walk. I can't invite you in. My landlady's respectable," she hurried to explain as she saw his arm fall to his side. "It's bad enough that I let you in the other nights—she's been looking at me oddly ever since. I know you only stayed a few minutes, but I'm in the theater, and she's not a theatrical landlady . . . I promised I'd only give lessons in my rooms during the day, and those with the doors open, but now that

I've actually taken to the stage," she said sadly, realizing what she said was truth, "I expect I'll have to move. The public may be more accepting of us these days," she added, shrugging, "but only so long as we don't live in their houses."

They walked down the street as a light snow fell over them. Gray shortened his stride to match the small steps Hannah had to take because of her tightly fitted, bell-shaped skirt. But she walked rapidly because she was cold, and soon was short of breath.

"Of course, when I'm rich and famous I can let far better rooms—anywhere, except in a respectable landlady's house," she puffed, as she clutched her hands together in her muff and tried to ignore the cold of the snow and his eyes, "and at the Player's Club, that is. Father belongs there, but even though he'd vouch for me, I belong to one of the only two groups that can never join or stay there: critics and females. But still . . ."

"This is damned foolish," he said, interrupting, turning and facing her, making her glad they weren't under a gaslight, because she couldn't see his expression clearly.

"It's cold, Lord, it's snowing," he exclaimed. "Kyle would be right to have my head if I got you pneumonia from this. We're only a few streets from your house, and we've got no place to talk. I've got an apartment, too, one with a fireplace I could roast an ox in, but you can't go there because I'm a man; I can't go to your place because you're a woman—where are we supposed to talk? In the street, until the snow covers us over? In your hallway so we can entertain your respectable landlady? Hannah," he said in a softer voice, "I need an hour to talk to you. Just that. You don't have to agree with me, either. But you've got to listen. I'll claim that much, at least, as my due."

When she didn't answer at once, he watched the flakes settling on her hair and said on a sigh, "Lord, Hannah—at least tell me why you've changed toward me. What did I do this time? Last time it turned out all I did was be a man, and you canceled dinner on me. This time you seem to be canceling everything. I thought,'' he said, looking down at her and trying to read her expression, ''you trusted me. Have I done anything to change that lately? Have I ever?''

She shook her head.

They stood facing each other on a dark downtown street, with only the falling snow to give them illumination.

''I'll come with you to your place,'' she said at last, because he did deserve that much. If she could give him nothing else, she decided, she'd give him her trust. ''I'm freezing,'' she admitted on a shaky laugh, as he stood and stared down at her, ''and you're right. Forget pneumonia—Kyle would kill you if I got the sniffles just before opening night. I can hide a cough as a sob,'' she explained, because he still hadn't moved, ''but there's no way to hide sniffle or a stuffy nose. Can you hear me? 'I lub you, darlinguh, I do,' '' she mimicked, doing a bit of dialogue with a head cold, and then grew still, hearing the unfortunate line she'd used, fearing he'd take her jest for truth, even if it was.

''Let's get a cab,'' he said.

The lights of the city died behind them the farther they rode uptown. And the farther they drove, the less they spoke. She was wondering at her rash offer to come to his rooms. She might think he knew her very well, but the fact was that she was an actress now, and she was going, alone, to a man's rooms at night. The idea of what she was doing—the words to describe it, made her forget who she was doing it with and why— and wonder if he would, too. He knew what she was thinking, but couldn't think of a thing to say that wouldn't make it worse, no matter how many times he opened his lips to try. If he said he wouldn't try anything, he'd only make her think about what he might try; and then, too, he was no longer sure of what he could promise her, not tonight.

She'd heard about ''The Dakota,'' and had been as amused by the name as she was impressed by what had been said of it. And so it was awe that kept her silent as they entered the main lobby. Then it was fear and awe that kept her still until they came to his door.

When he rose from his knees after igniting a fire in his fireplace, she went straight to the hearth, drawn by the cheery flames. And then at last she spoke.

"I don't know if it's big enough to roast an ox, Gray," she said, "but it will do for me."

He let her stay and warm herself. When he returned from hanging up her coat, muff and hat, he watched the firelight play over her. She sensed his presence and turned so the fire could warm her back.

"What a lovely place!" she said. "The ceilings are so high. And the rooms so spacious. Just as everyone says. It's too bad it's dark, I hear there's a splendid view of the park. Does this side face it?"

"No, my bedroom does, do you want to see?" he said. Then watching her face, relented, and smiled wearily as he added, "If you try to say only the most innocent things you can think of, you'll find yourself in trouble, Hannah. Better off talking the truth. I'm sorry you're so scared to be here. Tell the truth—I am, too. Does that make you feel any better? Come on, I'll light a lot of lamps so you know I can't sneak up on you, and we'll sit and talk it out. Then, if you want, we'll talk about my apartment and its furnishings, all right?"

"All right," she said and sat on a couch close to the fire, smiling back at him, thinking of how well he knew her, and how good he made her feel—before she grew frightened again, just exactly because of it. She looked anywhere but at him when he sat next to her, because he was so very good to look at, too. She wasn't used to seeing men so tanned or scarred, yet on the other hand, all the other men she saw literally paled in comparison to him. She sat up straight and put her heels and toes together on the floor in front of her, and clasped her hands in her lap.

"I still want to marry you," he said before she could draw another breath. "I guess I backed off before because of a whole lot of reasons. Mostly, I think now, because I was so surprised at what you told me. After that, I guess I was confused—and then I wondered: I wasn't sure I could be faithful to you, not knowing just exactly what your problem was . . . That's only natural, I guess. But it sure isn't nice,'' he went on, shaking his head, so that his flaxen hair shimmered in the firelight. "Still, I'm only human, so that's all I'll ask you to forgive me for. I had to think about it. And whether I could handle it. Because I don't believe married folks ought to cheat at anything with each other, or else it all becomes a lie, and I sure couldn't ever tell you about things like that; so even if you agreed I could stray, it would still be cheating.''

"And now,'' she asked stiffly, "after talking with your doctor-friend, you've changed your mind? Since you still dislike the idea of 'straying,' I suppose you've decided that perhaps it may not be quite as bad as I've said?'' She didn't know whether to be thrilled or angry at that idea, but he gave her little chance to entertain it.

"Lord no!'' he said in surprise. "It could be terrible. But whatever it is—it's not likely anything that we can't work out. That's the point. Hannah,'' he said, not allowing her to escape his steady gaze now, "I don't know what's wrong with you. Nobody does. Point is, it don't matter. See, I never met anyone like you before, and I know I never will again. You're smart and beautiful and good. You make me laugh, and it feels wonderful when I can make you laugh. If it wasn't for whatever it is, I'd never have had a chance to even know you. So I'm grateful for that, at least.''

Her eyes widened. "You'd marry a woman you're not sure you can—make love with?'' she asked in a rush.

"Well,'' he said, sitting back, stretching out his legs, watching her, loving the way the firelight made her eyes glow, as if with sudden fox fire in their brown depths. "Way I figure it, most men I know don't know—if they marry a good woman, that is. I just have a jump on them,'' he said.

He was impressed by the way her breast rose and fell with her emotion. "Don't try to make light of it!''

she cried, "You may never be able to . . . to . . . you know," she faltered, becoming both alarmed and delighted by the warm look in his eyes.

"Yeah," he said, "I do. But you don't. That's part of the answer, too. Ah," he said, digging his hands into his pockets and staring at his boot tips now, momentarily disconcerted, "but see, there's all kinds of ways to get around that," he said. "There's more than a dozen ways to skin a cat and believe me, there's more than that when it comes to making love . . .

"Anyhow, if it has to be," he said, glancing up, his face flushed by firelight and something else he hadn't felt since he was a boy, "trust me, ma'am, I'll think of something. And it'll likely please you, too, of course," he said quickly, seeing her expression, "or else we won't do it, honest. You don't know what I'm talking about, do you, darling?" he asked with tender amusement.

"I know you're talking western," she said in agitation. "That's like Kyle starting to pace. It makes me nervous. Answer me straightly—don't you want a normal wife?"

"Well, just supposing I had a way of knowing that before I married her," he said reasonably. "What if something happened after we were married, so she wasn't anymore—do you think I'd throw her out? You take me for a eastern potentate? I'd stick with her, and I'd hope she' stick with me if it was me that had the problem. That's what it's all supposed to be about, isn't it? Otherwise, why bother getting married?"

"What about children?" she asked breathlessly. "Oh Gray, you'd have such beautiful children!"

"Well, not by myself," he said, "and maybe not even with a wife. That's one thing no one can predict. Since we're talking so straight, I'll tell you I haven't had any before, that I know of. And you know I'm not up for sainthood. So how can I tell if I ever would? Besides, look around, there's maybe just about a half a million kids without parents right here in this city of a million, or didn't you take a good look around Peggy's neighborhood? Royal's already making noises about importing a slew of them.

"Hannah," he said seriously, sitting upright. "It's you I want."

When she didn't answer immediately, he asked, "Is it because you don't want to give up your career now that you've decided to be an actress? That might be a problem, I mean, if you become as famous as your father. All I can say is that we could figure something out about that, too. If it's that important to you, maybe I'd stay here with you when you were in a play, and you'd come home with me when you weren't . . . I don't know. We'd work it out. If you loved me. You've never said so," he said, touching her for the first time, picking up her hand, "but I thought you did."

"Oh Lord, Gray," she said, and came into his arms.

"Even starting to talk like me," he whispered into the pouf of hair she'd drawn up on top of her head as she burrowed into his chest. "Start to look like me in no time, poor girl—now that's something to give you pause. But only that," he said. Then kissing the top of her ear, he asked, "Will you answer me?"

But she only raised her head to look into his eyes, and saw them gazing at her lips, and offered them to him. He kissed her for a very long time, breaking off only to taste her neck, or her cheek, or her ear, before he came back to her lips again. Her mouth was warm and open beneath his, and if the touch of his tongue made her stiffen at first, it wasn't long before she was tentatively offering hers to him, as well. And if the feel of her in his arms was everything he wanted, the shape he felt beneath his searching hands soon showed what else it was that he wanted.

There were a dozen mind-boggling, tiny, slippery pearl buttons at the back of her gown, and yet it wasn't long before he'd conquered them. The sight of her bared breasts as they rose above the tightly laced bosom bodice that she wore made his breath catch in his throat, as hers did when he lowered his lips to them, at last.

There were eighteen narrow laces at the back of her

bosom bodice to patiently undo; he knew because he silently counted them so that he wouldn't be tempted to force them apart, and frighten her. When the casing that had held her so fast finally fell apart, he found his hands could do as good a job and better for her, because she never whimpered with shocked delight when it upheld her before.

John had taught her how good a man's hands and lips could feel. But John was a memory. He'd made her squirm with frustrated pleasure before they'd been married. But only then, because after that everything had been tempered by apprehension and fear. As began to happen now. Because now she gazed down to see Gray's big, sure hands and what they held so reverently, and her fears banished her pleasure. The white of her skin against the tan of his hands was as shocking as the sight of what was happening. She was only glad that though her shamefully bared nipples were puckered tight, he'd never know it was because of fear and cold now, and not delight. And so when his warm mouth finally left them, she had to remind herself to deliberately open her lips again to receive his kiss, because this was all for him now, and all of it deliberately so.

Because though she'd never said it, so as to embarrass or shame him with the memory of it later, she loved him very much. And so had decided, somewhere between the moment she'd seen him at the theater and the moment his lips had met hers tonight, that she'd give herself to him now, if she could, before she lost the courage to. So that he'd never have to make the sacrifice he'd offered.

She'd bear the shame of his shock if her condition was, indeed, something terrible. She'd bear his triumph if it was not. But she'd never let him throw himself away blindly, because she'd never stay and wait to watch his love turn to resentment, or hate. Although her shame was the thing she'd feared the most all these years, now she knew, as she let him lower her to the couch and draw off her gown, that it would be nothing at all; nothing compared to his hate.

She shifted so as to help him. There were a great

many garments to help him remove from her. Yet it seemed that somewhere along the way, he'd also wriggled out of his own jacket; sometime when she'd not noticed, he'd opened wide the high stiff collar of his white shirt. She noted the tense muscles in the strong neck, and though her hands were trembling with the desire to stroke that bare flesh, she put them on his shoulders, and waited. That was what John had always wanted her to do.

His hands trailed along her ribs, reached her waist, traced and cupped her hips and buttocks, and paused. She was entirely bared to him now, and dared not look where he did, but only at his hair. Inconsequentially, she noted how his part was crooked, toward the back, as she awaited his next move.

He suddenly raised himself on his elbows, and only gazed down at her.

"They were wrong," he said gruffly. "There is something very different about your body—you're perfect," he said. "Absolutely perfect. Ah," he groaned, and wrenching his gaze from her, levered himself up and pulled her up from the couch and back into his arms.

"What is it?" she asked, terrified, when she felt him shivering. Her heart was racing as fast as his was as he sat holding her, his hands stroking her bare back, "You can tell me, honestly."

"I tell you honestly you're perfect," he said hoarsely, "that's why I stopped. I thought I could go on, and bring you some little foretaste . . . but I'm not so good as I thought I was—or maybe it's because you're better than I could've guessed. Damn," he said, as he felt her tremble, and he held her at arm's length and gazed at her with hungry eyes. "You're just too beautiful. Come on, I'll help you get everything hitched together again."

"No. I mean," she said, squeezing her eyes closed. "It's not necessary—you can—go ahead, if you want. Really."

"The hell I can!" he exclaimed angrily. "Excuse

my language," he said more temperately, "but what do you think I am?"

"I thought," she said, her own hands coming up despite herself, to cover herself, as he turned and fumbled among her discarded garments to find something for her to put on again, "we would . . . I thought it would be best if we tried it now."

He stopped and gazed at her, astonished.

"Well, it wouldn't be," he said.

He looked at the pile of clothes on the couch and carpet, "Lord, what is it that you had on first?" he asked, fishing up her chemise.

"No, it would never be best, or ever better," he continued, picking up the pair of cotton drawers she pointed to with a shaking finger, "if we finished what we started. What would we gain? You'd know you could marry me with a clear conscience? Yeah, sure. And then spend the rest of our lives together thinking how I covered all my bets first, how I had to be dead-certain sure everything was perfect before I said 'I do'? And maybe, just maybe, hating me a little for it, huh?

"And if it didn't work, Oho!" he said vehemently, as he tossed her chemise over her head and picked up her corset. "What about how shamed you'd feel then? Even when I insisted we marry, wouldn't you just spend the rest of our lives wondering if it was pity or guilt, not love, that made me insist? And I'd insist, either way, believe me. But if you refused no matter what I said—and I won't take a bride to the altar with a gun at her back—who would you hate more all your life—yourself or me?

"No," he said a little more calmly, as he turned her around and started lacing her up. "No way. You're a fine little actress, but we can't pretend we're just some hotheaded young courting couple that got carried away, either. Though it was a near thing," he muttered. "No. If we marry, it's going to be like regular folks, with half a heart full of trust, and the other half full of hope.

"The only guarantee I want is that you love me.

Saying yes is the only way to show me that. You never said anything,'' he said seriously, his hands pausing on her corset strings, before he pulled them so tight she gasped. ''Don't think I didn't notice it. I may talk West, but I know East, North, and South, too. You love me—you marry me. That's all there is to it.''

''I won't be able to do anything if I can't breathe,'' she said, springing up from the couch and taking the laces in her own hands. ''A tiny waist is one thing, strangulation another,'' she complained, glad of something else to talk about as she scrambled into the rest of her clothing. She was almost done when she turned around to see him holding her puffy, lacy demi-bustle pad at arm's length, like Hamlet with Yorick's skull, with a bemused expression on his face. She laughed, only stopping when she managed to snatch it back and tie it on again. Then his tender expression made her want to weep.

''I don't know,'' she said at last, looking down at her toes, ''I don't know. What I want to do, and what I ought to do, and what's best for both of us to do— ah, Gray, I have to be sure they're all the same thing.''

''Now, here's a funny thing,'' he said, rising, coming to stand before her, and holding her hands, ''for all I want you, I won't wait forever. I can't. It's not just desire, I guess it's pride, too,'' he smiled crookedly. ''There's nothing so sappy as a perennial suitor. I won't wait backstage with roses until I look old enough to look right doing it. I'll need an answer soon.''

She nodded and swallowed hard.

''You'll have one,'' she promised, ''soon. I've got tomorrow night to get through. Then I'll be able to decide about the rest of my life. Only, Gray,'' she said, bowing her head until it touched his chest, ''I can promise you one thing right now. If I don't say yes to you, I'll never say yes to anyone—except maybe for business reasons.''

''Now that,'' he said, sighing, ''don't make me feel a whole lot better.''

He kissed her hair and let her go.

''Now you're going home to your respectable land-lady,'' he said, plucking her outer garments from his hall rack, ''because tomorrow night, you'll be making the most spectacular debut ever seen in New York City.''

''Do you know?'' she asked, pausing at his door as he helped her on with her coat. ''I'd forgotten that entirely. I was so anxious about tomorrow night, but now its the least of my worries. I don't think it will be any problem at all now, because suddenly I've got a much bigger one to think about. I suppose,'' she said with as much wonder as slowly dawning delight, ''it's cured my stage fright altogether!''

She would always remember the smile he wore at that moment, because it was a bittersweet mix of love, laughter, and pain.

''Glad to be of service, ma'am,'' he said wryly, and took her arm and ushered her out before she could think of a thing to say to heal the inadvertent wound that truth had given him.

Chapter Nineteen

The only odd thing about the audience was that such a crowd should flock to this theater tonight. It was almost as if the audience had been attracted by itself. After all, there was no famous name on the bill except for one which graced an unknown actress. No re- knowned actor was performing: Edwin Booth was home, ill; the Divine Sarah was somewhere in Paris, the lovely Lillian was playing elsewhere, Mr. Mans- field was in England. Other great names were per- forming at other equally great theaters in the city tonight.

But that was only how things appeared at first glance. Because, as everyone in the house knew, the famous father of one of tonight's performers was pre- sent in the audience, and the well-connected suitor of that same performer had a front seat, too. Together, those gentlemen had drawn such a crowd behind them, like comets trailing stardust, that the audience could be forgiven for dreading the moment when the house lights would be dimmed, and they'd be left to be en- tertained only by what would be going onstage.

After all, whatever fare was on the stage could scarcely compare to the famous profile of Blayne Dar- ling, which he was kind enough to show by standing to greet all his friends and anyone who looked like he might be a friend, while constantly rotating so that no one in the crowd could miss him in the fifth row, center. The fabulously wealthy Dylan brothers, as tall and handsome a pair of gents as anyone would wish to see, were there in the orchestra as well. Gray Dylan was the fellow with an eye for the actress, his brother already had his won—for there was Josh Dylan and his spectacularly beautiful wife—she'd been an actress once, too, the whispers informed anyone who didn't know—which would be anyone who was from out of town or dead.

There was a sprinkling of famous fellows from the Players Club and clutches of elegant ones from other exclusive gentlemen's clubs, some accompanied by ladies, and some by women who were somewhat less than ladies and even more expensive; as well as ladies and gents from diverse mansions on Fifth Avenue: the rich and the dramatic were there in numbers. Who could blame a ticket holder for staring at a sultan's hoard of diamonds and rubies, emeralds and pearls, and a trapper's winter supply of lush, exotic furs rather than his program? And that was only what the gentlemen were wearing.

It seemed a pity that the ladies would have to remove their hats, because they were concoctions of plums and feathers, flowers, fruits, laces, and gauze that would rival the intricacy and daring of any stage set that might yet be unveiled. Their gowns defied description, although members of the yellow press, in inferior seats, strained their eyes to try. Whether they bore famous names or were only angling to acquire them from their escorts, the ladies dressed to the hilt and carried themselves with as much grace as sureness. They either had a great deal of money or cost a great deal of it, and everything about them proclaimed it.

The audience itself ensured that the production it had come to see would be famous, whatever happened onstage. Or infamous. Which was the same as famous in the theater, and perhaps even better. Or so, surely,

Kyle Harper's greatest idol would have said, and what was good enough for P. T. Barnum was perfect for him.

Kyle stood in the wings and gazed out at the crowd. He sighed as sorrowfully as anyone in the audience did when the houselights went down, the footlights were lit, and the orchestra leader strode to his podium. Soon enough, fear and dismay, disappointment and fury would come as he watched the performers ruin his dreams—as they always did, however good they were. Yet now, in this scant blink of time between the dream and the telling of it, as always, he rejoiced in the only real joy that he knew—the joy of perfect illusion.

And then the curtains pulled back.

Lester Claxton pranced out and made them laugh, the singers got them to join in on the choruses of even the newest songs, the dancers kept their feet tapping in time, and the stage sets and effects for every number made them gasp and applaud even more than the prestidigitator and the acrobats did. By the time the comic dogs had paraded around the stage in fancy dress, the audience was clearly pleased. When the intermission lights came up, they could be seen to be chuckling and smiling. But it was equally clear that they wouldn't remember a thing they'd seen. An "Agreeable Entertainment" would be a fair review of the night's fare, but it would be as bad as an epitaph on a gravestone. None of it had been either excellent or deplorable enough to chat about at tomorrow's dinner. That was as deadly as outright failure would be.

But the night wasn't over yet.

Hannah stood in the wings and waited for intermission to be over. She was dressed in a long white nightgown, her hair hanging in carefully disordered gleaming waves, her cheeks pink with rouge, and her eyes wide with expectation: the very picture of the distraught daughter awakened in the night to hear dread news—as she was supposed to be. Kyle studied her; for a scant moment, he felt a stirring of regret, even pity. She was good. Not spectacularly so, but good enough. Of course, the tensions of the night might destroy her resolve again, as they had that time in the West. But what Kyle knew, and doubted that she did, was that it hardly mattered what she did when she got onstage, so long as she got there. She was Blayne Darling's daughter, and so whatever she was, she'd be talked about; and being talked about, for good or ill, would keep the box office open.

Keeping the show alive so that it would make enough money to finance another was the only thing Kyle was concerned with. Yet, just now, as he heard the audience settle in its many seats after intermission, Kyle had the wild urge to rush to her side and beg her not to go on. He'd the sudden impulse to take her costume and play her part again, as he had once before, to save her from herself, lest she freeze with fear again, but this time—onstage. But then he remembered it was her choice, and one she had to make. And calmed himself by remembering that he'd offered her his name and his hand, whatever transpired tonight.

Gray smiled. At intermission he'd greeted acquaintances with ease and grace, now as the houselights dimmed, he stopped trading quips with his brother and sister-in-law, and settled back in his seat with an expression of polite interest. But Lucy Dylan saw his tanned hands clenched to fists in his lap, and Josh Dylan saw the muscle working in his clenched jaw, and husband and wife exchanged soft sighs as they glanced at each other.

Gray was willing his lady to wild success with every nerve in his body, even as he was dreading it. He didn't know if he was more anxious for her or himself, since he knew all too well that her success might signal his failure. But one thing he did know, now at the last—and it amazed him to know it—was that whatever it meant for his future: she must not fail tonight. Because he doubted she could bear it, and if she couldn't, so then, neither could he.

And Blayne Darling, in the unfamiliar anonymous darkness of a theater audience, sat up straight and leaned forward, his body tense, his eyes glittering as he waited for his daughter's debut.

When Polly finally cried out, pleading with the villain, ''Oh sir, desist! Pray be still, for I fear you'll wake my dear sister from her well-earned slumbers— Oh, heavens! See, she comes!'' Hannah stepped out to take the stage.

Kyle took a step back. Gray let out his breath at last. And Blayne Darling stopped breathing so he could listen to every nuance of her speech. It was her moment, for good or ill. And there was nothing any of them could do but watch.

She looked wonderfully well. There was no doubt of that. Whether it was the makeup or her own inner calm, her face was refreshingly lovely. She didn't freeze up, so her movements were graceful and easy. Her voice didn't shake or quiver, and came out sweet, strong, and low, projected just exactly as she'd always taught her pupils, so that it reached every member of the audience. She used every nuance in the script and added some of her own. As the drama went on, she was touching as the distraught daughter, tempting as the shy lover, sympathetic as the endangered beauty, and laudable as the intrepid rescuer. She was very good.

Kyle sighed with relief. Gray wore an increasingly sad expression, even as his heart rejoiced for her. But halfway through the drama, Blayne Darling sat back and relaxed. Because she was very good indeed. However, she was not great.

The play ran just as it ought, and soon the more susceptible members of the audience had handkerchiefs in their hands and ready tears in their eyes. At times, they were concerned for the distressed father. At other times, for the cunning little sister, the worried mother, or the handsome, bold, but doomed lover. At times they hated the vile seducer to the point of audibly hissing him, even some of the more sophisticated of them. And they always sat up straighter and paid close attention whenever Hannah appeared, which surely signified her utter triumph as an actress. But Blayne Darling knew better.

Because sometimes, when Hannah was onstage, the audience's eyes and ears were elsewhere, as the playwright intended. She didn't dominate the action every moment, demanding every second of the audience's attention; she didn't seem to glow even when she stood silent, so that she had them glancing at her to see her reaction even when another character was speaking. When she left the stage, the stage didn't dim because of it; the audience could forget her now and again, when the action called for her to be forgotten. She was in the play, but she was not the entire play, as befit a good actress. But as never befit a great one. She was young, it was true. And time could teach her many things. But never that. Either it was there from the start, or it was not. And it was not. She was good, but she was not that rarest and most wondrous thing: the stuff of stars—the sort of performer who dazzled so that she cast all others on the stage with her into the dark.

The audience didn't seem to care, they applauded madly at the end. Encores were taken again and again, so many roses thrust into Hannah's arms that she took to plucking them and throwing them back at the crowd. Kyle winced, thinking of how much they'd cost him, and Gray collected one to present to Lucy, glad he'd thought to order so many, after all. And Blayne Darling stood applauding, every comment he caught of "She's got her father's eyes!"—"She's got his hair!" making him smile wider.

He was still grinning as he waited for the aisles to clear so he could go backstage. His wife looked to him with worry, and then relaxed when she saw his famous, mischievous smile, and the excitement in his eyes. Hannah had been good, and that he could bear. But she hadn't been great, for that he could not. Still, the one thing she'd been that he could never be was soon borne in on him again.

"Blayne," an actor friend of his crowed, as he pushed through the crowd to be one of the first to congratulate the new sensation's father, "I guess we've seen the last of the Darling 'Hamlet'—it's 'Lear' or nothing now, eh, old chap?"

"Old friend," "old man," "old fellow,"—he was called all of those things and more, many times, as he had been before. But tonight the words took on new meaning. By the time he made his way backstage, it was as well that he was a great actor. Because he had to congratulate everyone, and take their awe and congratulations in turn, and was used to the awe. But it took all his art to appear to welcome the congratulations for his beautiful, young, young and talented, clever young daughter.

"Thank you, thank you," he cried with every evidence of gladness, "and where is our bright new star?"

"Elsewhere, sir," Kyle said, as he took his own congratulations. "She won't be long. She's just taking care of old business before she meets her new public."

Kyle smiled with expectation as well as triumph. He'd seen Gray. How could he not? Gray had been the first one backstage, and so he'd sent him to wait for her at her dressing room, to get that out of the way first. Now Kyle waited for her to be done with that interview, so she could get on with her life.

Hannah fled to her dressing room at once, running light-footed, as though the applause was thunder that was threatening her. He was the first thing she saw when she got there, and without breaking step, she ran to him and cast herself into his arms. She stayed there, silent, hugging him as tightly as he held her, as though all the world were tugging at them, trying to pull them apart.

"I did it" she finally said, in wonder and in relief. "Gray, I did it, didn't I?"

She looked up and saw him nod.

"You did," he said softly. "Honey, you surely did."

"Are you proud of me?" she asked with such shy delight in her face that his arms tightened further around her.

"Absolutely," he said, "but I always was."

"Still, my father was there," she said, laying her

head on his shoulder. "I saw him watching and even so, I never missed a line. I did it, Gray. I really did."

He might have said "of course" again, or maybe he only thought it, but they stayed there, holding tight and silent, listening to the applause until it ebbed and broke into the several small sounds of a crowd of people milling together, and they remembered where they were again.

"And now? Now what do we do?" he asked, although he wished he didn't have to. But he knew waiting for tomorrow wouldn't change things.

She paused, her head against his chest. Then she raised it, and noticing how her face paint had got on his jacket, began to brush at it with her hands, until he grasped one and held it tight. She looked into his eyes and said, "Well, there's a cast party . . ."

"No, Hannah, that's not what I mean," he said gravely. "I know it's soon, but it's not too soon. It's now or never. Will you have me? Or have you found something more? Whatever it is, please don't tell me you don't know yet."

She took a deep breath.

"I won't" she said. "Because what more is there? You mean the applause?" She frowned. "It's very nice. But did you think it would replace you? Did you think I'd find that a lot of people I don't know clapping for me would be as good as one man I love loving me? No, I grew up in the theater, after all, and saw it all before I could read a line of script, so I know better than that. That was never what was delaying me. I only needed to concentrate on tonight before I decided, as I said. And now I have. Yes, please, thank you, I will."

Before he could say a word or draw her close, she put a hand on his chest and looked directly into his eyes.

"You know all my problems, and if you still want me, then yes. Or rather, *now*, yes. Because at least now I know I'm not just all problems. It's not because of what I did tonight. Or because Kyle proposed to me the other night, even knowing what you do about me.

Yes, he did,'' she said, grinning. ''I confess that's very nice to know. But it's not why, either. Or maybe they're all the reasons why together. It's because I finally know I'm worth something to myself. You see, now,'' she said, raising her chin, ''I can understand why you want to marry me, after all.''

''Oh, the conceit of it,'' he said, laughing.

''Yes,'' she said smugly, while she still had her lips free to speak.

There was nothing leisurely or tender about their kiss, even though they'd both just declared for each other, there was a desperate longing and lingering fear of separation that kept their mouths hungrily searching each other's. When he raised his head at last, he became aware of how heated she was, and the stage makeup she wore bore a faint, unpleasant oily scent, nothing at all like the usual floral essence he associated with her. It reminded him of a thing that must be said at once.

While he tried to think how to phrase it, she saw how her lip rouge had stained his face, and rubbed at it with her fingertips, flushing redder than the rouge he'd worn off her cheeks.

''About your career,'' he said helplessly, as she grinned despite herself at how oddly the tender tones of her cosmetics looked on his high-boned, tanned, scarred cheek, ''I guess we can stay here in New York when you've got a part you like, but . . . do you think we could spend some time back home, too? I'll buy you music boxes and player pianos to keep you entertained there—a whole Riverboat Calliope if you want,'' he said anxiously as she grinned the wider.

''Gray,'' she said seriously, though she wanted to laugh aloud at the sheer pleasure of his offer, ''I told you before—I'm not an actress. No, and I never wanted to be one. I'm still not one. I just had to prove I could do it if I wanted to. And I did.''

''You did, you were great,'' he said.

''No,'' she said quietly, kissing the cheek she'd just scrubbed relatively clean. ''No, thank you, but I'm not. If I were great, I'd be an actress. I was good, but that would never be enough for me. Father's great. I decided long ago that I'd never settle for less. How could I?'' she asked, as he appeared to protest, ''. . . unless, of course,'' she said with a sudden fearful surmise, ''you want me to—that is, some men like having actress wives onstage for others to admire . . .''

''Lord! Such a lovely fool,'' he whispered, cutting off her words to her absolute delight.

''Oh!'' Kyle said with enough projection in that one exclamation to snap even their intense concentration on what they were doing. ''Beg pardon, I do indeed! It's just that we were all looking for our new star!''

They sprang apart, and looked at the crowd of people that accompanied Kyle.

''Sir,'' Gray said at once, when he saw Blayne Darling in the group. ''your daughter's just consented to be my wife.''

''Indeed?'' Blayne said, pleased that he'd not have to play either the outraged father or the tolerant man of the world—since he'd no idea of which one he was supposed to be here. And smiling, because Gray Dylan was as wealthy as he was influential, he asked, ''When?''

''Soon as we can—before she comes to her senses and changes her mind,'' Gray said, accepting his brother's handshake and then his offer of a handkerchief, as he tried to erase the color he saw everyone smiling at on his carmine cheeks.

''Maybe even New Year's Day, if Judge Wilson is willing?'' he asked Josh.

''If your lady is, he'll be,'' Josh answered, as he saw Hannah's smile. ''Might be nice at that—a New Year's party and a wedding . . . We can do it, but can we do it up right this fast, Lucy?'' he asked his wife.

''It would be beyond wonderful!'' Lucy Dylan cried. ''We'll let Delia stay up to be bridesmaid—we'll invite everyone, just everyone. We've got champagne on hand already, and I can order more, and flowers; we can have the wedding before the new year or just after it. Of course, it would depend on whether Hannah wants to be married this year or next. That is to say, one way

she could be married a year by next week, and the
other she could be a newlywed for a year. Of course,
it all depends on what she says, although what a party
it would be, I mean . . .''

"Take a deep breath," Kyle commanded, just as he
used to do all those years ago when he'd taught her to
act. And though they hadn't spoken in nearly a decade, she immediately did as he asked. Then, on an
expelled breath she said, with evident relief.

"Yes. We can do it, and I'd love to."

Then she grew still, staring at Kyle, realizing how
well that admonition worked and how it had always
calmed her. Hannah grew even more still, remembering him at last.

"Oh, Kyle," Hannah said, her eyes wide with grief,
"I'm so sorry, what a way for you to find out! I never
meant . . ."

"Indeed," Kyle said swiftly, his dark face smooth
and calm, for whatever expression had come over it,
when he'd heard the news, had been as quickly erased,
and no one had seen it, being intent upon the newly
engaged couple. "What better way? It's novel, most
theatrical. My congratulations. Am I invited?"

But before she could answer, he added just as
smoothly, "I applaud the drama of it, of course. But
what a dreary honeymoon for your bridegroom—with
you on the stage here every night of it."

Hannah's parted lips closed. She spun around and
stared at Gray.

"I never thought about it," she confessed. "It went
right out of my head. But, of course, I have to play
the whole run of the revue."

"And," Kyle put in quietly, "it does look to be a
good long one. But I'll never be the one to ruin love's
young dream. Go along, Hannah, with your beloved,
I'll find a replacement."

Hannah stared at him. He shrugged and smiled
sadly. It was the best present he could give her, and
they both knew it, and it was difficult to tell which of
them was more surprised by the offer.

"No need," Blayne Darling spoke up. As everyone

turned to him, he seemed to enlarge, until everyone wondered why they'd ever looked away from him. "There's another Darling willing in the wings. I'm between engagements at the moment—such, alas, is the fate of the aging thespian, I suppose," he said coyly, as they all grinned at the ludicrous thought, as he'd intended them to do.

"Oh, I don't mean to don a wig and play my dear daughter's part—as if I could," Blayne said at once, as everyone, except for Kyle and some of his cast, chuckled at that, "but now, that Father's part in *Curfew* is a meaty one . . . My dear sir," he said to Kyle, "would you take one Darling in place of another? Let my Hannah have her brief engagement of another sort, as well as her honeymoon, and you—take me in her stead? The publicity might just make up for her absence, do you think?" he added with just the right touch of humility to take the foolishness from such a rhetorical question.

"My dear sir!" Kyle exclaimed, all personal pain forgotten as the aching, empty places in his hungry heart filled with another kind of profound love. "Harry, what say you?" he called to the actor who'd played the part.

The actor, knowing future victory could be snatched from the jaws of this inevitable defeat, bowed and said quite humbly, "I'd be honored to have you take the part, Blayne."

"We'll enlarge it, of course," Kyle said to Blayne, who nodded and said, "Of course." And as Kyle began to pour glad murmurs about the marvelous publicity into his inclined ear, Blayne nodded again, to signal his wife to take notes, and they strolled off to plan their revised production, leaving the company to begin toasting the success of the revue, the coming marriage, and the new year.

But for the first time that Hannah could remember, her mother didn't follow her father immediately. Instead, she came to Hannah's side and kissed her cheek, and gave her hand to a bemused Gray. As he looked down at the slender, dark-haired woman, she said in a

quiet undervoice, ''Congratulations, my dear. I'm
Hannah's mother, by the by. You've done very well for
yourself, she's a good girl. Ah, he looks for me! I'll
see you again, no doubt,'' she murmured, before she
hurried away.

There were real tears in Hannah's eyes as she
watched her go. She looked up at Gray, her eyes shining.

''Ah! Wasn't that wonderful of her?'' she asked with
such sincerity that all he could do was nod and put his
arm around her, silently promising her, whatever happened, a very different future from her past.

Chapter Twenty

"You," Gray said accusingly, as Hannah clung to his arm, humming a tune from the show as they left the theater after the cast party, "are tipsy."

She slowed her steps and glanced up to him.

"Yes. Quite so. Tipsy," she said, reaching up to touch a gloved forfinger to the tip of his nose, "Perspicacious of you, sir. But since I said that so very well, you will note that I am not drunk, or soused, or dreadfully inebriated. So you see, you'll have to leave off your vile plans to seduce me, villain. Because I know just what I am doing, and I love doing it, because I am merely merrily tipsy, thank you very much."

She missed a step and giggled. He helped her into the hackney coach, and when they sat back, kissed her. When he stopped, he sighed.

"It's hard being a really good vile seducer when I live so darned far off," he complained, as he nosed her ear. "By the time I got you back to my place way out there at the top of the park, you'd be stony sober, and with your hangover already starting."

"But I'm not drunk," she protested in a soft little voice. "I really do just feel giddy. It's not the champagne—although that does help," she admitted so prettily he moved to kiss her again. Before he could, she said wistfully, "But seducing me, drunken or sober, might be quite impossible, you know, however good a villain you may be."

And then he did kiss her, to silence her and all her fears, for the moment. Her mouth was so warm, her body so pliant, her response so eager—as eager as his own, that he tried to disregard the taste of champagne on her lips and believe it was all honestly for him. Because even though he knew it was perfectly honorable to hold her and kiss her now, he'd a personal code, and making love to drunken women was not part of it. That thought was the only thing that could take his mind from the sweetness of her mouth. Then the faint taste of alcohol reminded him of something his old friend and physician back home had said only days before. He thought of the future and drew back, considering it.

"Not drunk?" he asked, grinning, his gaze lingering on her plump lips. "Now how would you know?"

"I'll have you know, sir," she said with great aplomb, "that I have been very drunk in my day. How else should I know how to play a sot? Father said he once got himself *blind*, as research. And so did I," she giggled. "It was ghastly. Not like this. I was sick," she said luxuriously, "for *hours*. But then I knew I could play a drunk as well as anyone."

"Uh-huh," he said as the coach slowed. "Now let's see if you can play a sober lady, because you're home. Are you going to weave up the stairs and shock your landlady? I see her curtains parting."

"I shall be a model of decorum," Hannah said with majesty, and immediately ruined the effect by giggling at the very idea.

But her laughter fled when they reached the small hallway of the brownstone, and she saw the look in her landlady's eyes as her door opened. Those small, knowing eyes took in her lovely lodger's blushed lips and slightly tousled condition, as well as the elegance of her escort's dress, seeming to see beneath his evening cape to the half-finished bottle of champagne

Hannah had insisted he secrete there—and those narrowed eyes said everything that had ever been said about the manners and morals of ladies of the theater, without a word being spoken.

"Ah, good evening, Mrs. Prescott," Hannah said with complete sobriety, for the situation had chased all her merriment away. "Allow me to present my fiancé, Mr. Graham Dylan, to you." She paused, the sudden realization that she'd really no reason to be shamed now competing with all her ingrained habits. "We are to be married soon—very soon," she said with dawning wonder. "Why, in fact, I'm giving notice that my rooms will be available to let right after the new year."

Mrs. Prescott squinted.

"Dylan? Gray-ham Dylan? Of the Fifth Avenoo Dylans?" Mrs. Prescott gasped, and as Hannah nodded, she went on excitedly, "I thawt so! Yez being in the theayter and all. It's like they sez in the papers," she breathed in delight. "How d'ja do, Mr. Dylan. Congratulations to yez, and a Happy New Year, and no hurry about vacating the premises, dearie, no hurry at all. Take yer time. Pleased to meetcha," she said again, adjusting her spectacles to get a better look at Gray, looking far more thrilled than pleased to see him.

"Madam," Gray said solemnly, bowing, before he turned to Hannah and said with an air of great command, "I'll just see you upstairs then, my dear."

As they went up the stairs, Mrs. Prescott called after them, "Anything yez needs, jist call on me, yez hear?"

It was only when her door was closed that Hannah dared to laugh. And then only when Gray, after suppressing several apt but shocking comments, said, mimicking Mrs. Prescott: "Anything yez wants dearies—anytime of the day or night."

He smiled down at Hannah, and opened his arms wide.

"You don't have to worry anymore. My money's made us respectable, no matter what she hears going on here. Lord,'' he said prayerfully as she came into his embrace, ''God bless respectable landladies!''

When he finally let her go, she stepped back, suddenly aware of the night, the time, and several other things.

''Gray?'' she said in a slightly quavering voice, her eyes wide, ''We're going to be married in three days' time? Three days? I suppose that with all that was happening tonight—my getting onstage and getting it right, and then getting out of ever having to do it again—I forgot that.''

''Did you want a church wedding?'' he asked, suddenly grave as she was. ''I didn't think. I really just wanted us married, and fast, because I was afraid you'd change your mind—I wasn't joking about that. But if you want more of a wedding, that's Okay with me, we'll just send word to Josh and your folks and . . .''

''No, no,'' she said. ''No, it's fine. Anyway,'' she added with a slight, tremulous grin, ''Father's probably invited half the world already and advised all the newspapers, too—it will make very good print you know, however famous he is, he always appreciates publicity. Such a dramatic thing, after all, with him stepping in to save the day, and a New Year's Eve wedding in a fine mansion . . . I suppose Father ought to have offered to make the wedding,'' she said as she realized it. ''But he doesn't know about such things, and was likely more impressed by your brother's offer. It's fine with me. Except the whole world will be there, won't they, Gray?'' she asked, the fine color fading from her cheeks, her eyes wide and frightened.

He stood watching her, frowning at the change in her.

''We'll be married in three days' time,'' she said wonderingly, and looked at him as though she were seeing him for the first time.

''Uh-huh,'' he said on a sigh, and then seemed to come to a decision. He cast off his cape and produced the bottle of champagne.

"You were right, darling," he drawled. "You're not drunk. Not half enough. Now, come on, we'll drink a toast to us. Fancy weddings are like funerals, they're not for the folks they're given for. They're for all the guests. Tonight will be for us. After all, a lot has happened," he said, thinking, as he knew she was, as she bit her lip, of all that would happen.

"And then," he said briskly, "we'll sit and talk about it until there's nothing scary left. If it takes all night. After all, we've got your respectable landlady's permission, haven't we?"

He grinned. "But yeah," he sighed as she came into his arms again. "You're right again. First, we do this."

"Yes, I suppose we can live part of the time in Wyoming Territory, and part of it in New York," Hannah said from where she sat snug in the circle of Gray's arm, on her comfortable old couch.

"By next year, we'll likely be a state of the union," Gray said proudly, "so you might even find you want to live there longer—at least until any daughters we have can grow up and vote. Yeah," he said, as she gazed up at him with widened eyes, "looks like we're going to be the first state to give you women the vote. Well, what can you expect of a bunch of lonely fellows who'll do just about anything to make you girls happy enough to stay with us out there?" he joked.

"The vote? Really? But how wonderful!" she cried, and then fell still, suddenly thinking about the prospective children he'd mentioned, even as he realized what he'd said and damned himself for bringing up such a touchy subject as this, of all nights.

"Too bad Royal and Peggy won't be able to come in for the ceremony in time," he said quickly. "I'll wire them tomorrow just to tell them about it, though. But beware his idea of a fitting wedding present," he added to make her smile. "Likely to find a cow on our front doorstep."

She chuckled, but then sighed. "Even though he may give us something lovely, I suppose I've already given my father the best wedding present of all, haven't I?'' she mused sadly.

His arm tightened around her and his thoughts were black. Of all the things he wished for tonight, and he wished for a great many, with luck being foremost, he'd time to wish his new fiancé were not quite so forgiving.

''After all, he gets publicity even when he's between important shows, and a chance to show his daughter's not a patch on him. But I sure had him worried for a time there, though, didn't I?'' she asked wickedly.

She giggled again as he turned to her, his blue eyes incandescent, alight with pleased laughter.

''And Kyle got a real star,'' she said, a momentary sadness passing over her as she wondered if Kyle thought he'd lost anything he couldn't replace. Now she remembered the sudden pallor beneath his dark complexion in that first instant she'd glanced at him after Gray had declared they were to be married. She raised her glass, drained it quickly, and peered into it.

''Empty,'' she announced, raising it higher.

''So it is,'' Gray agreed. ''No more,'' he said. ''I know you've had gallons more in your dark past, ma'am, but two glasses are enough now. They're not even champagne glasses. When we get back to Wyoming Territory, don't you let it get out that you've been swilling champagne from tooth glasses, or there won't be a ranch hand who'll talk to you. Sure, we're rustic, but we're not peasants!''

She laughed with him, but then asked, frowning with sudden worry, ''Will your friends like me, I wonder?''

It was exactly that same slightly exaggerated emotion that had marked all her statements in the past half hour that told him she had, indeed, had enough for now. He only hoped it was enough for what he had in mind. Tomorrow and tomorrow and tomorrow, he thought—with a fine flair for drama she'd have enjoyed if he'd dare share his thoughts with her now—and then they'd be married. But from everything she'd said tonight, and every emotion he could read on her face—

and that was every one that came to her—she was preparing to be panicked, as well as married. And who
could blame her? he thought, remembering her past
experiences.

So tonight he determined he'd seduce her.

If he succeeded, in all ways, she'd never have to
worry about it again. Even if he failed, it was far too
late for her to back out now. He knew it was taking
advantage, because no matter what happened she'd
never want to disappoint her friends or embarrass her
father, but he was sure that if they left it to tradition
and their wedding night, she'd be cold as ice by New
Year's Eve. In fact, it might be well into the new decade before she'd be able to relax like this with him
again. Thinking about it would only make it worse for
her, and him. And being married would mean that
she'd be thinking about it every day and night. He
certainly would be.

Now he remembered every word Doc had said to
him, and just looking at her face when she even said
the word "marriage" made him think of all those dozens of secret, tiny, hidden muscles already beginning
to tighten up against him. If she could drink just
enough to relax enough tonight, and he could ease his
way . . . He wasn't sure he was doing right, but he
was sure he couldn't be that far wrong.

"Sure, all my friends will purely hate you—just look
how Royal feels about you," he said tenderly, gazing
at her, glad, at least from the way his body was accepting his plans, that he'd made them.

"You," she said, pointing to his untouched glass,
"aren't drinking. Isn't it bad luck to not drink a
toast?"

Worse luck to drink them, he thought, wondering
about the story of her first husband again.

"Mmm," he said, wetting his lips with the wine,
before taking hers again.

She despaired, even as she rejoiced in his kiss. He
wasn't drinking enough, he was as amusing and con-
trolled and sensible as ever. And she'd never take him
off guard if he were so sober. There were only three

days left until their wedding. There was still time. She hoped he wouldn't back out, whatever happened tonight. But at least she was determined that he know all the facts so he could, if he wanted to. It was only fair.

She'd decided to seduce him tonight.

She'd never had to practice such arts on John, but she knew what had made him want to do what he couldn't do with her. Kisses had been enough at first, taking off her clothing had been sufficient at the end. She'd done both with Gray, though, and failed. Still, she'd seen enough plays on the subject to know how it was done. And with enough wine, she could surely enact them. Although she realized she was a bit dazed now, she worried, thinking she could use a jot more champagne just so she could lose her last fears and cautions. But the bottle, she noted with a distant sort of grieving, was being emptied into Gray's own glass even as she stared at it longingly, though he hadn't so much as sipped what remained of his first share.

Gray saw her petulant expression as he put the empty bottle down, and moved his filled glass far out of her reach, knowing he'd done the right thing. She needed to be a little more relaxed, not limp as a dishrag and out of her mind.

"Well, now, what else is bothering you, honey?" he asked, as he wrapped his arm around her again. He scarcely heard her answer, he was so appalled at how false he sounded, as if he really was one of the villains in a melodrama. All he needed, he thought with some disgust, was a nice smoking jacket and a big mustache, and he'd get the part exactly right.

Hannah murmured something about when they'd go shopping for something or other, as her mind worked as furiously as it could under its twin burdens of champagne and self-doubt.

"I don't suppose I need many new clothes," she said, "because winter is winter whether we're in New York or Wyoming Territory. Heavens!" she exclaimed suddenly. "That's why I feel so warm, I'm still all dressed for a blizzard, and here we are so warm and snug inside. I wonder if I ought to slip into something more comfortable,'' she said too brightly, blushing a little as she blatantly parroted the most famous line in the seduction scene of *The Bridge at Midnight, Her Fatal Lover,* and a dozen other plays she'd seen, as she fidgeted with a button at the throat of her high-necked frock.

She'd gotten four of them undone when his hand came down over hers on the buttons. Her heart picked up it's beat as it raced in triumph, even as it did with sudden fear; she hadn't thought she'd get such immediate results.

"Now hold on, it isn't *that* warm," he said with grim dislike. So she'd had experience with liquor, had she? She was on her ear after two glasses, he thought angrily, now he'd have to wait a while for her to sober enough to make it a fair encounter. Knowing how it was with novice drinkers, he heaved a sigh as he removed his hand, for there was every chance she'd fall asleep before that happened.

As best Hannah could remember in her shaken state, her next line had to do with asking him to make himself comfortable, too, but from the look on his face, she was afraid to ask him the time of night. There was only so much her experience in the theater could do. She had to rely on her own intuition now. So she brought a hand up to the side of his grim face. And then bereft of easy words, and too frightened to think of difficult ones, she lifted her face to his and kissed him.

It felt like nothing he'd ever felt before, but he was fairly sure that it didn't feel like the kiss of a drunken woman. After one moment of hesitation, he decided he didn't want to analyze it anymore, whatever it was, he was sure he couldn't go on living without more of it. She was warm, willing, and entirely relaxed in his arms, and when he could think at all about his planned seduction, he could only think that it was well underway.

She burrowed into his embrace and tried to bury all

her fears in his arms, as his lips silenced all her doubts. This was her Gray, and he'd make it all, all right, she thought, as his hands covered over her breasts, and his mouth left hers to the mundane business of drinking air, as it got on with the life-supporting business of sipping at her neck. There was no doubt that it was far too warm in the little parlor now, but she'd not the words to ask to slip into something more comfortable, because the only comfortable thing she could imagine was to be deeper within his arms than she was, and she knew that to be impossible. And though she was upset at first when his hands left her, she soon realized, as they began to work at less rewarding, but more vital tasks, that he was quite right, her clothes were definitely in the way.

She'd only a moment to realize she was sitting in her parlor, entirely naked, when she discovered herself clothed again, with him, in his arms. But now, although his mouth was more than enough attire for her breasts and his stroking hands sufficient to blanket all her body, she found his being dressed unfair and unjust. He laughed when she managed to say something to that point, and obligingly struggled from his jacket.

It was when he'd finally thrown off his shirt and emerged from his undershirt that he saw her eyes losing the sweet glaze of shocked sensation that they'd worn, and take on a sudden, stricken look of doubt and fear. He saw it clear, because in their haste, they'd forgotten to turn down the lights.

"No, and no," he said at last, shaking his head, his bare chest heaving from the effort of not reaching for her, where she sat, naked, frozen with indecision, staring at him. "This is not the place," he said.

Oh damnation, she thought, and tried not to weep. A moment before when he'd left her to her own thoughts and the accusing light, she'd been terrified of his continuing. Now she was horrified at the thought of his stopping. His eyes were brilliantly blue, and his face as taut as her nerves were as he stared at her. He hesitated, and then bent to her again. Only this time one arm went beneath her legs, the other around her shoulders, and he lifted her high and easily.

He walked straight to the closed door of her bedroom with her, and turned the knob to let them in.

She'd a moment to be glad it was such a small room that he couldn't miss the bed, and another to be distantly pleased that she'd made her bed this morning, before he murmured with satisfaction, "Now this is the right place," let her down, and followed her as she came to rest on the high feather mattress. Then she thought of little but what he was doing with her. She'd been married, had laid with a man before, but no man had ever touched her as he did, or how he did, and even more—she thought with sudden shocked pleasure that set off a wave of terror that ebbed to sheerest delight—where he did.

His heart rose when he finally touched her where he'd yearned to, because his blind fingers found no fault, only warmth and the damp heat that told him he was wanted. But not so much as he wanted her, he was sure of that. He wasn't sure she could ever match his longing for her, but went on kissing and caressing her, determined that her desire at least come close to equaling his before he sought to end it.

Her world shrank to the size of his hands; its perimeters, the height of his wide, hard, smooth shoulders; its depth, the endless plumb of his kisses and its sound, her pulse and his soft breathy inchoate murmurs of praise and encouragement. His world was measured by her slowly deepening kisses, bordered only by the swelling curves he found and claimed and charted, as he reached his limit and went beyond it in order to ensure that he found hers before he went further. Because for all his delight, he never dared lose himself in it, being constantly aware of how soon it might end in a discovery that would be the death of it. With all that he'd done in a hard life, he'd never known a harder thing than to stay aware of this, when he found her so intoxicating. But he was determined to be as an artist, allowing himself to be caught up in the creation of what he was doing, while all the while remaining ever vigilant, aware, in some small part of his mind, of the result he must work toward.

Still, there are certain mechanics involved in any art, and he could only hope his skill was sufficient to get them over and done with quickly enough to escape her notice. Because for all his need, he had to draw away so that he could draw off the last of his clothes—he would not come to her like a hasty stranger paying for quick pleasure in the night. Only as he did, did he realize that she'd left a small lamp glowing in the room. Because after he'd rid himself of the troublesome garments and looked back to her, he could see her eyes widen as she looked down at him. He drew up his leg as he sank back to the bed, trying to conceal himself. But her face was still, and her eyes full of pain.

She'd hinted that her husband had always kept his clothes on, but he didn't know what else he'd done, or she'd seen. Once again, Gray silently cursed a world that had made her so close to him and yet so far from him in freedom of expression.

"I can't help that," he said, leaning toward her, kissing her forehead, as he yearned to do more, but dared not when she looked so stricken. "It's how I'm made. I'll go turn down the light, if you look away," he offered. "It don't feel half so bad as it looks," he said a little desperately when she didn't answer him.

"Oh, but I'm sure it does," she breathed, as he damned her dead husband to the last circle of hell. "How dreadful," she cried softly.

This wasn't the time he wanted to explain the workings of his body to her. Words would end what they'd begun, because it wouldn't be long until she'd be thinking about her own body if he started discussing his. He sat back, careful to keep his knee raised as a barrier against her fascinated stare, and ran a hand through his hair in frustration, trying to think how to distract her. Obviously, seduction wasn't his game. It was for colder-hearted men than himself, he decided in despair, as he realized the needs of his body and the wants of his soul were clouding his mind and deadening his usually glib tongue.

"Oh, poor Gray," she said softly, her hand coming out to tentatively touch the foremost of the great welter of scars on his flexed leg. "How it must have hurt you! I'd no idea."

"Well, it wasn't so bad, and it doesn't bother me much anymore, although it isn't pretty," he said in confusion. Then he fully realized what she'd meant and added incredulously, "You mean—it's my leg you were staring at? My leg? And not my—ah," he groaned, realizing his mistake as her wandering hand stopped caressing his scars.

"Oh," she said, lifting her hand and lowering her eyes. "No, not your—ah," she said, and then distinctly giggled. "Not that I've ever seen anything like—in real life," she added scrupulously, "because Father has a book, a very naughty one—although he says it's art—about the history of acting, and there's an illustration of an ancient Greek production of *Lysistrata* where the actors strap on big, wooden—ah . . ." She paused, merriment and embarrassment vieing for ascendancy in her eyes. "Anyway," she said, her lips quivering from the effort of keeping them straight, "that's more frightening, I promise you. You are . . . actually lovely, I think," she said before her voice died to a whisper and faded away.

But so everything about him was lovely to her, this stranger who'd become half her life. He seemed so perfectly made; so powerful, clean, and right in his nakedness that the only shame she felt at being with him like this was that she couldn't hope to compare to him.

She sat up in bed, her hair barely covering over those high, uptilted breasts he'd so lately held, her own leg tucked sideways to hide her last secret from him, and he thought his heart would melt with love for her. It didn't matter what hidden flaw nature had given her, she was, whatever it was, enough perfection for him.

And when she looked into his suddenly grave and adoring eyes, she saw it.

It was impossible to say which of them moved first, or which of them held the other harder, or whose need was stronger. She felt no fear when he lay down with her, and he felt no doubt when he turned her to him so they became one writhing form on the bed; one newly created being seeking peace.

But there were some things even love couldn't change. Despite all her desire, she couldn't help but know what he was finally attempting to do with her, and for all the words at his command, he couldn't ask her to do more than what she was already doing at his touch. But she didn't yield.

He paused, his desire pure pain now. She lay beneath him, accessible to him, but entirely closed to him. At the final moment, she'd locked against him. How much of it was her doing and how much nature's, he couldn't know. He stroked the hair back from her moist forehead, and put his own damp one against hers as he rested for a moment, wondering what in heaven's name to do next.

"I was just thinking how we got here," he lied, breathing hard, trying to buy time before all their time slipped away. "How I picked you up and marched in here. Now, what if you'd had one of those new kind of beds that fold right up into the wall? I was trying so hard to be the hero, I'd have walked smack into it. And with what I was leading with, it would have made the damage to my leg look like nothing in comparison!"

He felt the tremor in her breast, and then the trembling in her throat, and worried as much as he cursed himself for his clumsy, stupid, barnyard attempt at humor.

"Oh Lord!" she whispered, shaking with mirth as she envisioned it. "Now how would you explain that?"

And then she laughed. And in that moment of laughter, she opened to him, heart, soul, and body— because there is no fear that doesn't flee in the face of laughter.

She felt the sudden pain, and it was considerable, but nothing to the pain in her heart. Her eyes flew open. Gray lay motionless above her, as though in worse distress than she was, his face strained and drawn, a previously unseen pulse beating in his forehead, his blue eyes glazed, and his breath coming with effort.

"Oh, I'm so sorry," she cried as she tried to pull away from both the pain and the knowledge that she was at this last extremity finally proven deficient, proven flawed.

"What?" he asked on a gasp, "What are you sorry for?"

He wouldn't let her move so much as an inch, and so she lay pinned beneath him, weeping, "Because it won't work, because I'm . . . imperfect," she managed to say, as the new pain ebbed and flowed away, overwhelmed by shame.

"Hannah, darling," he breathed in her ear with effort, somewhere between a chuckle and a sob. "It worked, it did, it is. There's nothing wrong with you. Oh girl, there's nothing wrong but my clumsiness. Everything's fine," he moved to show her. "It couldn't work better, ah," he said as his movements caused him to let go of his hard-held control. "Ah, love, it's fine, it's so fine, it's too fine . . ."

She didn't feel the ecstasy he did as he moved in her, or more than a dim burning ache as he did so, or more than the faint beginnings of a keener, shimmering sensation as he continued to. She felt something that dimmed all bodily pleasure and pain. Because there was no doubt, he was actually making love to her: Gray was really making physical love to her, he was deep within her and he'd said she was fine, and she could see that it was. The thrilling joy of that overwhelmed all else. So that when he came at last to his convulsive release, she was already beyond more ecstasy.

"I did it!" she whispered, when he rolled to her side and held her close. "I did, didn't I?"

"No, ma'am," he said on a weak chuckle. "We

did. Just like an actress," he added, kissing her damp hair, "taking all the bows after all my work."

He was more than content; he'd been startled by the intensity of his pleasure, and was now stunned with gratitude and slow dawning joy. He waited to lie beside her, hold her, and take time to believe his good luck. But still, he raised himself on one elbow and looked down into her face, all seriousness now, because tired and sated as he was, the thing should be said to bury it for all time.

"There's nothing wrong with you, and never was. Mind, you weren't easy," he said on a crooked grin that moved something in her heart. "Lord, no. I guess all your medical books have a thing or two to say about that. No, it wasn't easy, but it wasn't impossible. But this time, you did the drinking, and I did some distracting, and we did it. Yeah," he said, smiling as he saw she did. "We did it, all right. I had the advantage of being sober, and knowing something might be needed besides desire," he added, unwilling to remind her of her late husband, but too fair-minded to forget him.

"See," he said gently, as she watched him with eyes as wide and deep as the night they were adrift in, "sometimes you have just got to get on that wild horse, no matter how scared you are. Because there's nothing worse than fear. It can defeat men as well as women. But it didn't get you," he said with pride. "You got on two wild horses tonight and beat them both. Although," he added with gentle rue, touching a feathery kiss to her cheek, "I suspect you feel more like one's ridden you just now—even though you sure conquered him, too. It'll never be that difficult again, I promise," he whispered.

"That's what you think," she said, so joyful she couldn't stay serious a heartbeat longer. "It will take far more than two glasses of champagne and a few kisses to get me next time. Yes," she said breathlessly when he raised his head from her again. "It will take that—exactly right."

"Hannah," he said at last, as he gasped with the

effort of stopping to get the words out again, "this is all a part of love, but it was never necessary for my love, you know that. Although it sure is good," he admitted. "Still, it was pretty rough for you the first time; we have a world of time ahead of us, you sure you want this again now?"

"Now," she insisted, "and later, and then again."

"Lord!" he sighed with pleasure and expectation, "the *Police Gazette* was right about you actresses, you're wild and wicked and depraved."

"Of course," she said smugly, "I just had to learn how to be. Show me again? Please?" she asked, suddenly shy, before he began to, and her words died against his throat, as he showed her how laughter could become something silent and even more pleasurable. And with all her lack of experience, she showed him what he'd always guessed: that their love would be something more than bodies meeting, and nothing less than beyond all his experience.

Mrs. Prescott woke, as usual, at dawn. She lay in bed, hearing the sparrows squabbling in the hedges outside her window, even though it had been closed against the December night. Mr. Evans, third floor, front, had begun his morning hacking and coughing in preparation to lighting up his first smoke of the day. And the milkman's horse came clopping up the street, she heard him stop in front of Mrs. Henderson's house on the corner, right on time. It was the usual morning song, muted by winter, but it woke her as readily as a rooster might.

But then she heard the gladsome sound of two people laughing uproariously: a man and a woman. Probably drunks coming home with the dawn, she thought with a sniff as she lay in bed, thinking of her morning's chores. She could understand if not approve that, she was in New York City, and not far from the theater district, after all. But she never knew why it was that she then heard them merrily chanting in unison: "We did it, we did it, we did it," until they stopped as suddenly as if they'd dropped down a well.

Because when she rose and went to the window to see what had happened to them, she saw nothing but the sparrows and the milkman's horse and wagon, and the morning light, coming up to warm the world.

Chapter Twenty-One

They threw rice and petals and words of advice and congratulations at the newlyweds as they raced down the stairs of the Dylan mansion to their coach, and then off into the new decade's first night. For once the wedding party lost none of it's zest when the bridal pair departed, because New Year's Eve was a time for both farewells and greetings, and there was still a new year to warm and welcome, even after all the good-byes.

The bride flung herself into the groom's arms and dissolved in merriment as soon as the coach door closed behind them.

"Your face," she chortled, "when he asked if I do!"

"Lord!" Gray laughed. "I was sure you'd say, 'I did!' like you threatened to."

"I was going to," Hannah lied blithely, "Except then I remembered that I'd have to say, 'I did, I did, I did,' if I was going to be honest."

"Add another 'I did' " he whispered before he kissed her. "Unless you're forgetting the morning."

She never got to agree, because he kissed the breath and the question away from her.

"It's very good," he said, when she lay her head on

his shoulder, as he stroked her hair and idly began to arrange the stray rose petals caught fast as stars in the dark cloud of it. "But darling, please believe its only part of why I'm so out of my mind happy now."

It was simply said, and yet for all the dramas she'd seen enacted, and all the ready answers a woman of the theater should have for any protestation of love, Hannah could only say, "Oh, Gray!" as tears filled her eyes.

"Of course," he added, "it's a mighty *big* part of it."

The sound of laughter poured from the closed coach as it rumbled off, mingling with the tolling of church bells that were still heard sporadically everywhere in the city. Hannah and Gray had taken their vows in the old year and had them consecrated in the new, as they'd felt was fitting for them, and now 1890 was well underway. Pans and pots were being banged by late revelers, and now and again firecrackers were still being set off to usher in the new decade. Yet their unbridled laughter rang out joyously, high and clear above the din, as though to also cheer the infant year.

Josh Dylan watched the coach go down the street, and was smiling widely as he came back into his house. His baby brother had never looked happier than when he'd kissed his new bride—except, Josh though as he kept his arm about his own wife's promising waist, for perhaps the moment just before the ceremony when he'd looked into his big brother's gravely serious eyes and murmured, "No need for worrying anymore. Everything's just fine. Everything's all right. Doc had words of advice, and turns out they're no longer needed. Yeah," he said, nodding at the dawning expression on his best man's face, "I'll be an uncle again before the summer, but there's no reason why, with any luck at all, you couldn't be one yourself, by next year."

He wouldn't say more, and he couldn't have said less, because he was as much a gentleman as he was about to be a husband. But neither would his brother violate either code of honor. Nor did he have to. Josh had understood right enough. Grinning from ear to ear, he swatted his brother on the shoulder hard enough to have sent him reeling halfway down the aisle if he hadn't been holding onto his other hand, shaking it. And he'd only said, "That's just fine!"

But it had been there in her eyes. All brides were beautiful, but Hannah was spectacularly so. And for those that looked for it, her triumph as well as her joy and satisfaction were there to see in the secret smile on her lush lips, and the dazed, slumberous look awakened in her great dark eyes. Newly lost innocence and newly kindled desire paired with love and made for a rare new beauty in an already beautiful woman. She dazzled so, in her cream-lace gown, with her black hair done up high on her proudly held head, that the guests hadn't an eye for her father or any of the other rich or famous that were there. And there were many of both in attendance, because the wedding list kept growing, until it became—as those members of the press that sneaked or were invited in were to write— possibly one of the most glittering affairs of the decade, even though it was held on its very first night.

"Everything will be fine with them," Josh whispered to his wife, but she only smiled, because she'd spoken a word to the bride before she'd left, and already knew it.

"Goodness! Look at Delia's face," she said instead, looking at her eldest girl, where she stood, petulant, in the hallway, staring after the disappeared wedding coach, stupified with sleepiness but too stubborn to show it. "I'll just go and get her to bed," Lucy murmured.

"You go sit down," Josh commanded as he unceremoniously hoisted his surly looking daughter over his shoulder, to the ruination of her frilly frock and her dignity. "She doesn't know whether to be angry at Gray for finding another girl, or amazed that she's got such a beautiful aunt now—an aunt who said she'd be more than willing to teach her acting someday," he added pointedly, and felt his burden cease wriggling. "But in the morning," he said as he began to climb the long circular stair to the children's quarters, "when she finds she can hold it over her sister and brother's heads because she was the only one awake enough to see the wedding, I think she'll get over it—even if she wasn't really awake enough to see it herself," he added, and howled convincingly when his cargo grabbed a handful of his golden hair to tug.

Josh came down the stairs again soon after, absently grinning at the way Delia had been asleep as soon as she'd gotten the "G'nite" out after she'd kissed him. As he descended, he could hear the sounds of the wedding-New Year's party in the ballroom still going at full swing, even without its guests of honor. The strains of "Oh, Promise Me" and "Love's Old Sweet Song" that had been played for them; "Down in the Valley" "Clementine" and "Whoopee-Ti-Yi-Yo" that had been requested especially for the groom and his brother, and selections from "H. M. S. Pinafore" that had been rendered in honor of the hostess, had given way to newer, more popular tunes for other guests.

Josh heard the lively finish to "Where Did You Get That Hat?" just before the raucous introduction to "Ta Ra Ra Boom Der Ay" was struck up again. He grinned, remembering that he had it on the highest authority—the bridegroom's—that the song was actually not new at all, but from a famous brothel in St. Louis. He grinned wider, remembering all the mock sorrow in Gray's voice as he tried to pretend regret for all he'd be missing now that he'd be walking the straight and narrow aisle of a groom—while all the time he could hardly keep his face straight for all the gladness in it.

But Josh's smile faded, and he paused when he came to the hallway. Kyle Harper was there, being assisted into his evening cape.

"Leaving so soon?" Josh asked with determined brightness, for he'd seen a fleeting expression on Kyle's face once at the beginning of the ceremony, and thought of it often throughout the rest of it.

"Indeed," Kyle said, taking his hat from the butler. "As you see. The party is over."

"The wedding's over, the party's not," Josh said. "Why, Blayne's just getting warmed up."

"Actors may carouse to all hours, alas, directors cannot," Kyle said, adjusting his top hat as adroitly as he avoided his host's eye. "Thank you for your hospitality, but I must go now."

"She'll be happy with him," Josh said.

"Indeed," Kyle said, "I never doubted it."

He had doubted it, of course. Until he'd seen her eyes this evening. He was a man who had learned to read every nuance in the human face and form. Whatever problem Hannah had thought she had, Gray Dylan had dispelled it beyond doubt. The emotions Kyle felt now were never doubt.

He allowed Josh one long, steady look into his own dark, solemn eyes, and then nodded.

"It is perhaps," he said softly, "that I am weary of being bested by you gentlemen. It will however, as all things must, pass. Good night."

Josh stood very still as Kyle adjusted his cape.

"I'd heard, in the street," Josh said as his butler opened the door for the departing guest, "that you've been looking for backers for a scheme to do with certain theaters in Philadelphia and Connecticut, as well as some out west. Albee and Keith have shown some concern over it. After all, it makes sense that a man who owned the theaters his troupe was to appear in would be in a mighty snug position. Is it true?"

Kyle hesitated. "It might be," he said.

Josh motioned to the butler, who immediately found other work to occupy himself with far across the wide marble hall.

"I also hear you've been making some inquiries about Mr. Eastman's new celluloid film process," Josh said. "Now, my brother and I are in a consortium that helps finance some of Mr. Edison's efforts, even though most of the men we know say we should stick to railroads, cattle, and mines. Still, we've not done badly with Mr. Edison. I'm curious. Edison says the possibilities of film are endless. You agree?"

Kyle swung around. His dark eyes glowed.

"Mr. Dylan," he said in his low, rich voice. "We enter a new decade and hurtle toward the millennium. We're richer and fatter than we've ever been as a nation, and we grow more so daily. We've earned the time and leisure to be entertained, at last. What the rich and fat need more than food or drink is entertainment. That's the industry of the future. Had I the capital, it would not end with theaters and touring companies. All of it—the recorded cylinders, the new films, the cameras and shortwave devices—anything that might entertain: those would be my gold mines and railroads."

"I see," Josh said thoughtfully, as though he'd never discussed it at length with his brother before this. "Now a man who owned hotels, as well as theaters, for his traveling troupes, and one who was on the spot to move in on other likely developments in the field, he'd be a man who was worth a lot. What would you say if you found someone willing to back you in these endeavors?"

Kyle drew himself up, and a small smile appeared on his dark features.

"I would be most surprised, Mr. Dylan, in that I'd not been looking for any more backers," he said sweetly.

"Ah, but what if one found you?" Josh asked. "Not only asked, but volunteered himself? We've known each other a long time, Kyle, and it was just the luck of the draw that you seemed to always discover what it was we wanted before we knew we wanted it. But now that my brother and I have both got that, we wondered if the same thing might apply to more monetary, speculative endeavors. To put it bluntly, we're in the business of making big money. You interest us because you seem on the verge of it. We'd like to be with you, rather than opposed to you, this time. And with you in a big way, because we're faithful as we are possessive. You might not need any of the other partners you've already found. Whether you like us or not, that would mean a bigger share for you, too."

"I see," Kyle said. He hesitated, and then turned

an oddly sweet smile on Josh, its power was such that Josh blinked for a moment.

"Ah—you don't happen to have any other brothers, do you?" Kyle asked.

"Not that we know of, and no sisters either," Josh said, grinning, "but we've got a passel of kids."

"I believe I can handle little Dylans," Kyle said.

"I wouldn't bet on it," Josh laughed.

"I believe I will," Kyle said, offering his gloved hand. "If you want in, Josh Dylan, here's my hand on it."

"Very good," Josh said with enthusiasm as he took the thin, but surprisingly strong hand in his clasp. "We'll discuss it further now if you want, or leave it until business hours in the new year."

"I'd rather leave it for now," Kyle said smoothly, "although tonight is New Year's and auspicious for new starts, this one is a wedding night, too, and so for celebrants of things that have happened—not for those that might," he explained on a sad smile that robbed the words of any rancor. "I'll see you next week, then. A very Happy New Year," he said, tipping his hat as he opened the door.

"To you too—partner," Josh said on a chuckle, before he returned to his company.

And so he never saw Kyle Harper as he stood poised alone on his doorstep, at the brink of a new year. Nor saw the way that Kyle finally smiled, too, as he glanced up at the waxing moon before he began to step out. Before—seeing his shadow outlined in the silvery moonlight, and superstitious as only a man of the theater could be, he remembered. And so did a quick reverse step in place—so fast it was as if he did a tiny two-step—so that he could step out on his right foot as he went into the new year. Alone, of course. But still, as though he was dancing.

The end.

About the Author

Edith Layton has been writing since she was ten years old. After getting a degree in creative writing and theater arts, she worked for a motion picture company, a television production company and in the newsroom of a radio station. She has also written publicity and worked as a freelance writer for newspapers and magazines. But history is both her hobby and delight, and so she was naturally drawn to writing her own versions of it. She has three children, and lives on Long Island with her physician husband. She collects antiques, books and large dogs.